50

FARRAR
STRAUS
GIROUX

BAKER'S DOZEN

BAKER'S DOZEN

A NOVEL

MICHAEL M. THOMAS

FARRAR • STRAUS • GIROUX

Published simultaneously in Canada by HarperCollins*CanadaLtd*
Printed in the United States of America
Designed by Jonathan D. Lippincott
First edition, 1996

LIBRARY OF CONGRESS CATALOGING-IN-PUBLICATION DATA
Thomas, Michael M.
Baker's dozen : a novel / by Michael M. Thomas.—1st ed.
p.   cm.
1. Corporations—Corrupt practices—Fiction.   2. Women in
business—Fiction.   3. Big business—Fiction.   I. Title.
PS3570.H574B35   1996   813'.54—dc20   96-2642   CIP

For two extraordinary people
my editor Elisabeth Sifton
my stepmother Poppi Thomas

CONTENTS

The man who gets angry at the right things and with the right people, and also in the right way and at the right time and for the right length of time, is commended. . . . The excess occurs in respect of all the circumstances: with the wrong people, for the wrong reasons, more than is right, too quickly and for too long a time.

ARISTOTLE

The Ethics (trans. J. A. K. Thomson)

Book Four

PRELUDE

In his hiding place under the wooden bridge, he feels the first faint pull of the lunar ebb eddying around his legs and checks his watch. Four-twelve in the morning. In exactly two minutes, the eastern sky will begin to lighten. How often it's begun this way, he thinks: with the sun coming up. Over Kilimanjaro, the Mexican Sonora, the Indian Ocean and, today, the Atlantic.

Still more than two hours to go, he thinks impatiently, then tells himself to calm down. It's always a waiting game, whatever the quarry. He feels stiff under the tight wet suit; the weight he's recently put on made it an effort to shrug himself into the twenty-year-old rubber garment, and it feels like it's cutting into his circulation. He rubs his thighs, strong fingers flexing stiffened muscles.

Off to his left, a pale fiery line spikes through the darkness and comes across the water at him as sunrise begins to divide earth from sky. In his imagination, he can picture day driving the night before it as a beater drives game, pictures the thinning darkness fleeing toward him across the surface of the sea, pounding up the sand and pelting across the land, returning the world to the consoling greens and grays of the great trees and "cottages" that dominate the surrounding landscape.

Dead ahead, just over the splendid dunes perhaps a quarter mile beyond the chosen killing ground, he can hear the ocean, a gigantic whispering presence whose smooth and steady rhythm marks the passing minutes with the precision of a metronome.

He waits and waits. The greenish numerals of his diver's watch, a hard-used stainless-steel Omega, now read five-fourteen. Another hour, he reckons. Already three and a half since he slipped into the water at the narrow end of the pond which twists in a flattish S-curve almost a mile from where the creek feeds into Hook Pond to where it dives under the dunes to seek the ocean.

He wiggles his flippered feet, keeping the blood moving. Despite his age, he feels alert and fresh.

Say five hours total, he calculates, from taking up position to the kill. No time at all, as stalks go. What was the longest? He reckons it was the eleven hours he and his guide once lay virtually motionless in the Wasatch Mountains waiting for the trophy bighorn. This quarry's no different: a creature of habit, it too will come.

The sky continues to lighten. A gull squawks somewhere off to windward. The specific familiar features of the landscape begin to emerge from the undifferentiating darkness: the ponds, the dark fairways and paler greens of the golf course. On the bluffs in the distance, he can make out the silhouette of the handsome Maidstone clubhouse. Five forty-six. Not long now.

He crosses his arms on his chest and massages his biceps. This'll be a disgracefully easy kill, he thinks. This quarry's not equipped by Nature with instincts built on wariness: it's never known danger worse than the possibility of being gotten the best of on a piece of paper.

Six a.m. on the dot. The sky's pale blue now, the air still unhazed and dry. As the day warms, the marshland around the pond will begin to reek. By then he'll be well away.

Another glance at his watch. Six-eleven. Any minute now. He takes a series of deep, slow breaths. His pulse feels steady and unhurried.

Time to get ready, he thinks, to lock and load. Floating easily at his side is a submersible watertight case of his own design and assembly. He picks it up, lays it across the bridge struts and unseals its outer two layers. He lifts out the rifle and strips it of its thick polyethylene wrap. He runs his fingers along the action, checking for moisture. Not a drop. From the case, he extracts a bulbous blued-steel tube, finely threaded at one end, about nine inches long, and roughly twice the diameter of the rifle barrel. This too is his own invention. He screws it on dead tight, then brings the heavy stock, dark and shiny as burnished ebony, to his cheek, resting the forepiece on the white polymer irrigation pipe running under the wooden bridge. He flips up the rear sight and settles the bead on the flag which sags limply on its stick across the pond. This morning, it's been positioned near the front right side of the fourth green, which extends into the pond as a semicircular peninsula shored up with railway ties. A tough pin position, he thinks: tough for a man with a six iron, that is, but not with this weapon.

Finger outside the trigger guard, he squeezes off a mimic round. "Bang," he murmurs.

All systems go, he thinks. Come to me, come to me, Poppa do. A few hundred yards from where he waits, a dairy truck clatters down the road from town and swings off eastward on Further Lane.

Time for a last run-through. A one-shot kill will give him at worst fifteen minutes—probably more like half an hour—before the quarry is missed, before someone's sent out to look, and the alarm is sounded. After that it'll be confusion for at least another twenty until any help arrives, and by then he'll have swum underwater a hundred yards diagonally across the pond to a place where the reeds converge with a neck-high cover of scrub running to the water's edge. His getaway outfit's hidden there. In the bank below the reeds, he's gouged out a pit for the rifle. There's a guesthouse set thirty yards up from where he'll emerge, but it's unoccupied. He's seen to that.

No one'll notice him. As Mao said, guerrillas must swim among the population like fish in the sea, and he looks as if he belongs in these parts. The club sitting proudly on the bluff numbers at least a hundred men of his general appearance and age among its members. Many of these get up early and take hearty constitutionals along the web of roads and fairways, listening on their Walkmans to Vivaldi or the latest London gold price.

In other words, it should be a piece of cake. An unwary prey with a fixed, solitary routine. An hour when few are about, since the very first golfers won't be coming this way for at least another hour.

He checks his watch again. Six-nineteen. He's starting to grow impatient.

In the middle distance, a couple of furlongs off to the left and beyond the green, he can see the quarry's lair, a tall white house set back about fifty or sixty yards behind the next tee. An important house, suitable for an important owner, a confirmation as much as a dwelling, lawn-moated and many-chimneyed, a habitation practically bursting its shingles with self-esteem. On the side facing the pond, wide french doors open onto a terrace encircled by a low balustrade. A pool house is off to the left. Beyond the terrace, high wire netting fences off a tennis court.

Suddenly there's a colorful flash of movement. One of the tall french doors opens. A small figure appears, in a white T-shirt and bright red trunks, a little boy with hair the color of August corn, and behind him, a larger, slightly stooped figure in a yellow short-sleeved shirt and florid pink trousers.

Goddamnit! he exclaims silently. He hadn't counted on a kid!

IIe takes a series of deep, pulse-calming breaths, watching the duo cross the lawn and clamber over the low wooden fence which bounds the golf course.

The little boy's presence causes him to shake his head reflexively, as if to clear his mind. He weighs up the various factors to be considered. At the heart of the hunter's code lies the imperative—*never* to be breached—to spare the young, never intentionally to take cub or kitten or fawn or hatchling. The point, of course, is to ensure the propagation of the species. And yet, and yet, he asks himself, staring across to where the two figures are clambering over a low rail fence, is this a species worth conserving, all things considered?

No quarter received, no quarter given. The air grows brighter by the second, burnishing the narrow band of water that lies between the hunter and his killing ground. The blood in his ears is noisy as his rage makes up his mind for him.

Che sarà, sarà. A man must do what a man must do. His cause is just—more so than the life of any one person, even a child.

And so he watches, breathing easily now, his conscience planed smooth by righteous anger, his senses, competence and intelligence drawn up and arrayed for the job at hand, as the man and the boy make their way down the path toward the destiny the hunter in the shadows waits to bestow.

PART ONE

BUYERS AND SELLERS

— I — The hammering in the sky grows louder. A large Sikorsky helicopter marked "United States of America" and bearing the presidential seal appears out of the fog cloaking the summit of Little Round Top and settles smoothly onto the National Park Service helipad. The nearside cabin door is flung open, an Air Force noncom starts to climb down but is gently edged aside by a square-built, sharply dressed man who looks to be in his late fifties. The new arrival drops to the tarmac, instinctively crouching to avoid the slashing arc of the main rotor, looks back up at the cockpit and snaps a firm salute to the pilots. Then, still bent, like an infantryman charging a pillbox, he hurries across to the two people waiting at the edge of the helipad while the noncom assists the other passengers: a strikingly handsome, suavely tailored although somewhat overweight African-American man in his late thirties or early forties, followed by a stoutish, matronly woman who juggles an assortment of file folders and datebooks and tries simultaneously to keep the prop wash from blowing apart her tightly pinned gray coif and chasing her full skirt about her neck.

As the chopper winds back up, greetings are silently mouthed and hands shaken, then everyone looks on silently as the chopper lifts heavily into the air, gains altitude and with a clattering roar banks into the fog and is gone from sight. Soon it is no more than a distant ruckus in the mist.

For a half minute or so, as people regain possession of their senses, no one says anything. Then the new arrival plucks a brightly figured silk handkerchief from his breast pocket and vigorously wipes his face.

"Noisy devil, that," he observes to no one in particular. Heads nod.

"Terrible weather, eh?"

He's right about that. It's a dull, dank, warmish, dirty yellowish morning that feels more like early September than late November, the week
before Thanksgiving. The earth is steaming. Overhead, a bleak sun
strains to cut through a pearl-hard overcast. The thick mist lying low
across the rolling Pennsylvania hills is just beginning to break up.

"Good flight, sir?"

The new arrival nods vigorously. He has what people used to call
"a noble head": with a deep broad brow surmounting sharp, clever,
ruddy features—a strong, pointed nose; cool, direct blue eyes under
eyebrows like charcoal slashes; an imposing mane of thick lustrous
black hair, dramatically grayed at the temples, thick at the nape, swept
back in Augustan curves. It's a head you'd expect to find in a
nineteenth-century statehouse portrait of a legislator or orator famous in
his time, a wise solon gazing out over great, timeless, visionary landscapes, one hand tucked in his frock coat, the other resting on a fat
volume of Seneca in a pose that dangerously skirts the nearmost littorals
of pomposity.

He's flashily dressed: floridly striped shirt with a white collar and
French cuffs, a vividly patterned Ferragamo necktie, an aggressively
tailored light-colored grayish-fawn suit, cut close to the body with un-
stylish high double vents. Natty in an old-fashioned way that rejects the
understated style preferred by most executives. Less a sartorial ensem-
ble than an aggressive declaration of independence. Nobody—no trend,
no person, no convention—is going to tell me what to wear, these
clothes proclaim—or tell me much else, for that matter.

He takes another look at the sky.

"Well, my bonny lads and lasses, looks like it's going to fairly piss
rain."

"Not as badly as the Street's going to piss on this deal if the numbers
aren't there," says the younger of the two women in the group. "I just
got off the phone with Fidelity. I played them 'America the Beautiful,'
but what they still want to know: have we—have *you*—lost our—your
—mind? Actually, my guy there used a kind of interesting adjective
before 'mind,' but knowing how you feel about bad language, I've de-
leted it."

The new arrival doesn't answer. There's a beat or two of uneasy si-

lence before the young woman continues in tones that leave no doubt
that she knows herself to be speaking in front of colleagues she can
trust to keep a confidence. Nevertheless, one or two glance reflexively
over their shoulders in the direction of the two drivers conversing idly
beside the vehicles parked a few dozen yards off, at the edge of the
helipad, matched Chrysler vans painted in improbable bumblebee
stripes of black and yellow.

"Lest you forget," she adds in a cool, precise voice that carries just
a hint of a Down East upbringing, "Fidelity Magellan just went up to
six million shares last quarter and until we announced this deal three
weeks ago, they were talking about adding to the position. There's a
million at Salomon that'll sure as shootin' shake loose if Buffett bails
out. Anyway, here we are. I don't smoke and I hate blindfolds, so I
guess I'll just grit my teeth and try not to cry."

She's a slim, good-looking young woman, in her early thirties, with
narrow, finely drawn features that are in keeping with her voice. She
might not be what everyone would call "a beauty," but she's certainly
handsome enough by most people's standards; very pulled-together, almost severe, nothing out of place, inside or out. The sort for whom "the
tailored look" is created: in her case a deep gray Bill Blass suit. The
narrow oval of her face is accentuated by a smooth, helmetlike pageboy
of dark blond hair; her eyes are frank, her gaze steady from behind
large, round, faintly tinted lenses set in punitively expensive high-tech
metal frames.

Her name is Lucy Preston. She is the senior vice president for investor relations of GIA, the $45 billion corporation of which John P.
Mannerman, the new arrival, is chairman, president and chief executive
officer. She is the third-ranking member of Mannerman's "Gang of
Four," as the legendary CEO's closest confidants are called inside the
giant, and as they proudly call themselves.

"Are you finished your wee diatribe, my bonny young lass?"

Mannerman looks around at the others, grins and shrugs. The gesture
says: what're we going to do with this one? It's a gesture he's so often
made, and they've so often acknowledged, that by now it's reflexive for
all parties.

"If you do your job, Lucy m'girl, Fidelity'll come to love this acquisition so much they'll *double* their position, will they not?"

The young woman pushes her glasses down her nose, and studies her boss with relish.

"Aye, that they may," she says, good-naturedly mocking the Scottish usages Mannerman uses within his inner circle, the affectation by which he tries to conceal his South Boston upbringing, as if Scots Catholic is somehow more couth than Irish, as if the Gaelic rather than the Celtic strain will make more respectable his overweening loyalty to Rome, which among American laymen can count on no son more true, more passionately devoted and more powerful. Sometimes Lucy wonders what voice Mannerman uses when closeted with the Cardinal—or with His Holiness himself. The man's a chameleon. That's his charm, that's his magic. He can sense a change in the wind or the color of the day a galaxy off, and alter accordingly. Lucy's not put off by this. She recognizes it for the strength it is, and besides, she spends most of her time among people—including herself—reinvented by force of circumstance or will, so who's she to complain?

"They may," she says a second time, "but if they do, you'll have to throw in a couple of those," and casts a flashing, look-yonder glance over her shoulder at the pair of vans.

"Great sainted Mary, Mother of our Lord Jesus Christ, what in heaven's name might those be?"

"Those, Peerless Leader, are courtesy cars furnished by our hosts and your soon-to-be vassals. Yellow and black—as in bee. As in BEECO, get it? It's kind of a visual pun. Bzzz, bzzz."

BEECO stands for Baker Extractive Engineering Corporation, which is scheduled by the end of the morning to be bought by GIA for approximately $300 million.

This will be the ninety-sixth acquisition to be closed in the course of Mannerman's reign. The consideration to be received by the Baker family, which after more than a century has decided to sell out, will be payable in GIA common stock. Three hundred million dollars may sound like a lot of money, but the sum in fact represents less than one-half of 1 percent of the aggregate market value of GIA, based on this morning's opening trade on the New York Stock Exchange.

Mannerman looks affectionately at the young woman with the expression an indulgent father reserves for a favored if mischievous daugh-

ter, a child who knows to a psychological millimeter exactly how far
she dare push it.

"As regards this morning's business," he says at length, "I'll thank
you to keep in mind that the heart has its reasons, which no one should
know better than you, you flibbertigibbet trifler with men's passions. Am
I not right, Grover, my lad?"

The African-American aide snaps to smartly.

"Yassuh, boss!" he exclaims. He touches a hand to the brim of an
imaginary cap and executes a deft shuffle while mimicking the wailing
skirl of a bagpipe.

"Down, boy," Mannerman says. "What must our hosts be thinking?"

His grin doesn't change. It's a famous grin, familiar from a dozen
cover stories, including one on *Time*, showing the gleaming teeth which
Barron's has described as "the biggest, whitest and sharpest since Little
Red Ridinghood's Granny."

It's obvious that these are licensed impertinences, and that these
people are comfortable in a way that belies the reputation for a prickly
disposition that has caused their boss to be known up and down the
Fortune 500 as "Cactus Jack" Mannerman.

"All right now," he says, more seriously. "I assume the lawyers have
all in readiness, from soup to nuts, one-two-three, quick as Billy-be-
damned? I've got to be out of here no later than two or someone's going
to turn into a jack-o'-lantern! I'm expected in Los Angeles for dinner,
and it's a date I really can't—won't—miss."

At this, Lucy, Spuds and Grover exchange significant looks. "Los
Angeles" is a nervous-making mantra, even for Grover and Roy "Spuds"
Spuddacker, who have some concrete idea of what's going on. Lucy's
not in the loop yet, which is fine with her. Until whatever's going on is
set in concrete, more or less, she'd prefer not to know. It makes it easier
for her mirror to tell her she's dealing with Wall Street on the absolute
up-and-up. This way, she and the Street are on the same side of the
table, privy to rational but uninformed speculation and rumor, and no
more than that.

"You'll be coming, too, Lucy, did I tell you? No? Ah, well, such is
the lot of the career woman. You can buy what you need at Magnin's,
I daresay, or that awful place on Rodeo Drive with the yellow awning

you frequent when you think I'm not looking. Now, now, Spuds m'boy, don't look so glum. I need you, but ye've other fish to fry. It's in New York that you'll be serving the cause this very night—to get Mrs. Mannerman through . . . what's it in aid of this time, Marie?"

"Bright's disease, sir."

"Ah, yes, Bright's disease. A noble cause, and close to my dear lady wife's heart because of her sweet mother, may the good Lord bless and keep her. Ah, well, no time like the present, is there? Shall we be on our way?"

Everything should go smoothly, Lucy thinks. The legal foot soldiers —in-house lawyers and a platoon of attorneys from GIA's outside counsel, along with GIA's and BEECO's accountants, and the proxies and representatives for various other parties in interest, principally family charitable trusts—have been in Bakerton for three days. Last night, a formal rehearsal was held, with an attentiveness to detail and protocol that would suit a royal wedding, and it went off without a hitch.

Mannerman starts to turn away, then stops. "Lucy, Spuds, you two should know that Grover and I had a very interesting visit with the Speaker this morning. *Very* interesting—the Speaker is a man whose genius is in the details; he and I understand each other to a T."

A *crossed* T, Lucy thinks, and then can't help adding: a *double-crossed* T.

"Afterward, we dropped by the White House and found the President in very good form, very good form indeed. Wasn't it grand of the Chief Executive to give us the use of his flying machine? Anyway, I'm bound to say that everything seems to be on the Yellow Brick Road, if you get my meaning."

Now he bounds across the helipad, yanks open the front door of the nearest van, then says over his shoulder, "Marie, I'll be needing you to ride with me. We've work still to do! Now when am I expected in Berlin, and did you talk to the Honorable Secretary at Muirfield about arranging a tee time for our friend Yoshi-san?"

With Grover and Spuds, Lucy climbs into the second van. They ride in silence. These are BEECO drivers, and one never discusses GIA business in front of strangers.

Well, well, well, she thinks: so the Speaker of the House *and* the President—to put them in proper order—have *both* signed off on our projected voyage to the Wonderful Electronic City of Oz, ticket largely to be paid for by the taxpayer. This morning's closing will pay off the Speaker; she's sure he's been promised that there'll be no "lean and mean" at BEECO, no cutbacks or layoffs before the next election, when the House leader presumably intends to trade up to a six-year Senate term as a springboard to the White House. Lucy wonders what the President's price was. The Catholic vote perhaps? A pat on the back from Rome?

TK will know, she thinks, but TK's out in Seattle, working with the Microsoft people on the joint-venture announcement.

TK is Tom Kennerly, senior vice president and director of communications and media relations, second-ranking of the Gang of Four. "Spuds" Spuddacker, whose title is senior vice president, community relations, has the most time in the outfit. He's been with Mannerman for almost twenty years, starting as a gofer back at American Standard, before Mannerman put himself on the map at Ford. Spuds takes care of Peerless Leader's personal PR: the Rome/Vatican/Papal Knight angle, the charity commitments, the gossip spin, which is fortunately light, since Mannerman's private life is above reproach.

Grover Furlong, riding up ahead with the boss, is the baby of the gang in point of service and perhaps the most powerful. Still shy of forty, like Lucy, he came to GIA just four years ago after stints with Billy Graham, the Murdoch organization and Ron Brown's Commerce Department. As senior vice president for public policy, Grover watches over Washington, with occasional statehouse forays. More important, he's the self-styled "Keeper of the Golden Faucet," the man to see about GIA political dollars.

The mainstream (nonfinancial) media, and lately the Internet, the Web and the wonderful world of "on-line," is TK's responsibility. Naturally, there's some overlap: if a story affecting GIA is being worked on by *The New York Times* or CBS, for example, TK and Lucy will team up—whereas if it's *Fortune* or *Barron's* or Bloomberg, she'll handle it herself. In addition, she runs her own update page on the GIA Web site.

Organizationally, the Gang occupies the box at the very top right on the company organization chart, the one designated "Executive Information Services Group" and connected directly—without passing

"Go"—to the box at the center top marked "Chair/Pres/CEO." Within GIA, everyone but the Gang of Four has to make an appointment to see the CEO; even to speak with Mannerman on the phone. Only the firm's dozen outside directors, the board and board-committee members who are his true power base, enjoy comparable access.

PL's door is guarded by a round-the-clock phalanx of administrative assistants, many convent-educated, who have to sign off before either Marie, who travels with him, or Betty—in New York—or Jean—in St. Louis—is even approached for final clearance to enter the presence. The vice-chairman and the executive VPs for operations and finance need to go through channels, as do the various group and divisional chiefs. But not the Gang of Four. To Lucy and Spuds, Grover and TK, Jack Mannerman is available without notice and without knocking, because they are the keepers of his and the company's image, and these, next to his family, rate highest in Mannerman's scheme of things.

When it comes to damage control, everyone grabs an oar. Fortunately, so far there's been no need for that. As Spuds has noted, the raw material they're working with isn't exactly second-rate. "Take any four great men you care to think of," he's fond of saying, "eliminate their weaknesses and peccadilloes—imagine Jack Kennedy without the nooky chasing, say, Churchill without the booze or Brando without the chow—and who've you got? John P. Mannerman."

For which, thinks Lucy, thanks be to God. PL's the ultimate control freak. She hates to think how he might react to a public relations disaster.

"Someone remind me," says Spuds, "where the hell's TK?"

"In Seattle, talking to the Microsoft people about on-line alliances."

Spuds looks like hell, Lucy thinks. When she left him in the taproom at the Bakerton Inn last night, he was just switching to stingers. This morning his capillaries are glowing like neon.

"Whatever the hell those are," Spuds comments. Mentally, he's a citizen of an earlier, simpler order of being.

Twelve minutes later, the two vehicles pass through tall iron gates and a guard post, all painted in the same striking alternating stripes of black and bright yellow. They follow a winding drive a half mile through open meadows and draw up in front of a low, handsome building which Lucy knows was designed by Frank Lloyd Wright in 1943 after the present Baker generation's father was knocked off his feet by Falling-water, the house Wright built in 1939 for the Kauffman family.

Looming beyond the executive offices is a complex of long-roofed, hulking assembly sheds, dominated by the mountainous bulk of the test pad and surmounted by a hundred-foot pylon wearing the same striping. As the vans come to a stop, the door of the low building opens and a welcoming party comes out, led by a tall, tweedy man about the same age as Mannerman. At that moment, the sun breaks through for the first time in a week. It seems a good omen for the business to come.

Mannerman darts from the first van, still talking rapidly over his shoulder to his secretary, who's cheerfully and deftly juggling the two electronic personal information managers, car phone, car fax, portable Bloomberg stock quote device and cellular pager which travel in the custom-designed Hermès case that meets PL wherever he alights.

As the reception committee approaches, Mannerman speaks urgently to Grover: "Grover my lad, best perhaps you skip the meet 'n' greet part and hit the phone. Lest the significance of this noble occasion be lost on the Hill, this being the Speaker's district. Let's not have it that the world little know nor long remember what we're about to say here, eh? So hold your hour and have another, my boy, and then rejoin us in time to hear the second-best short speech ever delivered in these parts. You'll not want to miss that, seeing as you're the lad who wrote it!"

This is the main reason for Mannerman turning up at the closing of a deal this small. Typically, his participation is limited to wooing and winning. He leaves the final dotting and crossing and bean counting to the technicians. Today, however, at the request of the Baker family, and because BEECO is a resonant name in the home district of a Washington politician crucial to Mannerman's grand design, the GIA chief executive will deliver a short speech welcoming the BEECO workforce to its new adoptive family. The former is understandably apprehensive at being handed over, after long generations—indeed, more than a century—of paternalistic family ownership, to a management reputed to suffer no fools and take no prisoners. A company that, some think, defines the popular current management philosophy known as "mean and lean." Many present, Lucy knows from past experience, will be wondering if they're being sold into bondage. It is not a question to which she is anxious to give an honest answer.

"OK, m'lassies and lads," Mannerman murmurs, "game faces, please!" Then he turns and enthusiastically greets the tall man leading the welcoming committee: H. A. Baker, chairman and chief executive of BEECO.

Spuds nudges Lucy as Mannerman grasps the much taller Baker's right hand with both of his, stroking as much as shaking it. It's a technique he learned back in the days when, just out of business school, he briefly worked for Nelson Rockefeller.

"Ever the consummate pro," Lucy mutters in reply to Spuds's poke. "PL's at concert pitch today. Look at him! You know what he reminds me of?"

"A pit bull about to chomp a greyhound?"

"Actually, I was thinking of *The Surrender of Breda.* "

"The surrender of what?"

"Don't be such a philistine, Spudsy. It's a painting. One of the most famous in the world. By Velázquez."

Spuds presses his fingers against his temples and screws up his large fleshy features in mock dismay. "Velázquez, Velázquez? Who's he? One of those Dominican shortstops? Who'd he play for?"

Spuds is a man of few interests. His devotion to Mannerman sops up his mental energies like a sponge. For the rest, he drinks late and deep and worries the night away.

"He was a Spanish painter. Born 1599, died 1660. *The Surrender of Breda*, also known as *The Lances*, which he painted in 1652, is one of his masterpieces. One of the all-time great paintings ever painted anywhere by anyone, period. It's the best depiction ever of how to make and receive a surrender graciously, how the victor should accept the vanquished party's sword without gloating, how the loser can hand it over without looking beaten. PL damn near plotzed when I took him to see it in Madrid last year. A transaction between gentlemen. You know how he is about style in all things. I think he's been practicing in his mirror."

"When were you guys in Madrid?"

"Last year, when we were screwing around with that Spanish bank that Herby Lamond tried to suck us into, the one he finally persuaded the Mellon to buy."

"Oh, that one. Which has so far eaten the Mellon's lunch for, what, two hundred big ones?"

"Closer to three hundred, actually. That's according to a guy I know at Salomon who follows the Mellon. Another Lamond blue-plate special! Anyway, I persuaded PL to steal a couple of hours and do the Prado with me. When he saw the Velázquez he literally wanted to climb into the picture, become part of it."

"The man likes his fantasies." Spuds looks at Lucy, smiles and makes a tiny gesture of benediction with his right forefinger. She grins back at the old, shared joke.

"Well," she adds, "you can say this for PL: he seems to know how to make 'em come true."

Spuds says something in reply, but Lucy doesn't catch it; her attention is drifting despite herself, drawn almost magnetically to H. A. Baker. A gorge-clenching shiver of unease courses through her. He's one of "them," she's thinking, and in the next mental flash tells herself to quit it! It's an old response, and she hates it, a reaction she's thought she'd suppressed.

Lucy grew up in a Maine coastal town with a very upscale summer colony. She was a slim, blond, handsome, well-spoken child, identical in most outward aspects to the slim, blond, handsome summer children, except that she lived in Paster's Point year-round while they lived in places like Shaker Heights and Chestnut Hill and came north only between July 4 and Labor Day. A "townie," in other words, who spent too many of her young summers taking orders, not giving them, until she couldn't help thinking of herself as coming from the wrong side of the tracks—or, more properly, the wrong side of the grill at the yacht club where she worked through high school.

Not the *wrong* side, the *other* side! It wasn't easy, not for a young person. Now that she's older, she understands how it was, how she was, but young people think reality's what they want it to be—that's the beautiful brief illusion of childhood—while grown-ups have to accommodate themselves to what it is. In Paster's Point, the summer colony was where the money came from that paid for the other ten months of the year, a truth as obvious to the town's adults as it seemed inexplicable to their children. Childhood notions can die hard, and it's taken

Lucy a long time to teach herself to say "other" and not "wrong," almost as long a time as it's taken her to realize that she's one of "them" now herself, with her fancy job, big-city life, money and clothes and the acquaintanceship of people who are by anyone's standards rich, famous and powerful.

But she's not entirely rid of the old bruises, she knows—to her immense irritation. A really perfect specimen of the type, as H. A. Baker seems in bearing and appearance to be, still produces a faint recurrence of that combination of abashed resentment and inferiority which eighteen summers ingrained.

"Earth to Luce, Earth to Luce," Spuds says.

"Yes?"

"I was saying, Velázquez, schmazquez! This isn't an unconditional surrender, this is a goddamn merger closing!"

"Oh, is it now?" murmurs Lucy. Well, we shall see.

Baker's right out of a Sargent portrait, she thinks. Or an Eakins. To the manner born. Or rather: born to the manor—which he's about to sell to Jack Mannerman.

More Sargent than Eakins, she concludes. Art history remains Lucy's principal frame of descriptive reference, even after her years in corporate life. It's not just descriptive. She doesn't say as much, except to her looking glass, but the fact is that Lucy feels her art historical training connects her to a past in many ways more honorable, more elevated than the present.

Art history's what got her here. A little over seven years earlier, after taking an art history BA from Bowdoin, followed by a three-year stint at the Portland Museum, she came to New York to work in the development office of the Metropolitan Museum, thanks to a trustee who was a summer resident of Paster's Point. She had a plan. The Met was to be a way station, a place to pull down a check while working for an M.A. or Ph.D. at the NYU Institute of Fine Arts, a few blocks south off Fifth Avenue, and—more important—a place where she could make connections that would open up the glamorous sectors of the art world: a job with a top dealer or at one of the big auction houses, or a corporate art advisorship. She had never wanted to end up as a junior curatorial or development-office church mouse. Whatever she might think of them, the Paster's Point summer people seemed to come from a bigger life, a larger world pregnant with excitement, action, self-realization. Lucy took the Met job as a springboard into that life.

Unfortunately, however, the Met seemed to be a dead end. The job was the yacht club snack bar all over again, although now the menu was denominated with three or four more zeros, and instead of a candy-striped apron and T-shirt from a Portland uniform shop, she manned her station in something the museum borrowed from "Oscar" or "Bill," as she referred to them in conversations with herself. She was still on the wrong—*other*—side of the counter. Not flipping hamburgers anymore, but poised prettily with her lists in front of towering flower arrangements whose cost would have bought her father's house ten times over.

Instead of "Two cheeseburgers rare, side of fries," or "What would you like to drink?" it was "Good evening, Mrs. Wrightsman, you're at Table Three with Sir John. Mrs. Heinz, you're at Table Six, next to Ambassador Annenberg."

This was not what she planned, but she seemed stuck. She began to wonder if the other side of whatever was forever to be her fate.

And then Jack Mannerman entered her life.

It was two years after GIA's banks and directors, reeling under hundred-million-dollar losses, imported him to St. Louis from Ford, where he had been senior executive vice president for international operations, and gave him carte blanche. Because he collected Scottish and Irish paintings in a small way, he was on the museum's national business committee, whose minutes Lucy was responsible for keeping. He liked her style at once, saw in her a kindred mind.

"You give great clipboard," he told her.

He'd seen right away that she shared his obsession with painstaking attention to detail, his love of exactitude, his enthusiasm for planning, his hatred of surprises. In Mannerman's philosophy, "winging it" was unacceptable. Targets were established in a manner that optimized the likelihood that they'd be met. Financial statements were scrutinized down to the tenth part of the tenth part. It helped that Mannerman could glance at a twenty-column spreadsheet footed to the billions and pick out a half-million-dollar anomaly. Spuds said PL had "an eye for financial detail like a housewife's for dust."

In this, Mannerman resembled her father, so she knew she could handle it. Chief Preston's methodical approach was a holdover from his FBI days, and he had passed it on to his daughter. One made sense of one's life and vocation, he taught Lucy, through microscopic attention to detail, by making lists and checking them off item by item by item, by respectful compliance with procedure and routine. "No shortcuts, no setbacks," is the Chief's way of putting it. "Battles are won before they're fought," says Mannerman. Her father and her boss are about the only two men Lucy knows who read the directions immediately after opening a box.

Six months after they met, he called Lucy from St. Louis and offered five times what the Metropolitan was paying her, along with the promise of excitement. She had what it took, he said; he could tell from the way she soft-soaped the Wall Street types who dominated the Met's board. The Met was a great product to pitch, he told her, but in GIA he'd give her an even bigger one, because at the end of the day, to the big shots on its board the Met was only a hobby, whereas a great investment story hit the big boys deep down where they lived: in their wallets.

"The Street'll be your beat, Lucy," he told her. "I speak globally, of course. Every market that prints a quotation. Lenders, stockholders, traders—they're all yours, from Toledo to Tokyo. Your job is to see they get with our program. That they come to love us with a consuming infatuation that only deepens with time and rising profits."

For years she's stoked that infatuation, and so far so good. At times, Lucy thinks of herself as a stylish bright spider paid a lot of money— more money than she once thought existed in the universe—for weaving a web of perceptions whose golden, seductive strands irresistibly draw in investors. Basically, however, she's at peace with what she does. At peace and proud: she's good—to last with Mannerman, you have to be. The man won't stand for a misstep, not so much as a mis-tiptoe. But it's getting harder. As GIA grows, as its CEO spreads himself more thinly, as investors and stockholders expect more, the tightrope gets narrower and narrower, there's less margin for error, the need—the pressure—for constant watchfulness intensifies.

PL and I really are brother and sister under the skin, she thinks uneasily, watching her boss converse with Baker. Mannerman is the world-famous chief executive of a services and industrial conglomerate doing $60 billion a year worldwide, and Baker merely the pro tem chairman of a venerable but limping capital-goods company doing barely $150 million, but a skilled reader of body language wouldn't have any trouble discerning who between that pair feels inferior to whom. Baker may not be worth a damn as a manager—the evidence is certainly there in the numbers—and he may represent a dying breed, the heartland WASP patriciate she used to read about in the dog-eared copies of *Town & Country* that constituted the library of the Paster's Point Yacht Club, but something about him sets him apart, something neither she nor Mannerman will ever attain. Something in his bearing, the way he dresses and speaks, the way he wears his *life.*

It's been quite a life, she knows from the FBI-quality workup Mannerman insists be done on the people on the other side of every deal GIA looks at.

Hobart Alexander Baker is within weeks of his fiftieth birthday, some seventeen years older than Lucy (in the way of women, she's noted that he's a Sagittarius and speculated how that might dovetail with her own Capricorn temperament). He's named after the legendary Princeton athletic star and military hero "Hobey" Baker, a classmate of his maternal grandfather's and a distant cousin. Baker himself would star in hockey at Princeton a half century after his namesake. Lucy's mental card file includes the usual biographical boilerplate of schools and clubs. There had been a young, childless marriage that failed after three years. The firm that GIA used for deep background checks has turned up an intermittent, long-running affair with a Chestnut Hill and Hobe Sound divorcée, although it seems to have petered out.

The man's passions are the great outdoors and painting. He's listed in Boone & Crockett, which keeps the official North American big-game records, and for a dozen years had conducted a "hunt 'n' fish" column in *Outdoor Sportsman.* Prominent in ecological and wildlife causes, he also served on the board of the National Rifle Association until a well-publicized dispute over the assault-rifle ban ended with his resignation.

A gifted artist, he's won the painting prizes at every school he attended. A knee torn up playing college hockey rendered him unfit for military service, but through a classmate's father he wangled an assignment as a *Life* combat artist, and he went straight from the pleasant shaded alleys of Princeton to the bleeding marshes of Vietnam, where he won a special commendation for noncombatant valor. On his return, he studied at the Pennsylvania Academy of Art for two years.

Until just a year ago, when his brothers perished in a plane crash, Baker's relationship to the family company was essentially tangential and nonexecutive. The BEECO annual report listed him as vice president for sales promotion. His degree from Princeton was in mechanical engineering, but basically Baker was BEECO's "Marlboro Man."

As a fabricator of images herself, Lucy could see how he was effective. On paper and in person, he projects the right qualities. Mining equipment is a high-end "guy stuff" kind of business. Expensive, complex, rugged, dependable. There's a kind of heroic, he-man aspect to it. Having a well-known sportsman making the sales pitch while on safari or fishing in blue water can only help.

The proof is in the company's boardroom. The past month, when the terms of the buyout were being settled, Lucy paid her only previous visit to Bakerton to get a feel for the new acquisition. In the boardroom, where the lawyers are now waiting with the merger agreement and the checks, she saw to her surprise that the walls sported rows of fish and game trophies instead of the usual photographs of past products and past presidents. A seven-foot stuffed polar bear menaced from a corner; an arching marlin surmounted a sideboard.

The BEECO functionary who took Lucy around—Baker himself was out of the country—called her attention to a tall Sheraton bookcase filled with row upon row of identical photo albums bound in heavy, rough linen. They contained professionally mounted and labeled photographs of shotgun-wielding Japanese clad in unlikely plus fours, stolid rifle-bearing Russians in parkas, rawboned Texans in jeans and vests holding bows and arrows, suspicious Frenchmen in tropical shorts brandishing fishing tackle, along with fishing guides, loaders, gun bearers, Sherpas, bush pilots. The photos showed a great variety of boats, aircraft, helicopters and all-terrain vehicles. All the pictures had two elements in common. Standing off to one side would be a tall, tanned man in an Indiana Jones fedora, smiling in an offhand, somewhat detached way, whom the aide identified as H. A. Baker. In the center foreground, stretched out on the ground or hanging from a hoist, would be a large, dead animal, reptile, fish or amphibian.

As for the paintings in the boardroom, they consisted of a series of large, well-framed naturalistic outdoor scenes, signed "HAB" in tiny copperplate letters, executed in flawless drybrush watercolor, the technique made famous by Brandywine painters like Andrew Wyeth. Each depicted a BEECO machine at work in a different terrain. Lucy fancies she has a reliable eye for what is "art." This work impressed her. It was closely observed, the underlying drawing confident and accurate, the medium applied with craft and skill.

At the narrow end of the room hung a pair of portraits: large full-face pen-and-gouache likenesses of Baker's two late brothers, the men who until their death had actually run the company. Baker was no mean portraitist either. He had an incisive grasp of feature that conveyed the whole of a personality: the brothers' careless, lazy intelligence and, equally evident, their boundless self-regard, the male equivalent of a woman's house pride. The sort of people who believed that name and reputation was all it took to get you through—because in fact that was how it used to be all over this part of the world. But now Bakerton was in the midst of an industrial graveyard. Like headstones, empty flyblown plants and sullen sooty towns memorialized the noble names with which the region was once dotted. Great names, symbolic of American industry triumphant, portents of the American Century.

Up ahead, Mannerman slings a comradely arm across Baker's shoulders, rising on the balls of his gleamingly shod feet to do so, and the two men make for the hangarlike indoor test pad where the GIA chief will address the BEECO workforce.

If Grover has done his typical clever wordsmithing, Lucy reflects, and TK has properly prepped the media, Peerless Leader's words will receive wide exposure. It won't hurt that Bakerton, Pennsylvania, not only lies in the Speaker's home district but is also right down the road from where Abraham Lincoln gave the most famous short speech in American history.

At least until today.

God, how I hate this deal! she thinks.

— II —

Inside the hangar, Lucy positions herself inconspic-
uously at the back of the crowd and looks around.

The sheer volume of the building is amazing. It's
here that BEECO's machines are put through their
paces for prospective customers from around the world. Today, a number
of the largest machines, forty-ton cranes, chain loaders the length of an
America's Cup yacht, shovels that can gulp up a house-size chunk of
earth at a single bite, all painted in the company colors, have been
drawn up at either end like a guard of honor.

As she generally does on these occasions, Lucy tries to gauge Mannerman's new subjects' emotional temperature. From the general pitch
of the buzz, she senses these people want to be receptive. They're floating on hope, and you hear it in their voices.

Mannerman's presence here today will help. It's clear to Lucy that
his appearance is part of whatever deal he and Grover have cut with
the Speaker's people. She figures the trade-off must go something like
this: GIA will make what sounds like a significant investment to the
voter and man in the street: $300 million to buy BEECO plus x million
in future capital expenditures, training, etc. These future expenditures
are "subject to . . ."—lawyerspeak for loopholes and outs large enough
to drive a forty-ton dragline through. In his remarks, Mannerman will
make it all sound like a ringing endorsement of the Speaker's ballyhooed
New American Agenda, a call for renewal and rejuvenation of America's
heartland industrial might. In other words: GIA's putting its money
where the Speaker's mouth is, about which Lucy's had to do some heavy
explaining.

And the quid pro quo? Lucy's guess is that the Speaker is committed
to deliver the legislative easements needed for Yellow Brick Road, Mannerman's code name for his projected transformation of GIA into an
enterprise whose massive feet will be planted firmly—and by the year
2000 almost wholly—in cyberspace. The amount of capital required
will be humongous—the number Lucy's heard is $50 billion—which
means Mannerman will have to go offshore to get it, probably through
a series of "strategic alliances" that will effectively transfer the ownership of huge blocs of America's media to GIA's foreign associates.

Considered strictly as a public relations or political outlay, $300
million is on the rich side, Lucy admits, but the pot of gold at the end

of the Yellow Brick Road is likely to be enormous. What matters is that BEECO serves both Mannerman's business objectives and the Speaker's political/ideological agenda, which is a lot of bang for not much buck.

Everyone at GIA knows the company is buying more history than earning power, but just now history is an easy sell. The text of the Speaker's "Declaration of Renewal" reads like a high school syllabus. In the sale of BEECO to GIA, one of the best-known of American industrial birthrights will change hands after a hundred and seventeen years in the hands of its founding family. Even in a commercial society whose real connection to its past—as opposed to lip service—seems to be melting away as rapidly as the morning mist on the surrounding hills, a tradition of twelve seamless decades of community-minded family ownership is worth a gesture. Grover and TK have worked hard to engineer the perception that Jack Mannerman's personal appearance is his way of paying homage to that history, that involvement, that leadership.

In its day, BEECO was a fine company, no doubt of that, worthy of its slogan: "The Name Industry Can Count On!" For more than a century, the company's equipment has gnawed, bored, reamed and gouged the earth to bring forth, on every continent, in every climate and from every kind of terrain, minerals susceptible of being converted into human wealth. The primitive dragline jury-rigged back in the 1880s by a young mining engineer named Caiphas Baker to deal with a recalcitrant seam of Youghiogheny anthracite has fathered a family of giants: monstrous augers and excavators, drilling cranes, draglines, backhoes and shovels, mobile and fixed-platform water jets, chain loaders. The trademark yellow-and-black honeybee striping in which the nacelles, booms, engine housings and fuselages are painted is recognized the world over.

The pride and ambition of five generations of Bakers have overseen the company's development and kept BEECO alive and thriving in Bakerton, where jobs at "The Plant" are still routinely passed down through families. The early years were bloody: there were strikes, lockouts, broken heads, even three killings, including one family member. But as the company grew and prospered, peace settled on BEECO and Bakerton, and right through the first two postwar decades, when America had all the money in what was called the free world, it seemed that everyone involved with BEECO, from the family to the factory hands, could take a rising of comfort and convenience for granted.

Now things have changed. The world is less friendly, less compliant, more expensive and tricky to do business in, more competitive. Profits are no longer adequate to support the technical investment and experimentation necessary to keep BEECO state-of-the art and competitively abreast of larger, state-subsidized European and Asian enterprises, not to mention domestic rivals which have moved their manufacturing operations overseas to cheaper labor markets. Last month, BEECO lost out to Komatsu on the $125 million ten-year contract to supply water-jet equipment to a giant copper project that Mobil is joint-venturing in Zambia. The news hit Bakerton like a bomb; for eighty years, if ground anywhere south of the Sahara was broken on a major hard-rock mining project, it's been a given that BEECO machines are "specced" by the consulting engineers.

The workforce is still reeling from the setback. And now, in the plant and the town, it's rumored that layoffs may be coming. People are starting to look shiftily at one another, wondering who among them, if cuts are made—the first since 1937—will be the first to go. Fingers are inevitably pointed. The "official" (from the top) explanation for the company's competitive difficulties is lack of investment; knowledgeable local scuttlebutt attributes it to lack of management. If only Laddie and Dick Baker hadn't been killed in that USAir crash, goes the gossip, if only they hadn't disregarded inviolate company policy about flying together, it'd be the Japanese pulling the long faces on the Zambian project. H.A. blew the bid: that's what people are saying, according to GIA's intelligence. If he'd moved quicker to bring in someone from Euclid or Caterpillar, BEECO wouldn't have lost out.

The buzz suddenly intensifies in pitch. The crowd shifts its attention to the front of the hangar. Baker leads Mannerman up the steps to the dais, joined by a number of other dignitaries identified in Lucy's poop sheet as Bakerton's mayor, the Pennsylvania Commissioner of Industrial Development (the governor's in Washington and the lieutenant governor is under indictment), and representatives of various local and regional commercial and booster organizations. As the men arrange themselves, Lucy feels the emotional barometer in the hangar drop sharply, the atmosphere turn thick with apprehension. Then there's a hum and squawk as the public-address system kicks in, and Baker comes forward to the microphone.

He looks around the hangar, as if to get the measure of his audience's mood, and then says quietly, "I don't have to tell you how emotional a moment this has to be for all of us in the Baker family. We've been together a long time. A hundred seventeen years. A long time."

His voice carries well and clearly. No "uhs," Lucy notes approvingly. He's a well-taught public speaker. Prep school did that for you, all that rote memorizing and debating-society stuff. She'd had a fling one teenage summer with a boy who was a senior at Loomis-Chaffee. Dumb as a box of rocks, he was, but he could quote half of *Hamlet* by heart, which had sufficiently impressed Lucy—once, and once only—to permit him to venture inside her bra.

"What's kept us together, kept BEECO moving forward," Baker is saying, "is a tradition of trust. We looked out for each other, and out of that built a great company. People were always our first concern here at BEECO. As Vince Lombardi should've said, in the BEECO family people aren't everything, they're the only thing!"

This draws a quick little ripple of amusement from the audience. They're not really buying this, Lucy thinks. It's Mannerman they want to hear. The Baker family is yesterday's news.

"When Jack Mannerman approached me about combining our two companies," Baker continues, "my first concerns had to do with people, with that heritage of trust. A mutual understanding, affection and respect that's taken a hundred seventeen years to build isn't something I could hand over lightly. But in Jack I saw someone who thinks as we do when it comes to people, but who also understands how to reconcile the new with the old, to bring the tried and true into line with the times. Jack understood the way we do things here immediately and instinctively. Jack respects tradition. He knows that it isn't necessary for us to throw out our traditional values to make ourselves market-worthy. Most important, he knows *how* we can make ourselves market-worthy. I think we all realize that times and markets have changed and that to maintain our place in the sun, we need access to resources and know-how that are no longer easily available to companies our size.

"I'm not talking about survival, mind you, which I know some people have been saying. They said the same thing about our friends at Chrysler and look at them! We've got the resources to keep going, and going well, but there's a tradition of pride around here, pride in the way we do things, in the way we treat each other, and pride, by God, in being the best damned producer of heavy mining equipment anywhere! With Jack, and with GIA, I am confident that all those proud traditions, what we think of as the BEECO way of doing things, will be well and honorably served. It's a big change, I know, and change always brings a spot of trepidation—but change is also the way the world works, and in this case I'm so absolutely convinced that this particular change is so much in everyone here's best interests that a year from now we'll all be wondering why we didn't think about doing something like this before."

On a scale of one to ten, Lucy grades Baker at perhaps a six. This speech is a deft piece of track covering, but despite all the "we" and "us" riffs, there's an invisible, impenetrable curtain separating speaker and audience. It's clear the workforce likes Baker well enough personally; GIA's intelligence is that he's admired for his sporting and artistic accomplishments and no one doubts his sincere interest in the community's well-being, but he's not really one of them, and they're willing to go down the road with him in charge only so far.

"You don't need to hear from me anymore," Baker says. "To everything there is a season, and ours—my family's—is over."

Ecclesiastes, thinks Lucy. At funerals and merger closings, which aren't all that different, come to think of it, someone always quotes Ecclesiastes. Just as nowadays you can't go to a wedding, of any denomination, without someone reading the Song of Songs at you.

"We've had a damn good run together," Baker is saying. "A hundred seventeen years. But the world's changed and we have to recognize that. I've done what I'm positive is best for all of us. If my brothers were still here, perhaps it might be different, but I can tell you with all my heart I doubt it. So now let's turn over that new leaf. Of course, I'll be around to help out wherever and whenever Jack and his people think I can be useful, but it's his show now, or it will be in about an hour, so let's give him a big Pennsylvania welcome. Jack Mannerman, it's all yours."

The applause from the audience is loud, but something is lacking,

Lucy's experienced ear decides. It lacks certainty. You're going to have
to earn your money with this crowd, she thinks, watching Mannerman
take the rostrum. Six weeks from now, H. A. Baker will be off on some
mountain shooting something, the immediate postmerger high will have
evaporated as surely as the bubbles from the celebratory champagne
now cooling in the BEECO boardroom, and the new regime will be
calling the shots. These people can read, Lucy knows, they watch CNN,
they own mutual funds, they're hip.

But they're also in a state of denial you could cut with a knife. It's
like a second layer of smog lying heavily upon this region, this valley,
this town, this plant. If they're applauding Mannerman at all, it's because they're praying that wishing will make it so, that he'll repay their
enthusiasm by keeping things the way they've always been.

Fat chance. It's all very well for these people to bitch about feckless
management, or lack of investment, or Japanese price cutting, or technological shortfall, but what no one talks about is BEECO's high-wage,
high-job-security, overpaternalistic employment practices. They're the
real killers. This is a spoiled workforce, accustomed to higher-than-
union pay scales, easy no-default mortgages from the friendly company-
owned savings association, a medical plan more generous than anything
at GIA. She can imagine that the GIA staff charged with mopping up
and regularizing the ancillaries and fringes at acquired companies is
licking its collective lips.

BEECO's workers have surely heard about "lean and mean." They've
got to have heard how tough Mannerman is on productivity and financial
targeting. It's common knowledge that GIA moved its own Pittsfield
turbine assembly operations to Guadalajara the day after the President
signed the NAFTA legislation. Many probably have a friend or a relative
somewhere in the rust-pitted Pennsylvania industrial belt who's been
laid off, probably the first of his or her family since the Depression to
be on the unemployment line, thanks to the labor economies which have
raced like firestorms across office and factory floors in the 1990s.

In the matter of jobs, guilt seems to be the central element in the
Baker family's management philosophy, as if to make up for the bloodshed and acrimony of early times. Indeed, H. A. Baker tried to insist
on a jobs-protection clause in the terms of the merger; for a minute, it
looked like a deal breaker, until Baker's investment banker, Herby La-

mond, talked him out of it and persuaded him to rely on Jack Mannerman's word as a gentleman.

Which is a laugh, Lucy thinks. Unlike the proverbial duck, Jack Mannerman may look like a gentleman, he may walk like one, he may even sound like one (thanks to an immersion course from the speech expert Dorothy Sarnoff), but a gentleman he is not. Nor does he wish to be.

"Gentlemen, like nice guys, finish last." She's heard him say that fifty times if she's heard it once. It's a quotation, more or less, of some baseball player Lucy's never heard of, another of the arcane sports references with which Mannerman studs his conversation. Mannerman uses Vince Lombardi too, but spins it differently than Baker had. "Return on capital isn't everything, it's the *only* thing."

Lucy herself can't remember—has never seen—a world in which people do deals on handshakes. She's had an earful on the subject from the few Street old-timers she occasionally indulges with a couple of Bankers Club martinis and a half hour's worth of attention just to keep her hand in, but privately her guess is that this dream world never existed outside their gin-soaked memories. The world she knows is one in which ten lawyers are hired to count the fingers on each hand, and then ten more to keep an eye on the first lot.

One thing Lucy's certain of: Mannerman will not mention the word "jobs." "Jobs" is a "people word," as Grover puts it, it's implicitly rich in human resonances and expectations, and as such it's fraught with potential problems. What PL will emphasize is how pregnant with renewed commercial possibility this merger is, thanks to GIA's investment and technological resources, how access to GIA's bottomless coffers will put BEECO back in the competitive forefront, and permit it to combine its updated technology with GIA's ability to offer prospective customers a total financing package. In other words, Baker has just talked about people, but Mannerman, more closely attuned to, indeed virtually incarnating, the spirit of the age, will talk about money. The trick, Lucy knows from her own spin-doctoring, is to sell the two as synonymous. At least for just as long as it's going to take to get from liftoff to destination.

From the beginning of the merger talks, on the table if ultimately not in writing, has been an undertaking that GIA will pump a substantial amount of new capital into BEECO. The figure which everyone seems to have settled on is $75 million, although Lucy, who's seen this a dozen times, knows that if you ask first one side of the table how firm the commitment is and then the other, you'll get two diametrically opposed answers. A skilled negotiator like Mannerman, ever mindful that beauty lies in the beholder's eye, will have a genius for translating verifiable ambiguity into perceived certainty.

Lucy knows it doesn't matter one way or the other. If she can't talk her way around $75 million, she doesn't deserve to keep her job. Even assuming Mannerman goes ahead with it, that kind of money is peanuts, even on top of the $300 million GIA is laying out to buy BEECO. The negative feedback from the Street—has Jack Mannerman lost his goddamn mind, buying goddamn mining machinery?—is strictly kneejerk.

That is, so long as BEECO is a one-shot deal and not the harbinger of a new direction. GIA now derives more and more of its profits from products and services smacking of high-tech. What's turned investors on is their perception of an Internet-driven future of fiber optics, digital compression, cellular communications, computer-driven financial services—business sectors into which GIA has diversified since Mannerman came in. If Yellow Brick Road gets implemented, the mix will be even more drastically weighted away from industrial production. The trick for Lucy is to make her "prize mullets"—GIA's biggest, most convinced stockholders—understand, without exactly saying so, that BEECO is no more than a political payoff on behalf of Yellow Brick Road.

To some people, a single zit on Venus's face is enough to ruin the goddess's beauty entirely. When the BEECO deal was announced, one of the Soros fund managers kicked out a block of close to a million shares and GIA made the most active list, down three-quarters of a point. Lucy doesn't want any more cyber-lemmings rushing for the exit. She needs to engineer a countervailing perception—which is tough, since she's not free to discuss what's really going on, other than in the spin doctor's symbolic vocabulary of shrugs and lifted eyebrows—that the BEECO deal is, in plain English, a $300 million bribe to a politician.

Lucy sees her world as defined by Price and Perception. She has a very precise mental image of how it works. It came to her a couple of years back when she and Mannerman were in Edinburgh wooing the Scottish investment trusts. On the way to lunch at a famous French restaurant in Gullane, about fifteen miles east of the Scottish capital, they happened to pass a flock of sheep being moved to new pasturage by a herdsman and a pair of Border collies. That herdsman, that's me, Lucy thought, noting the way the dogs responded to the virtually imperceptible commands of their master. Price and Perception are my dogs, and together we drive the market before us like a herd of sheep.

The herd is not always tractable. Certain of the Street's more finely tuned antennae, people with their own spies on Capitol Hill and elsewhere, have sensed that's something's afoot that's a hell of a lot bigger than BEECO. They're not buying what Lucy's limited to selling: really far-out technical synergies, mostly involving highly contingent applications of BEECO's water-jet know-how, the smooth way BEECO can be folded into GIA's Industrial Products and Services Group. Certain big hitters—the ones enthroned at the key interstices of Lucy's carefully crafted and polished filigree of insiderness—aren't fooled by this at all: they keep asking: What's *really* going on? They see what Lucy sees: the BEECO acquisition lacks a readily graspable logic; it's too much of a stretch. They're free to ask. She's not free to answer. She hates being at a disadvantage. She hates this deal!

She can live with the numbers. She's studied the analysis prepared by Mannerman's "gravediggers," the internal analysts who construct the worst-case scenarios on acquisitions. The gravediggers' spreadsheets show that not much can be milked out of operations as they stand, although some current savings can be generated by folding BEECO's indulgent health-care plan into GIA's managed-care HMO. But if the plug has to be pulled, then after a decent interval BEECO can probably be broken up and sold off in pieces, with a maximum hit to GIA's bottom line of no worse than $100 million, including the $75 million new-investment hickey—and a loss this small can be hidden away in pockets stitched here and there on GIA's balance sheet by clever tax lawyers and accountants, and the net perceptual effect will be minimal.

The real problem Lucy's looking at—worst case—would be the effect on PL's image of infallibility. And that—for a company like GIA—could be a very big problem indeed. She would have preferred it if PL

had left today's closing to a subordinate—say the senior executive VP
—so that when BEECO craters, she'd have someone else at whom to
help the Street aim its pointing finger. Mannerman's personal participation implies his personal sponsorship; she can only assume this is
something the Speaker's people insisted on.

She watches as Mannerman acknowledges Baker and the other noble
presences seated on the platform, and looks out at the crowd, playing
his presence over it like a spotlight. He can be counted on to give a
virtuoso performance. He's got the best, most instinctive sense of an
audience Lucy's ever seen, whether he's chatting one-on-one or speaking to a large crowd like this, on a factory floor, or a black-tie VIP
group in a bouquet-bedecked grand ballroom. Grover, a would-be actor
himself, calls it "natural-born stage genius," a set of instincts its owner
probably doesn't fully understand, which may account for Mannerman's
ability to connect with concerned human beings despite being as cold-
blooded and calculating as anyone Lucy's ever known. He sees life as
a series of equations derived from the known facts—which, by his definition, includes living, breathing, feeling "facts," several hundred of
whom are now gathered expectantly at his feet. In his calculus, Lucy
might be x and BEECO might be y with the Fidelity Funds being z;
you combine them with factors 1, 2, and 3—say, various market
patterns—and by Mannerman's calculation you will get—with Einstein-
ian certitude—result α or β.

"It would be easy to describe what Mr. Baker and I are going to do
later this morning as just another business arrangement," Mannerman
begins, "and the fact is, it *was* business common sense and a feeling
of business community that caused us to find each other across a
crowded room. But underneath all the papers and the lawyering, he and
I want you to know, is a real commitment by the two of us to all of you,
and for all of you, for all of *us*, that with this . . . well, this exchange
of vows, you might call it, we're going to light a small but brilliant torch
that's going to light the way for the resurgence of American competi-
tiveness in the global market for industrial machinery!"

Here he pauses, measures his audience, obviously likes what his
oratorical telemetry is feeding him, and continues in a softer voice.

"Now I know what's foremost on your minds," he says. "The same things are on my mind too. The economy, the political situation, GIA. My guess is you've probably been exposed to the conventional wisdom about us: that we're strictly a high-tech outfit. I can't blame you for that, because no matter how hard we try, and believe me we *try*, the gosh-darn media are going to paint us the way they see us."

Nice touch, that "gosh-darn," thinks Lucy, very down-home, just right for a pious, praying community where Norman Rockwell's *Four Freedoms* hangs back of the diner's cash register. She shoots a teasingly knowing look at Grover at the very back of the shed, but he's muttering into a cellular phone and doesn't catch it.

And a nice twist, too, for the CEO of a company that spends roughly $10 million a year to see that the media paint it just so, to complain about how it's painted.

"So naturally you're wondering," Mannerman continues, "where in tarnation an outfit like yours will find its place with us, given what you've probably been told about our high-tech bias. It's true we do have some meaningful interests in that area, but you should also know that we have important heavy industry commitments of our own, and not just as a matter of history, any more than is the case right here in Bakerton!"

He doesn't seem to raise his voice to make the point, but his words carry clearly to all corners of the cavernous building, and take on an added ring.

"The fact is," he continues, "man doesn't live by digits alone."

This is a breathtaking bit of hypocrisy, Lucy knows, but the crowd doesn't know that. Mannerman now flashes his famous smile, and draws from his audience a nervous small laugh which ripples briefly around the test pad. The man's sheer force of personality is extraordinary and undeniable. Spuds has sworn to Lucy he's seen Mannerman literally *charm* a thirty-foot putt into the cup.

He's beginning to reach them, Lucy thinks. She looks around. People are standing easier, facial muscles are relaxing.

"Another fact is," Mannerman says, moving his eyes right to left, left to right, sweeping the room, but now and then pausing on a single listener to give his remarks a tighter, more personal focus, "another fact is that you know, and I know, and Mr. Baker here and his family know, and certainly the Speaker of the House knows, at least that's what he told me last night when I stopped off in Washington on my way up here from Atlanta, that without a strong capability in heavy industry, this country of ours will go straight to the dogs . . ."

He lets his words trail off, holds the silence a beat, looks around the audience, and then above and past it, as if addressing a higher power, and then pushes a button guaranteed to detonate his listeners' frustrations and uncertainties. ". . . or straight to the damn Japanese and Koreans!"

Us against "them," thinks Lucy. Blame and anger are the straws that stir the Molotov cocktail of national politics. Once you get your audience's mind tuned onto the resentment frequency, Mannerman and his presenters know, all other transmissions are drowned out. Your listeners won't listen carefully to what you may, ever so subtly, be saying about something else.

As she looks around, now only half attentive, her eye lights on a large, well-lit opening cut into the shed's west wall about two stories up. It reminds Lucy of the GIA skybox in Madison Square Garden. This must be the booth from which BEECO's customers, like prospective bidders at a bloodstock auction, are shown the great machines in operation.

Today the booth is occupied by two women. "The Widows of Bakerton," Lucy guesses, H. A. Baker's sisters-in-law, the wives of his late brothers. Between them, they control 23 percent of the voting stock. It's they who have relentlessly pressed Baker to sell the company. From what Lucy's heard, Medea could've taken lessons from this pair. As Grover puts it: "BEECO's only one witch short of the first scene of *Macbeth*."

She studies them briefly. Cookies from the same cutter, she decides. WASP to the last centimeter, right out of the Talbots catalogue—until the check clears, after which it'll be: Paris, here we come! What's on their minds is clear on their faces; Lucy's seen that expression on the faces of many sellers' wives and girlfriends. Psychologically, they're already outta here: on the high road for Palm Beach or Southampton or Newport or wherever they think their own personal golden highways lead.

Standing with them is a man Lucy recognizes from long acquaintance. Herbert Lamond, investment banker and merger specialist, has represented BEECO in the negotiations with GIA. Give credit where it's due, this is Lamond's deal, a monument to his opportunism. He picked up on a casual remark of PL's and got his people to run a computer screen on every company in the Speaker's district that GIA could use as a vehicle for its grandstand play. BEECO stuck out; Lamond brought it to Mannerman's attention; GIA ran its own deep background checks, then gave Lamond the green light to churn the waters. As it happened, Lamond knew one of the Baker widows from East Hampton, where they both rented houses in August. Through her, he was introduced socially to H. A. Baker, and planted the seed that GIA was looking to add a few choice marques to its heavy industry group, price no object. A couple of weeks later, Baker signed up Lamond to explore the matter with GIA. In the final negotiations, Lamond represented BEECO and its selling stockholders; when the deal closes, that's what Lamond & Co.'s celebratory "tombstone" ad in *The Wall Street Journal* will surely say. It's the sellers, after all, who pay the lion's share of the fees in any deal.

Still, it's a nice point, Lucy thinks, as she contemplates the investment banker, whose sallow, rodentlike face and trademark unruly winglets of stiff gray hair are practically quivering with anticipation. One man's buyout is another's sellout. Only Herby Lamond knows whom he thinks he represented: was it BEECO and the Baker family, or was it GIA, with whom he hoped to have an ongoing relationship? Or was it the deal itself?

One thing is certain: without Herbert Lamond, there wouldn't be a deal. He persuaded Baker to pull back on a whole bunch of potential deal breakers: not only the job-security gurantee but also written commitments by GIA regarding future capital investment, fringe benefits, corporate "lifestyle" and so on. Once or twice, when Baker seemed ready to walk out, Lamond kept him at the table. No wonder he's beaming like the cat who swallowed the canary. More like the Rat who swallowed the Golden Goose, Lucy decides, considering that once all the signatures are on the contract of sale, he stands to earn a fee of $10 million for his part in the transaction. That is a large fee for a deal this size, but Lucy knows how investment bankers think: It's one thing to get paid x for "representing" one side of a deal but if in fact you end up "representing" both, why shouldn't you get $2x$?

At her back, she's aware of the looming presence of the great machines drawn up at the rear of the hangar. They're arrayed in a rank which spans the building's entire vast width. Freshly painted, polished and oiled, they're like everything else about BEECO: spick-and-span. You could eat off the floor, and Lucy senses it's this way every day. She wonders what these plant-proud workers would think if they got a look at GIA's Guadalajara turbine plant, where a week's pay is coffee money in Bakerton. Or the heavy cable facility near New Delhi, where skilled foundrymen make a third of what *maquilladora* workers do.

Mannerman is "pedal to the metal now," moving full-bore from buzzword to buzzword, from concept to concept. As he arrives at a riff about "the GIA family," he makes a characteristic gesture, one Lucy's sure he's probably unaware of by now. He opens and spreads his arms, as if to take his audience into a welcoming, sheltering embrace.

He's mentally back in Rome, Lucy knows. Back on the balcony overlooking St. Peter's Square on Easter morning, standing in the shadows behind the Pope. Hell, he probably thinks he *is* the Pope!

The greatest thrill of his life, that was. Two Easters ago, when Pope Leo XIV overruled his Curia and invited Mannerman to stand behind him, to get a sense of what it was like to command an audience of over a half million people crammed in the curving embrace of the colonnades of St. Peter's Square.

It was the Pope's way of saying thanks. His Holiness Leo XIV is, some claim, in Jack Mannerman's pocket. The two men met a decade ago, when Mannerman first became involved in Save Venice and raised huge amounts for ecclesiastical restorations dear to the heart of the present pontiff, who was then merely His Eminence the Cardinal-Patriarch of Venice. By the time the old Pope's interminable last illness drew to its end, Mannerman, now at GIA, had seen to it that promises had been made to other influential princes of the Church concerning projects close to *their* hearts. On the third ballot of the College of Cardinals, the smoke from the Sistine Chapel chimney puffed white for the man from Venice.

The relationship between the two men remains close. Mannerman's commitment to Rome is deep, genuine, visionary, doctrinal. He's a true son of the Church, born in South Boston, raised in the very shadow of the College of the Holy Cross in Worcester, the only child—thanks to postparturitive complications—of parents who between them supplied their son with five uncles who were priests and three aunts who were nuns. Mannerman Senior held a political appointment as assistant post-master of Worcester, thanks to excellent Boston and statehouse con-nections (he was on familiar terms with a chief aide to "Honey Fitz" Fitzgerald, Rose Kennedy's father, and a cousin worked for Mayor Curley).

It had been Mannerman's mother's wish to farrow a brood of strong sons to carry the colors of the Church Triumphant, but Jack Mannerman would twice be a vessel for her disappointment. His maternal uncle Ted, Monsignor Theodore Macdougal, S.J., was treasurer of Fordham. An intimate of the worldly circles centering on Francis Cardinal Spell-man of New York, he was in a position to further his nephew's career after ordination, but ironically it was Uncle Ted who diverted the prom-ising lad's steps from the priestly path. According to Mannerman, what pulled the switch had been a story his uncle liked to tell about His Eminence, an anecdote he'd invariably repeat on his thrice-yearly visits to Worcester. He'd been driving up Fifth Avenue with the Cardinal, back in the era when the great thoroughfare ran both ways, when Spell-man had looked out the limousine window at the Plaza Hotel and com-mented that Conrad Hilton had gotten himself quite a deal. Then he'd turned to the young priest beside him, placed an avuncular hand on Father Theodore's knee, and observed with considerable pride, "You know, Ted, I'm quite sound on doctrine, but what really counts is that I know *everything* about Manhattan real estate!"

It's a story Mannerman likes to tell. Lucy's probably heard it a dozen times. Mannerman never tells it without setting the scene, which he does with evocative relish, painting a word picture of a murmurous Sunday late afternoon in his parents' parlor, the dinner dishes done and put away, the blackberry cordial going round and round while the re-flected sheen of the great dome nearby turns the motes in the fading drowsy sunbeams into gleaming nuggets. It's the only occasion when Lucy can honestly say she hears something like nostalgia in the voice of a man who lives exclusively in the present and future.

As Mannerman tells it, he was fascinated that something so worldly as real estate should absorb one of the lordliest princes of the Church. So he asked his uncle, who set about teaching him the ways of finance—Father Theodore's specialty was long-term corporate bonds—

and found him such an apt pupil that money was located in a slush fund to pay for a scholarship to Fordham and thence to the Harvard Business School, with the understanding that the call to Holy Orders could come later.

The rest was history, ecclesiastical as much as secular: today Mannerman is acknowledged by everyone from *Time* to *Commonweal* to be the most influential lay Catholic in the United States, possibly the world. Holder of every papal honor there is, including—highest of all—the ear of the Holy Father himself, whom Mannerman serves as principal unofficial advisor on economic issues. When the Pope came, twice, to the White House, the ceremonial photographs showed Mannerman between the President and the Holy Father.

The papal connection will hit the spot with this crowd, Lucy guesses. The preacquisition study made by GIA's demographers shows almost 30 percent of BEECO's workforce to be Catholic. Poles and Italians mostly, with a smattering of Croats. Fourth, fifth generation. Yearners after the old ways. Loyal, proud, trusting. People who instinctively cross themselves, always sing the national anthem, go to mass and confession.

Mannerman's going along nicely now, talking about American renewal. Across the way, Grover, face intent, has his cellular phone jammed so tightly against his head the tip of his ear is white. Even unbuttoned, his Burberry looks as tight as a sausage casing. You're getting overweight again, Lucy thinks. Well, it goes with the territory: the checks Grover picks up aren't for sprouts and tofu; Capitol Hill only trades its soul for prime rib and caviar.

Of the Gang of Four, TK—absent today—has the hardest job, in Lucy's opinion: Mannerman is a hardnose who has reduced all existence to a procrustean calculus but TK must project him as Mr. Average, a regular guy who puts on his Superman suit one leg at a time, a kindly, fifty-eight-year-old softie, married to the same woman for thirty-six years, father of five, grandfather of two, golf nut, Cardinals and Rams fan (at Ford, it had been the Tigers and Lions), collector of microbrews, recondite malt whiskies and nineteenth-century beer steins from his paternal grandparents' native Bavaria.

It's all true, but who's going to believe it? That's TK's gripe.

Lucy sees Mannerman's wife perhaps once a month. She shows up at most big GIA functions, the stockholders meeting, the annual board get-together at Cypress Point, the pro-am banquet at the GIA St. Louis Open golf tournament at Bellerive, and she waves the right charity flags in New York and Washington. Mainly, however, she stays at home: spring and fall in a smart exurb of St. Louis, where she gardens and plays bridge; summer and winter on Fisher's Island, New York, and Boca Grande, Florida, respectively—old-money, old-blood resorts where she plays tennis and bridge and the grandchildren come to visit. Mannerman goes home religiously every weekend—touching ground by dinnertime Friday, aloft again after an early Sunday supper. With a life like that, it's a wonder he hasn't played around, but there's never been a whisper of scandal; certainly he's never come on to Lucy.

The fact is, it's true what someone said: "Jack Mannerman's a monk for Mammon." His commitment to the money god's earthly cathedral— GIA—is priestlike and total. The man, in his way, is unreal. But then, you can't run something like GIA, or at least run it *well*, and allow more than 10 percent of yourself to be standard-issue human—at least, so people think. The fact is, the 90 percent that sets Mannerman apart isn't some publicist's fabrication, it's just something he's *got*.

When she has to, Lucy can conceptualize and subliminalize with the best in the business, but she knows that the trick is to have a genuinely superior product to begin with, and that she has. "Investor relations" are no use at all unless the investors are already halfway converted. In GIA's case the quotient is close to 90 percent. This company is run 110 percent for its stockholders. Not for its executives, not for its employees, and only as necessary for its customers. Investors know that, and they *believe*. Mannerman's yet to shake that belief.

They say a shark can sniff out a micron of blood in a million parts of seawater. Mannerman's like that. He has a sixth sense of where he has to take GIA for the market to keep loving him to death, and to keep expressing that love by buying more stock. It's an infatuation which over the past six years has quadrupled GIA's stock price even as the company passed through one after another level of critical mass or financial sound barrier, benchmark quanta of sales, assets and profits beyond which sheer size is supposed to impede growth. With that kind of record, Mannerman and GIA are a ridiculously easy sell. That's why there isn't an investor relations honcho in any other Fortune 500 company who doesn't envy Lucy and her colleagues.

Mannerman cracks a little joke, and a ripple of friendly laughter courses easily through the BEECO hangar. Lucy looks quickly over at Grover. He's smiling. We're home free, she thinks. She wonders how these foursquare folks would react if they knew they were nothing more than a short-term down payment on Yellow Brick Road. As the laughter subsides, Mannerman turns up the intensity knob. Lucy returns her full attention to the platform.

"Stretching back over these hills and fields," Mannerman says, "I see the long parade of all those souls who've made this company what it's been and what it is. Standing before me, I see the living folks who're going to make it what it's going to be."

He's very solemn now, very focused, very—well—presidential.

"To achieve that goal, you have my undertaking that we at GIA will do what's necessary and appropriate to help get you there. To keep BEECO right at the forefront. Competitive and innovative and—as your company motto puts it—*the* name that industry can count on. A proud place to work. A great company.

"The last few years have been hard, we know that. Global markets are more competitive than ever. In the four corners of the earth are people—skilled people, hungry people—willing to work for less than it takes to put a good meal on the table here in Bakerton. Technology is moving ahead on winged feet; just to keep pace has become enormously costly. And for the last few years there've been people in Washington who frankly haven't seemed all that interested in the lives and livelihoods of working Americans."

By now, you could hear a pin drop.

"These are concerns we at GIA feel as much as you. Despite what certain naysayers in the media may say, 'lean and mean' hasn't been our style. We want productivity, we need it, but people are still our most important product. Fortunately, we have the resources and we have the commitment to make our people as productive as they can possibly be by putting the very best tools in their hands. That goes for our involvement here at BEECO, assuming things work out as we foresee, and frankly we can't see any reason why they shouldn't, especially now that, at long last, there are good people running things in Washington —people like your congressman, my friend the Speaker of the House, people whose concerns are the concerns of every working American.

The grand BEECO parade that's marched on steadily for a hundred and seventeen years. Now we at GIA look forward to joining it and marching shoulder to shoulder with you! Together we'll consecrate ourselves to making BEECO a light for all American industry to follow, a triumph of its people, by its people, for its people!"

He turns away abruptly and sits down, leaving the audience hanging.

It's a hoary public-speaking trick that never fails. For a beat, there's silence, then the applause breaks out. At first tentative, then full-palmed, enthusiastic, convinced, relieved. The Pennsylvania commissioner bounds out of his folding chair and crouches at Mannerman's knee, pumping his hand. Then Baker and Mannerman shake hands while a photographer clicks away. The applause ripens and swells. Lucy turns and stares at Grover. He's grinning like a banshee.

It's all in the eye of the beholder, she thinks. What PL has just said about "lean and mean" is a lie. It's that simple. In the last four years, GIA has eliminated nearly five thousand jobs at all levels. The average job "haircut" for new acquisitions averages nearly 20 percent. But if it's a lie, who's going to call Jack Mannerman on it? These days, nobody thinks twice about lying. Facts mean nothing, and truth is a relative thing that people like her are paid big money to "position." Job seekers lie to employers, scientists lie to colleagues, politicians lie to the voters, financiers lie to everyone. It's the way it is. It runs against her Yankee grain, but what are her alternatives? At least, she can tell herself, she hasn't gone as far as many people she knows in accepting this state of affairs. She does her damnedest not to lie outright. And she's resisted the current gospel that claims that if everyone's lying, no one is.

So far.

— III —   "You really have got the balls of a brass monkey," Lucy says to Grover as they trail PL and Baker toward the executive building. The closing will shortly be held there, followed by a ceremonial lunch. " 'Of its people, by its people, for its people,' my sweet Aunt Fanny!"

"Cut the crap, Luce. You think with Gettysburg just a half hour over the hill I was about to leave that out? Anyway, you think they bought?"

"I do. Hook, line and sinker. So tell me. What's the deal with the Speaker? How long do we have to sit with this one before we hook up the euthanasia tubes? The Street is not happy with this acquisition and they haven't seen the gravediggers' report—which I have. This patient is terminal. How long before we can tell the family and call the undertaker?"

Grover looks at her with amusement.

"Lucy, Lucy, Lucy," he says in a creditable imitation of Cary Grant, "whatever makes you think such things?"

"Anyway," Lucy says, proffering her hand, "congrats. It was a great speech. I thought they'd be more hostile, especially after those Westinghouse layoffs last week over in Lancaster. But you won 'em over. You got them by the short hairs of their hopes."

"Ah, hope," Grover says in a musing tone. "Hope—hope—hope: it's the spackle that smooths out the surface of the mind for the whitewash of credulity."

"Who said that?"

"I did," Grover replies. "I'm just waiting for the right chance to use it. I wasn't about to waste an aphorism worthy of Oscar Wilde on this bunch of bohunks."

Lucy scowls at him. "I didn't hear you say that," she says sharply.

"Well, ex-*cuse* me! I didn't realize I was speaking with little Miss PC."

"Cut the crap, Grove. You know what I mean."

Actually, Lucy's not sure he does, because she's not sure *she* does. It has nothing to do with political correctness. She feels something about this Baker deal and these people. They never had a chance. Only a year or so from now, when they're trying to figure out what hit them, will some of them see that. Between H. A. Baker's naïveté and the duplicity ranged against him on the other side of the table, BEECO was dead on delivery. Perhaps this is one reason she dislikes this deal all out of proportion to its significance. Maybe at long last, the job is getting to her.

"As you wish," Grover responds, sounding not the least bit apologetic.

"The Baker guy leading off the way he did really set the old man up. I gather he's kind of a jerk when it comes to nuts and bolts, but I got the feeling these folks trust him."

"In my opinion, it's the Baker name they trust."

"Whatever. You may be right. With these dipshit little companies, family pride counts. Anyway, the bottom line is, they aren't going to let themselves think, not for a minute, that Baker'll do a deal with anyone he doesn't think'll play by the rules and do right by them, which makes them grist for our rhetorical mill, if you will."

You've got a point, Lucy thinks. It was a clever, well-turned little speech that Mannerman delivered, but it was H. A. Baker's credibility that put it over. Grover's right: the BEECO workforce are "Baker people" not simply because of his heroism, his style, his dash. They trust his loyalty to them because he's part of a family whose devotion has always been—literally—bankable. The problem is, even the most bankable commodity can be overdrawn, and there's powerful evidence that's been the case here at BEECO.

When they reach the door of the executive building, Lucy tries again.

"You still owe me an answer on Washington, Grove. I don't need you to cross all the *i*'s and dot all the *t*'s, but anything I *can* say about what you've got going with the Speaker will help soothe the Street's savage breast. What's the arrangement? We're talking strictly broad-brush, of course. Some kind of recip—we'll do this for you, Mr. Speaker, and you'll see to it that we get pick of the litter when the next lot of frequencies and channels is parceled out? That there'll be no problem with foreign ownership if we team up with, say, Berlusconi to go after one of the webs? Something like that?"

Grover places his forefinger against his lips. "Luce, what's done is done. Time now for the coup de grace. And I can really use a drink. C'mon."

Inside, it takes less than forty minutes to end a century-plus of Baker family ownership. Mannerman and Baker sign and shake hands. At a nod from the presiding attorneys, aides on cellular phones trigger preformatted wire transfers and share releases. The sisters-in-law depart, each richer by several tens of millions, as do the representatives of the Baker Extractive Enterprises Employee Profit-Sharing Fund, and the lawyers for the various schools and hospitals sharing in the liquidation of the Baker Charitable Trust. When only the principals and their chief courtiers remain, the champagne is opened and poured, and while the table is cleared of documents and signing paraphernalia and is set for lunch, people stand around sipping bubbly and making the conversation people make when their minds have already moved on, like nomads leaving one oasis to search for another.

At lunch, Lucy finds herself placed next to H. A. Baker. She suspects it's PL's doing: Mannerman's always flinging men at her.

The fact is, however, she's secretly pleased. Baker intrigues her. Of his High WASP type, he strikes her as an unusual and interesting specimen, several cuts above the usual Racquet Club run that she's encountered in her travels. He's the real thing. Compared to Baker, Spuds, who spends about $50K a year at Ralph Lauren to create the impression he went to Yale and belongs to Piping Rock, looks like the impersonator he is. Baker's tweed jacket seems of a piece with the man; Spuds is merely draped in something he's bought.

She likes his looks. Nearing his sixth decade, he seems the proverbial ten years younger, not that an age difference has ever bothered Lucy. His profile is aquiline, his skin reddish dark and weather-roughened, although with his sort it doesn't have to be weather. She finds herself wondering how much he drinks. His eyes are hazel running to green, his gaze shrewd and cool. His hair is thick and dark, with not much gray; people like him let life and nature take their course, it's one of their seemlier virtues. There's something about the man that hints of Indian blood, of the heroes of the James Fenimore Cooper novels Lucy's father—something of an outdoorsman himself, a keen pistol shot and foul-weather sailor—used to read to her. Baker must have been really handsome when he was young, she thinks, not that he's going to seed now.

When he holds her chair for her, she feels those familiar uneasy resonances of her Maine girlhood, but as lunch progresses, these fade away. Baker doesn't talk to her right away. At first he sits, subdued, studying his plate, trying to focus on whatever the Philadelphia attorney on his left is saying and obviously not succeeding.

Lucy can't escape the feeling that he's in fact homing in on her. Almost to her astonishment, the notion detonates a shivery little thrill.

Say something, she thinks. Go on, make your move. If you wait for him to initiate things, you'll be here until the year 2000. She's experienced the notorious WASP reticence with other men—"reticence" if you're feeling charitable or open-minded, "emotional strangulation" if you're not. By whatever name, a pain in the psychological keister. Why is she thinking this way?

There's something straight and forthright and substantial about him, she thinks, the quality in a man that an English friend calls "bottom." None of that country-club crap and swagger. She likes his half-rueful expression. She tells herself it means he's a caring person.

Baker's probably having second thoughts, she says to herself, those "staircase thoughts" many sellers have, wondering if one's done the right thing, when the sheer weight of the zeros in the bank account hasn't really hit home, hasn't quashed once and for all the awareness of ghosts at the banquet—all those people whose lives and efforts paved the gleaming pathway leading to this hour and this wealth. A pensive frisson that'll fade soon enough, she guesses. Why should Baker be different? Still, it's nice at least to sense it even briefly. Nowadays, most sellers just take the money and run.

Maybe I'm making this all up, she tells herself. Still, when she looks at him she sees a different kind of value system from the one she and Spuds and Mannerman represent. A different America, for that matter, a country of open space and open faces, of straightforwardness and hope, the America pictured in her current favorite paintings: the nineteenth-century American landscapes at the Met and in the Brooklyn Museum, images very like what Lucy can see through the wide windows across the room, where the sunlight seems to caress the softly contoured hills and the world seems at peace.

Innocence isn't the right word for what Baker seems to project. "Purity" is more like it. A freshness of spirit uncontaminated by hustle, or by money, or by calculation. Galahad in buckskin. Rough-worn and unspoiled. Compared to a man like this, the people in her world seem old in spite of their youth; they seem jaded and cynical. Unless something carries a gigantic price tag, they shrug their shoulders and ask: Why bother? Theirs is a desiccated world without ideals, and living in it is like living in a desert.

Hey, hey, hey, she tells herself, breaking into her own riff. Down, girl! No more wine for you! And at just that moment, Baker turns in his seat and says to her, "Well, Miss Preston, it seems you've brought good weather. We can use it. Let's hope it's a good omen for the future."

She likes his voice. It has a well-bred confident quality, smooth and precise, but without the pursed vowels some Ivy League types affect.

"So it seems," she says, and smiles back. "At GIA, contentment is our most important product."

"See that white object at the top of the hill over there, to the right?" he asks, gesturing beyond the window with a forkful of smoked salmon. "That's the Tomb of the Known Executive, my great-granduncle Abel Baker—no pun intended. Shot dead in his carriage in 1887 on his way home from work. Our only martyr."

"Who shot him?"

"Someone whom he locked out. During what we call the Difficulties."

"Labor strife?"

"Precisely. Great-granduncle Abel had the idea of bringing in Central European workers to replace the Irish, who were getting all sorts of terrible ideas about workingmen's rights from the Molly Maguires out in the western part of Pennsylvania. There were walkouts and lockouts. Then Abel was killed. Three men were hanged for it. A local version of Sacco and Vanzetti, you might say. To this day, no one knows if they were guilty, but those were retributive times and someone had to pay. Abel's brother wanted to do what Frick had done at Homestead: call in the Pinkertons and slaughter the lot. Anyway, the monument's a useful reminder that this company wasn't built simply with capital and ingenuity. A hell of a lot of bloodshed and anger also went into it."

A hell of a lot of guilt forever after, Lucy thinks. "Has that made a difference in the way later generations have run the company?" she asks disingenuously. The guilt coddled the workforce into thinking of its pay envelope as an entitlement.

"I suppose it has." Baker doesn't want to speak of this. He takes another mouthful of the starter course. "Say, this salmon's pretty good."

"It ought to be," Lucy comments, "it's from '21.' "

"Is it really? My goodness—'21.' It's been five years—no, more— since I darkened the doors there, although in my wild, rambunctious youth, about a hundred years ago, it seems, I practically lived in the place. How is it these days? Probably like everything else: not what it used to be. Nothing is."

Oh, please, thinks Lucy, not one of those. Spare me. She's had her fill of people whining about how great everything used to be.

"Actually," she says, "it's still pretty good."

She should know. Every Thursday without fail, in rain or shine, war or peace, she eats there with Mannerman and one invited guest. Same time, same table, same food. The sameness appeals to PL, adds a pinpoint of continuity to a life that's a whirlwind of flux, change, new faces, new circumstances.

She doesn't want to pursue this line of talk any more than Baker wanted to talk about BEECO. "Now that your time is your own, Mr. Baker, what are your plans?"

"To tell you the truth, I haven't gotten that far. Africa, I suppose, after a little R and R at my place in the Adirondacks, alone with nature and the Internet."

Lucy looks at him curiously, drawing a chuckle, and Baker asks, "Is your expression saying you're surprised that I'm—as they say—computer-literate?"

She smiles, looks vague and encouraging.

"Well, even an old goat like me has to make some concessions—as few as possible, believe me—to the times one finds oneself living in. And the Internet, computers in general, reduce one's dependence on others. Anyway, I think I'll hole up at Two Moose until I get used to the idea that I don't have a job anymore, and then sometime after the turn of the year, I'll pack up my kit and head for the Dark Continent. It all depends on whether this cease-fire in Rwanda holds."

Lucy tries for flattery. "I know we're all supposed to know, so promise you won't tell anyone I'm asking, but where exactly is Rwanda?"

"In East Africa. That's my beat. Rwanda and Burundi and the country west of Lake Victoria. The wildlife there is taking a terrible beating from the tribal wars and from total social chaos. The poachers have been given virtually a free hand. Something has to be done, and some of us are trying to do something about it. A number of species, the giant yellow crocodile of Lake Kivu, to name one, could be facing extinction."

"I take it you're what they call an animal person."

"I'm becoming one. On the whole, I do find animals preferable to man, certainly to modern man. They're more dependable and trustworthy, they display superior family values and they're seldom predatory just for the sake of it."

He smiles at Lucy. She can't tell if he's kidding. She thinks about asking why, if he's such an animal lover, the walls of this room are studded with the heads and horns of beasts he's killed.

"And you, Miss Preston," he says, "what about you? A city girl born and bred, I suppose?"

"Actually, I come from a small coastal town in Maine. My father was the chief of police there; he's retired now. But I guess you could call me a city girl—person—now. Ten years in New York will do that to you. The place takes you over."

"I suppose it does. Outside of New York, what's your favorite city?"

"That's easy. Venice."

This elicits a strange reaction from Baker, a look almost of pity. He studies her for a moment, then asks, "Do you know it well?"

Lucy shakes her head. "I've only been there twice. Once right after college, one of those nine-countries-in-eight-days tours, and once again in a more civilized way, two—no, three—years ago."

"Alas, you never knew Venice when it was really Venice."

Oh, please, thinks Lucy again. "I guess not." It's her guess that people have been saying that about Venice for centuries. Self-styled old-timers say it about New York. Everyone says it about everywhere.

Baker shakes his head slowly, as if he's having trouble accepting what he's thinking. "You know," he says with a touch of bitterness, "twenty-five years ago, perhaps only twenty, before the damn Japanese took over the world, if you'd asked me that question I'd've answered Venice too. It was my favorite place. My God, I can still taste the Bellinis at Harry's Bar! Bellinis, the cuttlefish risotto and afterward a few Titians to remind one that this too shall pass. There was nothing like it." Again he shakes his head. He speaks with surprising vehemence. Lucy can't help thinking that Mr. Reticence has a certain anger simmering down there under the surface.

"But the place has been ruined, Miss Preston, ruined!" he continues, face and voice slightly flushed. "Tourism—tourism and greed, that's what's done it!"

He looks around and drops his voice. "Look, I know your boss is a leading light in Save Venice, but if you knew it as it was when I first went there with my parents in the 'fifties, when it really looked like the Queen of the Adriatic, not a ten-thousand-lire *puttana*, and compare that with what Venice has become, you'd organize a reverse charity called Sink Venice, because nowadays it's nothing but a tourist trap! You know what the problem is, Miss Preston? Too many people! In Venice, everywhere! Too damn many people in the world! The earth is strangling on its own population. How anyone can oppose birth control is beyond me!"

Lucy cocks an eyebrow at Mannerman. Baker catches the hint and lowers his voice. "Don't worry, Miss Preston, I may hate the Pope and his Church and his scheming priests, but I'm not stupid enough to raise the subject with Jack. It's just that it breaks my heart to think I'll never take the Bellini walk again!"

"Bellini as in Harry's Bar?" Lucy has a vision of Baker, tanked up on Prosecco and peach juice, stumbling along an intricate route that winds along fuming canals and through narrow alleys from Harry's Bar to God knows where.

"No, no. Bellini as in the painter. He made a series of great altarpieces, each in a different church in a different part of town, in which you can trace his development. He's my favorite Venetian painter. Who's yours, Miss Preston?"

"Titian, I guess."

"And which is your favorite Titian in all the world?"

Lucy thinks for a moment. "I guess *Rape of Europa* in the Gardner Museum in Boston."

"Here's mine," says Baker. From a pocket he produces a small sketch pad and a draftsman's pen. He works furiously for less than a minute, then rips the sheet from the spiral binding and hands it to her.

Considered simply as a parlor trick, the drawing's quite something, but it's better than that. She doesn't recognize the painting—the subject's obviously an Annunciation—but Baker's sketch itself is fine indeed: livelier, richer and more essential than an artistic parlor trick has any right to be.

"I don't know this picture," she says. "Where is it?"

"It's in the San Salvador, just on the San Marco side of the Rialto Bridge. If you didn't know the picture was there, you wouldn't give the church half a look."

They talk about Titian and Venice and art for a while, then he switches the conversation to his sporting life. It seems that, come spring, when he returns from Africa, he has a date with a sheep in the Sonora Desert of Mexico.

"A *sheep*?"

"Well, not just any sheep. A desert ram, to be exact. To complete my grand slam."

"Your grand slam?"

There are four North American trophy sheep, he explains: the bighorn, stone, desert and Dall rams. Baker lacks only the desert, which is now hunted exclusively in Mexico. Hunting permits are issued by lottery. It's been ten years since he last won one, and even then he never got a shot.

"It's not cheap," he tells her, "not that cost seems to matter anymore, not after today, but I'm going to get a desert ram or go bust trying."

"You sound compulsive."

"On some things, I suppose I am. The fact is, I'm a nut on completeness, I can't help it. Once I make a list, I don't sleep until everything on it's checked off. See those mounted fish up there? The ones with the spots? Those are the six salmon of British Columbia. All of them. It took me ten years to complete the set. If I get a ram in Mexico, it'll have been twenty-one years end to end, twenty-one years since I got my first ram, a bighorn in Alaska."

He seems ready to go on, but hunting and fishing bore Lucy, and there's a question she's dying to ask.

"Tell me, Mr. Baker, how do you think it went back there?"

"Back where?"

"In the hangar. The boss's speech. Your people must've been pretty anxious to see what kind of folks we are."

Baker considers his answer. "I think it went all right," he says finally, but his voice is not exactly teeming with conviction. "I wish he'd been a bit more specific. About jobs and investment, I mean. These people are nervous, especially after what happened this summer up the pike at Owens Corning. Two thousand jobs just disappearing when they closed down. Not just at the plant. It was the ripple effect. Stores closed. Service stations laid off. You couldn't have damaged the community worse if you'd dropped a bomb on it."

He pauses, takes a sip of the wine, flashes that half-rueful little smile and shakes his head at some thought before continuing. "On the whole, though, I think my people are happy to be with GIA. You're obviously pros. You know how to make things happen in a way that I don't. My brothers had what it takes. I never learned. Funny: the people here don't really trust me to manage them—I'm sure you could sense that —but they do count on me, my family, to look out for them. Just last night I woke up shivering, wondering whether it wasn't wrong of me not to have insisted on written guarantees on employment and investment, on sticking to my guns and having it all spelled out in the contract, not just taking Jack's word for it. Everyone tells me that handshakes aren't what they used to be."

"I don't know about handshakes, Mr. Baker, but Mr. Mannerman is a man of his word."

"Can I take *your* word for that?"

"You can." Lucy's voice is firm, but the declaration makes her uneasy. Another twenty minutes, she thinks, and they will all be out of here, Baker and all this will be just another file folder.

"I hope so," Baker says gravely. "In a way, that's *my* word he gave too. He has to live up to it for both of us."

There's movement at the end of the table; Mannerman pushes his chair back and stands.

As Baker pushes his own chair back, he smiles at Lucy and says, "I don't go to New York very often. As I get older, city life seems too wearing. But if I do, I'll call you. Perhaps you can guide me through the dangers of the new '21'?"

"It'll be my pleasure," says Lucy.

— IV — GIA's No. 1 jet, a spanking new Gulfstream IV with only fifty hours of airtime, has been done up by the old-line decorators McMillen in various permutations of pale gold and deep green that give the cabin the cool, still feeling of a private chapel. Affixed to panels on the teak-veneered bulkheads on either side of the narrow passage leading to the cockpit are gifts from the Pope: on the left, a fifteenth-century bronze plaquette depicting the Crucifixion, attributed by some scholars to Donatello's workshop. It formerly belonged to the cathedral treasury of an ancient village in the Veneto. Across the way hangs an eleven-by-fourteen photograph, in a fine Renaissance frame, of His Holiness blessing a model of the aircraft. Lest these accoutrements prove offputting to VIP passengers whose sympathies with or commitment to Rome are not as deep as Mannerman's, the panels to which they are attached swivel smoothly to reveal a TV monitor permanently tuned to CNN and an array of instruments displaying the aircraft's position and progress.

The front cabin seats ten: four on a long, leather-covered settee along the port side, four individual seats grouped opposite, configured for a confab or a bridge game, and up forward, separated by a half-bulkhead with an instrument display that shows the plane's course and progress, facing seats in which Mannerman conducts private audiences.

A galley administered by an Armani-uniformed attendant is located amidships. Next is a telecommunications cubicle that rivals the setup on Air Force One. The rearmost cabin is partitioned into a lounge with settees that make up into beds for long flights, a dressing room and a fully outfitted head with shower.

The $40 million plane is used exclusively by Jack Mannerman and invited guests from the world outside GIA. Lesser lights in the corporate constellation make do with the twenty other aircraft, ranging from choppers to a pair of G-IVs, that constitute "Air Mannerman."

Now and then Lucy asks herself how investors might react if they knew that she and her three colleagues are the only GIA employees who travel regularly on the CEO's flying sanctum sanctorum. Would they latch on to the symbolic irony that in what is unarguably the best-managed major company in America, according to the price of the stock and a dozen major cover stories a year, the only executives who can claim the CEO's immediate, urgent attention are his personal flacks!

GIA is run on the same principles as the late Communist Party, divided into autonomous, discrete administrative cells and subcells scattered around the world: groups and subgroups organized according to whatever makes the most managerial sense to Mannerman: line of business, geography or language, market, technology. Only Finance and Law in New York City have anything approaching an overview. BEECO, for instance, will be run out of Industrial Products Services headquartered in Columbus, Ohio, although its "ancillaries"—the credit and thrift unions and the First State Bank of Bakerton—will be taken over by GIAFin, the separate $20 billion finance and insurance subsidiary, along with the benefit and medical plans.

The operating groups keep out of each other's hair and each other's business. Mannerman alone has the whole picture. Every Thursday he spends the morning in New York reviewing the present state of affairs with Finance, which will have pulled together current operating figures, sees if Law has anything pressing on its plate and then has lunch at "21" with Lucy and a Wall Street guest. Afterward, he returns to Finance, this time to go over the future. What Finance's dry spreadsheets and layouts indicate, it's Lucy's job to translate into something that will play on the Street. Essentially, she's the point woman for a perceptual juggernaut which, based on today's closing quote, is valued by investors at something over $52 billion.

They're now three hours out of Hagerstown, about halfway to Los Angeles. From the time the Gulfstream attained cruising altitude, Mannerman has been on the phone. Now he's finally off. For a moment he lays his head back and closes his eyes—he has a yogi's ability to put himself into a quick and rejuvenative trance—then snaps awake and beckons Lucy to the seat opposite his. She and Marie, busy back in the telecommunications cubicle, are the only passengers on this flight.

"Now wipe that surly expression off your pretty face, my dear girl," he tells her, "or did you have a heavy date in New York? If so, my advice is to reorient your heart, lass, because you're going to be spending a great deal of time in California. How about a wee dram?"

"Nothing for me," Lucy says sullenly. She thinks she knows what's coming. "No blindfold either."

"As you wish. Feel free to change your mind at any time."

Mannerman presses a button on his armrest. Moments later, the cabin attendant arrives with a silver tray bearing a stem glass half filled with Tullamore Dew, the Irish whisky which is PL's favorite, although in public, in keeping with his image, he drinks single-malt scotch. Using small silver tongs, Mannerman extracts a single ice cube from a crystal bowl engraved with the GIA logo and deposits it in the whisky. He twirls it briefly with the tip of a perfectly manicured forefinger, then takes a deep, savoring swig. Smooth as the whisky is, it still bites. PL harrumphs and gives his chest a series of quick soft punches.

"Nothing like the Dew to soften the catarrh, I always say." He leans forward and speaks in a confiding tone, not that there's anyone around to overhear, but it's his style when he wishes to be emphatic. "I suppose you'd like to know why you've been shanghaied?"

"I can guess. Los Angeles means Hollywood. Hollywood means movie stars and shiny cars—and you-know-who who's been observed sneaking into your suite at the Waldorf Towers at odd hours of the day and night."

"My dear, you make it sound positively illicit! Like a love triangle!"

"Well, it is, isn't it? You—the Speaker—and he whose name I dare not speak. Plus, given one or two things I've heard, what you're up to may be not only illicit but illegal, given whom the gentleman is said to number among his more influential friends."

Mannerman grins. "Gracious," he says with a chuckle, "such passion!"

"I'm just telling you, PL. First there's this Baker deal, which has the Street pulling a long face. And now—if I get your message—we're off to cloud-cuckoo-land. Telecommunications, cyberspace, the Internet, even cable—they're OK. There I can walk the walk and talk the talk. But Hollywood? That's a no-no! After what's happened to Sony, I hate to think how they'll take it if they get a whiff that we may be looking at motion pictures. The day's long past when anyone, us included, can peddle the notion that a film made by some neurotic ditz at sixty million over budget can somehow be classified as software!"

"I can assure you, my sweet darling, Yellow Brick Road has absolutely nothing to do with films."

"What does it have to do with, given that Robert Carlsson's been seen riding up the back elevator of the Waldorf Towers? Mr. Carlsson is not exactly known as a prime mover in the area of heartland industrial renewal! I believe *Time* called him quote the king of Tinseltown deal-makers unquote."

"Aye, and so they may have, but there's more to Bob than his film interests. The picture shows are what he uses to pay the overhead. As you said, my lass, they're not for us. It's indeed the Information Society that we're going after. The Internet, the World Wide Web. Global telecommunications. Satellite and fiber-optic broadcasting."

He reels off all the buzzwords as if he really believes in them. "A lot of people think this is all so much BS, but you and I know it isn't. There's a reality out there, and I want GIA to be a major player. It's going to take money, to get money requires confident investors, true believers, and that's your job. Now that most of the money in the world is outside our own fair land, much of what we'll be needing will have to come from overseas, which raises certain legislative perplexities, let's call them, but those are for Grover and me to deal with. Correct me if I'm wrong, dear heart, but over eighty percent of our shares are owned onshore, isn't that so? The Street must get with the program, which is, of course, your responsibility. And there will be larger perceptual rows to hoe, as you'll see, and those will be your responsibility as well. You're to be our principal liaison to Robert Carlsson and his principal conduit to us, as I'll not have it perceived that our signals are being called by a Hollywood agent! So welcome to showbiz, my dear!"

"I'm honored. Would you press that button and tell Melanie to uncork a bottle of the Widow? I think I could use it."

"A pleasure. Now, Luce, tell me true. You seem to know who Carlsson is, but do you know the man himself?"

"No. All I've heard is that he's a genius professionally and an animal personally." Melanie appears with a bottle of Veuve Clicquot and a Baccarat champagne flute, and puts them on Lucy's tray-table.

"Ah, the familiar stereotype, complete with casting couch, no doubt?" asks Mannerman.

"That, too." The champagne is cool and fizzy. Go to my head—quickly—Lucy thinks.

"Well, I can see you're in for quite a surprise. From what I've heard, the man has as little time and taste for hanky-panky as I do; perhaps that's why he and I seem to get on well, although, of course, I'm not privy to his private moments, and he is a bachelor. About such men, there's always gossip, and I've heard it about Bob, but never with a name put to it, and thereby, in my own humble experience, lies the tale—or lack thereof. The man I know is extremely focused and reten- tive, does not suffer fools gladly, but then only fools do, and we've no time for fools in our enterprise, do we? He has made a great career and name for himself not merely by being brilliant and deft and quick, but by realizing that great visions, like my dear lady wife's prize roses, need careful tending and time to blossom. He's a patient man, Bob is, attentive to the smallest detail in the largest picture. It's for those qualities that I've retained him—for quite a pretty penny, may I say, indeed for several billion pretty pennies—to hold our hands as we venture off on the highway that'll take us to the wonderland of cyberspace and our destiny in the stars."

"In other words, he's going to honcho Yellow Brick Road for you?"

"For *us*, dear, for us. For our stockholders. Not honcho, m'dear. He'll simply be an advisor, a consultant."

Lucy nods, but she isn't buying this—not quite yet. Robert Carlsson, technically an agent, is the reigning power in Hollywood, although "Hollywood" is too narrow a term for the scope of his influence. When it comes to the multibillion-dollar interfacing of entertainment and telecommunications, he's become the man to see. Since Yellow Brick Road will bet the entire $50 billion GIA store on Mannerman's conviction that media-entertainment-telecommunications-financial services is where it's going to be, to be a player on the scope he intends dictates that he involve Carlsson or quit before he starts.

"I want you to liaise with Carlsson," Mannerman repeats, "and we'll channel his fee through you guys as a PR advisory. Think of some title to shut up the accountants. As for what we'll be working on with him, I don't want that getting around the company and making our—well— more *traditional* sectors antsy. Don't want 'em feeling that we've lost our hearts to a flashier sort of lass."

Lucy's read perhaps ten profiles of Carlsson in everything from *Vanity Fair* to *Business Week*. She's seen him in the flesh at a couple of screenings. He scares her. He has a cold, glittering, reptilian eye. He may have a Harvard PhD in Romance languages, a point the profiles always like to emphasize, but the word is that his rapacity and cynicism make Rupert Murdoch look like Pollyanna.

"I think you'll like working with Carlsson," Mannerman continues.

"Really?"

"In my few meetings with him, I've found Bob to be the soul of civility and cultivation. He went to Harvard, as a matter of fact. Just your type, I should think. He quotes Dante and Petrarch as readily as the weekend grosses. A truly smart man."

In other words, Lucy thinks, just lie back, close your eyes and think of Tuscany. "Street smart or smart smart?" she asks.

"Is there a difference?"

Lucy thinks there is. Smart smart is about absolute values; it's about truth and beauty; it produces art, philosophy, poetry, science. Street smart is entirely relativistic; it's about hustle, about working the system, about what plays right now. Einstein, who discovered relativity, was smart smart. PL is street smart; Lucy's lost somewhere in between.

"I've also heard that Mr. Carlsson's name wasn't always Carlsson, and that he owes his present eminence to certain connections in Sicily."

Mannerman shrugs. "Everyone must come from somewhere. Only a fool doesn't take advantage of his birthright."

Don't play innocent with me, Lucy thinks. Carlsson shot to prominence by arranging a bailout for Goldscreen Productions. It was said the money came from a big French bank, but the word on the Street was that the real source was Colombia via Palermo cleared through Rome.

"Be that as it may, you'll find him a regular fountain of erudition and judgment. Who knows, you might fall under his spell yourself. You must be about ready to give love another try, dear heart. How long has it been since the last one? Don't think I didn't see you trying Mr. H. A. Baker on for size back there. Lipscombing again, are we?"

"Cut that out!" Lucy says sharply, but she smiles in spite of herself and shakes her head. "Lipscombing" is Mannerman's catchphrase for the serial character of Lucy's so-called love life, a staccato parade of fluctuating, inconclusive involvements that prance onstage with a peal of angelic brass and—in most cases—limp off with a whimper after a couple of months. Like so much of Mannerman's rhetoric. "Lipscombing" derives from his sports-besotted boyhood. There was a professional football player named "Big Daddy" Lipscomb, he told Lucy, a legendary defensive tackle in the National Football League in the 1960s. As Mannerman tells the story, Big Daddy was once asked to give his theory of playing defense. He thought for a moment, then replied, "I tackles 'em all, and then I goes through 'em 'til I find the one with the ball, and I keep him!"

Lucy's gone through a lot of them, no doubt of that, and has yet to find the one with the ball, but she's still optimistic, still consoles herself that it's only a matter of time, *has* to be only a matter of time. As each involvement peters out or blows up, she consoles herself with pride in her patience and discrimination, with the supposition that with every failure she's learning a bit more about herself, that every "Sayonara," "Let's be friends" or angry exit nudges open the door of possibility a little bit wider for the prince who will someday come through it.

"OK," she says, "if you want me to do this right, you have to put me in the loop, so I know when to take and when to swing. Yellow Brick Road is going to take a whole bunch of foreign money, right?"

"I'm talking to people. Lining up a few strategic affiliates."

That's all she needs to hear. "Strategic affiliations" is PL-speak for heavyweight foreign partners who'll put up the money and let him run the show. That involves cutting a deal with Washington just so, a deal that'll let the overseas money in, but only provided it works through Mannerman, to give the appearance of domestication. Lucy can guess who PL's "people" will be: overseas holders of huge quantities of badly depreciated dollars—Koreans and Taiwanese, maybe Japanese, maybe Chinese, people in Europe and South America, Russians, possibly, via Zurich.

She can begin to see how Grover must be working it on Capitol Hill. Right now, foreign ownership of U.S. broadcasting's a no-no. For someone seeking a congressional by-your-leave for a really big media play involving a foreign partner, it'll help to have flown the flag for American industry. We tried, Mannerman'll be able to say, but it didn't work, it's too late in the day, all the money is overseas and you've got to cut us loose to go where the money is. To get back all those dollars that went overseas when Americans bought Toyotas and Italian pasta and Swedish furniture and Chinese everything else.

"I dig," she says.

"Good. So it's on your way to Hollywood, you are. Now primp, and straighten your seams, and give us a big smile." Mannerman looks away, snatches up the armrest phone and punches out a number. As far as he's concerned, the conversation is over.

Lucy sips her champagne, starting to feel the buzz. She gazes out the window and asks herself: Are we going *to* Hollywood, PL, or just "going Hollywood"?

She feels really beat. The mere idea of having to liaise with Robert Carlsson is tiring. I need a vacation, she thinks. Maybe I need a total change. Seven years of never quite telling the truth has worn me down, seven years of dealing in deflections and obliquities. I need some R&R. A pause to smell the moral roses.

It amazes Lucy that she gets away with what she does. If the public could ever really understand how life's ultimate arrangements came to be, how wealth was "created," there'd be no end to the outrage. But thanks to hundreds like her, and thanks most of all to television, which has acclimated people to thinking in sound bites and flash bits, the rich keep getting away with it. And she keeps her job. At what cost? Who knows? What does a pennyworth of soul look like?

Somewhere over Nebraska, she dozes off. When she wakes, it's still light outside, but the sky is deeper in color and the brilliant orange of the declining sun makes the leading edges of the wings appear on fire. Her mouth feels dry, her mind dull. She goes to the galley and pours herself a cup of coffee.

When Lucy returns, she sits herself down across from Mannerman and asks a question that's taken on new significance for her since lunch: "How long are you going to give those people back there?"

"Who? Back where?"

She nods toward the rear of the plane, in the direction of the eastern night they're trying to outrun. "The people at BEECO. Remember? The company we paid $300 million for just five hours ago?"

"Of course I remember! What about them?"

"C'mon, PL, you and I know they won't hit their CRONI. Not in a million years!"

CRONI stands for Cash Return on Net Investment. It's the sum of all things at GIA; it's the company mantra, credo, First (and only) Commandment. It's the inflexible standard by which every line of business, every individual, every particle and atom of the great corporation is judged. CRONI is to GIA what the Code is to the Marine Corps. You don't screw with it. One rule for all; no exceptions after the grace period—which means that two strikes and you're out. It'll be OK for

Mannerman to cut BEECO a little slack, but not so much that he risks letting the word get around that some people get to play by different rules. You either hit your CRONI or your head rolls. Only Jack Mannerman can grant a stay of execution, and he seldom does.

At present, CRONI is set at a 15 percent rolling average return—pretax—on assets. BEECO hasn't done anything close to that in a decade. On the numbers Lucy's seen, the new acquisition's pro forma CRONI would be on the order of 10 percent, tops.

"Why would you be asking that question now, Luce? Have you suddenly taken a special interest? It's that Baker fella, isn't it? You *were* trying him on for size, you little Lipscomber, you! I knew it!"

"Forget Baker, boss. That's your fantasy, not mine. But you did all but promise those people back there that we're in for the duration."

"Promises, promises . . ." Mannerman rolls the word over thoughtfully. "Well, you know how it is," he says finally, "you told me so yourself. Remember? You said, 'Anyone can make promises, but it's Wall Street that decides which ones get kept!' "

Lucy says nothing, watches him closely.

"If I cut them some slack, Luce, the Street'll have to go along, right? CRONIwise, that is. Those people have taken at face value our assertions about internal financial discipline. If I make one exception, allowing for a reasonable turnaround period, they'll take that as a sign of weakness. And that doesn't even address what would happen elsewhere in the company if it got around that certain animals are less equal than others."

"What do you think is a reasonable turnaround period?"

Mannerman looks at her curiously. Why are you asking me this? his face says. It's a question she can't answer. "Normally a year, but in this case, let's say two," he says.

"That's a long time." A very long time, she thinks, to ask the Street to ignore its misgivings about GIA's going into the mining business. A *two*-year respite before the CRONI ax descends on BEECO? Before budget scalebacks, investment reductions, layoffs, facility shutdowns, asset sales, spin-offs—actions that amount to a confession of error but also a stiff-spined willingness to cut losses soon and mercilessly? Once the news gets out—and somehow it will, it always seems to—investors will want to know why BEECO got a special deal.

"Well . . ." Mannerman lets his thought trail off. He looks faintly embarrassed. Finally, he shrugs and says, "Well, there's an election to consider. Let's leave it at that. Do your best," he continues. "Play the usual cards, the old synergy ploy, what's there that BEECO hasn't taken advantage of, what we bring to the table. The boys in Tech-Ops report there may actually be something to this water-jet stuff—that's an angle you can do something with. We'll give it a jazzy new name. Something that starts with 'hydro' and ends with 'ic.' Then there's always the financing angle, how GIA Credit will help BEECO penetrate new markets, tailor financing packages, blah-blah, efficiency through new plant investment, et cetera and so on, blah-blah-blah."

Everything, in other words, thinks Lucy, except what BEECO's business really is. Lousy.

"Besides," Mannerman adds, "Baker's nothing. We'll tighten it up, get the credit union current, replace their medical plan with our HMO—"

"Have you seen their plan?" Lucy interrupts. "It is not exactly managed care."

"That's their problem, not ours. As for CRONI, we'll eat the shortfall. As we project, it's nothing to our bottom line. If it gets out of whack, Finance can bury it in the reserves."

I don't know, she thinks, something here is bothersome. Maybe it's the cynicism. But she feels a kind of partisanship for this little company she hasn't felt for any other GIA acquisition she's shilled for.

The phone on Mannerman's armrest buzzes. He listens for a moment, then says, reluctantly, "OK, you might as well put him through."

For an instant he listens, then winks at Lucy and says, in a voice just a half-tone too loud, "Good to hear your voice too, Herby! Say, old man, your efforts on your client's behalf were much appreciated. By *our* good selves perhaps even more than him. *Et tu,* Herby, eh, what, *et tu?* . . . No, no—just kidding!"

He winks at Lucy again. Lucy finds the arch tone unbecoming. To joke about Herby Lamond's duplicity is to endorse it, to co-conspire, to be smeared with Lamond's own slimy values.

After a pause during which Mannerman silently shakes his head at whatever's being proposed, he finally nods dubiously. "OK, Herby," he says, barely disguising his impatience, "I get the picture. But that's one

I think we better back-burner for the moment. Tell you what, though, what say we get together, chew it over. How about breakfast next Thursday? I'll buy. The Gorse Club OK with you? I'll get a room, you bring whoever you want from your shop and I'll have one or two of my planning people in tow. So you check with your secretary if Thursday's OK and she can get back to Jean in St. Louis. . . . What? You are? Really? . . . Sure we will. Of course we'll take a table. What're you going to talk about? . . . You don't say!"

When Mannerman hangs up, he grins at Lucy. "Try this on for size. The Council for Morality in Business has named as its Man of the Year none other than H. Herbert Lamond! He's to receive the award at a grand whoop-de-do at the Pierre in January. He wants us to take a twenty-five-thousand-dollar table."

"And we will."

"Aye, that we will. In fact, we'll take two. One for you to preside over and one for Spudsy. You'll find it enlightening. Herby's amazing, how he can pound the pulpit with the same virtuous hand he uses to endorse his merger-fee checks. Some people call it hypocrisy, but to me it's nothing shy of sheer genius!"

Lucy will deal with this vexation when the time comes. Her mind's elsewhere.

"Just one thing," she says absently.

"Yes?"

"If I were you, I'd be careful on this one," says Lucy.

"Which one? Herby Lamond?"

"BEECO."

"Meaning what?"

"Meaning I think Mr. Baker and his people believe we really are in for the whole nine yards."

"Ah, come now, Lucy, that may be today, but tomorrow's another day, as Rhett Butler's estranged wife notoriously remarked." His tone is flip and confident. "And who's to say Mr. Baker won't see it the same as others have? As a fine fair morning full of joy and opportunity for a lad with coin in his pocket and the past a way, way back in another country. It never fails, lass."

Suddenly it seems terribly silent in the cabin. The only noise is the smooth roar of the Gulfstream's engines. Lucy looks out the window.

They're descending now. Up ahead lies the great sparkling earthbound galaxy of the Los Angeles basin, a vast bowl lined with velvet the color of twilight in which a million twinkling diamonds nestle. She studies the shadow-ravined foothills fleeing under the wing and tries to sort out her thoughts.

When she turns back, Mannerman has another glass of whisky on the tray-table in front of him, and he's peering into it as if hoping to find revealed in its amber depths the answer to a troubling question.

"Look, PL," she says, "about BEECO. Don't get your guts in an uproar. I just want you to be aware that I think you're looking at a real throwback: an old-fashioned duty, honor, country guy who really believes all that. I know the type. I've got one for a father."

Mannerman looks at her, then picks up his glass and raises it. "I thank you for your support," he declares. "And now, here's to Hollywood, and the Yellow Brick Road!" He clinks his glass to hers.

As they drink, it occurs to Lucy that this is the first time she can recall PL having a second whisky.

PART TWO

A BAKER'S DOZEN

— I — It's the week before Christmas and "21" is typically packed. A Salvation Army brass quintet has set up shop in the lobby and is blasting away with "God Rest Ye Merry, Gentlemen." The air is thick with the festive scents of holly, ivy, money and self-regard. It's been a big year for the New York scheme of things: the market's risen by nearly 30 percent, stockbroker bonuses are being paid at record levels, office space is back renting at over $100 a square foot and well-heeled tourists are flooding Manhattan's poshest shops, hotels and restaurants with cheap dollars.

Lucy's exhausted, running on the fumes, and she finds the heavily perfumed din almost unendurable. But it's Thursday, and Thursday means "21."

What a fortnight it's been! A week of last-minute negotiations, shuttling back and forth with Mannerman between four continents, covering his flanks with volleys of denial as markets around the world are swept by rumors that something very, *very* big is up with GIA. Finally, Tuesday a week ago in Beijing, the Chinese finally initialed the agreement, the Argentines came in the next day, GIA's lead law firm pushed the button on the word processors and within forty-eight hours Yellow Brick Road became a $100 billion reality called UnivCom Group at nine simultaneous closings around the world.

On Friday, at a press conference in the grand ballroom of the Istanbul Four Seasons, the approximate geographical center of the brave new cyberworld he had fathered, Jack Mannerman had "cut the ribbon" by going on-line via a platinum-plated laptop crafted for the occasion by IBM. He was flanked by high-ranking functionaries of GIA's fourteen "name" partners: major Japanese, Korean, Australian, Indian, Chilean,

Argentine, Turkish, German, Chinese, South African, Hungarian, Israeli, Saudi and Dutch telecommunications and media enterprises, both private and state-controlled. Scattered through the room, unrecognized by the several hundred members of the world press dispatched on one day's notice to the Golden Horn to cover the occasion, were dull-suited lawyers from Liechtenstein and Hong Kong, along with bankers and accountants from Zurich, the Isle of Man and Aruba, giving presence by proxy to clients who wished their participation to be masked.

Lucy's coordinating a worldwide public relations effort, guiding the global "Street" and the financial press through the interlocking joint ventures, cross-investments, reciprocal minority stakes and control-option purchases constituting UnivCom's first stage. Ninety-one market-dominating public- and private-sector enterprises have been knit into a globe-blanketing web of strategic commercial alliances that add up to the largest and most potent telecommunications-entertainment-media combine the world has ever seen, involving software, cable and satellite image/data transmission, computer networks, broadcasting, films, television and recorded music. The result is a vast octopuslike enterprise—the image chosen by *The Washington Post*'s irate editorial cartoonist—whose globe-girdling tentacles curl around and grasp the entire known universe of human sentience and useful commercial interconnection.

UnivCom is a monument to the cleverness of lawyers, accountants, financiers and lobbyists, already variously described as the legal and financial equivalent of building the Pyramids, as commercial diplomacy's equivalent of the Congress of Vienna. Competing and contradictory interests have had to be nicely balanced. In some cases, eyes have looked elsewhere as scrupulousness has been put aside to make way for expediency. Various heads of state in a position to do so have granted ironclad licenses on their governments' telecommunications monopolies while becoming substantial investors personally. The Vatican is a major behind-the-scenes player, as are six different states of the former U.S.S.R. A hundred sixty-eight law firms in ninety-three jurisdictions around the world have erected legal fire walls. The hedge funds are in, the great state and national pension funds, the banks, the shadowy Cayman and Macao trust companies, everyone. Being just about the biggest deal in history, it has spun off more than $2 billion in fees to legal and financial intermediaries.

As with every massive deal, Wall Street's initial reaction is a giddiness verging on intoxication, with the press keeping the drunk's glass full. Then, as the news seasons and the realization sets in that someone's got to figure out what the damn thing's worth to whom, it's hangover time.

Lucy has to deal with the Street's recognition that UnivCom materially alters GIA's direction and focus. Investors are trying to determine what price to put on that change, and it's up to her to push for an upvaluing. It's not easy. As they do with so many other equations in the calculus of global finance, increasingly computer-driven yet still at bottom instinctual, the markets have to decide which financial numbers to emphasize and how to weight them, how to assay the potential enlargement of GIA's profit stream against the effect of its UnivCom commitments on its balance sheet.

So far the jury's out. Lucy's worked like a slave to get the big hitters to buy the official GIA line, that this is nothing but good for GIA and its investors. But GIA stock hasn't taken off. The longer the lag, the deeper and harder the doubts are likely to be. The big hitters see what Lucy knows but isn't saying: that GIA's participation in UnivCom involves significant contingent obligations which it'll need a significantly higher stock price to meet.

Still, there's plenty of time, and right now Lucy is more exhausted than discouraged.

When rumors that something really big was in the works had ignited a conflagration of investor curiosity six weeks earlier, she had already decided which analysts to huddle with, whose hand to hold, where best to leak counterrumors. In the first three weeks, she commandeered GIA's No. 2 Gulfstream and—before Mannerman summoned her back to hold *his* hand—managed to hit Chicago, Omaha, Boston and San Francisco, followed by Milan, Zurich, Geneva, Paris and London, and then raced east to Bahrain, New Delhi, Hong Kong, Singapore, Tokyo, Taipei and Brunei, with a final touchdown in Nassau before realighting at Teterboro. By the time she had gotten to Tokyo, she was tired of washing her underthings in the aircraft's head, and she spent $1,000 of

GIA's expense money for three pairs of panties and a couple of bras. She figured the deal could stand it.

The interest swirling around UnivCom makes the buzz generated by earlier media megadeals like Disney–Capital Cities seem, well, a mere mouse squeak. The bon mot is Robert Carlsson's. On this particular Thursday, he's joined Mannerman and Lucy at "21." Unlike them— even PL is picking listlessly at his smoked salmon—he seems fresh and vigorous. The ink is barely dry on the first $100 billion, the Street's still half agog, and already Carlsson's projecting Stages Two, Three and Four.

Lucy doesn't like him, but she has to concede that the man is amazing. In some ways, her initial impression hasn't changed: he's manipulative, ruthless, sexist, peremptory—a total control freak, with the shortest fuse for fools that Lucy's ever seen, shorter even than Mannerman's. Not someone you *ever* turn your back on. But at least he's a subtle sort of control freak. He isn't crude or coarse in speech or behavior. Indeed he's rather cultivated. And his unremitting mental and physical energy is admirable.

She sips her Bloody Mary, scarcely hearing what Carlsson is pitching to Mannerman in a low conspiratorial voice, and looks idly around the crowded room. At that moment, the cluster at the bar parts like the Red Sea, and to her astonishment she sees H. A. Baker standing there, martini in hand, talking in that easy, familiar way of his to the bartender.

How long has it been? she wonders. How long since they sat together at the BEECO closing? Reflexively her brain supplies the answer: one year, six days and change.

Her next thought combines several strains of mild irritation. Irritation that the man's in New York and hasn't called. Irritation that she's irritated. Further irritation when she finds herself worrying: My God, I look like hell!

She puts a hand to her face and sneaks another peek in his direction. Baker's still chatting away. Lucy's a good, experienced reader of the faces men display in bars. She judges that the drink in Baker's hand isn't his first.

She gathers herself, puts on a businesslike expression and returns her attention to her companions. Carlsson's saying something about Cabinrock Productions.

Lucy's heard the Cabinrock rumors. On that subject she's decided to keep her thoughts to herself—at least in front of Carlsson. She'll talk to Mannerman later, if at all. She's not about to go head-to-head with Carlsson, not just now, when the man is definitely the flavor of the decade at GIA's glass-and-timber Versailles outside St. Louis. So much so that he's somehow managed to stake out an orbit for himself that's even closer to the GIA sun than hers.

But from her reading of the Street, this is not the time for GIA to be going after Cabinrock Productions. Not with UnivCom barely put to bed. To lay out $2 billion-plus for a Hollywood production company with no hard assets would be a big mistake, she thinks. Whatever the business merits of Cabinrock, and the company has a hell of a recent box-office scorecard, there's only so much the markets can absorb. To overload their crowded plate might prove an expensive mistake.

Mannerman nods as Carlsson expounds. He stirs a runny canary-colored tassel of egg yolk into the chicken hash the waiter's just brought. PL really does look beat, Lucy thinks. Is it possible that UnivCom's just too big for any one individual, even Jack Mannerman, to get his arms around?

At that moment, a voice behind her says, "Well, well, well, Mr. J. P. Mannerman, as I live and breathe."

Lucy turns around, the two men at the table look up. H. A. Baker's standing there, martini in hand, a mean smile on his lips.

"Mind if I join you?" he asks, but doesn't wait for an invitation. Ignoring the people next door, he pulls an empty chair from their table and sits down.

"You know, *I* used to sit at this very table," Baker says cheerfully. He looks around the room with a proprietary air, the air of someone born and raised as an owner or lord by right of whatever he happens to survey. Lucy has a sudden uneasy feeling that this is not a chance encounter.

"When the place still had a little class," he adds. "Who *are* these people? I asked Bru up at the bar the same thing. He said he was damned if he knew!"

What a snotty remark, Lucy thinks. It doesn't square with the man she recalls talking about Titian with. There's something going on here —or perhaps he's a little tanked.

For a moment, Mannerman stares blankly at Baker, as if he's trying to put a name to the face. After the last few weeks, even PL's commodious mental software is probably running short of RAM, Lucy thinks. She wonders if she ought to fill the gap, but then Mannerman makes the identification, and the familiar chain reaction is set off: first the on-demand guy-to-guy grin, then the two-handed shake, then the name repeated as if to fix it on the screen of present attention.

"H.A.," he says, "H. A. Baker. Well, I'll be damned. How the hell are you? Shake hands with Robert Carlsson. I'm sure you two know each other. Robert, this is H. A. Baker, whose company we merged into GIA, what, a year ago, was it?"

"Just about," says Baker. His expression remains wintry, and his voice seems about ten degrees colder than his face.

"A lot of water over the dam since then," says Mannerman pleasantly. "You remember Lucy Preston here?"

"How could I forget?" Baker reaches across the table and shakes her hand. "You look enchanting, Miss Preston. A Circe dressed for success."

He's pulling something, Lucy thinks, taking her hand away. This is definitely going somewhere. She doesn't like it. She hopes PL's spotted it. She glances at Carlsson and sees that he has.

"So what brings you to Gotham, H.A.?" Mannerman asks.

"Oh, this and that. I had a couple of hours to kill, so I thought I'd look in on the old stamping ground. But except for a couple of people like Bru there behind the bar, and Walter and Remo, I don't see anyone from the old days. Everything's changed. Jesus H. Christ, will you look at that!"

He points a long forefinger at the ceiling, from which dangle dozens of models of airliners, trucks, private jets, oil derricks, bulldozers and what have you, all conspicuously marked with their owners' or manufacturers' logos. Lucy and the two men follow his gaze. Just above their heads, alongside a garish plastic replica of the MGM lion, hangs a model of a large, tanklike machine painted in vivid yellow and black stripes.

"Our first Eight-Ton Mobile Power Auger," says Baker. "The machine that tamed the Arctic tundra for the Aleyaska Pipeline. I remember my old man giving that model to Bob Kriendler back in '73 or '74. Bob's dead now—along with everything else."

He sighs, shrugs and lowers his gaze, seeming to study the bright checkerboard of the tablecloth.

"Anything we can do for you while you're in town, H.A.? Theater tickets, anything like that?" asks Mannerman.

Baker shakes his head. For an instant, no one says anything, then Baker's eyes light up, a very faint smile forms on his lips and he looks at Mannerman.

"Come to think of it, Jack, there is. I had a call from Bakerton yesterday. There seems to be some scuttlebutt to the effect that you're cutting back your investment, that you now may not commit more than fifteen million dollars. That's not true, Jack, is it? I certainly hope not, because it certainly wasn't our deal. Our deal—your commitment—was seventy-five million."

Mannerman's eyes widen slightly.

Baker doesn't wait for a response. "Jack, anything less will leave BEECO in big trouble."

He's still smiling, but there's something in his eyes that's a warning signal. Instinctively, Lucy looks at Carlsson, sees his eyes narrow, jaw muscles tighten. Mannerman, toying with his food, doesn't catch it. He lets Baker's words hang in the air for an instant, then looks up and smiles back.

"I'd have to correct you, H.A. You and I had an *understanding*—not a contractual commitment—that we'd go up to seventy-five million provided the results justified it. They haven't. You can look it up—or your lawyers can. It's Subappendix One B, paragraph six—headed, as I recall, 'Supplemental Undertakings.' "

"Never mind Subappendix One B, paragraph six, Jack! You and I had a deal! We shook hands on it." There's a very faint quiver in Baker's voice, just the hint of a flush under the weathered tan.

Mannerman shrugs. "With all due respect, these things tend to blur after a while. It's been a year and then some, don't forget. What is certain is that we—you and I—signed a contract that was very precise in terms of who is obligated to do what. If you review that contract—or, better still, have your lawyers review it—I think you'll find there's nothing in there about being obliged to invest a thin dime in BEECO."

The smile on Baker's face is gone.

"You had expert professional advice, H.A., both legal and financial," Mannerman adds. "They—"

"*They*—well, Herbert Lamond to be exact—assured me that I could rely on your good faith, Jack." Baker whirls on Lucy. "So did you, Miss Preston, if it comes to that!" He looks from one to the other. Lucy tries looking back, can't, drops her gaze to the tablecloth and starts counting the squares. "*They*—Lamond, that is—told me that to insist on getting it in writing would complicate things and possibly break the deal, and that it wasn't necessary because your word was like gold. Fool's gold, it would seem!"

"Now wait just a minute!" Carlsson interjects.

"You keep out of this, sir!" Baker's look is like a dagger traveling through the air. Carlsson seems unfazed.

"It's all right, Robert," says Mannerman, bestowing his best seigneurial smile on the others. "H.A., I'm flattered that you prize my word so highly, but I have my stockholders to consider. Based on what we've seen so far, additional investment simply isn't justified, although frankly, it can't all be laid at BEECO's feet. None of us saw this global recession coming."

You wouldn't know it from the bully atmosphere in this place, Lucy thinks, but elsewhere in the world's economies, where people dig in the ground for a living, or stoke foundry fires, or man dry-goods cash registers, there's been a major lull.

Baker says nothing. He looks at Mannerman, then at Carlsson and Lucy, and then transfers his attention to the ceiling, as if Truth is hanging up there somewhere amid the miniature bulldozers and the football helmets.

Does he understand? Lucy wonders. Mannerman *did* give his word, no doubt of that, but in business what's the half-life of a promise? If you can get six months out of a deal before having to amend, you're ahead of the game. Of course, at BEECO there've been no surprises, so technically Mannerman's being cute. They knew BEECO was a dog going in, and Mannerman gave his word with that knowledge.

"I think I get it," Baker says finally. He looks at Mannerman. "Didn't I see somewhere that Herbert Lamond is now *your* advisor? Didn't I read somewhere that he pocketed close to a hundred and fifty million as a finder's fee—or whatever you call it—on this TV deal you've just announced?"

"Telecommunications, H.A., telecommunications and multimedia."

"A hundred fifty million's a pretty penny, Jack. Is that what thirty pieces of silver comes to these days?"

Mannerman grins and starts to reply, but Carlsson interrupts. "You know, Mr. Baker, you're definitely off base on this one. I think you'd better show Mr. Mannerman where exactly he's failed to live up to the words of the sales contract you both signed."

Baker's eyes shift momentarily and contemptuously to Carlsson before he returns his attention to Mannerman. "Jack, I was brought up to believe that inside every legal contract there's a moral compact. That's what handshakes signify. That's what I thought you and I had. That's what I was *told* we had."

"Robert's right," says Mannerman patiently. "What you and I had— *have!*—is a legal agreement." But there's steel under the velvet. "On paper and vetted by your attorneys with your approval. If you felt there were aspects you wished to have covered, you should've insisted. If you felt as strongly as you claim you do, you could even say you had a moral obligation to walk away from our deal. But you didn't. Why? Well, to use your own words, perhaps you weren't so keen to risk terminating a transaction that would put in your own pocket stock that today is worth forty-odd million. Perhaps you're right, perhaps that *is* what thirty pieces of silver is worth today, but in whose coinage? The sale relieved you of obligations and responsibilities you didn't much care for, and which, by your own word, you weren't very good at. You left your people, as you call them, in our safekeeping. We have lived up to our end of the bargain. There have been no layoffs. There's been some belt-tightening, principally in the area of fringe benefits. I know this last has caused a reaction in a workforce that by today's standards appears critically, if not terminally I use the word advisedly—overentitled. Some of this reaction has doubtless reached your ears. Indeed, I know it has, and I know from whom."

Don't overplay it, PL, thinks Lucy. She knows that Mannerman is bluffing, building a story on the probabilities, because there are only about six postmerger scenarios and Baker's said enough to tell the GIA chief which one to choose.

"May I add," says Mannerman, full of confidence now, "that your gossiping behind our backs with the people at Bakerton is a clear violation of our contract. Our *written* contract!"

Which is true. When you sell out to Mannerman, unless otherwise specified in the contract, you're history. Still, Lucy thinks, seeing Baker's expression darken, it'd be a mistake for PL to push that point.

Mannerman seems to read her mind. "Look," he concludes in a friendly, conciliatory voice, "nothing's been decided one way or the other. All we're doing is reviewing our position."

"Reviewing your *position*! For Christ's sake, man, you have no need —no *right*, for God's sakes—to review your position! You gave me your word!"

"I gave you a strong indication! Do you want me to spell it out?"

Both men's voices are rising. The nearest tables get interested.

"A strong indication? A strong indication! That's not what I heard. It's not what I told my people! It's not what you said—implied—in that speech of yours!"

Mannerman grins, but it's a nasty grin, nasty and triumphant and hurtful. "*Your* people, H.A.? *Your* people! They're my people now. You sold them to me, or have you forgotten?"

"Selling is one thing, selling out is another!"

"Is it really?"

People at other tables are starting to look over. Baker lowers his voice.

"These are simple people, Jack. Loyal, decent, hardworking." His tone is urgent, man-to-man. For the last time, Lucy thinks. "They trusted me, I trusted you. When you gave me your word, in effect you were giving them *my* word, don't you see? My word of honor."

Before Mannerman can respond, Carlsson breaks in. "Mr. Baker," he says, "I don't know you, but it seems to me you've confused the issues. Honor has its price, which is one issue, and honor has its costs, which is quite another. I think you had better sort out which is which in your own thinking before accusing Mr. Mannerman of breaking faith."

"Look," Mannerman interjects, "I can understand your concerns. But I have the interests of nearly two million stockholders to consider. The fact is, BEECO hasn't met the targets set for it. The ingrained habits of your people are largely responsible. They're not good, H.A., not good.

The productivity is terrible. I hate to have to say it, but there you are."

Baker leans forward, slowly chopping the air with both hands in tandem for emphasis. "But you knew that, Jack! That's why you committed to invest!"

Perhaps it's the repetition of "committed" that's the last straw, but suddenly Mannerman's face and voice turn pugnacious. His patience and urge to conciliate are all used up, Lucy sees. Any other time, it would be different. "I don't invest in shit, Baker, and shit is what it turns out I bought! A workforce that's coddled. A plant that's in worse shape than even our worst-case analysis! It's clean, but that's all it is! I made a mistake, and until I see some improvement, I'm not going to take one cent's hit more than I absolutely have to. Now go take your forty million and be happy in Palm Beach, there's no more to be said, and I have business to discuss with Mr. Carlsson and Miss Preston here."

Baker says nothing for a beat or two. Only a slight narrowing of eyes and mouth betrays what Lucy guesses must be absolute fury.

Finally, lowering his voice to a half-whisper, half-hiss, he says, "I should have known better than to do business with a lace-curtain mackerel snapper who can't take a leak without the Pope's say-so. Now listen to me, you goddamn jumped-up bog-trotting mick bastard. Let me make myself perfectly clear. If you screw my people over, I . . ."

Lucy knows that tone of voice. As a girl working at the Yacht and Swim Club she'd heard it over and over again, berating a waiter, cursing a clumsy busboy, dressing down a lifeguard, often flushed with alcohol, always dripping undisguised class-ridden contempt. Normally she hates talk like this, but in this instance something about Baker's wrath is different, a tinge of high-mindedness, of principle, of—well—*honor* that captures her sympathy. He's in the right, she thinks. Not technically, not legally, probably not rationally. But isn't there a point—beyond technicality, beyond law, beyond even reason—where decent people have to live, as it were? It can't always be like that quip of Mannerman's: "Show me a principle that's worth a dollar of principal."

Mannerman looks at Carlsson, as if for moral support, then back at Baker. For some reason he never turns in Lucy's direction.

"You'll *what*, you whining white-shoe WASP son of a bitch?" sneers Mannerman. "Write a letter to the *Times*? Or a sob-sister Op-Ed piece?

Go on *Larry King* or *60 Minutes*? Write your congressman? Complain to your headmaster?"

Baker smiles to himself, shakes his head and says to no one in particular, "Come to think of it, that wouldn't be much help, would it?" He shakes his head again, sighs and gets up.

"That's right," Mannerman says, in what Spuds calls "the voice of PL Triumphant." "Get out of here. Slink back to the Racquet Club and leave the men's work to real men, you blue-blooded sellout!"

For an instant the only sound at the table is the drumming of Carlsson's fingers.

"You know, Jack," Baker says, almost casually, as he looks down at Mannerman, "there was a time in this country when people like you were dealt with in a direct and simple way. That era's dead and gone. Still, if only as a matter of common courtesy, and in your case I emphasize the word 'common,' I think you ought to smile when you call me such names."

So smooth and seamless are his next movements that there's a gap of a second or two before anyone really comprehends what's happened. Lucy's looking away, wishing herself a million miles from here, and it takes a gasp from the next table followed by a sharp little cry that causes her to look up.

The blue-black snub-nosed revolver whose muzzle is a rock-steady two inches from Mannerman's nose looks like a howitzer. From her angle, Lucy can make out the copper snouts of the bullets in the cylinder.

Mannerman doesn't move. He tries to force a grin and fails. The muscle under his jawline starts to twitch. His face suddenly sags. He looks quickly down at his lap. An unmistakable acrid smell fills the air.

"Pissed off, are you, Jack?" says Baker. He seems to tower over Mannerman like an avenging angel. "Think how lucky you are. This is how it was once upon a time when someone broke his word, back when a man's honor was often all he could boast of."

The restaurant has fallen utterly silent. One of the captains edges toward the table, a hapless hand raised.

"It's all right, Walter." Baker lowers the pistol and slowly thumbs the hammer down. It makes a faint chocking sound; in the silence, it's like steel on a muffled anvil. "I'm going to repeat this one last time," he whispers in a voice audible only to those at Mannerman's table. "If you break *your* word to my people, you are also breaking *my* word to them, and I will not have that. Do you understand?"

He puts the gun away. For an instant, Mannerman stares up at him, trying to match Baker's fierce smile with his own. Then he gives up and drops his gaze.

Carlsson hasn't moved a muscle or made a sound since Baker drew the gun. Lucy has the feeling this isn't the first time the agent's seen a pistol drawn in anger.

"Mr. Carlsson," Baker says curtly, then: "Miss Preston, Jack, a good day to you both. And best wishes for the holidays."

He turns away and passes quickly through the crowd of waiters, who shrink back openmouthed to clear a path. For a minute the room remains frozen, as if in fear that the merest outcry will bring Baker raging back, revolver blazing. So quiet is it that Lucy can hear all the way out into the lobby. She hears Baker speaking with the maître d', then an exchange of low chuckles, the unmistakable sound of a joke shared between two men, followed by the clunk of the restaurant's heavy iron-and-glass door.

Hearing it close, she feels a strange emptiness, but it vanishes in the next instant as the restaurant resumes its babble, now pitched an octave higher than before, and the brass quintet strikes up "Adeste Fideles." Captains and waiters descend on Mannerman's table with napkins and excited apologies that the GIA chief executive accepts in good grace while Lucy, pleading a spilled Bloody Mary, discreetly cell-phones the office for a clean suit. Peace and goodwill are speedily restored to this particular place on earth, to this particular gathering of mankind. In a matter of minutes, the great sea of material contentment once again rolls on untroubled.

— II —   Lucy hands the car keys to the parking valet along with a ten-dollar bill.

Ten dollars—ridiculous! And there'll be another ten on the way out, she reflects as she enters the restaurant. Twenty bucks to park a rented Taurus! It offends her Maine sense of thrift; that it's the GIA stockholders' money provides small comfort.

Well, she thinks, that's the way it is, because this *is* Morton's, and it *is* Monday night. Morton's on Melrose: the only place in Hollywood to be on Monday, after lunch at the Ivy. Tomorrow night the caravan moves on to the Grill.

"Miss Preston, nice to see you again. Right this way, please."

She's seated right away, drawing glowers from the lesser souls consigned to wait in the purgatory of the bar. A few diners look at her curiously, and a little extra buzz stirs the busy air when it becomes clear that this comely yet interesting-looking young woman is being led to *the* table. Lucy doesn't make much of this, one way or the other. She's past the point in her career where the recognition of restaurant captains sets off tiny sparks of self-esteem.

Of course, she thinks, it might be that my inner glow is shining through.

"Mr. Carlsson phoned, Miss Preston," the captain tells her. "He'll be a few minutes late."

Lucy orders a vodka and tonic. She's curious why Carlsson has asked for this urgent meeting. Well, what Carlsson wants, Carlsson gets. That's become the order of the day around GIA.

Up to but not including Lucy herself, that is, although Mannerman hasn't exactly been explicit on this point. Not that she sees any cause for alarm. Like PL, Carlsson acts as if any diversion of energy away from business—to, say, sex—would be an unforgivable dissipation of a prize corporate asset.

She looks around, trying not to stargaze. The restaurant is packed in the noisy, self-aware manner of all places where influence, ambition and fear circle each other like predators disputing carrion. A man a couple of tables away looks familiar. Who is he? She squeezes her memory like an orange and finally has it: he's the actor who was in that movie she saw the other night on cable in her hotel in Singapore; the only one she could find that wasn't kung fu or Bruce Willis being blown up. What was it called? *Ferris Bueller's Day Off*, that was it. He played a teacher; it was a stupid little picture, but this guy had been pretty funny, even dubbed in Chinese.

Other faces around the room strike faint, unplaceable chords. In the flesh, few stars resemble themselves. That blond woman with the killer cheekbones, for example. Michelle Pfeiffer? Or no one?

She forces her attention back to her own business. The one thing I must avoid is confrontation, she tells herself for perhaps the hundredth time today, and that's not going to be easy, because she truly loathes this new idea of Carlsson's.

Loathes and despises it: not for Street reasons, although the preliminary feedback is strongly negative, but because it takes GIA in a moral and ethical direction she's not sure she can live with. Up to now, whatever her private reservations, Lucy's been willing to defend GIA resolutely no matter what, willing to subordinate personal conviction to the profit motive, willing to accept that GIA's overriding raison d'être is to make money for its stockholders, no matter what that involves, as long as it's not illegal. But there are points at which one has to think twice.

The Individuality Channel strikes Lucy as being just such a point. It's Carlsson's baby, his inspiration, his pet: a worldwide cable and satellite hookup offering exploitation of every conceivable form of human ugliness, every hatred, resentment, anxiety, anger and self-pity that this psychologically ingenious, narcissistic, paranoid age can cook up.

"We'll get every sicko, wacko and hater from Boston to Bombay," Carlsson had asserted in his initial pitch. "Keep the flame turned up nonstop round-the-clock, round-the-globe with simultaneous translation. You know how many people that is today? Probably billions! Take America alone, Jack: my guess is, the way things are these days, two out of every three Americans are looking for someone to shoot or rat out!"

It's Lucy's view that absolutely the last thing GIA ought to be doing right now is adding to the psychological violence permeating life in America and elsewhere. There may be good, even big money in mass anger, but it's the devil's gold. Everyone in the for-profit world may be walking tall, but Lucy worries that the footing may grow uncertain. Markets look their brassiest just before they fall out of bed, she knows. Grover may strut and smile in his *Time*-cover-anointed role as "the King of K Street," unelected leader of the Washington lobbyists' lobby, and the new Speaker may privately tell a $10,000-a-plate breakfast group that the business of Congress is "to keep the American people sullen but not mutinous," but all this can backfire.

So why, thinks Lucy, and she says so to Mannerman, take a chance, no matter how glowing Carlsson's projections of global audience share may be. It worries her that a Hollywood "above the line" mentality, couched in terms of Nielsen points and grosses, may be seeping into PL's thinking. Not that he isn't still running GIA as CRONI-tough as ever. UnivCom is a huge success. But it's also a ravenous consumer of capital, requiring massive new investments in fiber-optic and satellite transmission, Web access and on-line capability and software. It's grown to the point where GIA is contractually obligated to dollar-match its overseas partners in growing UnivCom, so every nickel's being squeezed out of GIA's core operations to feed the beast.

Lucy's pretty certain that Carlsson wants to pitch the Individuality Channel to her one last time before going to Mannerman. Carlsson's a subtler sort than she expected, no bull in a china shop, crashing old loyalties like crockery. It's clear he considers internal dissension a capital waste of time. She guesses he respects her, and respects the bond she has with PL. She isn't absolutely sure whether Carlsson knows that it was she who essentially persuaded Mannerman to back off on the Cabinrock acquisition and settle for a 20 percent silent-partner interest through UnivCom, but it's likely he does.

She has to admit that, if you can keep morality out of the equation, Carlsson's idea seems on the money in terms of the way we live now. His plan involves a continuous twenty-four-hour rota of talk shows, possibly as many as a dozen, scheduled on a two-repeat rotation. To keep the stew simmering, the Individuality Channel would establish and support several hundred forums on the Internet where every form and variety of self-expression, including, of course, sociopathic rage, can indulge itself to the outermost limits. To anchor the channel, Carlsson proposes to steal Betti Jo Barnum and General Chadbourne Tinkry from the Mutual and Fox networks.

To anchor something like the Individuality Channel, short of prying Oprah loose, it would be hard to imagine stronger leads than Betti Jo and General Chad. A much-decorated hero of Vietnam who'd lost a son in the bombing of the Marine Corps barracks in Beirut, Tinkry had retired from the Marines in 1985 full of honors and rage after being passed over for the third time for Marine Corps Commandant, and had promptly made himself into the media nightmare of every sitting President.

Chadbourne Tinkry is the hero-figurehead for the millions of Americans whose political philosophy comes down to one word: *against*. Against this race or that tribe or that faith, against war, against peace, against the rich, against the poor. It's clear from the famous monologues that open his nightly television stand-up routines that combine the opening scene from the film *Patton* (Tinkry in uniform in front of a giant Stars and Stripes), the opening routine from the *Tonight* show (a scorching jeremiad against pantywaist, draft-dodging politicians and civil servants) and the final scene of the film *High Noon* (Tinkry ripping his star-laden epaulets and his chestful of ribbons from his uniform and hurling them to the ground in the manner of Gary Cooper while the audience, unprompted, goes wild).

People fear Tinkry as a would-be Man on a White Horse, waiting to be summoned by acclamation to the presidency. It's obvious he's convinced that the electorate cannot be led effectively except in ways for which the Constitution makes no provision. Twice the Republicans have offered Tinkry the White House on a silver platter; twice he's rejected them. He's a man of the mob, of the despised, the outed, the marginal, and he calls himself "the walking Rainbow Coalition in khaki," being, in fact, of mixed descent, half Shinnecock Indian—which, as he proudly points out, marries African-American and Native American strains— and half Polish-Welsh potato farmer. It will cost UnivCom a ton to buy him away from Murdoch, with whom he has a $15-million-a-year personal-services contract due to expire shortly, but it will be worth it. General Chadbourne Tinkry, USMC (Ret.), is a very shrewd demagogue, rousing his rabble by understatement and indirection, and his audience is huge, restive and devoted.

Betti Jo Barnum trades on a rare empathy with women confused by contemporary gender politics, stereotypes and antistereotypes. In her own case, this confusion finds expression in avoirdupois. Betti Jo Barnum's gig is weight: violent oscillations, near-hundred-pound swings, between anorexic, bulimia-abetted scrawniness and cellulite-raddled obesity. She has turned her gain-loss cycles into a conglomerate of signature diet plans now emphasizing homeopathy, now emphasizing prescription drugs, cookbooks to make you fat, cookbooks to make you thin, each pitched to current food fads. At present, Betti Jo Barnum's *Fat and Happy* stands—as it has for nineteen weeks—atop *The New York Times* hardcover "how to" best-seller list, while last year's *Think*

Thin and Live Good heads the paperbacks. Then there are franchises, videos, lectures and over-the-counter diet aids—the whole anchored by Betti Jo's top-rated daytime network talk show. According to Carlsson, whose client Barnum is, the whole adds up to a big number—he hints at a quarter billion annually in gross revenues overall—that is closing fast on Oprah.

Most important, the lady's audience, according to Carlsson, numbers "ninety-four million slobs and pukers, self-haters, in other words, ninety-eight percent female. Women control the money in the world. We exploit the self-hate to get at the money."

And there was more.

"What's been missing," Carlsson said, "is the third party to our little equation of misery—namely, the kids. So what Betti Jo moves into now is to get children to rat out their parents! Take some twelve-year-old fatty who weighs two hundred pounds, who's to say it isn't because Daddy showed her a thing or two? Or his thing. And to keep the legal eagles off our collective ass, we make sure every show with kids— maybe *every* show, period!—has a couple of shrinks sitting by scratching their chins and nodding gravely, which any one of 'em'll do, provided the money's right."

Lucy's no feminist—she's never met an "ism" she could be made to care for—but afterward she speaks up strongly to Mannerman. "It's not just me, PL. Wall Street will hate this idea. Especially the part about the children! Some things in this country—few, I admit—are still sacred!"

She left it at that, but PL must have said something to Carlsson, who's like the princess with the pea under the stack of mattresses when it comes to a dissenting voice. The merest murmurous hint of disagreement roars in his ears like the ocean. So here Lucy sits, in Morton's on Monday night, under virtual orders—unspoken orders—to settle things with him.

She's thinking this over disgustedly, staring into her glass, when she senses a change in the atmosphere of the restaurant, a diminution of chatter, a shift of attention.

She looks up. Robert Carlsson is making his way toward her, shepherded by Pam Morton, seeming to cut a visible swath through the fog of striving self-regard that fills the restaurant. Like Moses parting the

Red Sea, she thinks, taking a quick sip and pasting on a pleasant, suitably welcoming smile.

It's impressive, the effect the man has on people who themselves aren't exactly chopped liver. Lucy's been around power; she knows what influence feels like, the sucking sound of deference, the bronzy, boomy clang that multiple zeros make in people's minds, but the Carlsson version's like nothing in her experience. She's felt it here, she felt it checking into the Bel-Air.

It's personalized, not like on Wall Street, with people sitting at computers, hidden away like the Wizard of Oz, tapping keys, sending out impulses traveling at the speed of light, creating financial waves that may be tidal in their effects but whose agents are just names on screens. She can see why a strong personality like Mannerman is excited by Carlsson's aura. It's personal, has a name, a persona, its own shape and odor and coloration: it's man to man, it's face to face, it's *mano a mano*. The other son of a bitch is out to get you—so you get him first. Winners get the good tables, losers kiss hands, or the hems of cassocks, or fat, pale behinds.

Versailles must have been like this in the days of Louis XIV: all hope and connection, possibility and destiny, dependent upon and groveling for the smallest gradations of royal acknowledgment, putting the emotional calipers to a faint kingly smile, the precise angulation of an imperial eyebrow, the tiniest incline of the royal head.

With a final wave to a young man who might be Keanu Reeves, Carlsson arrives at the table.

"Ah, Lucy," he says, "how nice to see you."

"And you too, Robert."

Placing a slim ostrich-skin briefcase on an chair brought over expressly for that purpose, Carlsson sits down. His own chair's placed at an angle, neither across from Lucy nor exactly next to her, not too close or too far away, positioned just so, in order to send a calculated signal of ambivalence to all those here at Morton's on Monday night. They'll toss and turn the ensuing night away wondering who she is, why she's there, what *he's* up to.

"So," he says, "how goes it?"

"It goes OK." She wants to sound guarded but not impolite.

A bottle of vintage Krug arrives, along with glasses. Lucy declines

—champagne goes too quickly to her head—and asks for another vodka and tonic. When it arrives, Carlsson clinks his glass against hers.

"Here's luck, Lucy."

"And to you, Robert."

He takes a sip and looks around the room. At one point, he lifts up the palm of his right hand in all but imperceptible salutation. He holds the gesture for no longer than a second or two, but Lucy notices that's time enough to bring a wide, nervous smile to the face of a dark-suited thirtyish man seated a few tables away.

"Do you know what you might like, Mr. Carlsson?" asks the captain, who hasn't left the table. "We have some nice specials."

"Two Caesars to begin, mine with extra anchovies," Carlsson says, "then, let's see, Miss Preston's a fish lover, so do the tuna and sand dab sashimi as a main for her, and I'll have the free-range as usual."

"One sashimi, one chicken. Very good, sir."

When the captain goes off, Carlsson gets right down to cases.

"I hear you don't like Individuality."

"It's not my call. I'm just passing along what I hear from the Street."

"Really? How odd."

"Well, you know how Wall Street is."

"Indeed I do. That's what's funny. The Street just *loves* me, or so they tell me. They think I'm a combination of Richie Rich, Mr. Magic and the Pied Piper! So why on this one—"

"This one is different," Lucy interrupts evenly. "The Individuality Channel is predicated on a lot of areas which make people uneasy, especially after Oklahoma City—"

"Still?"

"Oklahoma City wasn't that long ago. A lot of our large stockholders are as hard-nosed as they come when it comes to making money, but a great deal of the money they manage belongs to people—institutions— who have an image they want to protect. They don't want controversy, and Individuality's bound to be controversial. It's like the tobacco business, or South Africa. There was money to be made there, but also things no one wanted to be connected with."

"You're telling me that Individuality's like South Africa? Or Philip Morris?"

Lucy shakes her head. Stay at his temperature, she urges herself. His phrasing may be contentious, but his tone of voice and attitude are cool.

"Robert, I'm just the messenger. My job is to—"

"Your job is to carry the bad news from Ghent to Aix, or whatever." His voice stays polite. "Still, sometimes if you don't want the message to get through, about all you can do is knock off the messenger."

What is she supposed to say to that? For a moment, she doesn't reply, and Carlsson simply sits there, studying her. I'm not in control of this conversation, she thinks with a shiver; he is. He knows where he's going with this; I don't.

"I gather a lot of the rest of Jack's businesses aren't going so well," he says finally.

"These aren't easy times, but basically we're holding our own."

He smiles at her and nods to the room at large. "This business is too. Look at these people! A bunch of adolescents who never read a book are running a quarter-trillion-dollar industry! Except they're getting older, the audience is getting older, and nobody knows what to do next, so they fall back on the only three truths they've ever been taught."

"Which are?" Lucy's relieved that he's taking the conversation away from Individuality, if only briefly. It gives her time. Of course, he knows that.

"When in doubt: go dumb, dumber and dumbest! Take it so far down-market you need a goddamn diving bell!"

Lucy says nothing.

"The thing is," Carlsson continues, his tone slightly warmer, "they've rinsed the brain of the audience to the point where maybe that's what *is* true. Hence the Individuality Channel."

"I'm not sure I follow you."

"I don't like the movie equation anymore. I don't see spending a hundred million-plus on pictures pitched to an IQ level of about the national speed limit. The dumber the audience is, the harder it is to figure. *Gump* does a billion dollars worldwide, so everybody thinks: OK, idiots are where it's at—and the industry promptly blows close to three hundred million proving that theory wrong. There's the beauty of Individuality. The audience will tune in to see itself. It's slob-to-slob, wacko-to-wacko communication, and it costs *bupkis*, as my competitors say! The talent's free, there's no location shooting, no stars, no agents, no studios socking the above-the-line with overhead, no egos in suits slowing you down just to show how important they are—in a business where time is money more than in any other. Lucy, believe me, I've been there, I put a lot of this shit we see around in place, but praise be to God, I've seen the light, and the light is the Individuality Channel! It can't miss. It isn't Shakespeare, granted, it isn't even *Seinfeld*, but we're living in a time when every jerk on God's green earth has been taught to believe that what she or he has to say is worth hearing, plus jerks love to hang out with other jerks, even vicariously, the same as billionaires do: what did Fitzgerald call it, 'consoling proximity'? Well, that's what Individuality'll give 'em, company for their misery, and we'll make a cool billion or so in the process!"

Lucy puts on an intentionally effortful smile and nods, hoping that Carlsson will read this as graceful surrender—giving her the chance to regroup to fight this particular battle in another way on another day.

It looks as if she's succeeded. With the arrival of the salad course, Carlsson's attention is diverted. As he chops his anchovies with his fork, he looks around the room and counts out loud, "One, two, three . . ."

Lucy shoots him a quizzical expression.

"Just seeing how many Grace Kelly look-alikes we have here tonight. Counting Michelle over there, I make it four."

"Grace Kelly? The star who married Prince Rainier? She died in a car crash just after I graduated from Bowdoin."

"That's the one. With the daughters who can't keep their pants on. I'm surprised someone as young as you knows her work. Video, eh?"

"Video—and my father."

The late actress was a particular favorite of the Chief's. He made Lucy watch all of her films.

"A great lady, Miss Kelly, at least on the screen. And the wave of the future, it would seem. I was over at Disney yesterday, and they're thinking about doing a one-eighty. Going upmarket. Apparently someone on Goofy Drive caught *Rear Window* on cable, and now the Junior League's the new flavor of the month, which means blond pageboys, good bones, pearls and twinsets and all the la-di-da you can swallow. Everyone's talking elegance, class, style, not that any of these people would recognize any of the three if they bit 'em in the backside! No more Ah-nuld, no more blondes with ice picks, no more beaver, no more bosoms, everybody back in their clothes! Girls, put your pants

back on! Boys, get rid of the stubble and the earrings. WASP is in! The
haute-er the better! It even applies to the suits. Someone told me the
word at CAA is that by July 4 no more Armani! Anyone not in Brooks
Brothers loses his parking space!"

He shakes his head at the ridiculousness of it all, and looks at Lucy.

"You know, Lucy, you kind of look like Grace Kelly. Matter of fact,
you look a lot like her. Did you ever think about going into pictures?
Anyway, fire and ice, that's the new gimmick: icy blond to look at, but
red-hot inside."

Lucy smiles, says nothing, sips her drink. He's probing, she thinks.

"Speaking of WASPs," Carlsson says lightly, "has anyone heard anything more from our friend from '21,' that guy—what was his name—
who made Jack pee in his pants?"

Lucy shakes her head.

"Jesus, was that ever some show! The OK Corral with a hundred-
dollar minimum! You got to hand it to the guy. It may have taken a
.357 Magnum to get the job done, but anyone who can—literally!—
scare the piss out of Jack Mannerman is some piece of work! Plus I
gather he also scared the seventy-five million out of Jack. I understand
he went ahead and ponied up the dough. How'd the Street like that?
Usually those guys go ape when they see good money thrown after bad."

"He would have done it anyway. He had made a commitment. He
kept his word. What happened at '21' had nothing to do with it. And
the jury's still out on BEECO."

Carlsson looks at Lucy with a snide expression that makes her feel
like a bug on a slide. "Is it now?"

Lucy nods the lie. The BEECO deal bought them the Capitol Hill
due bill they had to have, but apart from that, GIA might just as well
have burned the money, because all it got for its close to half billion
was a company that could turn out one picture-perfect—by 1990
standards—nine-axle auger every six weeks while Komatsu or Caterpillar were producing three that were state-of-the-art in half the time
and at a 20 percent lower price. GIA had acquired a workforce that
might have stepped out of a Norman Rockwell illustration but was protective of its "entitlements," work and pay practices going back more
than a half century, and by modern productivity standards all but useless. Just another spoiled, overindulged and undermanaged remnant of

the postwar Pax Americana, when America ruled the world and all its markets because we had all the money and we alone weren't in ruins. Another good old name running on the fumes of its reputation and the goodwill of its old customers, taking its market for granted, chewing up its order book without building backlog except for parts and service.

Carlsson looks at Lucy doubtfully and continues. "But I don't think Jack's going to forget that, do you? Someone makes you piss your pants in front of *tout* New York, you're not going to forget him."

"I doubt anyone noticed."

Carlsson's grin changes quality, takes on a more malevolent cast. "*You* did," he says. "*I* did. Not to mention God. That's three. Surely enough for Jack. I'm surprised he didn't take revenge. The way the Nazis used to. You know, the guerrillas would knock off some high-ranking Gestapo type, and the Germans would exact reprisal by destroying an entire village."

"Jack's no Nazi! What a thing to say!" Her voice is full of righteous indignation, and she is certain Mannerman would never let what happened at "21" influence his business judgment, at least not the Mannerman she knows. But she also knows that with the Speaker safely reelected, and BEECO's grace period about to expire, the company's for the chop.

BEECO's lucky to have stayed untouched this long, but everyone's mindful of what happened to Standard Utility when it tried to cut its losses by closing down, virtually overnight, a gray-metal castings plant in Kentucky. The simpleminded-looking hillbillies who made up the workforce put on their Sunday best, went up to New York, hired a hotshot PR firm to handle their tale of woe, and the next thing anyone knew, they turned up on public television and then on *60 Minutes*, which led to Standard Utility's chief executive spending two of the worst days of his life before a minority-dominated Senate subcommittee holding hearings on "the hollowing-out of American industry." At the end of the day, SU had to pay an extra $40 million to shed a lousy two hundred jobs; it lost a $95 million Ex-Im subsidy when the congresswoman fronting for the company suddenly wouldn't return calls; its CEO found himself on the cover of *Newsweek* over the headline "Is the Business of America Too Important to Be Left to American Business?"

The BEECO closure is planned to be so gradual it'll seem almost gentle. First, the bean counters and cost cutters will weed and winnow the fringe benefits that GIA's left alone so far. There'll be a little tactical tweaking here and there that may suggest to certain marginal members of the workforce the wisdom of early relocation. A few product lines will be shut down, a few thousand square feet of factory space will be vacated and left fallow, here and there scattered handfuls of jobs will be eliminated.

The eviscerative process will begin with another Group-level task force's reorganization of BEECO into clearly separable core constellations of operating and nonoperating assets. These will be priced for sale by Lamond & Co.'s cheerless M.B.A.s with laptops, who'll move through the company putting tags on various pieces, turning BEECO into a multimillion-dollar yard sale. Brochures will be put together and likely buyers identified and approached. Komatsu will be talked to, as will Caterpillar and Euclid. Finally, whatever's left will be shut down. GIA will walk away, eating whatever write-off has to be taken, and that will be that.

Carlsson studies Lucy with that same steady smile. She replies with a bright little smile of her own. He's definitely taking this somewhere, she thinks, and feels a chill on her spine, a prickly adrenal warning to keep on her toes. She wishes she hadn't had that second drink.

"Marlboro Man turns Wyatt Earp in '21,'" he says finally. "What a total weird-out! I can't get it out of my head. A guy like that pulling a gun!"

He falls silent. Lucy's thought a lot about that episode herself. For her, at least as recalled, it has taken on some of the qualities of an epiphany. Time and recollection have invested Baker's actions with a certain desperate Tory gallantry she finds just about irresistible. Her father, however, didn't agree. As a lawman, he loathed the very idea of people waving guns around in public, no matter how expert they might be. On the other hand, the Chief conceded that, taking all into account, Lucy's Mr. Baker seemed like the sort of fellow modern life needed more of.

"You know, these old-school WASPs fascinate me," Carlsson says at length. "I went to Harvard myself, did you know that?"

"As a matter of fact, I did. Romance languages, wasn't it?"

"Very good. You surprise me, Lucy, that you know that. The way you look at me, I figure you think I'm some sort of Sammy Glick."

"Sammy Glick?"

"You don't know *Sammy Glick*?"

"I'm afraid not. Should I?"

"Lucy, everyone who basically is on the hustle for a living, as are thee and me, no matter what we call it, should know Sammy—not that we should do as he does, however."

"So who is he?"

"A character in a book by Budd Schulberg called *What Makes Sammy Run*."

"I think I've heard of it."

"I should hope so." Carlsson pauses, and in response to some signal imperceptible to Lucy, the captain materializes at the table. Carlsson instructs him to send someone to an all-night bookstore over on La Cienega and fetch a copy of Schulberg's novel.

"I read it when I was at Harvard—when I wasn't in the Houghton Library closeted with the *Roman de la Rose*; I wrote my thesis on the Influence of the Troubadour Poets on Petrarch. I'll bet you don't believe it, but I did. Since my old man was a chiropodist to the stars, who took care of half the fallen arches between Hancock Park and the Santa Monica pier, I figured I should know what there was to know about the local turf. I read a lot of Nathanael West and Dreiser too, and Sherwood Anderson and Faulkner. As an antidote."

"Antidote?"

"To Harvard. To this place. To the cancer of unmitigated bicoastalism. You know something? Looking back, I wish I'd gone to some place like Oberlin or Ohio State. Especially as I went to school on the East Coast too. St. George's in Newport."

"Why Oberlin?"

"I wish I knew just a little bit about what this country's really like. I've lived my entire life perched on the doughnut. A doughnut baked in never-never land. Well, I tried to make up for it. I did an informal minor in sociology, or—if you prefer—zoology."

"Are you serious? Really?"

"Well, *not* really. But I observed and classified the habits and characteristics of a dying breed, the offspring of the old WASP officer class that won World War II so that their kids could dodge the draft in the future. Back then, they still owned most of everything big in this country, unless they thought it was beneath them, like making money, in which case they let the Jews have it. Those WASPs . . ." He shrugs, smiles, shakes his head.

"Yes?"

"Took me a long time to figure them out. Then I finally got it. Point one is they're programmed never to grow up. Prep school is about as far as most of them ever get in the way of personal development. Who can blame 'em, when from the cradle people're filling their little blond heads with all that for-the-good-of-the-team crap: play up and play the game, lose gracefully, ladies first, and never, but never, vote for yourself! It's all rubbish, because it's not the way life works! They're not stupid, but they have a hell of a time accepting that life is what it is. Poor buggers, they start out with the assumption that God'll keep an eye on them no matter what as long as they're good little boys and play fair. Nobody warns them that there's going to come a day when the Big Teacher in the Sky no longer calls on the brightest or politest kid in the class but the one with the most money or the loudest voice."

"I'm not sure I follow you."

"Sure you do, you just don't like my theory, 'cause it won't be romantic enough. Give you an example. What's the hottest sector right now on the Street? Don't answer, I'll tell you. Derivatives. Now, what are derivatives except an elevated form of Monopoly played with real-live stocks and bonds and dollar bills? And who's getting killed in derivatives? Just look at the names—WASP, WASP, WASP. Bankers Trust, Procter & Gamble, Piper Jaffray, Barings Bank. This guy in Orange County looks like a vestryman in a goddamn Episcopal church! You think there's a Jew or an Italian in the world dumb enough to let some kid bet a billion dollars in an electronic blackjack game against guys he can't see, guys who're dealing from decks that have fifty-three or whatever number of cards they need to win?"

"You don't need a Harvard degree for that," she observes.

"Hell, you need an *un*-Harvard degree! I look back and, as far as I'm concerned, I only learned one really useful thing in all those years at school in the East."

"Which was?"

"I'm too much a gentleman to be explicit. Let's just say I learned how to sublimate certain drives that otherwise get in the way of clear thinking."

Carlsson pushes ahead. "You know, Lucy, I've been studying people a long time now. No better way to get a line on what a guy's about than to cut a deal with him. Well, I've cut 'em with you name it—the Wall Street rich, French lawyers so cagey they make your teeth hurt with all their subtleties, *campesinos* who walk onto a location with machetes and want fifty thou or they cut off the leading lady's bazooms, and very, *very* tough union guys. I've seen 'em all: Irish, Sicilian, Mexican, Jewish, WASP, French, Brits, you name it. I've screwed them over and they've screwed me over—at least a few times. You know what I've concluded about what makes this guy tick, or that one? What jerks his chain? The way I see it, it's a kind of tribal thing."

"Tell me more."

"I mean, every tribe has its own shtick, what it does best to get what it wants, the natural element for its desires—like water for fishes. Here's where I come out. For the Irish, that element is bullshit, what they call blarney. Sometimes it's just whisky talk. Sometimes—Jack comes to mind—it's as calculated as nuclear physics. Jews? Jews like really clever deals, a lot of angles to figure out and play with. Italians? Italians like secrets, conspiracies, Godfather-type stuff. And WASPs? What do you think it is for WASPs, Lucy?"

Carlsson eyes her carefully. Lucy looks at him frankly, shakes her head and smiles.

"C'mon, give a guess! You know these people."

Now, what could he mean by that? Another needle of apprehension digs at her. She ventures, "Honor?"

He grins. "Not bad!" he says. "But if you ask me, honor's nothing but vanity in a cheap suit—at least most of the time. But honor's part of the equation, no doubt of that. Now, think hard, Lucy!"

This isn't give-and-take between two people shying away from a big disagreement, Lucy thinks. Carlsson and I are creatures in a script. His script. She knows they're not all that far apart in age, but she feels like a child next to him. A child perhaps about to be cruelly punished.

Where *is* this going? What's his point? How can any of this relate to Individuality?

"You tell me what you think it is," she responds in a cheerful firm voice, but with a complicitous smile.

"I think it's one of the two things that all's fair in."

Not love obviously. "War?"

"You got it!" beams Carlsson. "Give the little lady a plush teddy bear!"

"Thanks. But tell me why."

"Easy. War combines the two things WASPs like best. Killing things—Jack told me the Baker boardroom looked like the damn Explorers Club, trophies and antlers and stuffed fish wherever you turned—and team sports. War's the ultimate white-guy team sport. It beats lacrosse and hockey hollow, provided you survive it. Win or lose, war lets you never have to grow up even if you make it back. It all goes together, don't you see? Honor, war, killing things. The way of the WASP. The thing is, you have to wonder what's going to happen to Brother WASP now that war seems to be a thing of the past, at least in this country, where your hard-core electorate and half of Congress were draft dodgers. What d'you do for your jollies now? Invent a war? Go find one? Do like Baker and shoot sheep?"

"There's always Wall Street."

"Nah! The Street's about money. WASPs like their action pure; they think money sullies it."

"So what do they do?"

Carlsson beams. "They try to wage war against time. Like those knights in Italy in the fifteenth century, with the Middle Ages on the way out and the Renaissance on the way in—hanging around in the woods ambushing merchants and cutting off their hands. Or those Japs they used to keep finding on those deserted Pacific islands: you know, thirty years since V-J Day and the guy's still prowling around in the jungle eating bark because he hasn't heard that Hirohito surrendered. It's kind of admirable in its way, even magnificent, and so was the Charge of the Light Brigade. But it's not real in today's terms, and real is the only game that pays. Funny thing, everybody wants to look like a WASP, maybe because they figure that being taken for a duty-honor-country schmuck gives you an edge against the hard boys, but I don't know anyone who really wants to go for the whole package and be a true-blue, white-shoe WASP down in his soul!"

Duty, honor, country. The words Lucy recalls using to warn Mannerman about Baker long before the episode at "21." To Carlsson, they're terms of derision. Grist for fools, to be pronounced with scorn.

"Anyway, Lucy, this is just a long way of getting to my point."

"I thought it might be!" Lucy has to be charming. "Your point is what, precisely? My feelings about Individuality?"

"You might say so. Actually, I think it's your *expression* of those feelings that's my precise area of concern." His eyes have taken on a glitter, a gleam, like light dancing on a scalpel blade.

"Expression to whom? PL? I can hardly see that it's made a dent. He's a hundred percent behind Individuality."

"That may be, but don't you see, I want him—I need him—to be a hundred ten percent behind it, two hundred even. Individuality is the first step in a grand design to convert GIA truly into a company—into *the* company—of the future. Tell me, Lucy, you're a historian—at least you were, of sorts—what do you think is the great chapter of history now unfolding?"

She looks intentionally blank.

"Let me tell you." There's a fierce certitude to Carlsson now. "It's the coming class struggle. The poor versus the rich. Things can't continue as they are now, with all the wealth in the world landing in fewer and fewer pockets. I wish they would, God knows, since one of those pockets is mine. But I'm no fool, and it seems only wise to plan for the day when power is denominated in something other than money."

Lucy's beginning to wonder if Carlsson's all there.

"Hatred." He lets that sink in for a couple of beats, and adds, "It wouldn't be the first time. Think about it. Beggary is now universal. Capitalism's seen to that. Beggars can't be choosers, but they can be haters. And there're as many types of rage out there as stars in the sky. Individuality will be a series of frequencies, if you will, each attracting—appealing to, reaching—a different band on the vast spectrum of hatred and paranoia. Comes the day when the basis of power shifts from dollars to voices, Individuality will be a preestablished rallying point, a staging ground for the great unwashed. The entity that controls Individuality will have a good shot at controlling what people think. What they do. What their agenda will be!"

"That's what Orwell called Big Brother."

"Aw, not quite. We're talking levels and degrees here, quantities of control, amounts, markets for systems of belief instead of VCRs. Especially if we have a good, solid tie-in with a major worldwide force for antimaterialism. Everybody else is talking about the future as business as usual according to Bill Gates, except with more zeros to play with. I think that's a grievously mistaken oversimplification. They're still thinking in units of production. I'm thinking in units of conviction."

"By antimaterialism you mean Rome, don't you? PL and his connection with Rome? You *are* thinking Big Brother—with a halo."

Carlsson smiles. "You said it."

And *you* will control PL, Lucy thinks. That's your game!

He obviously grasps what's on her mind. "So you see," he says amiably, "I can't have the road to Jack's brave new world contaminated by even the tiniest sliver of doubt. To get from here to there will require unbounded, unshaken confidence."

"Are you nuts?" Lucy is both candid and playful.

"I don't think so. Was Columbus? Galileo? Freud? Was Christ or Muhammad, to put it more appositely?"

"Or Hitler? Or Stalin—or Mao?"

"What about them? You can disagree with what they did, but you can't say they weren't damn good at it. Isn't that the point? The trick is not to press it." Carlsson's tone is infuriatingly bland. So, for an instant, is his expression, but then it darkens, and when he next speaks, his voice has a dangerous edge.

"Lucy, I made straight A's in school, and I intend to make straight A's in life. Unfortunately, I can't pick and choose my course of study, but I do have options. I've made a choice. I have a goal in mind. I intend to get there. The world is moving faster than any of us thinks, hurtling toward destiny at a rate that doesn't permit the luxury of dealing with obstacles—real or perceived—in any other way than getting rid of them."

"And you see me as an obstacle?"

Carlsson doesn't answer.

"And so you intend to blow me off?"

Carlsson grins. "My goodness, no! What a thing to say! Well, only if you choose not to step aside gracefully."

Lucy wants to stay very cool. She hasn't studied Jack Mannerman for years for nothing. "And why should I?" She looks right at Carlsson, smiling.

He seems to ponder her question as if he has no really good quick answer. He examines the room, the ceiling, his expensive briefcase lying on the chair between them—and then he finally picks the briefcase up and places it on the table in front of him, pushing aside his plate and coffee cup. He studies Lucy across the table, hands resting on his case, steepled index fingers tapping reflexively.

Carlsson has a good sense of the moment, Lucy thinks, as all great negotiators have. He's setting her up, but for what? What can she do?

"You know what I mean by *son et lumière?*" he asks her at last, face deadpan, voice flat. "Ever been to Versailles, the châteaux on the Loire?"

"Yes, I've been to Versailles. Yes, I've been to the châteaux on the Loire, at least some of them. Yes, I know what *son et lumière* is," she replies evenly.

He unsteeples his fingers and unzips the leather briefcase. "Well," he says, "I've put together a little *s* and *l* for Jack. Here's the *son.*" He takes out a recording cassette and hands it to her. The label reads "Conversations of subject with H. A. Baker" and shows a series of dates, about sixty in all, going back to earlier in the year, beginning about two months after the incident at "21."

She reads the label twice, very carefully. Then she lays the tape down beside her plate and looks at Carlsson expectantly.

"Wiretapping is a federal offense, Robert," she says.

"Is it, now?" he answers, sounding disgustingly—and, Lucy's certain, intentionally—like Mannerman. "Would you like to hear it? I'm sure one of the boys in the kitchen has a Walkman we can borrow. It would be an interesting demo of the Information Age in operation."

Lucy doesn't respond. She is numbed by the cool amorality of what's being done to her, and no less by the realization that this is a logical working-out of tendencies she herself has managed to live with for close to a decade now. She's not certain for whom she feels greater contempt: Carlsson or herself.

"The *son* part alone will probably suffice to get Jack fired up," Carlsson says chattily. Nothing in his demeanor or expression would suggest to anyone more than ten feet distant that he's just drawn a knife across the jugular of his handsome dining companion. "But just in case, as a fallback, you might say, I thought a touch of *lumière* might harden his resolve—and whatever else. Jack's a bit of a prude, Lucy, as I'm sure you recognize. All those priests and nuns in his family, no doubt. And, of course, he's always had you on a pedestal. He thinks of you almost as a daughter, at least that's what he told me. Anyway, take a peek."

From the briefcase he slides out an ordinary letter-size manila file folder and flips it open. It contains a thin sheaf of color enlargements of a picture, variants of the one on top, which Lucy can see upside down. He turns it around so that it faces her. It shows a bedroom surveyed from an oblique angle, down and in, as if the photographer had peeked in from a perch outside the window from a distance of some fifteen or twenty yards. From its reddish cast and rough image, it appears that the picture was taken with a medium telephoto lens at maximum aperture in dim light, with the photographer pushing high-speed color film to the limit, although the lighting is odd, almost as if it had been brighter at the focal plane of the camera than at the subject.

The room is occupied by a man and a woman, both naked. The man is in the background, off to the left and behind the woman, and seated on a bed. Legs asplay, in a state of unmistakable arousal, he touches himself as he studies the woman—who is focused on something outside the image frame—studying herself in a mirror perhaps? Her hands cup her breasts, small in size but with amazingly large nipples and areolae, and it is clear from her face, from her half-closed eyes and drowsy, slack mouth, that she too is in an advanced state of excitation. It is both reflexive and logical to project that the other photos in the sheaf record succeeding stages in the erotic drama that is depicted here.

Lucy looks coldly at the picture. She recognizes the room, recognizes the man and the woman, recalls the exact occasion. The man is Baker, the woman is herself, the setting is the master bedroom at Two Moose, Baker's Adirondacks camp, a dramatic log-raftered chamber with a splendid view down the length of Lake Massee. And the evening, the mere recall of which now sets the insides of her thighs aquiver, had been just a month earlier, when a noble spring full moon had lit up the night like an inextinguishable flare. She knows things the photograph doesn't show. There is a mirror just outside the picture plane in which she's studying herself, having momentarily disengaged from Baker thanks to a sudden impulse to see what a woman in love (perhaps) and about to make love (surely) looks like. Outside, just down the dock, is a boathouse in which Baker keeps his Adirondacks guide boats and a Sunfish. An enterprising photographer who conducted a proper reconnaissance would have discovered that by lying on the uppermost rack of the boathouse he could command the bedroom from an aperture through which a block and tackle could be deployed.

Lucy goes on studying the photograph. She's aware that Carlsson's looking at it too, but that doesn't bother her. There's no prurience at work in the man, she somehow feels; sex doesn't come into it. For him, this is just a document in a negotiation, just paperwork incidental to a transaction.

There *is* something about the photo, something about its mood, that bothers her, but with so much else to think about, she can't spare the mental energy to chase it down. Finally, she looks up, flips the folder closed and stares at Carlsson.

"So?" he says.

She shrugs. He has all the chips. Let him open.

"Well," he says, "you know how Jack is. About loyalty, stuff like that."

There's a lot Lucy could say to this, but she keeps silent.

"You step aside, set up for yourself—it's probably time anyway— you won't lack for business. I'll see to that, believe me."

Now she has to smile. This situation is so utterly preposterous it has to be true. There's no escape for her. Yes, she does know how Jack is. Check and mate.

"Robert, I believe you. You're definitely a man who can see to whatever he wants to see to."

The odd thing is, at the back of her emotions she senses a shadowy feeling of relief, ever so faint—but unmistakable. Carlsson may in fact be right. It probably *is* time.

He sticks out his hand.

"Deal?"

"Deal."

She takes his hand without rancor. She's at a point where nothing she feels—or doesn't feel—surprises her. Perhaps this is what shell shock's like. Euphoria without the glow.

"You decide how you want to handle it with Jack. Of course—"

Carlsson is about to go on when the captain appears at the table. "Your book, Mr. Carlsson."

Carlsson looks at the Budd Schulberg paperback and hands it to her. Lucy studies the cover, turns it over and examines the blurbs on the back.

" 'Ruthless,' " she quotes. " 'Scheming,' 'ambitious.' Robert, are you sure this isn't about you?"

The agent looks at her for a moment before replying. He shrugs his shoulders and eyebrows, then cocks his head and smiles. "Only when I laugh," he says.

— III — At three-thirty, when the shooters take their stations for the last drive of the day, the late-October light is beginning to fail. A fitful, nasty little breeze is blowing off the Alps, driving its damp chill like a poniard into the very marrow. Lucy clasps her arms around herself and shivers under her waxed-cotton shooting jacket, wishing she'd thought to bring an extra sweater. As the whistle blows for the beaters to begin the drive, she presses close to Baker, using his tall, wiry body as a windbreak.

The line of shooters—six "guns" and their loaders spread out in an irregular line that stretches roughly a quarter mile from end to end—faces a deep stand of alder and hemlock, from the far side of which there now arises a fearful din: whoops, squawks, clucks and shrieks, accompanied by pails being banged and tree trunks whacked. This racket will drive the game from cover, send the pheasants clambering heavily into the air and the hares racing in terror along the ground toward the sulphuric embrace of death.

Today, the six guns comprise five men and one woman, the latter a Spanish *marquesa*, a world-famous shot who Baker says is as good as he's ever seen. She's next down the line, a tall, fierce-chinned woman of about sixty with a scary, ascetic, half-mad El Greco face; when she brings her gun up, her features take on a feral, teeth-bared expression that suggests a devouring skull. Standing beside her is her personal *segretario* (loader), a bandy-legged runt peering into the gloaming, one of his mistress's matched 16-bore Ayala shotguns cradled in the crook of his elbow. She's insisted on bringing him from Seville, even though it's an unspeakable breach of wing-shooting etiquette. There has already been one dispute over credit for a bird that nearly ended in fisticuffs and required the shooting party's host, the industrialist-financier Giovanni Zingori, to pacify his own staff with thick bundles of thousand-lire notes. It's clear to Lucy that the Marquesa de Andaluciensa, like Baker, is a trophy in her own way, and that it's a useful thing to be able to declare at Turin dinner tables that the two graced Zingori's most recent outing at Villa La Clemenza, the exquisite retreat nestled in a pleasant declivity of the Pennine foothills between Bergamo and the Swiss border.

The presence of Baker and the Marquesa lends a sporting gloss to an occasion that is otherwise palpably commercial. Apart from the host, the three other guns are the proprietor of an important Milan journal of opinion, whose influence may help Zingori with problems he has with overzealous investigators from Rome; Sir "Jim" Pullsborough, chief of Euroloans for a big London merchant bank, whose footings include some tens of millions of pounds, dollars and D-marks in short-term and derivative credits to various Zingori enterprises; and Herr Grussli, Zingori's Swiss lawyer, whose Lugano computer files, Lucy guesses, can pinpoint exactly where purported billions of unreported Zingori treasure are buried.

A wet, flood-ridden winter and spring followed by a merciless summer and fall have decimated the hatch, and the shooting has been poor, the birds few and scrawny, and frequently too high, quick or tricky for the quality of their opposition. Pullsborough's made a real ass of himself. Like many Englishmen—so Baker says—the Eurobanker fancies himself a rather better shot than his bag indicates. He's complained or made excuses almost continually since arriving: about his stations on the drives, his loader, the quality of the wine, the weather, the sparse supply of birds. At lunch today, he got quite drunk and unpleasant with his new wife, an American woman trying desperately to look no older than fifty who talks constantly about her late husband's money.

Lucy'll not be sad to see the last of the Pullsboroughs—or any of the others. Zingori's a smarmy, plump little man, a stereotypical "operator"—Spuds would call him a *hondler*—a deft schmoozer quick with flattery who's obviously a specialist at putting the fix in. His industrial-financial conglomerate, which has acted as BEECO's Italian sales agent since World War II, is currently under investigation for corrupt practices ranging from bribery to tax laundering. To be placed at his right at dinner makes Lucy feel vaguely unclean.

Still, according to Baker, an invitation to La Clemenza is worth it. It's one of the great Continental shoots, with no expense spared to make it—as the host has pointed out at least forty times—*"esattamente come a Biddick,"* the legendary English shoot run by the Marquis of Lambton. Even in a bad season, when birds are scarce, the food at the villa is three-star.

There's a cry down the line as the first game breaks cover, and the nearest guns open up. A few birds fold and fall, but most of the pheasants get by the first three stands, wings beating bravely as they squawk bootlessly and fight for altitude. Fewer make it past the Marquesa. She and her loader make a very efficient killing machine, smoothly and calmly exchanging guns, firing and reloading, exchanging, firing and reloading, exchanging. A hare races from the copse, zigzagging across the stubbled ground, making for a farther copse; almost casually, the Marquesa lowers her shotgun and fires; the impact of the heavy charge sends the animal flip-flopping crazily for several yards before it comes to rest, sides heaving, hindquarters twitching. Lucy squeezes her eyes shut and turns away; she hates killing. Yesterday a falling bird nearly clobbered her, dropping right at her feet. She'd nudged it with a foot, ruffling the brilliant plumage going dull in death; it seemed impossible that such small wings could bear aloft so heavy a body. To see such a lovely creature dead nearly broke her heart.

Baker's playing center field, as he puts it. Not entirely by choice, Lucy suspects. At yesterday's first drive, Zingori, apparently wishing to show off his American friend's famed ability, put him in the middle, in the plum position, where the birds funneled helplessly out of a long pine-filled channel straight onto the guns. Baker had taken six doubles in a row, a bird with each barrel, before sportingly letting a few by to ensure there'd be some left for today. He shoots with practiced ease and grace: cheek laid on the stock, arm extended to direct the shotgun's muzzle like a pointing finger, rotating easily from the waist, as smoothly as if his torso is mounted on gimbals. When he fires, the birds fold up and drop straight down like sand-filled stockings.

Baker's confessed to Lucy that shooting game birds is the only blood sport in which he actually enjoys pulling the trigger. For big game, it's the chase that's the thrill, the stalk, the tracking. He doesn't pull the trigger unless the animal in his sights is an obvious Boone & Crockett trophy. He's not a killer at heart, certainly not like the Marquesa; nor is he like the metaphoric predators Lucy's known—Mannerman and Carlsson.

I'm no killer either, she thinks. I might have become one, but no longer. With every passing minute away from the staccato, hard-edged world of Jack Mannerman and GIA, Lucy feels herself softening. In this frame of mind, she thinks she's never been happier in her life—not as an adult at least. Now and then, if she lets down her guard, she even feels a surge of gratitude to Carlsson.

Next to her, Baker suddenly tenses. A lone pheasant has somehow made it past the Marquesa. It cries exultantly as it beats higher and higher to an altitude at which it seems impossibly small and distant. Baker's gun comes up, shooter and shotgun coalesce, and with a flexibility that's indecent for a man over fifty, Baker swings back and around and fires once. For an instant, the pheasant continues on its way, then hits the wall of mortality, stops dead in the sky, folds up into a compact packet of feathers and death and plunges earthward in a swift, shallow arc.

Baker looks over at the Marquesa, a dozen yards away, grins and sweeps off his hat, an old, soft trilby of dark purply-brown Austrian velour banded in pheasant feathers. He bows deep from the waist. He looks courtly, elegant and handsome, very *comme il faut* in his shooting kit: loden jacket, tattersall shirt, nondescript club tie; full-cut plus twos of dark, fat-waled off-green corduroy ending in thick wool stockings brightly ribboned at the band. With this crowd, Lucy's learned, how your clothes fit and where they're made—preferably by Davies, in Lon-

don's Hanover Square, or at a Milan sporting tailor in the Via
Fatebenefratelli—can be as important as how well you shoot.

That's what's bothering her. The house is beautiful, the food is indeed
spectacular, the scenery's great and every pain has been taken to make
the guests comfortable. And yet the hoity-toity quality to the overall
scene suggests a phoniness that's hard to take. Lucy feels as if she's
been imported into a weird, archaic game that uneasily mixes up *ancien
régime* snootiness with nouveau riche pushiness, and everyone's trying
to be someone else in a contest for undefined rewards. It's all confusing
and pointless, and it bothers Lucy that Baker condescends to play the
game at all. Even though he'll pretend he's just playing along to be
polite, it confuses Lucy's feelings for him, and when he now and then
throws himself into it with real gusto she finds it profoundly unsettling.
Two nights ago, when they got started after dinner about how Capri's
been ruined, and the Costa Brava, and St. Moritz, led by Zingori, who
Baker says got his start running a sausage cart outside a Modena box
factory, all she wanted to do was to rush back to the room, throw her
things into a bag and get the hell out of here!

Another whistle sounds. The day's shooting is over. Baker breaks his
gun and slings it over his shoulder. He throws his other arm about Lucy,
bends to her, nuzzles her gently and kisses her just under the ear, and
then they join the others making their way toward the covey of Range
Rovers that waits to return the shooting party to the villa. At a moment
like this, she feels absolute bliss.

An hour later, Lucy lies soaking in a scalding bubble bath, still
utterly content. This may not be love, she thinks, but it's close enough
and will surely suffice for now.

She rinses her hair, checks her pink and glowing self in the mirror,
which briefly bestirs memories of Carlsson's *"lumière,"* and wraps herself in a thick towel big enough to cover three of her. In the bedroom,
she finds Baker stretched out on the bed in his bathrobe, scratching
away at a sheet of the heavy, crested *castello* stationery, no doubt
sketching something that caught his eye during the day. It's a sketch
—more caricature than portrait—of the Marquesa.

"Mmm," she says, "very good! Scary!"

Baker holds it out at arm's length and studies it over his half-glasses.

"Do you think so? What a hawk she is! She practically scares the birds out of the sky! I must say the old girl reminds me of what Shelley wrote: 'I met Murder in the way. / He had a mask like Castlereagh.' "

"More like a buzzard, if you ask me."

Baker looks up at Lucy and examines her. His gaze is bold, frank, appraising. "You look *très* Grace tonight."

Like Carlsson, Baker's a big Grace Kelly fan. He has everything of hers that's out on video at Two Moose. Lucy's watched them all. She thinks both Carlsson and Baker are nuts. She doesn't look at all like Grace Kelly!

"Come over here," he says, putting aside pad and pen, and removing his glasses.

Baker's hand steals up under the towel, which soon comes off, then she parts his dressing gown, and one thing follows another in due and thrilling course, and afterward Lucy lies worn out and naked beside Baker, eyes closed, mentally drifting away, oblivious to everything except her own huge satisfaction and the busy scratching of Baker's pen. As always, sex—which wears her out—seems to reenergize the man.

Pretty soon, maybe in another month or so, she's going to have to think seriously about what she's going to do with her life. The business part'll be easy, a matter of choosing between eager would-be clients. Carlsson's seen to that, and even without his interest, once it got around that Lucy Preston had quit GIA "to pursue other interests," the offers would start to come in. It will be easy for her to make a good living without ever again working a hundred-hour week.

Where Baker will or won't fit into her life, or she into his, is quite another matter. She likes everything pretty much as it is, and she suspects he does too, but where feelings and habits are involved, nothing stands still. If they keep their distance, she's sure they'll drift apart, and it'll be back to Square One. If they "consolidate," if they merge their lives on some basis, there will be problems. It's only been eight months.

So far, it's been quite guarded. From their very first "date," they operated on unspoken takings-for-granted. The L-word and its cognates have never figured in the discourse. They never talk about their "relationship." What's between them just *is*. The future's not discussed except in terms of travel arrangements. They travel well together, so that's what they do. Both are highly organized, unflappable, meticulous, flexible.

So far, so good, then. They've taken stock of each other and each other's lives and preferences and found no insuperable obstacles. It surely helps that she's no longer affiliated with GIA. For a while, in the beginning, when they were still operating undercover, before she was, so to speak, blown by Carlsson, Baker would ask her about Mannerman and GIA. He seemed obsessed with her ex-boss in the way new lovers, still feeling their way and wary of comparison, tend to dwell on old boyfriends.

It's also helped that it's been quiet on the BEECO front so far. She tries not to think about this, but any day now Mannerman's likely to pull the plug, especially since he now knows she's "with" Baker. "With" is a bit of a stretch, of course. Baker can't handle New York for more than three days at a clip, which is how Lucy feels about his place in the Adirondacks. At first, Two Moose seemed sensational, a miracle of clear air, cool water, wide vistas of water and forest and mountains, of privacy and silence. Within hours of waking on her first morning there and seeing the red dawn's blazing reflection on the lake, Lucy was ready to close up her Sixty-seventh Street apartment, call in the Salvation Army for her Oscars and Bill Blasses and dial the 800 number for L. L. Bean.

After seventy-two hours, her attitude changed and she got real. Do it once—one trek through the woods, one canoe portage to the far shore of the lake, one more postprandial pot of coffee out on the deck under the stars listening to the loons call each other across the water—and you've done it forever. The trees begin to loom in on top of you until you feel they may pounce. On cloudy days, the lake's dark water is threatening, ominous. The silence starts to deafen.

Baker turns out to be the original practice practice practice practice man. "If a thing's worth doing at all, it's worth doing well," he tells her again and again.

He wants to teach Lucy everything about the Great Outdoors. To cast from shore or boat. To tell one bird from another. To sketch from nature. To shoot—which she likes best, as long as it's confined to plinking empty tin cans with a vintage .22 caliber Colt Woodsman pistol he keeps for varmints. She likes it because it comes naturally: she has her father's naturally good eye and steady arm. "If you worked at this, you could be another Annie Oakley," Baker tells her.

It's all fun for a while, but Lucy also needs people: cities, crowds, noise, restaurants, variety. Baker tries to sell her on the Internet, but talking to someone that way is worse than not talking at all. Life in the woods is too narrow. Lucy's programmed her existence around options and choices, she needs crossroads to choose between, a full panoply of buttons to push. The luck of the draw and serendipity aren't to be discounted, but it's best if there's a palette or smorgasbord to select from, a full deck to play with. Room to choose, room to maneuver.

Baker's more focused. He keeps life in the crosshairs. He knows what he's after, but all his extensive and expensive preparations can come to nothing if the game—the beast, the bird, the fish—fails to show up. Or if it does, then something else goes wrong: the angle of attack is poor, the shot's too difficult, the range is too great, someone coughs, there's a tree in the way. After nearly forty years of trying, he still doesn't have his damn desert ram! Forty years of lying on cold, stony ground at a cost of God knows how many cumulative tens of thousands of dollars, and never one killing shot! Lucy guesses she's seen more desert rams on PBS than Baker's seen in all his fruitless time in the Sonora. For all his preparations, it still comes down to blind luck. Lucy can't channel her life that way. In her world, the Picassos are where you expect to find them; in the restaurants, the Dover sole will be on the menu; if you run out of Clinique, Boyd's or Saks will have what you want.

She loves variety, but she also likes the variations to be as neatly and understandably laid out as in a Bach score. She prefers to bet on expectations that have proven themselves through repetition. That's Jack Mannerman's influence, although she's nowhere near so mechanistic as her ex-boss, who operates on a near-mathematical reduction of human nature that takes the variables into account, subjects them to certain observed or wished-for constants and produces equations on the order of $(X + Y \times Z)/B = A$, with A being what Mannerman wants. These "equations" are really fables, little stories Mannerman tells himself to prove that the world indeed works the way he believes it does. After all, Mannerman himself puts his trust in absolutes: in the ruling sacraments of Church and Company, in the eucharist, in CRONI. The thing is, so far it's worked out. Mannerman will tell you it should: after all, he'll argue, you're dealing with herd mentalities, with Wall Street and Washington groupthink as predictable as the tide tables.

Well, Lucy thinks, listening to Baker scratch away, we'll just have to see how it works out. After eight months, she really hasn't a clue.

Baker had called her in early February, the week of Valentine's Day, as it happened. Lucy hadn't expected to hear from him—not after the business in "21." When she picked up the phone, he didn't identify himself, simply asked if she'd like to have a drink. And she said why not, even knowing she shouldn't, knowing that she could be putting a great deal at risk.

Baker had humiliated Jack Mannerman. Baker had caused Jack Mannerman to pee in his pants at "21." And Carlsson was right: it didn't make any difference that only three other people knew it. To a man like Mannerman, humiliation—assault and battery of the ego—was worse than death and called for an unconditional declaration of war. H. A. Baker was now officially an enemy of the Mannerman state. To associate with this agent of Mannerman's humiliation would be treason, and treason was a capital crime punishable immediately by corporate death.

Lucy knew this, and yet when Baker called, she still said, "Why not?"

Drinks turned into dinner, as she'd somehow known would happen, and after that, as she'd somehow thought might happen, she invited Baker upstairs for a brandy. What happened thereafter still seemed by turns a little confusing and utterly clear, but when she woke up next to him the following morning, she hadn't a worry in the world.

They were able to keep their affair secret for three months, until Carlsson decided to get on her case, which she later figured out was sometime in late April or early May, when her computer files dated a memo to PL setting forth her objections along with negative Street feedback—to the Individuality Channel. That had been her first substantive expression of opposition—and her first take on the Street's reaction, with the murdered children of Oklahoma City still burning holes in everyone's mind—so it would have been about then that Mannerman might have mentioned her views to Carlsson.

Mannerman was stunned—and wounded—when she told him she was leaving GIA. He couldn't plead, that wasn't in his nature, but he offered her the moon and the stars. Her story was that she was just worn out, that once she recharged, she might well be back. He seemed to accept this, at least the first part, but both of them knew that at the pace Mannerman was now moving GIA along, to step out of the loop even for a fortnight—in eight years, Lucy's longest continuous vacation had been six days!—would be to banish oneself forever. To lie to the man who had given her a ticket to life was a shameful business; it was like lying to her father, she felt. And yet, the fibs positively tripped off her tongue. The fact was, once Carlsson had cast the die, she couldn't wait to be on her way. Still, her first day out on the street was a shock, like being ejected from a plane: a sudden violent centrifugal displacement, confusion, surprise and vertigo—and then, gradually, a segue into an easy descent to welcoming earth.

She dozes off, and when she wakes up, steam is flooding the room, and she can hear Baker crooning Italian in the shower.

It's intervals like this, moments of easy, instant intimacy, of close-mated contentment, that make it worth the effort. Their trip hadn't started well—not compared to her expectations. The five days in Venice had definitely been a mixed treat, when they should have been unremittingly marvelous, should have been filled with continuous gaiety and pleasure. Baker knew Venice intimately, the out-of-the-way restaurants, the seldom visited churches, and he did his duty by that knowledge but took all too little joy from it, Lucy thought. Even in November, Venice was thronged with tourists, a circumstance Baker seemed to regard as a personal insult.

He acted as if the city were his personal property and everyone else a trespasser. He displayed consummate, gracious courtesy to servers and servants, to waiters, gondoliers and porters. But let some hapless tourist get in his way and he blew up in a small puff of muttered curses. He incessantly reminded Lucy that nothing was what it had once been, even on a beautiful Sunday, when they walked from the Cipriani to the Palazzo Volsi while the two great bell towers of San Marco and San Giorgio sang to each other across the lagoon.

"Damn Krauts!" he huffed as they edged around a group of sturdy, florid-cheeked men and women elbowing into the Zitelle water-bus station. "Goddamn jumped-up stockbrokers!" he cursed as a gleaming motor launch bore a madly overdressed couple toward the landing for Harry's Bar.

For him, Venice may have been ruined, *ruined*, but for Lucy, the city was a miracle. She said as much over lunch in the garden of Villa Volsi, an elegant small mansion on the island called the Giudecca, whose easternmost tip was occupied by the Cipriani Hotel. The day itself was perfection, their hosts—old, old friends of Baker's—charming and generous, the house and garden spectacular, especially the dazzling Tiepolo ceilings in the large salon, and it surprised her to learn that the Volsis occupied the place only three months a year, shuttering it from December 1, when they decamped to the chic ski resort of Cortina d'Ampezzo in the Dolomites, to September 1, when they returned from Porto Ercole, the no less fashionable seaside retreat north of Rome, having sojourned in Milan, Fez and Paris in between.

If I had a place like this, she'd thought, I'd never leave it. Over coffee, she'd lost herself in hazy, wine-oiled daydreams while Baker and the Volsis engaged in a contrapuntal lament for the Venice that once was, Venice before it was wrecked by tourism, pollution, profit seeking, greed. Lucy had returned from her woolgathering somewhere in the middle of this requiem and remarked absently how perfect she found everything, at which the others looked at her as if she were mad.

But now it's different. Baker's in his element. Lucy's content. Very, very content—but cautious. Now is perhaps the last phase before the relational point of no return, before declarations from which the turning back will be hard. Now is the time for taking it carefully. She's been in enough entanglements to know that love affairs at their outset are conducted by people in masks, that courtship's a kind of fraud; only with time and familiarity will the killing true facts of personality and habit emerge to do their deadly work: the farting, the couch potatoing, the drinking—all those qualities that are by turns and degrees grating, unappetizing, difficult, impossible and, ultimately, lethal.

The next morning, they bid La Clemenza goodbye and drive northwest to Cernobbio, on the shore of Lake Como, where they check into the Grand Hotel Villa d'Este. The setting is spectacular, although the first real frost of the year has come and they're obliged to dine indoors, and the hotel is luxe to the point of embarrassment. There's nothing much to see hereabouts, but the main reason Baker's chosen this spot is that the drive to the Malpensa airport, from which they'll fly back home in three days, will be infinitely easier than from Milan.

They spend the first day puttering around the lake, visiting the town of Como, finding little to see and not much to buy. The following morning they hit the road early, arriving in Milan as the shops are opening. Baker's promised to let Lucy "destroy the Via Montenapoleone," which she's heard is one of the great shopping streets in the world but which turns out to be Madison Avenue at twice the price. After forty-five minutes, she's had enough. They take a quick tour of the Poldi-Pezzoli museum, a little gem of a collection just around the corner that reminds Lucy of the Gardner in Boston, and then grab a taxi and make for the Brera, Milan's principal fine arts museum.

Much of the Brera is, as seems to be usual, "temporarily" closed, so Lucy and Baker spend the balance of the morning prowling the galleries and *antiquari* of the quarter around the museum. In one dark flyblown little shop in a side alley, Lucy comes across a promising trove of Renaissance-style majolica. It's no earlier than mid-nineteenth century, she decides, and not bad value—allowing for the reduction she expects to haggle off the price tag. She's trying to make up her mind between a *palla*, a ball-shaped vase decorated with a Hercules scene, and a pretty blue-and-yellow drug jar, an *albarello*, that she thinks can be made into a lamp, when Baker calls out to her from a corner of the shop.

"Hey, come look at this!"

He's studying the contents of a marbled-paper folder, its worn and rubbed boards held together by fraying pink ribbon: a set of unsigned engravings of the Seven Deadly Sins. Lucy's eye marks them as late eighteenth century, probably executed in or around Venice, since in style and spirit they seem to borrow from Tiepolo. Artistically, they're fairly crude, but they're engaging: lively and lighthearted. Whoever made them perceived sin as a sort of advanced naughtiness rather than mortal dereliction. The sow on which "Gluttony" rides is actually a grinning pig with wings, and the mirror studied by "Pride" reflects a devilish simper. These personifications of evil aren't deadly, simply the patron demons of human frailty.

Baker has to have them. Haggling ensues, a price is agreed, then

Lucy negotiates for the *albarello*, and finally there's a cheerful skirmish between Lucy and Baker about which of them will pay.

She insists. The engravings will be a suitable thank-you for a wonderful trip. Baker, always the gentleman where a lady's wishes are concerned, yields, and the lire equivalent of roughly $1,600 is charged to Lucy's Platinum Card.

Over lunch, she and Baker pass the drawings back and forth.

"You know," he says, holding up "Sloth," a bulging figure hideously hermaphroditic, with a glum, self-mocking expression, "this slob could go right on . . . what the hell was the name of that awful woman you made me watch at Two Moose last August? The day we had that big lightning storm?"

"Betti Jo Barnum. I saw her picture in the *Trib* the other day—apparently Individuality's cut a deal with that SkyTV operation of Murdoch's, and she's telecasting out of Liverpool for a couple of weeks—and she's on the way down again. She's already taken off fifty pounds. I wonder what the gimmick is this time."

"Who cares?"

"Only about a hundred million people around the world."

Getting Baker to watch *The Betti Jo Barnum Hour* had been an attempt to bring Baker into the orbit of modern life. It seemed ridiculous to her that someone who constantly griped about how America had changed should be ignorant of a likely root cause—or, at best, a defining symptom. The evening they tuned in, the program was about men who committed adultery with their fathers-in-law. Baker's reaction was livid. From the range of expressions that crossed his face, it was obvious to Lucy that he really didn't have an inkling that this sort of thing was now routinely permitted to be talked about in public. Odd for a man who knew his way around computers and spent a lot of time on the Internet—where, if the news media were to be believed, every grudge-artist had his say. But perhaps Baker never connected with the seamy side of the Web, confined himself to rod-and-gun and environmental forums.

Individuality was turning out to be everything Carlsson had predicted. Just three months old, it already had a virtual monopoly on the anger, antipathy and self-pity that filled the American air like pollen. Chadbourne Tinkry, hired away from Murdoch for what Spuds whispered was close to $100 million, delivered a mostly male audience that nicely balanced Betti Jo's "Barnumettes." The latter hated themselves; Tinkry's squeezed white audience, comprising the entire middle-class spectrum, hated all forms of otherness. "Like every phony patriot," a *New Republic* columnist had written, "Chadbourne Tinkry wraps himself in the red, white and blue: red as in neck, white as in skin, blue as in collar."

While they wait for their first course to arrive, Lucy takes a closer look at the engravings.

"Who thought up the idea of the Seven Deadly Sins in the first place?" she asks Baker.

"Haven't the slightest. Someone like St. Augustine? I seem to remember Aristotle had something to say on the subject in a course I took in ethics sophomore year. How about Dante? The *Inferno*'s chockablock with sinners, isn't it?"

Throughout their trip, Lucy's been reading Dante. She expects it's an avocational disease with Italophiles like herself when they travel to what they regard as the mother country of their true selves. She fishes in her shoulder bag for the one-volume *Divine Comedy* she picked up just before leaving New York and skims through it until she finds a chart that shows, canto by canto, the Circles of Hell and lists the sins and other forms of evil associated with each circle, along with the specific individuals Dante chose to exemplify those sins.

She studies the chart, then skims through the engravings, and then looks at Baker.

"This is interesting," she says. "Of the original Seven Deadly Sins, Dante uses only four: Lust, Gluttony, Avarice and Anger. He left out Envy, Sloth and Pride. And the four he identifies are all in the first circles, which means he regards them as relatively mild."

Baker spears a forkful of oil-soaked Bresaola and chews it thoughtfully. "So what are his big hitters?" he asks.

"Well, there's quite a list. Heresy, naturally."

"Which today some of us would consider a virtue."

Lucy greets this interruption with a sharp glare. She's heard quite enough of her lover's views on the Catholic Church and the population explosion.

"Do you want to hear this or don't you? OK, then you have people who were violent against others, against themselves and against God and—this should please *you*—against nature."

"Dante was an environmentalist? Bully for him!"

"Let's see about that." Lucy goes to the back of the volume and locates the notes to the eleventh canto of the *Inferno*. "Well, not exactly. It seems what Dante means is what's natural, so crimes against nature include sodomy and . . . Hey, this is interesting, usury. Lending money at excessive rates. Listen to this: 'The Greek word for interest was *tokos*, literally "offspring," so that usury was thought of as the breeding of money from money and therefore against nature.' "

"Sounds like a perfect definition of capitalism. I wonder how that would go down with your friends on Wall Street. What else?"

"Next we have various kinds of fraud, which seems to cover everything from seduction and flattery to soothsaying and alchemy to corrupt politicians and clerics. Also—I'll buy this—hypocrites, deceitful advisors and sowers of discord, which I assume is the same thing as rabble-rousing, and other forms of thievery and deceit. Then, moving on, further into the depths, we have treason, people who betray their kin, like Cain, or their countries, or their guests—this is where the Macbeths would go if Dante'd known about them, I guess—and last and worst of all, Judas and Brutus, who betrayed Christ and Caesar."

"Interesting," Baker comments, studying the dish of pasta that's been set before him. "So how do you suppose Dante'd handle it if he was plopped down on earth today? Where d'you think he'd stick Henry Kissinger, for example? Or your ex-boss's great pal the Speaker of the House? Or about a dozen others I can think of?"

Before Lucy and Baker realize it, they're deep into making their own definitive list of modern deadly sins and vices. Baker supplies the working definition: "Whatever either of us thinks makes the world or life significantly worse for everyone except the sinner. Tendencies, traits, cultural stuff, doctrines—we can invent a few 'isms' of our own if we need to—the most regressive things we can think of."

There's no way, both agree, that seven will suffice. They settle, more or less arbitrarily, on a limit of twelve. After the best part of an hour, through two courses, dessert and coffee, after a good deal of bickering, they finally settle on a list:

Some, like Treason, Violence, Nationalism and Anger (which both agree may be the cardinal vice of all, since it seems to be destroying the world), are no-brainers. To these they quickly add Greed, which seems more to the contemporary point than Avarice.

As to specifically late-twentieth-century vices, there's little argument over Exhibitionism, the phenomenon, as Lucy puts it, of "everybody pushing to the front of the stage to claim their Andy Warhol fifteen minutes like the louts that turn up on talk shows!" They agree that "celebrity culture" on every level is a manifestation of this particular vice. Hypocrisy/Duplicity is also quickly agreed on, provided, as Lucy insists, that it be understood to exclude Public Relations—at least *some* Public Relations.

Saying, "People who know nothing can be made to believe anything," an obvious pointed reference to his favorite target in the Vatican, Baker proposes Ignorance.

"OK with me," Lucy replies, "provided you open it up to include dumbing down and downmarketing in general." In her opinion, television alone would be good for at least fifty fully qualified deadly vices.

She has no trouble with Relativism, which is Baker's shorthand for "the denial of all fixed values, making everything subject to change or disposal, especially if there's a buck or an ego trip in it."

"I assume you're throwing political correctness under this one."

"Absolutely!"

The disagreements start when Lucy proposes Individualism.

"Individualism's not a vice," Baker retorts, holding his glass of wine up to the light and studying the deep straw color approvingly. "It's a virtue."

"Once upon a time, yes. When it meant self-reliance, go-getting. But the version we're living with now is nothing but pure self-centeredness. You know what I mean: if consensus, say, or convention, or due process, or even the law, doesn't happen to fit your own personal agenda, the hell with it!"

"I take your point. Wouldn't Narcissism be better? That would allow for all those jerks who seem to think that anything they have to say is something the rest of us should be obliged to listen to."

"Narcissism is OK with me. Solipsism wouldn't be bad, either."

The last two are more of a stretch. Baker wants to readmit Gluttony, arguing that Western Man is eating himself to death, but Lucy persuades him that overeating simply isn't a *big* enough evil to make the top team.

"How about Capitalism, then?" he proposes.

"Don't be ridiculous! There are bad capitalists, and we cover them under Greed, but that doesn't make the system itself a sin!"

"Come back in twenty years and tell me about it, sweetie pie. Anyway, maybe Capitalism isn't what I mean, not exactly. Your guy Dante's Usury comes closer, but that's not quite what I want either. Give me a hand here, Lucy. You know what I'm after: money madness in a way that Greed doesn't quite cover. The notion that the only thing that matters is how much money you have. That the only way to value anything that happens in life is how much paper wealth it creates. That absolutely everything is for sale—at the buyer's price. What about Milkenism? Or—better yet—Mannermanism?"

"Very funny." Lucy screws up her face and thinks for a minute. "How about Aureopantheism?" she says brightly, feeling very pleased with herself. "Gold—that is, money—as the universal deity, present in all things. I bet Dante'd like it."

"Dante's not writing out the lineup card in this game," says Baker, obviously wishing he'd come up with the word himself. "Still, let's put it in. At least until I come up with something better. So now—how many have we got?"

Lucy's been writing them down. "Treason, Violence, Nationalism, Anger, Greed," she reads. "Exhibitionism, Hypocrisy a.k.a. Duplicity, Relativism, Narcissism"—she pauses—"and—ta-ra-ra-ra!—Aureopantheism. Eleven. One to go."

"You won't give in on Gluttony? I'm getting bored."

"Nope. If we're going to go back to Square One, I'd vote for Envy over Gluttony. It seems to me an awful lot of the world's troubles stem from someone wanting what someone else has. Or wanting to be what someone else is."

"Well, if it comes to that, what about Lust? In my own limited experience, a great deal of the trouble people make for themselves, and others, comes from an uncontrollable wish to see what someone else looks like without any clothes on."

Lucy brightens as a lightbulb clicks on in her mind. "How about Trespassism?"

"What?"

"Maybe there's a better word for what I'm getting at, but it's what you're always complaining about, how nobody seems to have a grain of respect for anyone else's space, or privacy, or right to tune out."

Baker doesn't put up much of an argument. It's growing late, they've both eaten too much and they want to beat the traffic. He nods half-heartedly, "Trespassism it is," and calls for the check.

As he waits for his change, he looks naughtily at Lucy and announces, "As the senior rank present, I am about to exercise *droit du seigneur* and add Lust, which happens to be very much on my mind just now, to our little list."

"You can't! That would make thirteen, and thirteen's unlucky!"

"Not for us, dear heart," Baker replies with a smile. "Thirteen is also something else."

Lucy looks puzzled.

"Come on," he prompts, "what is thirteen of anything called?"

She shakes her head.

"A Baker's dozen, get it?" He chuckles at his own joke.

"I think I'm about to throw up," Lucy says, but she dutifully adds Lust to the bottom of the list.

On the drive back to Cernobbio, the lunch and the wine finally do Lucy in and she barely remembers the trip. In their room, she flings herself on the bed and goes right out. When she awakes, it's morning. She reaches for Baker and finds the bed next to her empty. She rolls over and sees him on the bedroom balcony, seated with his back to her. From his hunched shoulders and the intent angle of his head, she guesses he's studying the morning papers.

She slides out of bed and tiptoes up behind him, naked and still sleepy. He's not reading, he's busy drawing. The engravings they bought in Milan lie next to his coffee cup on the glass-topped table.

She stands quietly behind him for almost a full minute. He's utterly oblivious of her.

"Good morning," she says at last, and kisses the back of his neck.

He looks up, startled, then smiles and tousles her hair.

"Take a look," he says. He hands her a sheet of the hotel's elaborately crested letter paper. "This is how we get the best of both worlds."

When she examines the sketch, Lucy's eyes widen in surprise and amusement. Baker's done an amazingly accurate pastiche, capturing the old engravings' flickery style perfectly, right down to the elaborate curlicues of the caption, which identifies the subject as *"Ignorantia."*

It shows a sinister figure, a tall man with arms outstretched in a gesture of benediction, whose vestments and headdress identify him as the present Pope Leo XIV, formerly Cardinal Fortebella of Venice. A scaly serpent's tail ending in a spadelike point curls from behind and lies at his feet, fencing in myriad tiny, negroid figures clustered at the hem of the papal skirts, an unmistakable visual allusion to Baker's passionate feelings about Rome's responsibility for the population crisis in Africa.

The figure's accessories constitute a second set of references. The papal miter bears the flag-and-sword logo of UnivCom's Individuality Channel, a dollar sign is superimposed against the shaft of the shepherd's crook held in the figure's right hand, transforming Hippocrates' caduceus into Mammon's. In place of the orb, the "Pope's" left hand holds an antenna dish emblazoned with the winged-eye symbol of GlobeStar, the UnivCom satellite telecommunications network, which now brings shows like *Dallas* and *Cops* into six hundred million homes from Peoria to Peshawar.

The zinger is the face. Instead of the aquiline lineaments of Mannerman's friend Fortebella, the sneering likeness beneath the miter is a devastating but dead-accurate caricature of Robert Carlsson!

"It's brilliant," says Lucy. "You ought to be a political cartoonist. You could make a difference."

"Don't be a dope! That kind of the-pen-is-mightier-than-the-sword thinking went out with the dodo. Anyway, I like the way I've combined Rome, Hollywood and Television—the Holy Trinity of Dumb!"

That night, after a day of lounging around the hotel's enclosed pool, they go over to Como for their last dinner in Italy, crossing the lake in a hired motorboat. It's nippy out on the lake, but the night is exquisite, starlight mingles with lamplight on the water and the restaurant bubbles with warmth and jollity. They put away a bottle and then some of Pinot Grigio; the light white wine goes down like Pellegrino water. When they climb into the car that's to drive them back to the Villa d'Este, Lucy's feeling sexy and more than half drunk. In the car, under cover of darkness, she feels her lover up; it's all she can do to keep her own clothes on. Even in her fuddled state of mind, she realizes she's never been like this before and rejoices at the realization that she's finally coming unbuttoned. This must be it, this *is* it! she thinks. It really, really is!

In the tapestry-bedecked entrance hall of the hotel, the concierge presents Baker with a Federal Express envelope. Baker looks at the waybill and curses.

"Damn!" he says. "It's from my lawyer in Bakerton. I told him not to bother me!"

Inside is a brief letter clipped to perhaps a half dozen photocopies of some documents. Baker starts to go through them.

"Upstairs," Lucy says. "Come on!" All she can think of is bed.

"Go on up," he says, surprisingly abrupt. "I'll be along in a minute. I just have to figure out what to do about these."

"Well, ex-*cuse* me, Mr. Nasty. See ya roun'." She executes a graceful little twirl which almost lands her on her nose. As she sashays off toward the elevator, she looks over her shoulder and glimpses his back disappearing into the bar.

In their room, she steps out of her clothes and slides naked under the covers. She feels feline, sexy. She wants him now and she wants him bad. She lies back and closes her eyes, waiting, purring.

The next thing she's aware of is the sound of the door being unlocked clumsily, the bedroom bursting alight, heavy footfalls dragging across the room. She sits up. Baker's standing at the foot of the bed, glowering at her.

Lucy realizes she's half naked and covers up. The clock on the mantel across the room says 1:17.

"Where the hell have you been?" she mumbles, mouth dry and sour. The white wine's worked its customary alchemy. The jolly light-headed buzz has given way to a vile sour-mouthed aftermood. She ought to say nothing, but she can't help herself. "Stop looking at me like that, damn it!"

He doesn't answer. There's a slack dullness in his face and bearing that tells her he's half in the bag. By now, she knows the symptoms.

"I was waiting for you, damn it!" she continues. "All dressed down and ready to come! Look!" She hurls the bedclothes aside and sits there naked.

Still nothing. He stares at her and she stares back, a contest of glares.

He looks a hundred years old, she thinks. He could be my father! Hell, he *could* be my father! What am I doing with this old man? She feels about as sexy as Mother Teresa, but to pull the sheets back over her would be an unforgivable sign of weakness.

Still wordless, he hurls his thin sheaf of papers at her, turns away and slumps off into the bathroom, slamming the door behind him.

For an instant Lucy glares at the bathroom door, trying to laser through it with her eyes and vaporize the man on the other side. Then her curiosity gets the better of her. She gathers up the papers scattered on the counterpane and begins to read. Almost immediately, her head clears.

Uh-oh, she thinks, studying the topmost enclosure, the solids are finally in the fan. It's a xerox of a lead story, dated exactly a week ago, from the Bakerton weekly paper, *The Valley Gazette-Record.* The story's head proclaims: "BEECO Hydraulics Sold to Korean Company / Four Hundred to Be Laid Off in Compressor Plant Closing / First Layoffs Since 1937, More Set."

She reads on. According to the story, GIA negotiated agreements to sell BEECO's Hydraulic Extraction and Compressor Division to Samchung Industries of Seoul, Korea. The Korean firm intends to maintain a sales office and limited research facilities in Bakerton, but to consolidate manufacturing and engineering operations at its new plant in Guadalajara, Mexico, producing a job attrition of 406 line workers.

It gets worse. The next-dated sheet reproduces a second story from the local paper tabulating further workforce reductions, a total of 540 jobs spread across the company, with the heaviest cuts coming in the Boring Machine and Crane divisions. Research and Development is also to be scaled back to a standstill. Lucy makes a quick calculation: if memory serves, this means that roughly a third of BEECO's factory payroll is being lopped off.

She hears the toilet flush, then the shower starting up.

The third and fourth sheets, bearing the same date as the first newspaper article, reproduce a letter addressed to "Dear GIA–BEECO Coworker," datelined Columbus and signed by the vice president for human resources, Industrial Products and Services Group.

"In order to make your company more productive and competitive," it begins, and goes on to outline a program of "Human Resources Re-engineering" that is being introduced "as of instant date" at BEECO. Lucy reads through it. Wow, she thinks, talk about Hiroshima!

The thrust of the letter is twofold. BEECO's employee medical-dental benefits plan is to be terminated. Henceforth BEECO employees will be covered, like the rest of GIA's "nonexecutive workforce," by the "GIA Employee Wellness Program," a health-management organization (HMO) administered by a Utah-based insurance company jointly owned by GIAFin's Bermuda reinsurance affiliate and a subsidiary of a Hong Kong financial group whose name Lucy recognizes as a major player in UnivCom.

It's hard to puzzle out the effect of this change, since the next sections of the letter are couched in highly technical language that Lucy imagines would baffle an actuary. What it comes down to, she concludes, is that henceforth, should a Baker employee require a prescription for any drug stronger than aspirin, or a hospital visit—or surgical procedure—involving more than two emergency-room stitches, permission must be obtained at least forty-eight hours prior thereto from the Human Resources Group (which, Lucy imagines, will itself have to clear with Provo) in order for "said covered employee to qualify for reimbursement review." As for ailments or afflictions of skin, teeth or eyes—well, as Baker, the old hockey star, likes to say, "It's shinny on your own side, buddy!"

The second part of the letter announces that the BEECO credit union and thrift bank are being folded, again "as of instant date," into GIAFin. "In order to comply with federal and state regulatory policies," the letter continues, "as well as the long-term interests of your company, all outstanding loans and mortgages will be priced to market, and all payments on such loans presently in arrears or overdue shall be given a thirty-day grace period to be brought current, after which GIAFin, or any party succeeding to GIAFin's interest in such outstandings, reserves the right to seek the appropriate legal remedies, including foreclosure or forfeiture."

Lucy knows what this means. She's seen GIA execute the maneuver any number of times. A straw company is set up, financed but not owned by GIA, so that there's no visible connection that might whet *60 Minutes'* appetite. The straw man buys the employee loans and mortgages that inevitably come with the acquisition of family-owned or closely held companies that have practiced an essentially paternalistic style of management. It then sets about collecting the overdue loan and mortgage payments, often in ridiculously small individual and aggregate amounts, that have built up in consequence of simple humaneness on the part of the old managers—not, as will be claimed by the new owners, sloppy or outmoded financial controls.

She hopes that all the BEECO people recently laid off are current on their loans. It's bad enough to lose the paycheck, but then to have Snidely Whiplash show up to take a big hunk of the severance package—or else!—strikes her as insupportable.

It's the final section of the letter, dealing with some sixty single- and two-family dwellings in and around Bakerton that BEECO rents to long-time employees, that makes Lucy whistle in disbelief. This is overkill, she thinks. Everything else so far is boilerplate, but this is definite payback for what happened at "21."

The plan outlined is simple. The BEECO houses have been sold by GIA to the mortgage-backed finance arm of GIAFin and will be offered to their occupants at prices reflecting current market conditions, with financing, subject to credit approval, at market rates. The word "eviction" doesn't appear, but it doesn't have to. The old carrot and stick, Lucy thinks, wondering how many of the occupying families, some of whom have been in these houses for years, will be in a position to take up the offer. Someone at GIA has no flies on him, she thinks; during her tour of BEECO, she'd been shown several clusters of company-owned housing. Many were fine old Victorian homes, for which a lucrative second-home market had grown up among the money-manager and lawyering populations of Philadelphia, Harrisburg and Wilmington, all within easy weekend driving range. And all the more desirable if the smelly and noisy old factory is shut down!

For her answer, she has to wait no longer than it takes to turn to the next sheet, another newspaper account. It concerns a sixty-year-old line supervisor at BEECO Hydraulics, a forty-year-service-pin man, a father, a grandfather, a churchgoer, a Rotarian, a pillar of blue-collar values in all ways. Despondent at being let go, confused by the apparent loss of the medical plan that had provided home care for an invalid wife and probably just plain scared to death by a brave new future that years and years at BEECO left him unequipped to deal with, this man had hooked up a hose to the tailpipe of his '86 Olds and done away with himself.

It's not an unfamiliar story to Lucy. She's a child of a working-class town brushed fitfully by the frantic wings of modern wealth. She remembers almost the same thing happening a few years back in Stenton, not thirty miles upcoast from Paster's Point. The Japanese finally fished out the cod banks and the cannery closed down. One old-time worker who'd been let go got stinking drunk and burned up his mobile home with himself and his dog inside. The town had gone into shock. In her mind, Lucy can picture how it must be in Bakerton: the family in deep mourning in the plain humble house in the plain little street with the 32-inch Mitsubishi in the parlor, comforting Gramma while Sister and the neighbor women bake pies and fry chicken for the folks who'll come back after the services.

And in the meantime, she can't help thinking cynically, everyone'll keep one ear cocked for the sound of Barbara Walters at the front door to bring this American tragedy to the awareness of the nation, because—unlike the first two newspaper accounts—this one makes no pretense of journalistic objectivity. It fairly reeks with what she can't help thinking of as "us-vs.-themism." And so does an editorial reproduced on the next sheet, deploring "the rape of heartland America," and practically calling on Main Street to arm itself and take to the streets to defend itself against Wall Street.

There's one last sheet. As she turns to it, she hears the bathroom door open.

This one's not a copy. Its message is composed of words cut from newspapers and magazines and is brief and explicit:

"To Mr. Judas H. A. Baker with blood on his hands. You sold us out, you bastard!!! I hope you choke on the money, you dirty sellout SOB!!! Your brothers must be turning in their grave!!! And may you too rot in hell with them!!! And soon!!! A curse on you!!!"

Jesus H. Christ, Lucy thinks, just as Baker roars, "You knew this was coming, didn't you, you damn lying bitch!" from right behind her.

Not caring about her nakedness, she turns slowly and makes herself look into Baker's face. "I don't know anything about any of this," she says. But she wonders as she speaks: How can I be saying this? She knew it *had* to happen, she knew it *would* happen. She had just put it out of her mind.

"He put you up to this, didn't he?" Baker asks. "This is all a setup, isn't it?" The initial fury in his voice has given way to loathing.

Lucy sets the papers carefully down on the bedcover.

"Up to *what*?" she asks in as calm a tone as she can manage as she thinks ahead. It's perfectly clear where Baker's going.

"Mannerman sent you after me to keep me quiet! To take me to bed and keep me out of the way and shut me up until after the filthy deed was done! Until in his own sweet time he could get around to butchering my company! Those are my people you're killing, you know! And I'm as much to blame! I might as well have attached that hose to the exhaust with my own hands! I gave my word of honor to those people!"

Honor, thinks Lucy furiously, honor! Without thinking, she cries, "Baker, I am so sick of you and your damn honor!"

He actually steps backward at this. Oh, Jesus, she thinks. "Forget I said that, please. It's nothing like you think. I have nothing to do with Jack. For God's sake, Baker, Jack *fired* me for being with you! I'm sorry for what I just said. I know how you feel!" Love, she thinks bitterly, is knowing how to say you're sorry.

"How can someone like you even use the word 'honor'!" he booms.

She sees that, far from alleviating matters, her apologetic words are taken as a white flag. Realizing this, Lucy herself starts to boil.

"How can people like you know what people like me feel?" Baker continues, sounding snide and superior, sounding very Paster's Point yacht club. "What's honor to you people? A joke, an inconvenience! You people think you can arbitrage everything—my word, your word, Mannerman's goddamn word! It's all relative, isn't it? From beginning to end you're the most devious bunch of people I ever met! You're all like spies, you're all traitors, all playing double games! You, Lamond, Mannerman, Carlsson, all of you! Two-faced the lot of you!"

"That's a lot of crap!"

"I should've shot that son of a bitch when I had the chance!"

"Yeah, yeah, yeah," Lucy says in a fired-up street-fighting voice. "Shoulda, coulda, woulda. Tell me about it!" She feels mean, feels like baiting him. Who needs this crap? She wishes she had had another glass of wine. There's white wine in the minibar, but she suspects that if she tried to get it, he might hit her.

"It was all so much snake oil, wasn't it?" he asks. He's used up his own buzz, she sees. He sounds weary.

"Snake oil?"

"Everything Mannerman said, everything you people promised. It was just to get the deal done, wasn't it? What I don't understand," Baker continues, sitting down heavily on the edge of the bed, "is why."

"Why what?"

"Why he wanted to take over BEECO at all. Why he—you—had to lie. Why you did this to me. To my people." His voice is now close to a whine.

Lucy too is exhausted. "I think PL believed in the deal," she explains. "He thought he could synergize it, get it back on its feet. The way you were going, there's no assurance those people would have had their jobs as long as they have."

Only the last part is true, Lucy thinks. Well, yes, in a way it's all true, at least enough so that it isn't an outright lie. Lucy's a firm believer that there are times when a fib—as white as you can make it—is the best, perhaps the only right, answer. Sometimes you just have to be prepared to "position the truth," as Spuds likes to put it.

"It just didn't pan out the way we all hoped it would," she adds, searching in her repertory of stock excuses for filler. "The market's changed too much. NAFTA, the yen . . ." she adds lamely. "Jack's under a lot of pressure."

"Liars, all of you, you're a pack of goddamn Judases!" Baker has his wind back.

Lucy doesn't answer. There's silence in the room. It seems palpable: old, musty, heavy—like the tasseled curtains the maid has drawn across the windows, the heavy nineteenth-century furniture, the ugly pastoral hanging above the dressing table.

Baker starts to say something more, then shuts down. He looks around the room in a wild rage, then throws aside the curtains, flings open the french doors and disappears onto the balcony. The chill off the lake rushes into the room; she shivers and covers herself, but her fury mounts, doesn't cool in the least.

"Damn you, Baker!" she howls at the open door. "Damn you! I lost my job because of you! I gave up my life! And as for your goddamn rotten company, you killed those people, Baker! You spoiled 'em rotten with your paternalistic goddamn noblesse goddamn oblige! We thought we were buying a company—a real making and selling company!—and what we got was an out-of-date sandbox! Perhaps if you'd bothered to learn anything about the business, instead of running around the world shooting things, if you'd stayed in Bakerton like your brothers, none of this would've happened. But don't blame us!"

It doesn't occur to her that "we" and "us" are big mistakes, but something inside her has got the bit and her mouth is running free and wild. "You should feel good, Baker, damn it!" She's practically shrieking now. "Because if we can't fix it, it can't be fixed, don't you see that! We bailed you out, damn it, we saved your lily-white butt from having to fire all those people yourself!"

There's no answer, just a rush of cold night air from outside. Lucy can imagine Baker on the balcony, scowling into the darkness, so hot with rage he can't feel the chill. She realizes how far she's pushed it, and all the energy just fizzles out of her. She flops back on the bed, pulls the covers up over her head and closes her eyes, trying to figure if there's anything she can or should say next. A vast weariness settles over her; in a few minutes she's asleep.

She awakes early in the morning to find the sheets smooth beside her. She jumps out of bed and looks around. Baker and all his things are gone. She dresses quickly and rushes downstairs. It's barely eight o'clock.

Downstairs, the concierge informs her that a car waits to drive her to Malpensa.

And the Signor?

Signor Baker, it seems, left early for the Linate airport and a domestic flight that would connect him with the noon Alitalia out of Rome. With an expression that combines deference and pity in precise proportions, the concierge gives Lucy her passport and ticket. The bill has been taken care of. May he send a porter for the Signora's luggage? It is best that she leave within the half hour.

He may, Lucy replies. Just give her twenty minutes to pack. As for the rest of her life, she reflects, she'll just have to deal with that later.

$= IV =$ Her flight out of Honolulu was two hours late, so when Lucy finally arrives at LAX, it's almost 8 p.m. Pacific time and she's missed her Boston connection. Finding a nearby hotel is no problem; she settles for a Marriott a bit up the coast near Marina del Rey. She's still on Hong Kong time, so her body thinks it's noon the next day and—although exhausted—she's not sleepy. In her room, she dons a hotel bathrobe, unpacks a change of clothes, makes herself a stiff scotch from the minibar and orders eggs Benedict and a salad from room service.

While she waits for her food, she dials her answering machine back at home in Maine. She doubts there'll be anything new. She cleared it earlier while waiting in Honolulu.

She's surprised, however, to hear Spuds's voice on the tape. "Gimme a call, urgent, soon's ya can." The message is time-stamped 12:14 a.m. Eastern time. His voice sounds bleary, which is no surprise. If Spuds is still up at midnight, it's a sure thing he's been at the whisky.

She debates briefly whether to call back now. She's bone-tired; the day's been long enough.

What can Spuds want? she wonders. Probably another overture from Mannerman to come back to GIA, all is forgiven. After a minute's hesitation, her curiosity gains the upper hand, as it always does, and she dials Spuds's New York number.

There are four rings at the other end, then Spuds's machine kicks in. Lucy starts to put the phone down, when she hears Spuds come on. They wait for the outgoing message to finish, then he asks, "Where the hell've you been?"

"Out on the rim." Lucy can tell he's half sloshed.

"Doin' wha'?"

"This and that."

Spuds has been hitting it pretty hard lately, she thinks. When Lucy last had lunch with him in New York, a week before she went out to Hong Kong, he put away three martinis before the soup. Apparently PL is having a bad patch and is on a real tear. UnivCom is beset by squabbles—the Dutch aren't speaking to the Japanese, the Chinese hate the South Africans, the South American satellite deal's a shambles—and rumors are sweeping Hedgefundland that GIA will be taking some pretty heavy write-offs in its other businesses. The shorts are cranking up. The stock's off 10 percent since Easter. That's a five-billion-dollar diminution of stockholder "wealth," enough to make even the biggest hitters restive.

Lucy worries about Spuds. As far as she's concerned, he's been stand-up for her from Day One at GIA, a friend, a colleague, a real trouper. He's a gentle soul at bottom, who lets Mannerman take him too much for granted, lets PL use him as a punching bag when the heat's on. Since leaving GIA—it's been just over a year—Lucy's stayed in touch with him, talking regularly on the phone, having lunch or dinner when-ever schedules permit—and not, she's come to realize, because she's avid for gossip about the old stamping ground, but because she values his friendship and counsel and because she flatters herself that her company softens the edges and fills a few potholes in his life.

"So, Spudsy, it's way past your bedtime," she jokes. "What's up?"

"Bad news."

"More write-offs?"

"Nope. Baker again."

"Really. What this time?"

It's been months since Baker's been heard from, months since Lucy's even thought about him. She's one of those souls blessed with an emo-tional circuit breaker that shuts down her heart even while her head is puzzling out the whys and wherefores of an involvement that no longer works.

When Baker walked out on her at the Villa d'Este something inside her clicked off and she went immediately into what Spuds calls her "postmortem mode." By the time she was halfway across the Atlantic, her relationship with Baker had been dissected like a corpse on a cor-oner's table, the lessons to be learned had been mentally written up and the report filed away, and Baker himself was just another name in her graveyard, another headstone marking the final resting place of yet another guy who turned out not to have the ball.

She had fallen for Baker for what he wasn't, she's decided. The volt-age of the infatuation was both positive and negative. He wasn't Carls-son, he wasn't Mannerman, he wasn't about money and power, all of which was a plus. But he turned out to be not what she had imagined him. At "21" she'd thought she'd seen a certain last-throw Tory gallantry that was very fetching, a knight riding out in blazing armor to do battle with Market Man and Money Man. He had those armorial qualities to some degree, to be sure; her passion had to have been based on *something*! But what she'd discovered about Baker, once intimacy caused the masks and scrims to fall away, was that every quality in the man was tempered by an unremitting resentment, an inner rage that sometimes simmered, sometimes boiled, but whose pilot light never went out. His anger, she would tell Spuds, was like an addiction. The urge was always there; now and then he could keep it in check, stay clean, as it were, but as often as not, it got the better of him.

Lucy doesn't practice amateur psychotherapy and, since the affair shut down, she hasn't given Baker's psyche much thought, apart from reflecting that the resentment must have been the product of some midlife crisis, of having to come to grips himself with who he isn't and what he's not.

Even so, in the months immediately following their breakup, it had been hard not to be aware of the man.

To begin with, there had been the episode in Bakerton. On returning to America from Italy, Baker had gone directly to Pennsylvania to attend the funeral of the BEECO worker who'd killed himself. According to Spuds, it had been catastrophic. "The services had to be held in the Polish Hall; the Catholic church down there wouldn't take a suicide. Apparently, before he crashed the old boy's funeral, Baker raised hell with the priest about *that*!"

"Where'd you hear this?"

"A guy who was there told one of our people—funny how some of 'em think that if they cozy up to us, feed us stuff, tittle-tattle, it'll save their jobs. Anyway, the funeral was a short deal, and afterward Baker goes up to the widow and tries to say something to her, and her kid knocks him down."

"What!"

"Yeah, a big strong kid who's on his way to Penn State to play DT for Joe Paterno. He pops Baker one that lays him out in the gutter, and then damned if the kid doesn't spit on him—along with four or five others who were standing there."

"God almighty!"

And yet Lucy somehow couldn't help feeling that Baker had asked for it.

Then he had launched a one-man war on Jack Mannerman and GIA. It was a sorry sight, like Sir Galahad transformed into Don Quixote, clanking hither and yon on the media battlefield, trying to fight the equivalent of tanks and rocket launchers with a lance. He tried to hire the big PR firms to represent him, but the pros knew a losing proposition when they saw one, and he ended up paying a has-been in Washington what Lucy heard was close to a half million dollars.

It wasn't a total bust. He got some national talk-show exposure— fuming appearances on *Larry King* and *MacNeil-Lehrer*—along with a scattering of rust-belt town meetings and cable shows. The *Times* printed an Op-Ed piece by him, and *The Village Voice* ran a profile, but these days people who stuck their heads up like as not got them chopped off, and eventually the campaign lost its tiny, frail grip on marginal public attention and petered out.

After that, Baker had popped up on Lucy's screen a couple of other times. A friend of Lucy's who was a documentary filmmaker passed along unconfirmed scuttlebutt that Baker was trying to hire the guy who did the Roger Smith hatchet job on General Motors to do a similar number on Mannerman, but nothing more was heard of that.

And then there was the curious affair of the California hacker who was caught trying to crash GIAFin's internal computer network. Had he succeeded, the result would have been an administrative nightmare and might well have caused hundreds of millions in losses. He turned out to be a hired gun who'd been contacted anonymously on the Internet, negotiated with over the telephone (the call turned out to have been made from a pay phone at Washington's National Airport) and paid five thousand in cash for the job, the money having been sent in a first-class Jiffy bag postmarked Raleigh-Durham. The affair was a nonstarter from the get-go. The hacker had no idea whom he was dealing with. To trace a month-old contact back through the Internet, which had become a regular bazaar for all kinds of shady arrangements, was impossible. As for people with a motive, Spuds had told Lucy over dinner at the Stirrup Cup that there were roughly fifty thousand debit accounts on GIAFin's books, ranging from a few hundred dollars in credit-card debt to upward of a billion owed by certain corporate borrowers.

"Plus you can throw in another nine thousand who've been downsized, plus their relations and sympathetic friends, and then there are the Luddites."

"The who?" Lucy practically had to shout to make herself heard. This might be Spuds's favorite restaurant, but she hated it—a famous Manhattan steak house with the atmosphere of a trading room, where the very air seemed beaded with testosterone and cigar smoke. Very guy-guy. Very noisy.

"People who hate everything we're doing and want to break it up!" Spuds had shouted back. "Including that damn Frog!"

She knew whom he was talking about. The Luddite factions comprised not only people who hated what technology was doing to the U.S. workingman but also the French Minister of Culture, who hated what the material transmitted over UnivCom's EuroSky satellites was doing to the collective mind of his great, cultivated nation.

"All in all, no way," Spuds continued. "We're just lucky we missed the bullet this time. In fact, even as you and I nosh on this delicious sirloin, IBM's got fifty people at GIAFin programming in fifty megagigs of new backup to the fifty we're already running."

For whatever reason, when Spuds told her about this attempt on GIAFin's computers, Baker's name had flashed in Lucy's mind. He certainly hated GIA and he knew his way around the Internet—and the way it was executed could have come right out of one of the thrillers Baker was fond of reading.

So what now? What new news?

"Baker's bought the farm," she hears Spuds saying.

"He's *what*?"

"Joined the circus, morted out, cashed in his chips! He's dead, stupid! I just caught it on the CNN late wrap-up. It happened in Africa this morning. Get this! He got eaten by crocodiles!"

The world doesn't explode black or yellow inside Lucy's skull. Her stomach doesn't turn into a bottomless gulf. But quick little waves of sadness race through her, tumble her feelings in their turbulent wash, momentarily suck her empty as they ebb and then leave her high and dry.

"Eaten by crocs? You're joking!"

"Tune in and see for yourself. You know how it is in Africa right now. Jungle bunnies running around with AK-47s, operating on the strategic premise that if it moves, blow the fucker away, including these special crocodiles that Baker went over there to try to save, although how you save a damn crocodile beats me! It seems he and a couple of boys went out in a boat and the crocs capsized it and ate them!"

Lucy, sorting out the impact of Spuds's newsflash, can say nothing.

"Anyway," Spuds continues conversationally, "it'll save us a bundle."

"Huh?"

"Baker checking out like this, I mean. I don't know if I told you this, but the guy was trying to get the Jesus freaks on our case. Writing to Pat Robertson about the quote immorality unquote of Individuality, asking for meetings. The Old Man's already got it up to here on the subject with you-know-who in Rome, so this isn't—wasn't—his idea of a good time. Anyway, he asked me to look into getting Scanlon or someone to do a Wigand on Baker."

"A 'Wigand'?"

"You know. The cancer scare last year? The clown who blew the whistle to *60 Minutes*. The tobacco boys hired the PR heavies to do a major number on him."

Lucy remembers. It had not been her chosen profession's noblest hour. In fact, it had disgusted her. Spin was one thing. Outright character assassination quite another.

"Anyway, kiddo, that's found money. Be that as it may, you have my condolences. I guess you liked the guy. At least once upon a time, eh?"

I guess so, Lucy thinks when she hangs up. She's not sure what she feels. She's often wondered what goes through the mind of a man or woman when, on turning to the obituary page of the *Times*, they read of the death of an ex-spouse. Now she knows. A numb confusion of self-neutralizing emotions. She turns on CNN and waits for the next news cycle.

When it comes on, the story's pretty much as Spuds described. Baker had gone to Central Africa, to Lake Kivu, between Zaire and Rwanda, to attempt to save a rare species of lake crocodile whose breeding grounds lay directly in the path of the region's latest tribal war. With two natives, he had gone down the lake to the habitat of the huge, murderous amphibians presumably to harvest some eggs or fledgling crocs to relocate. Baker was an old Kivu hand, he'd done this a dozen times, and his helpers were equally experienced. His boat, capsized, was discovered washed up on the shore of the lake the following after-noon. The remains of one of the natives, badly croc-mangled, came ashore a day later. The other bodies had not been found.

The next night, back home in Maine, Lucy reads through the obit-uaries—which dwell on the late H. A. Baker's accomplishments as artist, sportsman and conservationist. Then, over a bowl of spaghetti and a salad, she raises her glass in a silent toast of farewell. Lucy's not one for might-have-beens, but she feels she owes some acknowledgment to Baker for helping her regain her own life. You may have wasted some of my valuable feelings, you old shit, she thinks, but by God you lib-erated me from Jack Mannerman, and that has been a big, big plus.

The first night back in New York after the Italian "idyll" had con-vinced Lucy that, however badly it had ended and however bumpy the relationship with Baker had been, something within her had indeed changed for the softer and wiser; that she was no longer suited for the hard-nosed, rat-tat-tat, twenty-hour-a-day world of New York business. Her country girl instincts had taken control. New York wasn't something you merely put up with or tolerated; to really make it here, you had to relish it, crave it, truly get off on its sharp-elbowed style. She no longer could.

Two weeks after that, she had her lawyer bust her lease on the Sixty-seventh Street apartment; a month later, she had moved into the cozy house on the bluff near Paster's Point that she'd bought two years earlier as a vacation place. Now she's continuing to earn a very handsome living doing freelance public relations, but out of her own home and hundreds of miles from New York, happier in her work than she's ever been. What with the fax, the scanner, the computer, the Web and the on-line services she's plugged into, Lucy is as much on top of things as if she were in her old office on Fifty-seventh Street. The only thing she misses is the daily buzz at the Four Seasons, "21," Le Cirque, but she has Spuds and a wide network of phone pals to fill her in. She's completely at peace here; she's come home. The ocean—even in its worst, roaring moods—is a familiar, steady presence.

Her life seems complete. She's still up to the odd bit of Lipscombing: currently a professor in the French department at Bowdoin—nothing serious, but agreeable enough. It's more a friendship with occasional sex than a romance. Maine is everything she needs: the house, her kitchen, her work, her telephone "sewing circle," the outside world no further away than her computer keyboard, her father just down the road, her cat, Lucifer. The inner softness that she traces to her "Baker interlude" continues to deepen. It doesn't seem to have affected her professional ability; asked to size up a public relations problem, she's as hard-nosed as ever. But when she returns from a business trip—her business takes her away perhaps ten days a month at most—and gets into her car at the Portland airport, it's as if she's been transported back to an earlier era that moves at half the speed, with half the nervous fuss and twice the moral integrity of her old New York life.

The shock of Baker's death is sharp but short. Lucy has too much going on just now to pause and mourn. What with one thing and another, he disappears to the back of her mind and she doesn't think about him until about three months after his death, when she returns from a two-day turnaround to Midland, Texas, exhausted by a difficult client and the one-hundred-degree midsummer heat, to find a Federal Express envelope inside the screen door. It contains an officious-looking envelope marked with the name of a Philadelphia law firm.

Inside is a letter advising her that the firm is acting for the estate of Hobart Alexander Baker, deceased, in whose last will and testament Lucy is named as a legatee. Another legatee, a foundation set up by the late Mr. Baker for the relief of disemployed employees of BEECO, has petitioned a Philadelphia court to declare Baker legally dead notwithstanding that his body has yet to be recovered from Lake Kivu. In anticipation of such a ruling, the estate is being prepared for distribution. The letter requests Lucy to contact the law firm.

She riffles through the will. It's a straightforward enough affair, dated about six months after she and Baker broke up, which means that he still must have had her on his mind well after she had more or less stopped fretting about him. To Lucy he's willed the .22 Colt Woodsman pistol. The remainder of the estate, cash and securities, his Bakerton house, the Two Moose camp are bequeathed to the foundation, as are his artworks and other personal effects, with the exception of his outdoor gear, fishing tackle and sporting arms. These are left to one Lewis L. Morland of Halifax, Nova Scotia, a name Lucy recognizes. Morland was Baker's favorite guide; the two had traveled most of the world together.

She calls Philadelphia and is told that an inventory and valuation of the Baker estate is being prepared for probate. She can expect her bequest will be shipped to her shortly, very likely before the end of the year.

Before hanging up, she lets her instinctive nosiness get the better of her manners and asks, "By the way, Mr. Dalrymple, just out of curiosity, what was Mr. Baker's estate worth?"

There's a pause, then the attorney answers, "Well, as you're among Mr. Baker's heirs, Ms. Preston, I don't suppose there's any harm in telling you. Excluding real property, we're valuing it for probate in the near neighborhood of $39 million. What we're able to get for the Bakerton and Adirondacks properties will, of course, increase that somewhat."

Thirty-nine million? That can't be right, she thinks. Even allowing for the recent fallback, Baker's GIA stock should be worth close to fifty million today!

"That seems awfully low, Mr. Dalrymple."

"Well, in the last year or so, as you may be aware, Ms. Preston, the decedent engaged in an extremely expensive public relations campaign. It cost over fifteen million dollars, according to his records."

Fifteen million? she thinks. That's impossible! Baker's "campaign" was the sort of thing the newest kid in the Ruder & Finn mail room could've handled with one hand tied behind his back. Lucy knows better than her own name what public relations campaigns cost. Even if she tripled going rates for space and time buys, and doubled agency markups, if he was out of pocket more than three million she'd eat her computer!

Something else occurs to her.

"One other thing, Mr. Dalrymple," she says. "I don't know if you're aware of this, but Mr. Baker and I . . . well, we kept company for a time. During that spell, we bought—that is, I bought—a set of eighteenth-century Italian engravings as a present for Mr. Baker. Of the Seven Deadly Sins. I think I paid around twelve hundred dollars for them; I can check my American Express bills. Purely for sentimental reasons, I'd like very much—if it's at all possible—to buy them from the estate at fair market value. I'm sure any knowledgeable print dealer in Philadelphia could put a price on them, or, if you prefer, I could ask Peter Kraus or David Tunick in New York."

It would be nice to have them back, she's thinking; they'd make an agreeable souvenir of a happy time.

"The Seven Deadly Sins, you say, Miss Preston? Let's see now. I have the schedule right here. No, I'm afraid I don't see them here. Are you certain?"

"I am, but it's entirely possible he gave them away."

Or burned them up in a fit of rage, she thinks, ringing off.

Shortly after Thanksgiving, a large manila envelope arrives with the Baker inventory. Lucy skims it, confirming both the attorney's estimate of the value of Baker's liquid assets and his statement that no engravings of the Seven Deadly Sins were among the decedent's personal effects. A fortnight later, a box bearing the return address of a Utica, New York, moving and storage company arrives. It contains Lucy's legacy: the Colt Woodsman pistol, carefully and professionally oiled and wrapped in thick clear plastic. On top of it is a sealed envelope with her name. In it she finds a single .22 long-rifle hollow-point and a slip of paper on which is written, in Baker's spidery handwriting, "This one's for you."

Even in death, you can't let go of the anger, can you, you poor miserable SOB, she thinks. She puts the weapon back in the box and shoves the box onto a closet shelf.

Once, during the week before Christmas, she thinks about her departed former lover. She and her Bowdoin friend, who's down for the weekend, are planning a barge trip through Gascony for the following summer. It's cozy in Lucy's living room, with a crackling fire, Lucifer on the hearth, maps and Michelins spread out, red wine in tumblers and a Ducktrap Farms pâté to nibble on. The itinerary they're working out looks wonderful: three-star food, noble churches, interesting towns, splendid countryside. And yet as fabulous as it sounds, Lucy suddenly realizes, with a stab that annoys as much as pains her, that not this, nor anything in the rest of her life, will likely ever approach the bliss she felt on some of those days in Italy with H. A. Baker. It's a horribly irritating thought.

PART THREE

=DAMN DEADLY=

=BAD FORTUNE=

— I —
"Daddy, you can't still be watching that!" Lucy exclaims, backing through the door with her arms full of grocery bags, stomping the snow off her boots.

The Chief doesn't answer. He remains stolidly planted in his chair at the kitchen table, staring at the television set on the counter next to the microwave.

"Unbelievable," he says finally. "Darned if I can understand what this country's become."

Lucy grunts her assent as she shifts her burden onto the counter and starts to put her haul away. Out of the corner of her eye she watches the whole deadly business begin to roll on-screen for what must be the nth-to-the-tenth-power time. Surely not in fifteen years, not since the space shuttle *Challenger* blew up on launch, can a single minute of film have been played so repeatedly on television. Probably, Lucy thinks, since around 1 p.m. Central time, almost six hours earlier, between cable, conventional and satellite transmission, not one second has passed without this loop being aired somewhere in the world. The woman, after all, commanded an audience estimated at nearly a half billion globally.

"Want a glass of wine?" she asks her father. "This Chardonnay I got doesn't seem half bad."

There's no reply. Once a lawman, always a lawman, Lucy thinks. How many times does someone who's spent his life fighting crime actually get to see a major crime committed live?

On-screen, a rail-thin woman, as vividly—even grotesquely—made up as a Fellini actress, is seated in a bookstore behind a yard-high stack of books with flashy gilded jackets. She's signing these for a line of fans who pass before her at the rate of one every thirty-odd seconds.

As Lucy starts to make dinner, which she does for her father every Saturday night if she's in Paster's Point, she can't help watching the television, even though she's seen the loop herself what must be a dozen times by now—ever since Spuds called in midafternoon to tell her what had happened.

Sixty-seven seconds. That's all it took. One minute and seven seconds from the time the young man entered the field of view of the videocam operated by the husband of the woman next in line to the moment he disappeared from view under a pile of bodyguards and security personnel. T minus fifty-eight seconds: the young man comes into view. Forty-three seconds of him waiting his turn patiently, until T minus fifteen. A nondescript young man, strongly built and stringy-haired, nothing unusual about him except, as it will turn out, the five-inch carbon-steel chef's knife honed to surgical sharpness that he's gripping under his coat. At T minus fourteen, he takes a book from the pile and hands it to the seated woman. She opens it to the flyleaf and, at T minus ten seconds, starts to write.

At this point, most telecasts shift to slow motion; CBS News—to which for old times' sake, out of reverence for Walter Cronkite, the Chief remains loyal—is no exception. The woman's head is bent, exposing a rice-white nape, in her current bulimic stage more a turkey's neck than a swan's, that vanishes in an upswept corona of frizzy, improbably orange hair. At T minus six seconds, the young man reaches over quickly with his left hand, grabs her topknot, pushing her head backward, and at T minus zero, as someone sees what's happening and screams, he swipes the knife blade across her throat in a savage upward diagonal. A fountain of scarlet blood jets from the lady's severed carotid artery and spatters everyone within a seven-foot radius. Five seconds later, the assailant vanishes beneath a half ton of late-reacting security people.

Sixty-seven seconds, Lucy thinks, as she spills the contents of a small jar of roasted peppers onto the counter and starts to chop them. Less time than it'll take me to dice these. She looks at her knife and notes the familiar trident mark stamped on the blade. It's been learned that the murder weapon was of similar German manufacture, and when Lucy examines the blade of her own knife, she sees there's nothing except the maker's mark and an item number. A knife like this would be untraceable, she guesses: imported in lots of several hundred at a minimum and sold coast to coast in hardware stores, kitchenware and cooking specialty shops, mail-order outlets. She recalls she bought this one from Williams-Sonoma—as part of a birthday set for the Chief. She doubts he ever uses them—other than to cut the foil on a TV dinner.

When a commercial comes on, she asks over her shoulder: "Any new developments?"

"Yeah," her father replies. "Apparently the kid's made a statement. Says the devil came and spoke to him on the Internet, on some kind of bulletin board the right-to-life fruits use to shriek at each other about how unfair it is they've all got AIDS."

Lucy hates it when her father talks this way. She can understand his homophobia—he's from a generation that had different limits—but his opinions have already cost Chief Preston dearly. Forty-odd years ago, he'd been one of the most promising young agents in the FBI, in charge of the Atlanta office and clearly on his way up, but then one night in some club he'd shot his mouth off about the relationship between J. Edgar Hoover and his deputy, Clyde Tolson. Somehow word got back to the Director and Lucy's father got the sack.

That was before Lucy was born, and his bitterness on the subject has been a part of her entire life. In every other way he's been a good man and a good father, a model of personal and departmental deportment, five times reappointed chief of the Paster's Point police department, who kept himself and his people up-to-date and state-of-the-art. Every Wednesday afternoon, as sure as the sun's coming up, would find the Chief down at the range, keeping his hand in with his venerable Smith & Wesson .38 Police Special. Even now, five years into retirement, Chief Preston is regularly called upon by the Maine state police up in Augusta when they hit a wall on a major crime.

She returns to her work. She's not a good cook, nowhere near equal to her late mother, but good enough, and she knows that just her being around makes a difference to the Chief, even if, in his taciturn New England way, he can't make himself say so. Her mother died eleven years earlier, just after her fifty-eighth birthday, and the Chief had been lonely since. By his own admission, he was a "one-owner dog."

Poor Betti Jo Barnum, she thinks. A girl from nowhere who'd

achieved celebrity, success and a fortune estimated by *Entertainment Weekly* at $200 million. You had to hate what she did to make that kind of money, the shameless trafficking in resentment and self-loathing. Nevertheless, there was a kind of pluck to her that you could admire.

The killer's motive is still unclear. Still, something like this had to happen. The cyberanimals among Lucy's chums report that the Internet is overrun with sociopaths feeding each other's fury. That's one reason Lucy doesn't use the Internet; there's something about it that scares her. She knows that bulletin boards and Web sites exist for every hatred, deviancy, socioeconomic grudge or crazy doctrine, and she's afraid of wandering onto one by accident and never escaping.

The Betti Jo Barnum show alone spawned six bulletin boards and nine "pages" on the Web. Now, the CNN anchor says, it was on one of these that Satan had reached out a digital claw and, like God tapping Adam's forefinger, gave flaming life to the pathology that wielded the knife in the course of those sixty-seven seconds in Houston.

The Chief flicks the television off and swivels his chair around.

"I guess that tape'll be for your generation what the Zapruder JFK film is for mine," he says. His broad face, ruddy under a full head of straight sandy hair, is wreathed in a naughty smile.

Lucy doesn't comment. She knows he's fishing for a rise. To suggest that the killing of a talk-show hostess somehow equates with the assassination of a President is ridiculous. Well, maybe.

The next day, the Barnum slaying obsesses the airwaves right through the late news. A hundred times it's repeated that Satan is the subject of a worldwide search being jointly supervised by the electronic auxiliaries of the FBI and Interpol. Barnum's murderer turns out to be a resident of a dreary suburb west of Houston, thirty-two years old, an unemployed design assistant and bodybuilder. His physician, a pathologist from Baylor Medical Center, states that his patient is in the middle stages of AIDs. That evening, on *MacNeil-Lehrer*, he will be described by a Houston court-appointed psychiatrist as manic-depressive, with a bitterness bordering on hysteria about what he sees as the federal government's failure to confront the gay health crisis. ABC breaks into the game between Michigan State and Iowa for the Big Ten basketball championship with a bulletin that a second man, apparently the killer's legal spouse in a gay marriage, is being held in Paris by the Sûreté.

By his own account, the assailant was contacted approximately four months earlier by telephone. The caller—using some type of aural scrambler to distort his voice beyond recognition—said that he had gotten the young man's number off the Betti Jo Barnum Web page devoted to gay concerns. The putative killer, it seemed, had written her several pathetic, plaintive letters requesting a loan of $10,000 for a special treatment available in France for his companion. Each request had been rejected via form letter. The caller identified himself as Satan and expressed sympathy for the young man's anger at the talk-show hostess. What sort of selfish pig, Satan had asked, would sit atop a heap of gold while decent people were dying for lack of just a few ounces? Two hundred million, all made off the misery and misfortune of others, and the woman couldn't spare ten thousand?

Satan called regularly after that, at first about once a week, building to two or three calls daily toward the end. Why not do something with what remains of your life, while you're still able to get around? Satan argued. Why not kill Betti Jo Barnum? Satan hates Barnum too, he tells the young man, for her greedy, uncharitable, un-Christian exploitation of the penniless and dispossessed and unlucky, but he's just too old and too weak to do anything about it. On the other hand, Satan reports, he has money. Quite a lot of money. He can afford to hire a younger arm to wield the deadly blade. He drags the sum of two hundred thousand in cash under the young man's nose.

That's a sum more than sufficient, Satan points out, to send the young man's lover to France, where they really care about AIDS and have spent vast sums of public and private money in an effort to develop new drugs. Unlike the giant profit-guzzling pharmaceutical firms in the United States, one of whom sponsors a line of diet pills endorsed by Betti Jo. Since you're going to die anyway, and sooner than later, Satan wheedles, why not serve a great cause well, and then die in comfort, in a nice hospital, not in prison, because Satan, who always takes care of his own, will see to it that the young man is represented by a famous Texas lawyer.

And so, on the Friday of the President's Day weekend, the official publication date of Betti Jo Barnum's new book, *Go Thin, Go Glad!*, already in its ninth prepublication printing, the young man made his way to Houston's America West Mall out on Memorial, where the talk-show hostess's autograph session was to be the crowning event of the opening of a huge new bookstore.

Satan was a man of his word. Even as the first ambulance screeched into the mall, the young man's lover, waiting by a pay phone in the parking lot of a McDonald's not far from Houston Intercontinental Airport, received the call his companion had told him to expect in the course of a long, often tearful, candlelit farewell dinner two nights earlier at Anthony's, Houston's most expensive and elegant restaurant. The dinner, as well as a number of extravagant gifts and a new traveling wardrobe, were paid for out of a fifteen-thousand-dollar earnest of Satan's good faith delivered three days earlier by Federal Express, one hundred fifty used hundred-dollar bills in an eight-by-ten padded envelope.

The lover confirmed that he had his passport with him. He was told to go to Section G2 of the long-term parking area at Houston Intercontinental, and to locate a 1977 Toyota sedan with Georgia plates parked in the fifth row. The keys to the car were in a magnetic box affixed to the underside of the driver's-side fender. In the trunk was a soft-sided drugstore-quality suitcase containing $100,000 in used hundred-dollar bills.

The young man took the night flight to Paris. There, after barely twelve hours of high life, he was arrested by the French police and returned to Houston, where he stands charged with conspiracy to commit first-degree murder. CBS reports that the defense of the two young men will be handled, contrary to Satan's assurances, by a court-appointed public defender.

Satan is never found. Surveillance is established for every likely Internet forum, but the efforts are fruitless. As Jay Leno will remark in his opening monologue: "Half the country is waiting for this guy to get caught, and the other half for him to call." There are, understandably, no witnesses. It seems obvious that Satan must have lingered close to the scene, in order to verify at first hand that the service he'd contracted for had been performed, but the mall and the bookstore were packed, and the call to the lover could have been made from any of the hundred sixty-eight pay telephones located about the mall.

Other leads go nowhere. The car in which the money was stashed was bought six months earlier for cash at an Atlanta police auction of some three hundred impounded and abandoned vehicles; no one remembers the purchaser; the barely legible signature on the receipt is a false name. The Federal Express waybill for the "earnest money" is traced to Gunch & Hosmeer, a large Tulsa law firm specializing in oil and gas matters. As the senior partner of the firm explains to CBS, its lawyers are involved in the conveyancing of several thousand oil and gas properties a year, which can mean obtaining waivers and transfer contracts from as many as a hundred fractional working and royalty interests. As a result, the firm sends and receives literally hundreds of communications a day, using preprinted waybills which it orders in 10,000-unit quantities. To abstract one from its mail room would be a simple matter, but in-depth investigations of the firm's past and current personnel roster and conveyancing records fail to yield a single useful lead.

Inevitably, the public's attention is claimed by other deeds of violence. Lucy herself loses interest, although at lunch with Spuds at the Four Seasons ten months later, she asks her former colleague how Mannerman has reacted to losing Betti Jo.

"Well, it was damn deadly bad fortune, by his lights, naturally," says Spuds, wading into his second martini. "There'll never be another Betti Jo. That woman had the skin of a rhinoceros. We think we've found a replacement, however. A woman at an evangelical station in Provo that our HMO people took a piece of. A transsexual Mormon with a heart of ice who sincerely wants to get rich. They ran her by a couple of fruits-and-nuts focus groups in the Bible Belt and the results were dyn-oh-mite! Total apeshit! They're flying her out to audition for Carlsson tomorrow. In my opinion, six months from now, no one'll know who Betti Jo was. By gum, there's a lot of money to be made from the short memory of the great American people! The other shows are filling their slots OK, and Super Cola just picked up Tinkry for the U.K. Wait'll the lager louts get into militia-ing! Carlsson's right. There's enough nastiness out there to keep us going for a hundred years!"

— **II** — The mountains which overlook the 38,000-acre spread of the X Lazy 9 Ranch are still wrapped in night when a tall figure leans over the end of the bed and gently touches the foot of the sleeping figure.

"Reveille, General Tinkry, sir," he mutters in a low, barely audible voice. "Oh-five-hundred hours, sir."

There's an incomprehensible mumble from the heap on the bed, then a groan as General Chadbourne Tinkry, star of America's most-watched television call-in show, emerges from sleep like a giant grouper ascending with borborygmous dignity from the ocean depths.

"Damn your eyes, Corporal," grunts Tinkry. "Can't a man sleep?"

He doesn't want to wake up. He's been having a delicious dream. He squeezes his eyes shut to preserve the fantasy. Pressed beneath his bulk, his right hand tightens around the erection which always sprouts in sleep when Chadbourne Tinkry dreams of power.

"Got your coffee right here, sir. Brewed just the way you like it. In a tin pot over a mesquite fire."

The general's penchant for things "home-done" in the good old American way has been the subject of numerous articles. Just now his agent is dickering with a major publisher, its lifestyle list critically depleted by the loss of Betti Jo Barnum, for a million-dollar advance for a book on Tinkry's favorite American things.

The sleeping man hears none of this, nor the sound of the bedroom door closing. He's sunk back in sleep, deep in his dream, standing tall and proud on a balcony overlooking a wide boulevard, a triumphal way with a marble arch gleaming white in the far, far distance. He's dressed all in black; his boots glisten like oiled steel, the silver ornaments at his throat sparkle in the sunlight. As far as—farther than—the eye can see stretches a sea of faces, several hundred thousand at least, probably closer to a million, possibly more. He raises both his arms in a victor's salute, and the crowd, those million throats, roars out his name. "Tink-ry! Tink-ry!! Tink-ry!!!"

"General Tinkry, sir!" the voice calls through the closed bedroom door. "It's oh-five-fifteen hours, sir! Mount-up's at a quarter to!"

"Thank you, Corporal," Tinkry mutters. He opens his eyes and snaps on the bedside lamp. He swings his feet out of the bed and sits hunched on the edge, rubbing his eyes and reflecting that a man's gotta do what a man's gotta do, but sometimes it's a pain in the keister.

He levers himself up and shuffles heavily over to the tray on the sideboard and pours himself a cup of coffee, then sets about getting dressed. In the bathroom, by standing this way and that, he manages to keep the needle just under the three-hundred-pound mark. Damn, he thinks, keep this up and I'll never see my pecker again. He's of two minds about his bulk. Privately, he's self-conscious, although the women he sleeps with don't seem to mind, and his handlers say it gives him presence.

Washed, combed and toothbrushed, he emerges from the bathroom, grunts into shirt, jeans and socks and looks around.

"Where are those damn boots?" he calls out.

"Right here, sir."

The bedroom door opens. Tinkry looks up. He doesn't know the man standing there, a stereotype cowboy, a regular Marlboro Man, rugged and tough, with a strong square jaw; the upper part of his face is hidden by dark glasses and the low-pulled brim of a squashed and stained Stetson.

"Who in tarnation are you? Where's the corporal?"

"My name's Smoky, sir, your cabin wrangler for today. Corporal's over at the vehicle center checking on your ATV. Anything you need, sir, just holler. Here're your boots, General, sir. That's a right smart shine. Maybe I can get the corporal to teach me how."

"Just put them over there by that chair, will you." Tinkry studies the ranch hand. There's something about this fellow. The kernel of a routine's beginning to germinate in his mind, a rant about the West as the last outpost of true American individualism, about men like this being driven into the wilderness by "libberbubbles," "ecofruits" and "clitclackers." Pretty soon, he'll tell his foaming audience, the only place you'll find real men like this'll be in a zoo!

"Listen, Smoky," he says, "you ever do any TV?"

"No, sir."

"Well, I just think you'd be a natural. We'll have us a little talk after the ride."

The ranch hand closes the door. Tinkry sips his coffee and thinks.

Of course, he muses, the guy's probably a poli-sci major from Arizona State and a fruitcake into the bargain, but who gives a damn! Chadbourne Tinkry hasn't built a radio-TV-print-video audience of ninety million by telling the truth, but by celebrating a rugged, apple-pie, gun-totin' individualism that derives almost wholly from old Clint Eastwood and Gary Cooper Westerns. By now, he's learned that truth is relative, that lies don't matter and facts don't count, not so long as you're giving your audience what it's tuned in to hear.

I can use this fellow to hit the beach first when Chadbourne's Commandos go after the Vice President's July 4 Environmental Telethon, thinks Tinkry, scratching his tummy. Chadbourne's Commandos have become familiar to most Americans, hatefully so if they're liberals. The commandos are the shock troops of Tinkry's Moral Militia, as his rabid followers style themselves. The commandos—the honor is entirely self-appointive—are responsible for spoiling any public meeting or forum that their leader goes on record as disapproving. Just two months earlier, they'd wrecked the President's Martin Luther King Day Telephone Town Meeting, stacking up on each incoming White House phone line to vilify the Chief Executive for six hours while other callers tried vainly to get through and finally gave up—as did the President.

Yes, he thinks, I'll just put that shitkicker on. The guy's perfect. Looks and sounds like a one hundred percent gun-rack-in-the-pickup, true-blue bowleggedy all-American white-bread shitass with gunpowder for brains. A type you can build a segment around, get him riled up on the air, get him going on gun control, feed his anger and resentment to the audience like meat to wolves. Perfect for Tinkry's Wyatt Earp constituency. It ought to be easy to get a crew down here from Tucson, be set up and ready to go when the annual Memorial Day sunrise trail ride returns at lunchtime.

He picks up the phone, punches out the number of the Tucson hotel where his personal assistant is holed up and—fully awake now and all business—gives a series of crisp instructions to co-opt a crew from the Fox local affiliate and be here at the ranch ready to go at 2 p.m. sharp.

He goes over and sits down by the boots. They're going to be a bitch to pull on, but not to wear them today might hurt his hosts' feelings, and a good commander is always mindful of his subordinates' sensitivities. These must have cost a couple of thou minimum, he thinks.

Custom-made by Lucchese in San Antonio: silver-toed, the uppers fashioned in red-white-and-blue vertical stripes, with incised white stars set in the red and blue, and exquisitely detailed American eagles worked into the front and rear shin pieces.

The boots, and the chrome-and-gilt spurs which go with them, were presented to Tinkry last night at the conclusion of his keynote address to the annual retreat of the Executive Council of the Security for America League, two hundred VIPs representing the nation's largest arms and defense manufacturers. Ordinarily, Tinkry wouldn't speak to an audience this small, even though he was paid his customary $100,000 honorarium, but he has large plans for his own future, and these people are likely to be willing to bet the tens of millions of political-action dollars they control that Chadbourne Tinkry's mouth can take him where they'd like to see him four years from now: 1600 Pennsylvania Avenue.

Well, might as well get on with it, he thinks. These may be my kinds of people, he reflects, but this trail ride is a pain in the ass. Fortunately, he's not going to have to get up on a horse, assuming there's one alive that could carry him. No, General Chadbourne Tinkry's going to ride the rugged Rincon trail and review the troops from the back seat of a Hummer. Thanking the Good Lord that made him for small blessings, he takes up the right boot and crams his foot into it.

The sudden movement and intrusion disturbs the tangled knot of baby western diamondback rattlesnakes snuggled in the boot's toe. There are five of them; they're ten weeks old, stolen from a large snake farm near Bisbee, and at the most lethally venomous stage of their lives. Between this lot and their littermates in the other boot, Chadbourne Tinkry's flamboyant new footgear shelters enough poison to kill an infantry platoon.

The tiny serpents' rattles have been amputated to conceal their presence, so Tinkry has no warning before tiny fangs easily pierce the thin cotton covering of his descending foot.

He gasps more in surprise than initial pain, jerks his foot out of the boot and then gives a roar of horror, half strangled by sheer terror, when he sees the tiny serpent clinging to his ankle. He kicks the rattler free, then notices another one. In his terror and confusion, he doesn't hear the door open and close at his back, doesn't see the tall Stetsoned figure glide quickly across the room.

A gloved hand closes on his windpipe, its fingers like steel cable under the leather, and shuts off his scream; a wiry arm circles under his chin, almost cutting off his breath, holding him stock-still and saucer-eyed as first his foot, then his ankle, then his lower leg swell bluish and grotesque as the venom boils up in his bloodstream.

It is finished in a little over a minute. Tinkry's heart, already pressed to the limit by the strain of his enormous bulk, yields to shock and goes into arrest. His body goes limp, his eyes lose expression and roll back, his tongue, swollen and discolored, bursts from his mouth, the air is suddenly foul-smelling as his intestines release. The iron gag and grip relax; gently, the stranger lowers the corpse to the floor and, for just a moment, studies his handiwork.

It's hard to believe that this beached, bleached, blue-faced whalelike lump lying contorted at his feet on the bright Navajo rug not two minutes ago possessed the power to sway the citizens of the greatest nation on earth; almost as hard—the intruder reflects—as it is to imagine the nation so out of touch with its historical meaning that it has allowed itself to be swayed by a pig like this.

A minute later, the stranger, carrying Tinkry's left boot in his right hand, crosses the living room to the closet, where a hardcase paramilitary type dressed in camouflage fatigues marked with a corporal's twin chevrons has been stashed, wrists and ankles bound with speaker cable, mouth sealed with duct tape. He's wheezing heavily behind the gag, sedated by the powerful tranquilizer with which he's been injected. The intruder looks down at him, face impassive, then upends the boot, sprinkling the second lot of tiny de-rattled diamondbacks onto the sleeping man's lap, and closes the closet door.

He snaps off the interior and porch lights and quickly checks the compound. Most of the cabins are still dark; a few are lit and in their windows vague figures move about with the wary stiffness of elderly men aroused too early. Over past the brightly illuminated cookhouse, where the corral is, voices mingle with the neighs and shufflings of horses being rounded up to be saddled. The now-purpling darkness wears the heavy perfume of frying bacon.

The man in the doorway satisfies himself, pulls the cabin door quietly shut, tests the knob to make sure the lock has set and melts into the night.

The body will not be found for another forty minutes, five minutes before saddling time, after repeated calls to Tinkry's cabin have gone unanswered, and a nervous scouting party has been dispatched to check on the great man, only to find the door locked; they will peer unsuccessfully through windows, and finally, at peril of disturbing the honored guest's slumber, will have Ranch Security summoned with its passkey.

By then, the stranger has regained the stand of cottonwoods a half mile down the highway from the main entrance of the X Lazy, where just after 1 a.m. he left the Ford Tempo he'd rented in Santa Fe a week earlier. The wrangler who knocked at the late Chadbourne Tinkry's bedroom door an hour earlier is now a trim-mustached, silver-braceleted, silver-coiffed type with an enameled flag pin in the buttonhole of a garishly stitched, fawn-colored Western-style business suit: definitely more on the order of a Phoenix or Albuquerque stockbroker or subdivision promoter than a paragon of the rugged Old West.

As he reaches the eastern outskirts of Tucson on his way to pick up 89 North, the first stage in a doubled-back route that will return him to New Mexico, flashing, yelping police vehicles stream by in the other direction, along with vans marked with call signs of radio and television stations. Two helicopters clatter past overhead, then a third. As he swings off onto 89 North, he flicks on the car radio and plays with the seek button until he finds a twanging country-and-western station; it isn't until almost half an hour later that an announcer positively squeaking with urgency breaks into a set of old George Jones songs with the first flash news of the murder of Chadbourne Tinkry and his bodyguard.

By now it's 6:30 a.m. Mountain time, 3:30 in the morning on the island of Kauai, in Hawaii, where Lucy has just fallen asleep. It's not until some five hours later, when she reflexively turns on CNN, that she learns of the Tinkry murders.

She's flown to the fiftieth state to meet her newest client, a financially beset Japanese company which is about to shut down a group of financially disastrous resort investments on the U.S. Gulf Coast. The presence of a representative of the Japanese Ministry of International Trade and Industry gives weight to the deliberations; MITI is concerned that this move, unless orchestrated with delicacy, which is where Lucy comes in, might set off a reaction which might endanger some important yen-dollar initiatives now under study in Tokyo and Washington. To announce the closing of four theme parks between Pensacola and Biloxi, with a loss of some five thousand of the marginal, low-pay-no-fringes jobs for which the "Redneck Riviera" is famous, could well incite violent protectionism in one of the nation's most xenophobic regions. Senators from Mississippi and Florida control two key subcommittees which the Speaker of the House is counting on to endorse critical parts of his recently announced Operation America Year 2001, the free-trade successor to the abandoned New American Agenda that Mannerman's purchase of BEECO helped to underwrite. The Japanese, with enormous ongoing investments in U.S. home satellite TV systems, have bet heavily on the Speaker being able to deliver.

It's not going to be easy, if it can be smoothed over at all, and the trouble is, Matuwa-san and his associates have somehow convinced themselves that Lucy possesses a magic wand she can wave over their predicament to make it go away. It was good of her old colleague Grover to recommend her so highly, but he may have overdone it. She's not having much luck making them understand that successful public relations is 90 percent the result of preaching to a congregation already at least halfway converted, of planting seeds in well-prepared and fertilized ground. She spent nine hours yesterday trying to put that point across, and despite all the grinning and nodding, she didn't get anywhere.

When she realizes what CNN is talking about, she turns off the bath and sits half naked on the bed, watching. My God, she thinks, talk about lightning striking twice! First Barnum, now Tinkry! It's as if Individuality's been kneecapped! What had Spuds called the murder of Betti Jo Barnum? "Damn deadly bad fortune." She looks at her watch and wonders whether she should try to call him. With what? Condolences? Mannerman must be shitting bricks!

In the way TV newscasters do when they have nothing hard to go on, the CNN people are in overdrive, on information and reportage overkill, but what's coming from the television is filler, an attempt to engender compulsive round-the-clock viewing from a scant foundation. The only solid information is about the gruesome manner in which Chadbourne Tinkry and his bodyguard met their deaths, and CNN's Phoenix stringer is breaking his back to fill the video waves with noise and motion until, as he repeats at least four times while Lucy watches, "Bernard Shaw can get here from Washington."

He's telecasting from in front of the guard post at the gate of the X Lazy 9. Shortly after Lucy tunes in, a herpetologist from the University of Arizona-Flagstaff is brought on. She points out that at this time of year rattlesnakes in the wild are breeding, not whelping, which means these snakes must have been bred at a commercial farm. Anyone with some knowledge could easily collect enough infant serpents to aggregate a lethal dosage of venom, and given the scale of some snake-farming operations, it's unlikely that a dozen tiny hatchlings would be missed.

The scene outside the gate of the X Lazy 9 is replaced suddenly by Wolf Blitzer patched in from Washington, live with the Speaker of the House, who is calling for a national day of mourning. The White House, a known nest of Tinkryphobes, is also said to be preparing an announcement. Over at the Department of Justice, yet another correspondent has braced a deputy director of the FBI, who confirms that the Bureau is checking with all commercial rattlesnake farms and reptile parks, running computer checks on known liberal organizations and bringing up dossiers on the membership of various snake-handling sects around the country which the late Chadbourne Tinkry may have in some way offended. As the FBI man makes clear, there are no clues and no suspects, although, with equal justice, it can also be said that there are millions. The victim was as hated on the left of center as he was revered on the right. Despite the—to Lucy—obvious Individuality connection, no one brings up the murder of Betti Jo Barnum.

This could really hurt GIA stock, she thinks. First Barnum, now Tinkry. Linchpins of a combined audience that must generate a quarter billion annually in revenues from advertisers and cable subscribers. Most of that would be pure profit to UnivCom, with a healthy slice ending up on GIA's bottom line. God must have it in for GIA.

Although it's Memorial Day weekend and the New York Stock Exchange is closed, she goes on-line and logs onto Bloomberg to see how GIA is doing in world markets. The early Tokyo screen shows GIA sharply lower, and the shares of GIA's Japanese and Korean partners in UnivCom are falling out of bed.

She watches until it's time to go across to her clients' lanai for a working breakfast. By then, Bernard Shaw has alighted from a chopper and is intently questioning a Pima County deputy. There are still no leads, no suspects: nothing. Just before she turns off the set, the screen switches to canned footage of an Alabama snake-handling rite. Lucy's finger pauses on the remote. She thinks she's experiencing déjà vu: something about this scene is familiar.

She catches the Saturday-afternoon flight out of Honolulu, having persuaded her clients to extricate themselves gradually, to start their withdrawal by inviting voluntary attrition, and saving the Mississippi and Florida parks for last. You never can tell; the two Senate committee chairmen are elderly, and it's not out of the question that the actuarial tables might kick in with the same deadly efficiency with which fate is cleaning out Individuality's locker.

She lays over at LAX at the same Marriott as before, this time intentionally. If everything goes as scheduled, she should be home by suppertime the next day, and the upcoming week is relatively free. She orders room service and a full range of newspapers and settles down.

As she's plowing through the *Los Angeles Times*, she comes upon a sidebar that sets chimes ringing ever so faintly in the back of her mind, a capsule history of the X Lazy 9 Ranch. The original buildings had been razed after the war to make way for the present handsome adobe complex, based on designs by Frank Lloyd Wright. In 1986, the property, famous for its hunting and fishing, had been sold by the family that had owned it since the 1880s to the present owner, a Houston-based operator of upmarket resort properties, who enlarged and expanded the facilities to accommodate up to a hundred guests in total luxury at rates ranging upward of a thousand dollars a day. The ranch was a favorite venue of groups of the sort that the late Chadbourne Tinkry had addressed on the eve of his death.

The sidebar is illustrated with a photograph of the wide adobe gates of the ranch, surmounted by a handsomely worked wrought-iron cartouche with the famous brand—an upright X and a supine 9. There's something familiar about this, Lucy thinks: I've seen that cartouche somewhere, I remember those tall white adobe gateposts, that curiously bent cottonwood off in the right background. And then, floating loosely to the surface of her mind, is a phrase she associates with the X Lazy 9 but can't get a fix on: it begins "have a . . ."—that much she can recall. But have a what? Have a nice day?

You haven't got time for this, she tells herself sternly, putting the paper aside. Her thoughts turn to the problems of Matuwa-san. Probably the best place to start, she thinks, is with the soft underbelly of the business press, *The New York Times.* She makes an entry on her computer datebook to set up a lunch for the following week at the Four Seasons. The X Lazy 9 is soon forgotten.

— III —
"Another steamer, it looks like," says the woman from Ernst and Young, gazing out the conference window onto the air high over Sixth Avenue. "This has been some summer!"

No one answers. Half the people sitting around the table have dozed off, including Lucy.

The accountant starts to burble something more about the hottest August on record when the phone on the polished Georgian sideboard rings.

"Aw, shit," mumbles the Merrill Lynch guy sitting nearest to the phone. He rubs his eyes and heaves himself out of his seat.

It's been a long night here at Hackins, Sparkin & Blake. At the eleventh hour, a Swiss bank acting for a Monaco trust came in with a demand for some modifications in the subordinated adjustable debentures. As in all deals as large and complex as this one, a domino effect ensued: changing any one element necessarily affected every other element in the vast corporate and legal calculus of the exchange offer, so it was almost 5 a.m. New York time when the final necessary consent was secured, grudgingly, from Zurich, and the five-hundred-page document detailing the offer could be sent to the law firm's word-processing center for retyping.

Lucy checks her watch. It's almost 7:30. The retype should be coming back upstairs for a last read-through before being transmitted to the printer and the relevant regulatory authorities. They're running out of

time. The UnivCom exchange offer has to be up and running before the
Euromarkets gear down for their annual August vacations.

She looks out the window. Across Sixth Avenue, the marquee of the
Radio City Music Hall is dark, but the early morning is already alive
with the sounds of Manhattan tuning itself to concert pitch. She can tell
from the dirty oyster sky that it's going to be another scorcher. She
longs to be back in Maine; just the thought of the cool Atlantic takes
a few degrees off her mental temperature.

Well, with any luck, by nightfall she should be. She has a noon lunch
at Alliance Capital, which owns over a million shares of Honamara
Holdings in its Japan funds, along with $60 million in various issues
of UnivCom Eurodollar convertibles and units. A meeting is scheduled
for either side of the lunch, one at *Forbes* and the other at *Business
Week*, to introduce Honamara's new CEO to the American business
press. There will be questions about the offer, and Lucy wants to be
letter-perfect down to the last dotted *i* and crossed *t*. The Japanese,
she's learned, will claim that their English is perfect and will insist on
working from the English-language offering circular, but the fact is, their
English is not that good, and Lucy wants to be in a position to gobble
up any fumbles. When she was at GIA, it was mostly selling the vision
thing, but with Honamara, it's 90 percent linguistic damage control:
"What Mr. Mitsuka *means* to say is . . ." Still, she thinks she ought to
make the 4 p.m. Boston shuttle.

As for the UnivCom offer, it ought to be boilerplate from here on out.
She's glad it's over. She hasn't been entirely comfortable hawkeyeing a
Mannerman deal on another client's behalf. And this one is quintes-
sential Mannerman, is it ever! "When in doubt about the Street's mood,"
he's always said, "give 'em action and complication!"

"Action" and "complication" are mainly what this new financing is
about, Lucy knows, even though "commercial utility and administrative
and financial efficiency" are claimed to be the purpose of the transac-
tions elaborated in the thick document that the twenty-odd accountants,
lawyers and investment bankers scattered around the conference room
have labored all night to put to bed. But Mannerman needs to do something. The old love affair between GIA and Wall Street is cooling.
Individuality's had another belly flop: first Betti Jo Barnum, then Chadbourne Tinkry, and now Barnum's replacement, whose ratings were

building nicely, has been arrested for soliciting a twelve-year-old girl in the ladies' room of a Denver hotel. Moreover, Tinkry's proved impossible to replace, and the rumor is that Mannerman's thinking about biting a $100 million bullet and going after Limbaugh, which will be read as a major admission of defeat.

Absently, she runs a finger across the cover page of the fat bundle of typescript on the table before her. How many trees for this one? she thinks. "The corporate form of recombinant DNA" is how it is described by the tough-mouthed woman calling the shots for Hackins, Sparkin & Blake, GIA's counsel on the exchange offer. More like a "shell game" or three-card monte is Lucy's opinion. What's been concocted is an investment banker's dream, and small wonder—what with Herby Lamond as trail boss.

A $27 *billion* exchange offer like this means *mucho* payola to investment bankers, lawyers and accountants, to what Spuds calls "the better class of parasite." UnivCom is to be "restructured": who owns how much of which part of the vast combine and in what form will be significantly modified. Parts of UnivCom are being exchanged for other parts, and still others are being recapitalized with newer, more exotic pieces of paper. Basically, as one skeptical money manager has told Lucy, "Humpty Dumpty's being taken apart and put back together. Let's just hope that at the end of the day, there won't be any pieces left lying around unaccounted for."

The finance houses will reap handsome commissions from soliciting exchanges and consents. The traders' hearts will be gladdened by the possibilities for swaps, strips and straddles; there will be enough of these to keep every beavering analyst and arbitrageur on the Street at the computer for a decade. All told, the "parasites" could be looking at upward of a billion dollars in fees.

The Merrill Lynch guy who answered the phone gestures with the handset at the Lamond & Co. partner across the table.

"It's for you. Your office."

Merrill Lynch and Lamond & Co. are co-managing the offer, coordinating the efforts of a global syndicate of several hundred firms: banks and finance houses domiciled in thirty-one countries. For this, the two firms will split fees exceeding $112 million.

The Lamond partner grins balefully, looks at his watch and shrugs.

"Later than usual," he remarks. "God help us if he wants to change anything!"

Everyone in the conference room knows what he's talking about. It's happened every morning this week. Technically, Lamond may be on vacation in East Hampton—he keeps the last week of July and the first week of August sacrosanct and inviolate for his two grandchildren's annual visit from Seattle—but he's hardly left the room in spirit. For the past week, he's been micromanaging by phone, calling twenty times a day, beginning at first light, with for-instances and revisions. It's his much-publicized habit to rise with the sun and putt for a half hour or so on the fourth green at Maidstone, which is just a couple of hundred yards from his summer home. He's told the *Times* business section that he gets his best ideas on the putting green, that putting is like high finance: a subtle business in which you have to take into account every last break and angle.

The Lamond partner takes the phone. He listens for a moment, his expression growing more grave by the second, and then suddenly he emits what sounds like a sob. His well-jowled face seems to melt and run right down the rumpled front of his stylishly striped shirt as he slumps back against the phone console.

Don't tell me the damn Dutch are balking at the eleventh hour, Lucy thinks.

The Lamond partner hangs up and looks wildly around at the others in the conference room.

"You're not gonna believe this," he croaks, "but the Old Man's been killed! Shot dead while he was putting. Dead on the fourth green. At Maidstone!"

There's a sharp collective gasp.

"It gets worse—" The young man breaks off. He's having trouble making himself say what must come next. As the others in the room watch, aghast, he pulls himself together and says very slowly. "The Old Man's grandson? Seven years old? The apple of his eye? You know?"

"Yes," says someone.

"They blew him away too!"

The room's reaction defines "stunned silence." It's as if everyone in the room has been felled by a single blow, so enveloping is the shock. For a long minute, they just sit there staring at each other. Then someone gets up and moves to the door. One of the Ernst and Young people asks, "You guys got a tube around here?" Half a minute later, everyone is down the hall, clustered around the 36-inch set in the partners' lounge.

When they tune in, NBC is transmitting a straight-down view of the crime scene from a News Four chopper. The green is crowded with police of both sexes, some in plainclothes, others uniformed. The bodies have already been removed, but outlines have been chalked on the grass, oddly white against the mottled rich green. The heads of the outlined bodies lie close together, the feet of the larger point back toward the fourth tee, of the smaller toward an inlet which the announcer identifies as Hook Pond, beyond which, as the camera pans up, one can see the beach and the sea. As the chopper gains altitude, the camera's vision enlarges to take in the whole neighborhood; sweeping around, it focuses briefly on the splendid east-curving scythe of dunes and beach, then on the pond, edged by the great lawns of the sprawling grand "cottages," on the fairways and greens of the two Maidstone courses, on the distant steeples of East Hampton rising above the trees, on the handsome spread of the clubhouse and its grounds and finally on a high, many-winged shingled structure, with a large swimming pool and a ten-nis court, that the telecaster identifies as the "mansion" of the slain financier—before launching into a breathless recapitulation of the net worth of the people who dwell in these fine houses.

Lucy finds herself thinking: God, what a beautiful day! The mere sight of the ocean, crisply furrowed by lines of breaking combers, fills her with a yearning for Maine. She hates the Hamptons, but this summer morning is pluperfect, the way it can be in late summer out there, cloudless and warm and bright, not a day for violence and death.

On-screen, the *Today* show is back in the studio. Katie Couric is saying that, as far as is known, Herbert Lamond left the house, accom-panied by his grandson Johnny, just after the sun came up—around 6:15—and that the slayings presumably took place shortly thereafter. The few people about at that hour, a *Times* home deliverer, an elderly couple taking their daily constitutional, various Maidstone employees, don't remember hearing shots, because according to a ballistics expert, the type of weapon used in the killing—assumed to be a high-powered sporting rifle, pending analysis of bullet fragments by the FBI ballistics laboratory—would have made a report clearly audible to anyone within a quarter-mile radius.

The point from which the shots were fired was still anyone's guess. Probably from the south, toward the beach, possibly from a thicket off to the left of the fifth fairway. From that direction, the steady drumming of the incoming sea might have smothered the sound of the shots. Possible, but a stretch.

This is absolutely unbelievable, Lucy thinks. Herby Lamond was what he was. A bit of a blowhard, perhaps, a bit of a hypocrite, a man who always went for the main chance, but *around*, seldom *over* anyone who might be in the way. Basically, as Spuds says, a parasite, a leech. Take away the zeros and what've you got? Nobody—not someone you murder! And what about the child! What kind of a psychopath shoots a seven-year-old boy in cold blood?

As Lucy watches, a really troubling thought steals to the forefront of her mind. Barnum, Tinkry, now Lamond. Each murdered, each associated with UnivCom. A common link. Is there someone out there who— like the French Minister of Culture—hates its vast web, hates it for what it's doing to culture, to civility, to values and standards? Of course, Lucy thinks, but a killer? If so, is everyone prominently associated with UnivCom at risk? This is an angle the FBI and others are bound to explore.

On-screen, it's being reported that Lamond's funeral is expected to be held in a few days in Manhattan, probably at St. Thomas's Church on Fifth Avenue, where the slain financier was a pillar of the vestry. Lucy can picture it: a real trophy funeral, an honor guard of TV cameras and celebrity watchers formed on the sidewalk to watch the great and famous gather, the neo-Gothic splendors inside packed with magnates and dignitaries of industry, definitely an occasion to be seen and recorded at. Mannerman will probably be a speaker. Grover's no doubt already hard at work with his Roget's and his Bartlett's.

The initial shock is losing its hold on the group clustered around the television. Someone thinks of breakfast. Coffee and tea, pastries and rolls appear. The revised exchange circular arrives back from the word-processing center. The people reassembled around the conference-room table remind each other that there's a job to be finished, a deal to be done. "Herbert Lamond would have wanted it this way," someone intones piously. All hands fall to work. By nightfall, Lucy is back in Paster's Point.

$=\mathrm{IV}=$ During the first week following the shootings, the only hard information to emerge is that the weapon used against Herbert Lamond was a .303-caliber sporting rifle. Unfortunately, this is a popular sporting caliber; more than three thousand rifles chambered for it have been produced by custom and off-the-rack gunsmiths since its introduction by Winchester back in 1966. The FBI is tracing these, but given the way guns circulate these days, it's conjectural that the search will be fruitful.

When Lucy reads this in *Time*, she sits up.

Baker owned a .303.

Or did he?

Lucy thinks she recalls his saying that one particular rifle was his favorite among all his sporting arms. "Light, but with a real knockout punch." She thinks—she's certain—that it was a .303 he was talking about. She even remembers where the rifle hung in the gun cabinet at Two Moose.

Or was it some other caliber? No, she's sure. By now, she doesn't get numbers wrong. It was a .303.

Still, to make certain, she searches out the inventory of Baker's effects that his lawyers sent her after his death and looks under "sporting and other gear." Eight guns are listed: a brace of matched 12-gauge Purdey shotguns, the 16-bore he shot with at La Clemenza, a Weatherby .454 rifle, a Winchester .270 and three handguns: a Ruger .357 Magnum, an S&W .32 Police Special—and the .22 Colt Woodsman which is in her closet.

No .303.

And yet, damn it, Lucy knows he had one! Eyes closed, she ransacks her usually reliable and powerful visual memory until it yields a picture of Baker's gun rack. Yes, there were nine guns, not eight. No—she thinks—there were ten! Ten in all: six long guns and four handguns, not three. She can picture them in her mind: at the top, the pair of English shotguns, racked stock to muzzle; below them, in descending caliber, the 16-gauge Winchester, then the three rifles, the .454, the .303 and the .270, and across the bottom, on pegs, the pistols: the Woodsman, the .357 Magnum, the .32 Police Special like her father's and . . . and . . . yes! The fourth handgun was a big brother to the Magnum, a .45-caliber—no, a *.44*-caliber Ruger.

Ten in all. And certainly three rifles! More information floods back. The Weatherby was used only for really big game, in Africa for elephant and Cape buffalo, in Alaska for Kodiak and polar bear. The .303, custom-made in New York by Griffin & Howe, Baker's favorite gun-smiths, he used for larger horned game, including the rams. The .270 was for deer and antelope.

She goes back and checks the inventory again.

No .303 caliber is listed.

Perhaps they made a mistake, she thinks. She pages through Baker's will, finds what she's looking for and calls Nova Scotia information. Be listed, she prays, then dials the Halifax number she's been given.

There's no answer.

The next day and the next, Lucy calls the Halifax number repeatedly without success. Finally, on the third day, when she's running out of time, about to leave for Seattle, she gives it one last shot and this time there's an answer.

"Is that Mr. Lewis Morland?" she asks.

"Who's this?"

"My name is"—Lucy hesitates, then, for no thought-through reason, says, "Martin, Irene Martin. You don't know me, Mr. Morland."

"Mr. Morland doesn't know anybody. At least, *that* Mr. Morland, Mr. *Lewis* Morland, that is, doesn't know anybody. Mr. Lewis Morland is dead. This is his brother Peter. How can I help you, Ms. Martin?"

Good heavens, Lucy hasn't expected anything like this. Another death! "Well, I don't know if you can. I'm so sorry to hear about your brother. When did Mr. Morland pass away?"

"A couple of months ago: end of May. Stomach cancer. Anyway, Ms. Martin, what can I do for you?"

"A corporate client of our firm—I work in financial public relations —wishes to make a present of a fine sporting rifle to a valued customer, something really out of the ordinary. It happens that my senior associate was talking to a lawyer friend in Philadelphia last week, and he mentioned our dilemma, and his friend, Mr. . . . I believe it's Dalrymple, mentioned that your brother had come into some very fine sporting rifles via a bequest about two years ago, I believe the deceased's name was Baker, and at the time Mr. Dalrymple spoke with your brother, he— your late brother, that is—seemed uncertain as to the bequest, that is, whether he might prefer to have the guns forwarded to a New York dealer for immediate disposition, but in the end the guns were sent to your brother." Lucy's web of semi-truths spins and spins. "That's why I'm calling."

"That's quite a mouthful, Ms. Martin. As it happens, I do know about the guns. Lewie had them and now I have them. Do you have a particular one in mind, or would you prefer that I tell you what I've got?"

"Well, as a matter of fact, the one our client seems to have in mind is a .303-caliber rifle with an engraved bolt assembly and a hand-checkered walnut stock—I'm reading from a description we got from Mr. Dalrymple—made in 1967 by Griffin and Howe." This is yet another fib, concocted from equal parts of recollection and whole cloth— Dalrymple certainly sent Lucy no such description—but it's worth the chance.

"A .303, you say?"

"Yes."

There's a pause—at the other end Morland is obviously checking something—before he says, "No such luck, Ms. Martin, I'm plumb out of .303s."

"You had several?"

"No, I mean I don't have any. In fact, and I'm looking at this old notebook of Lewie's where he kept his records, including an itemized list of his arsenal, there's no mention of a .303. The other Baker guns are here. Let's see, there's a .454 Weatherby, a .270—"

"No .303, you're sure?"

Morland finishes reading off the list. It's the one Lucy got from Dalrymple. She knows there's no .303 on it.

"No, ma'am," he says when he finishes. "No .303."

"That's incredible!" Lucy kicks herself mentally for not keeping her surprise out of her voice.

"Maybe, but them's the facts, ma'am."

"Mr. Morland, I'm sorry to have troubled you," Lucy says, back in control of herself. "I imagine my associate misunderstood something Mr. Dalrymple said. You know how men are about guns."

"That I do. I had my first rifle in the cradle."

"Oh, are you a guide like your brother?"

"In a manner of speaking. I'm what they call a location scout."

"A location scout?"

"For movies. I help find the right place to shoot what the script calls for. Generally speaking, that is. Sometimes you find a location that's so ripe you rejigger the script to fit the place. I guess you might say that most of the time I fit the scene to the crime, but sometimes I fit the crime to the scene, if you follow."

"That must be fascinating work."

"It has its moments."

"I'm sure it does. Well, Mr. Morland, I apologize for troubling you—"

"No problem. Listen, maybe Baker sold the .303 himself—you could check with Griffin and Howe in New York. From what Lewie told me about Baker, it's likely he'd've done anything like that through them. Anyway, I hope you run it down. It must be some kind of rifle, at least that's what Lewie said. He was dying to get his hands on it and was disappointed when it didn't turn up."

"Why? Was there something special about it? Did your brother say anything?"

"Matter of fact, he did. Apparently Baker invented a suppressor for it that actually worked for big game, although he had to increase the load to compensate."

"A suppressor? I don't understand these terms."

"Most people call it a silencer. Usually it'll kill the report but also mess up the accuracy and muzzle velocity. Not this one, or so Lewie said. He told me Baker invented the damn thing so he could get in a second shot."

Lucy can hardly speak. The hand holding the receiver is shaking. "Well, thank you very much, Mr. Morland," she finally says. It takes all her self-control to manage her voice. "Again, I'm sorry to have troubled you."

Lucy sits down heavily. It can't be, she thinks.

Yes, it can!

Or not. It's possible, isn't it, that Baker took the .303 to Africa with him, and that it's now at the bottom of Lake Kivu? Of course it's possible!

Indeed, it's more than possible; it's likely.

Isn't it?

Barnum, Tinkry, Lamond—and now the .303. To account for the first three murders leaves a wide choice: someone out there among the tens of thousands who hate UnivCom—or Mannerman or GIA for that matter. But add in the .303 and the field narrows exponentially.

In Lucy's mind, it narrows to one.

No, no, no! It's merely an overresonant coincidence, she tells herself. Didn't the FBI spokesman say there were several thousand rifles of that caliber in existence? Just as, she tells herself in the next breath, there were thousands of Mannlicher-Carcano .30-.06s—but only one Lee Harvey Oswald.

By now, she supposes, the authorities will have tracked down and run ballistics tests on all of the .303s they can locate, which, just for argument's sake, she tells herself, may amount to as high as 90-odd percent of all the rifles known to have been manufactured. That will still leave a great many untraced.

Exactly 643, she soon learns. The source of this information is Lucy's father. The Chief has former colleagues who've kept their lines to the Bureau open; it's one of them who comes up with the fact that roughly 9 percent of the .303s of all makes known to have been manufactured remain unanswered for.

Chief Preston's taking a real interest in the Lamond murders, bringing to bear the same intensity he'd earlier expended on O. J. Simpson. He and his old police and FBI chums have a regular phone bee going. The dismissive analysis they'd heaped on the LAPD in the earlier case is now reserved for their successors at the FBI. "These clowns couldn't catch a cold," they wheeze gleefully to each other.

The connection Lucy can't help making, all leading to a man who died three years earlier, is faint and farfetched. Could anyone other than her begin to see it? For instance, if she were to raise it with the

Chief, he'd laugh her out of the house. Take the the silencer-suppressor mentioned by Peter Morland. To her it's a remarkable and meaningful fact that makes sense of the curious truth that no one heard gunshots in connection with the Lamond murders. But if—as is her habit with everything—Lucy in the next instant second-guesses herself, if she's perfectly logical and clear-minded about it, it's equally probable that Baker might have passed on the ideas for such plans to someone else, either back in the days when he had his hunt-and-fish column or during those long hours on the Internet discussing the best caliber for oryx or which lures worked well with steelheads.

And yet her intuitions won't go away. She simply has to find out more. But how's she to do that?

The next day, an idea comes to her. She takes down the box containing the .22 Colt Woodsman. The name and number of a Utica moving and storage house are on the label. Nothing ventured, nothing gained, she thinks, as she dials. If they sound suspicious, she can simply hang up.

Once again posing as Irene Martin, whom she's now made into a paralegal at Dalrymple's firm, she asks to speak to whoever's in charge of document storage. When he comes on, she tells him what she needs. A matter of estate tax, she says, and afterward scolds herself for once again giving in to her tendency to gild the lily.

He assures her there'll be no problem. They'll have everything out and waiting for her. Three days later, having cleared her schedule, Lucy's in Utica.

At the storage company warehouse, she's shown to a large cubicle where some forty cartons holding the residue of the life of H. A. Baker, deceased, are neatly stacked on pallets. What had she expected? she wonders. This is going to take some time.

It takes her three days, in fact, to go through box after box, file folder after file folder, album after album, scrapbook after scrapbook, journal after journal, page by page by page. She can only put in about six hours before her eyes grow bleary with checking and double-checking. Her art historical studies have taught her to be thorough and methodical, to make sure she looks carefully at everything, not to bypass or overlook anything, to give luck, happenstance and serendipity every opportunity.

Lucy's never lonely on the road, not as long as there's some place—not a gym!—where she can go off by herself and think through the business she's involved in. In this regard, Utica turns out to be an agreeable surprise, a compact city, pleasant and leafy and well furnished, with plenty of good walks, especially along the Mohawk River and the old New York barge canal, where Lucy strolls uninterrupted as she ponders the terrible implications of H. A. Baker. There are several perfectly decent restaurants and an excellent small museum, the Munson-Williams-Proctor Institute, whose interesting collections, housed in a Philip Johnson building, include a series of allegorical paintings by Thomas Cole, the Hudson River painter, who's one of Lucy's favorites. In late August, the air-conditioned galleries are relatively deserted, and when she's not walking out-of-doors, she can find solitude on a bench in front of the Coles. According to a guidebook in her hotel room, as recently as 1970 Utica was a bustling little industrial city of almost 100,000; now the population's down to 75,000 and the city's economy is based largely on Adirondacks tourism and a regional campus of the State University of New York. Is this how it will turn out for Bakerton? she wonders.

She goes through the book cartons first. There's nothing much there: sporting books, old plate volumes, biographies and travel books; very little fiction except for thrillers, which she knew Baker devoured. In a box packed with old magazines and stationery—piled in a way that suggests to Lucy they must have been found together elsewhere than on bookshelves—are five thrillers: three by John le Carré—*The Spy Who Came In from the Cold*, *The Little Drummer Girl* and *The Night Manager*—as well as two published in the year of Baker's disappearance: *Vanishing Act* by Thomas Perry and Lawrence Block's *A Long Line of Dead Men*.

Lucy's read the le Carré novels, but she doesn't know the books by Block and Perry, so she slings these into her shoulder bag. She can skim them tonight in her hotel room.

Two cartons contain folders of miscellaneous correspondence dating up to a month before Baker's death, now almost three years ago. In one of these, Lucy happens upon a letter, from just about the time BEECO was sold, requesting him to sign off on the proposed unitization of certain oil royalties in which he holds a tiny fractional interest; the signed consent, the letter closes, is to be returned using an enclosed prepaid Federal Express waybill.

The name of the law firm, preprinted on the waybill, is Gunch & Hosmeer. It's an unusual, ugly name and Lucy's sure she's heard it before. Where? She jots it down on her legal pad and moves on. By the end of the first day, her pad is half filled with notes of interesting facts and omissions that may mean something.

Most of them turn out to mean nothing, go nowhere. But when she taps into Nexis from her laptop, requesting a search for references to Gunch & Hosmeer back to the date of Baker's death, what she learns sends a real chill through her. It was a Federal Express waybill prepaid by Gunch & Hosmeer that "Satan" had used to send $15,000 to the young man who had slashed Betti Jo Barnum's throat!

Which means that "Satan" could be . . . ?

No! Don't be ridiculous, she tells herself. The man is dead!

So what exactly does this waybill signify, then?

Nothing—that's what! Unless she can compare the serial number on Baker's waybill with Satan's: it means nothing. Stop overexciting yourself, she remonstrates. All you have so far is a wild hunch inside a crazy guess.

She stretches out on the bed and flips through the two thrillers she's brought from the warehouse. After about an hour, she's got the main idea, and the now-familiar chill is back. Thrillers? she reflects. Or how-to manuals—because the Block novel is about someone faking his own death, the Perry about someone doing the same with professional help, and now her mind is chasing itself in wild circles.

OK, she tells herself, this may *mean* something, but does it *prove* anything? You have to have known Baker to see how it all might fit and Baker's—

Baker's dead, isn't he? Isn't he!

In Lucy's mind, the line joining the dots emerges more clearly by the second, and the dots themselves glow brighter. Spread across her mental landscape, they shine like neon, so bright and insistent and disruptive that it is well past midnight before she can make herself go to sleep.

The next morning, however, reason has regained the upper hand. As she's showering, she tells herself that she ought to chuck this. She's just being . . . is "paranoid" the right word? Baker took the .303 with him to Africa, along with the silencer; they would have been in the same gun case, wouldn't they? As for Baker's choice of thrillers, well, it was just an accident that two about false disappearances came out the same year, but both authors were well known and Baker owned other thrillers by them.

As she dresses, Lucy decides to make this her last day.

At the warehouse, she begins with a large crate containing his computer along with several file boxes filled with 3.5-inch floppy disks. She flips through the disk files quickly. Most seem to be system and installation floppies for various software programs that are presumably on the hard disk. In one box are a dozen or so diskettes labeled, in Baker's distinctive spidery printing, "corres," "fish and game," "World Wildlife Fund" and so on.

She lugs the computer over to an outlet, plugs it in and boots it up. In short order, the DOS prompt appears. That's strange, she thinks. Baker used a number of Windows programs; the machine would normally go straight into Windows. She knows it does, she's worked on it herself. She types "win" and waits. Nothing happens. She presses Alt-Ctrl-Del to reboot the machine and types "win.exe." at the prompt. Nothing happens: the monitor is blank save for the C:> prompt and the blinking cursor.

Again she reboots. This time, at the DOS prompt, she checks the hard disk.

There's nothing there. No files, no applications, no programs, no nothing. Apparently it's been completely erased.

Now, this makes no sense at all. Baker used his computer a lot, both in-house and on-line. Why would he trash all his files and programs before setting off for Africa?

One answer's obvious. If he knew he wouldn't be coming back, he would want to cover his electronic tracks.

You're crazy, says one voice in her head. No, you're not, rebuts another.

She supposes it's conceivable that somehow the hard disk was erased by accident, that it crashed, that Baker didn't have time to recover the lost files, that some freak mischance occurred when Two Moose was being packed up. Possible, but farfetched. This time her intuition prevails over her tendency to rationalize. Anyway, there'll surely be a computer store hereabouts where she can pick up software that will let her recover anything that's accidentally glitched out of sight.

She sets aside the diskette files. She'll get back to them later. If she can't restore the hard disk, she can run them through her laptop.

Now she turns to Baker's photograph albums, journals and scrapbooks. She'd seen a number of these already, on her weekends with Baker, but her interest had been mainly courteous, not curious. This time she scrutinizes each photo carefully.

Most of these are carefully annotated as to where, when and whom. In a number of them a balding, squat and swarthy man is identified as Lewis Morland. His and Baker's reciprocal body language suggests a relationship that's equally personal and professional; Morland is confidant as well as guide. If Morland had lived, she can't help thinking, he could have really helped her. What she lacks is insight into the Baker she realizes she barely knew: the stalker-hunter-killer.

In the album for 1991, she comes across a photograph of Baker with a group of middle-aged men brandishing lever-action carbines like characters in a Remington painting. Despite their confident, macho smiles, they look ridiculous in their oversized Stetsons, fringed vests and chaps. City mice passing as desert rats. The caption identifies the other men as an Undersecretary of Commerce and the CEO of a major copper company. It's datelined "Caballeros del Cielo Easter Roundup, Vail, Ariz, 4/6/91."

It's the background that engages Lucy's attention. Tall white gates, a cattlecatcher on which the men are balancing uneasily in their cowboy boots, a strangely twisted tree in the near distance, a now-familiar cartouche.

The X Lazy 9 Ranch, she thinks. She *was* right when, watching the report of Chadbourne Tinkry's murder, she thought she'd seen that gate before!

She comes across the X Lazy 9 several times in other albums. Baker had been there a good half dozen times. With his instinct for terrain, he'd have known the place like the back of his hand. Known where to lurk, watching in the dark. Lucy'd followed him through the high, close pine forest surrounding Two Moose; the man could move as silently and stealthily as an Indian.

Suspicion is hardening into conviction like a tumor. Here and there she encounters empty spaces in the albums. In most cases, the photos have simply come loose from their mounts, but one or two seem to have disappeared altogether. She scribbles the details of the captions for these on her pad.

The journals are not much more than extended footnotes to the albums—accounts of various hunting and fishing sorties, recapitulations of catches and game bags, reports of weather conditions. Nothing here that she can see.

The scrapbooks are much the same, although there are a couple of breaks in sequence that cause her to pay attention. Do they mean anything? For instance, in an album devoted to Baker's occasional pieces, there's a two-week break in the sequence of pasted-in monthly columns he wrote for *Outdoor Sportsman* in the mid-1980s. Why? She examines the album closely; it looks like the page on which the missing columns would have been pasted has been carefully excised with a sharp knife. She makes a note of the missing dates. It will be easy enough to find the columns in the Portland Library or at Bowdoin. Maybe I'm being silly, she keeps thinking, but there's an investigatory logic which she's now committed to pursue to its end and which allows no scrimping on details.

Then there's something else: the break in the sequence of columns covers the same date as the hand-printed caption under one of the missing photographs. Lucy checks her pad: "May 14, 1986, Sweetwater, Tex, HAB, Bob Dubow, Frank Sinclair."

Going through Baker's written and photographic remains uses up the whole of Lucy's energy for today. She takes the afternoon off, visits the Munson-Williams-Proctor and her friends the Cole paintings, along with a Pollock that's also pretty wonderful. She walks along the riverbank, imagining the countryside as it must have been when the Erie Canal was dug, wishing she could whoosh herself back through time to see it. At the end of the afternoon, she walks over to the SUNY campus. As she expects, the college bookstore carries an impressive array of software. She buys Windows 3.1 and a file-recovery program that the young man in charge assures her is the hottest thing going, capable of "retrieving Lazarus from the dead." She has an early dinner at a sushi place near the college, walks back to her hotel and watches *Seinfeld* and *E.R.* in her room until she can't keep her eyes open.

She returns to the warehouse the next morning. Her new software and her laptop are in her shoulder bag. She reinstalls Windows on Baker's computer, then installs the file-recovery application and sets to work.

It's a bust. She draws blank after blank. Doubtless some computer whiz could manipulate this stuff and possibly dredge up something, but that's not Lucy. She plugs in her laptop and turns to the three clear plastic file boxes which contain Baker's floppies.

Frustrated by her failures with Baker's computer, Lucy's tempted to skip, but habits well learned die hard, and she examines each disk carefully, running it through File Manager and checking its contents for anomalies—anomalies that she can identify, that is. Again she finds herself wishing herself a more adept hacker.

Then it suddenly doesn't seem to matter, because on a disk labeled "Undo," she hits pay dirt.

Lucy's familiar with Undo. It's a backup you create mainly because you're told to by a popular disk-checking utility that she along with thousands of others uses. It has something to do with "corrupted data strings," whatever they are.

The names borne by Baker's Undo files mean nothing to Lucy—except one. There, nestled incongruously among files with ".bk" and ".ini" suffixes, is a file called "Qdata1." Lucy knows "Qdata1" as well as she knows her Social Security number.

Lucy's a "Quickenhead," an addict of the Intuit financial-management program with which she manages her personal and business life. Quicken keeps Lucy's bank balances, maintains her tax records, sorts her bills and pays them electronically, invoices her clients. Lucy—and a lot of people she knows and has talked with—can't imagine life without Quicken: "Once you start using the damn thing," one friend's remarked, "you don't see how you ever lived without it."

Lucy no longer thinks of Quicken as a computer program. It's a central fact of her daily routine, it's a friend. So user-friendly and well designed is the program that Lucy is by now, well, *fanatical* about keeping it up-to-date, about inputting every single datum of her financial activity, and so are the other Quickenheads she knows.

Quicken isn't a robot, however. It doesn't back itself up automatically. It asks its users to execute the backup command. Lucy supposes it's another way the program keeps in touch.

The thing is, however, that now and then, if she's hurried or distracted, if the phone rings, say, while she's working in Quicken, or the pasta water starts to boil over, or the in-flight movie comes on, Lucy won't bother to hunt up her special Quicken backup disk, she'll simply back up on whatever floppy disk happens to be in her backup drive.

Unless modified, which she's certainly never bothered to do, Quicken backup files are labeled "Qdata," with "Qdata1" being of most recent date. That's what Lucy's looking at now. Short of access to a computerized diary, Lucy can imagine no richer source of information about a person's life than his or her Quicken files, so it's with hugely mounting excitement that she copies the "Qdata1" file to her laptop *and* to an extra floppy.

Back at the hotel, she orders dinner from room service and goes to work on her laptop.

This file was backed up approximately three months before Baker's death, which means there will likely have been subsequent activity in Baker's accounts, even from Africa—with a modem and a laptop, a person can lead as varied and full an electronic life in deepest Rwanda as in brightest Manhattan—but this is all Lucy's got.

She breaks out the entries over an eighteen-month period, roughly, going back to the episode at "21," and runs through a short list on her yellow pad of the obvious entries to look for. She finds no entry for a deposit from Griffin & Howe, so if Baker sold his .303, it wasn't to the New York gunsmiths with whom he religiously, virtually exclusively, had done business for thirty years. Which doesn't mean he mightn't have sold the rifle elsewhere. Or given it away. After all, it occurs to her, it wasn't specifically mentioned in his will. Only the Woodsman bequeathed to her was. She still thinks the likeliest answer is that he took it with him to Africa, intending to use it later. Elsewhere.

She next studies the record of transfers out of Baker's various accounts, at banks in Philadelphia and New York, a cash-management account at Merrill Lynch and a managed-investment account at a New York firm called Bernhard & Co. In the ten months before the last entry

in the backup file, starting some sixty days after his angry return from
Italy, his records show an almost continuous flurry of activity involving
very large sums.

Almost four million dollars, drawn from all three accounts, is shown
as paid to the order of "GK-CHUR," whatever that is. He has borrowed
eight million dollars against the securities in the managed-investment
account; the drawdowns on this loan match up by date with credits in
the Merrill Lynch cash-management account. From various accounts,
significant sums are shown as having been disbursed to Loomis Associates for "BEE/PR," presumably Baker's code name for his short-lived
PR campaign against Mannerman. Who the hell is Loomis Associates?
Lucy knows every serious public relations shop outside the Third World,
and she's damned if she's ever heard of one called Loomis Associates.

Using the on-screen calculator, she adds up the Loomis payments.
They total fifteen million two hundred thousand dollars and change!
Fifteen million dollars! The number the lawyer Dalrymple had used!
Fifteen million for PR? Not in a million years! Well, maybe if you
locked up Hale & Boggs or John Scanlon for a couple of years. But
some no-name firm that Lucy's never heard of? Never!

Just to be sure, she goes to the phone and calls Spuds. He's never
heard of Loomis, nor has Grover in Washington, nor has Lucy's friend
Molly in Burbank, who's just moved from PMK to do in-house PR at
Disney for Michael Ovitz.

This is totally weird, she thinks, after Molly finishes telling her a
particularly juicy anecdote about the proclivities of an English actress
that Spielberg is said to be thinking of casting as Mother Teresa. She
has to think about this.

She checks her pad a last time and sees she's skipped one question
mark. Her first run-through yields an answer, maybe: there are entries
reflecting monthly royalty payments from a Tulsa oil and gas firm on a
lease whose designation and tax number match those in the letter from
Gunch & Hosmeer. Apparently, Baker had never conveyed his interest,
which means that he probably hadn't returned any papers to anyone,
which in turn means, at the very least, that the prepaid Federal Express
waybill might not necessarily have been put to the use for which it was
intended. Which means it could have been used to send fifteen thousand
dollars in cash to a raging young man in Houston!

For the first time Lucy is fearful. Where is this taking her? No sense of imminent physical peril—not yet. She's told no one of her suspicions and searches, hasn't really thought about telling anyone. If she does, she'll obviously start with her father.

But this is leading into territory where she feels hopelessly at sea. She fears she'll go out of her mind trying to figure out what to do with what she knows.

That night she sleeps uneasily. The next morning, before heading back to the warehouse, she ticks off the last item on her pad and telephones a friend in New York who works for Hearst and asks him to dig up and Fed Ex her the two *Outdoor Sportsman* articles missing from Baker's scrapbook.

At the warehouse she saved the best for last, five cartons marked "art." She opens her late lover's artistic remains first and sorts them on the long trestle table—sketchbooks and watercolor pads in one pile, some dated but most not, ribboned and zippered folios and folders of loose watercolors, drawings, scraps and sketches in another. Baker's painting and sketching materials she sets to one side, along with framed certificates, engravings and watercolors she knows from the walls and tables at Two Moose. These are truly the leavings, she thinks. The really high-grade sporting art—the two Homer watercolors, the Ben Marshall, the Eakins and Mount oils, the Stubbs prints and the little Landseer—had been sold at auction for the benefit of the BEECO Relief Foundation. The Pleissner scenes of fishing for Atlantic salmon now hang in the lounge of the fishing camp on the Restigouche River in New Brunswick where Baker went for many years.

As Lucy meticulously goes through the piles, she becomes increasingly tired and impatient. She's anxious to move on to the next stage, whatever that is. Still, she's made a pact with her suspicions to be absolutely thorough, to examine every last scrap and shred. By lunchtime, as she picks up what must be the fiftieth pocket sketchbook she's examined, Lucy's just about had it—and there are still two piles to go!

This particular sketchbook is like the others, six by nine inches, wirebound with stiffened covers—vinyl "leather" over double-thickness cardboard—bearing the name of a Philadelphia art supply store. Only the first few pages appear to have been used—they show quick, offhand, undated watercolor impressions of men with shotguns in a field, presumably sketches for a larger painting but not one that Lucy recognizes.

The rest of the sketchbook looks blank, but Lucy, ever diligent, goes through to the back cover, then flips the book and starts in on the verso pages. On the second, she comes on something that makes the breath stop in her throat.

It's a sketch in pencil of a hydralike monster with innumerable faces. Underneath is penciled "Narcis."

The lower heads—Lucy counts thirty-one of them—are little more than blank-faced, generalized circles and ovals. Rising above these, however, like monstrous towering flowers, are three larger faces swaying above scaly, serpentlike stalks—easily recognizable faces. By the time he drew these, Lucy can guess, Baker would have contemplated his subjects so long and intently that he would have had them down pat.

Flanking the topmost head in the middle, which is slightly larger, are the unmistakable faces of the late Betti Jo Barnum and the late Chadbourne Tinkry. The topmost face is also well known to Lucy. It's Robert Carlsson.

As she studies these, she remembers the engravings of "the Seven Deadly Sins." Like the .303 rifle, they're also missing. Baker might have burned them out of pique. The thought had occurred to her. Now she's certain he didn't.

She turns to the next leaf.

This also bears an image Lucy recognizes. She's seen an earlier version before, on a sunlit balcony overlooking Lake Como, on a sparkling, happy day that might as well have been lived in another geologic era. It's mostly the same as the first one. Starving multitudes still claw at the central figure's skirts, whose miter still bears the insignia of the Individuality Channel. The outspread hands still hold "Mammon's caduceus" and a satellite dish marked with the UnivCom logo.

But the "Pope" 's face has changed. Now it's Jack Mannerman who smirks at her.

The first thing that catches Lucy's eye on the next leaf is the word "Duplicity" scrawled at the bottom. As she lifts her focus to the drawing of a two-faced demon, Lucy senses what she's going to see.

One face is instantly identifiable from the trademark winglets of hair floating above the ears. It's the late Herbert Lamond.

The other face she knows even better.

It's her own.

— V — The timing is lousy, thinks Lucy, but what choice do I have? For months she's been stewing, going this way and that, even considered dropping the whole business. When she finally has her mind made up, it turns out that today is the only day Carlsson can give her an uninterrupted two hours.

She couldn't have just walked away from her final deduction. But what should she do, to whom can she turn? She can go to the authorities with what she has, but will they find her chain of circumstantial evidence as binding as she does? And if they do—*if* they do—what then? The FBI's record is hardly good. The Unabomber is still at large. That Timothy McVeigh was captured after Oklahoma City seems sheer luck. The only time the Bureau seems to catch anyone is in the novels of Thomas Harris, and even the archfiend Hannibal Lecter is still on the loose. And if she goes to the FBI—or to any lesser agency—the odds are there'll be a leak that'll drive Baker into cover so deep he'll never be caught. The positive side is that publicity might stop him from further killing, but who's to say that some other nutcase—or several—mightn't take him for an example and pick up where he leaves off. Possibly on a more lethal scale, since who's to say that a leak across the world's media—Lucy can just imagine the headlines—couldn't inspire a whole litter of would-be Bakers.

Lucy has been thinking and thinking of talking to her father, but she's held back. If she confides in him, he'll surely tell her to go to the authorities, and that if she won't, he will. The Chief's a law-and-order man from the get-go. She's heard him on the subject of vigilantism, on what he saw when he was attached to the FBI's Atlanta office. She could try to convince him that she and he alone could somehow bring Baker to book, and the notion of embarrassing his "alma mater," with all its highfalutin high-tech crime-fighting resources, would surely appeal to him, but he'd be the first to recognize what meager resources they command.

She needs an ally. Someone with the right resources and connections, including extralegal contacts if it comes to that, to run Baker to ground and then deal with him. Someone with the kind of twisted imagination or whatever other mental qualities it takes to believe as she does. Robert Carlsson has those. Carlsson is the man to see. If there's anyone Lucy knows who commands the right fire- and airpower, it's Carlsson.

To run Baker to ground and deal with him. There's the rub. In her mind Lucy's formed a plan based on one of those thrillers of Baker's. If everything in it were to go right, she imagines, it should be possible to deal with Baker without either turning him over to the authorities or—

She can't make herself think the "or." Lucy now accepts that Baker still has a hold on her. She can still reimagine that heroic aura she saw rise like sacred flame around him during those ten minutes at "21," that epiphanic knightliness that touched the depths of her romantic soul. Later she was disappointed, and yet there had also been moments in Italy when it all seemed wonderfully right, moments that she can't help recalling with the same clarity with which she remembers the anger and cursing.

Her plan needs an ending. She needs to find a sanctuary, a place where one could set up a private Alcatraz from which escape is impossible, maybe a remote island somewhere surrounded by sharks or freezing waters. One of the "disappearance" thrillers she'd read at Baker's ended like that, with the villain being taken off to end his days chained to a wall in a blockhouse on a private island, watched over by a caretaker. Couldn't one do the same with Baker? Not kill him, not hand him over, but spirit him away to some distant, isolated place, some uncharted island or perhaps a private sanitarium in some mountain fastness?

How much would it cost? Where would the money come from? How could it be done? What would be involved in the way of transport, documents, medication? The financial and logistical problems seem insuperable, but Lucy won't let go of the notion.

Still, she needs someone who has the material resources to bring it off, who appreciates the complexities, who like her reveres the sanctity of secrets, who knows—as they say on the Street—that "a closed mouth gathers no feet." And if the plan can't be carried out and a hard choice about what to do with Baker has to be made by someone, that someone had better be ruthless enough to make a call Lucy knows she can't make.

Again, the name that pops up is Robert Carlsson. There are good reasons why he's ideal for her purposes. The first is motive: If Baker isn't stopped, Carlsson's great dream itself will die. Already it's suffered serious setbacks at Baker's bloody hands. If he isn't stopped, it's Good-bye, Cy! Which is why she's agreed, to her father's chagrin, to spend Christmas Eve in Aspen as Robert Carlsson's guest.

Until she called him a week ago, Lucy had barely seen or spoken with the mega-agent since their dinner at Morton's almost—can it have been?—four years ago. Whatever anger she felt then has long since evaporated, thanks to the same realism that tempered her reaction to Baker's raging departure from her life. She loves what she's doing now, and she knows she probably wouldn't be doing it if Carlsson hadn't forced her out of Mannerman's orbit.

Although nothing's been said or even hinted at, her instincts tell her that Carlsson's been behind some choice pieces of business that have come her way. The last time she saw him was at a top-level meeting in Atlanta with the Turner-Warner people in connection with a new public-service adjunct CNN was thinking about. Out of the blue, they hired Lucy to consult on the Wall Street implications: the fee was good, and for once the project was utterly beyond criticism. To her surprise, Carlsson had turned up in Atlanta. From his expression it was clear he agreed with Lucy's analysis: that by now, anyone with a big position in T-W was permanently fed up, essentially anesthetized, and new management should feel free to do whatever made sense as long as it fell somewhere short of betting the company. Afterward, Carlsson gave her a ride back to Washington in a T-W jet he'd commandeered. He scarcely talked to her, spent most of his time on the phone and shook hands perfunctorily when they parted company at Dulles.

What a strange man. Lucy never felt he was about to come on to her, never had the feeling that he needed to prove something to himself— like so many men she met—by covering Lucy's pale body with his own. He struck her as basically nonerotic. Perhaps some almost allergic reaction to the constant company of beautiful women and handsome men, objects of desire for millions of people, had excised his sex drive? Without, however, expunging his sexuality. Of his maleness there is no doubt; driving back to the Bel-Air Hotel after breakfast with a client in Beverly Hills, Lucy wonders what would happen if she were to come on to Carlsson. Not that she's in the least attracted to him.

She looks at the clock and sees that she's in good time to make a couple of calls, close her bags and check out. Carlsson's plane, a Falcon he got from MGM/UA, is scheduled to depart for Aspen from the Aero Services terminal at the Burbank-Glendale-Pasadena airport at 11:45 a.m. But when she crosses the hotel lobby, the concierge calls to her and waves a folded message slip.

It's from Carlsson's office. He's stuck at Universal, and takeoff has been pushed back by two hours, to 1:45. That's cutting it close, Lucy thinks. By her quick calculation, and allowing for the one-hour time difference, the plane will arrive in Aspen just before dark. It's well known that Robert Carlsson won't fly into any airport much smaller than O'Hare after sunset.

Che sarà, sarà, she thinks. She picks up the phone and dials her friend Molly's number at Disney. They were supposed to have dinner last night, strictly girl talk, but Molly had to cancel at the last minute —Ovitz is apparently on a real year-end tear—and Lucy ended up eating in her room and catching up, on cable, with a couple of movies she'd missed. To her delight—Lucy cares about her friends and keeps in touch with them—Molly's lunch has just been shifted to the following week, and they make a date for noon at a place in the Valley. By ten, Lucy's headed up into the San Fernando Mountains on her way to Burbank.

To her surprise, she's looking forward to Carlsson's annual Christmas Eve party in Aspen. When Lucy told Liz Smith about it over lunch at the Four Seasons a week ago, the columnist's eyes widened appreciably. Two days ago, Smith's column had reported: "Flying in with host and mega-agent ROBERT CARLSSON will be super-hot New York public relations whiz LUCY PRESTON." Lucy was sure Carlsson wouldn't mind—to be "itemed" in his company could only be good for business.

These parties of Carlsson's were legendary, for both the quality of the guest list and their style and inventiveness. When he invited her, Carlsson had told Lucy, "You can consider this year's blowout strictly a warm-up. Next year, I'm going to switch it to New Year's Eve and throw one that'll be the bash of both the old millennium and the new one!"

Lucy promised to save December 31, 1999.

She turns her thoughts to her upcoming presentation to Carlsson. This is unlike anything she's ever pitched before. There are gray areas, pieces of the puzzle she's unequipped to deconstruct or run down. Yet somehow she thinks Carlsson will get it, that his devious imagination, his enthusiasm for secrets and conspiracies, will yield conviction and a willingness to get involved. The problem is that for every clue, there's an opposite explanation that on the face of things destroys her "case," though each disproof goes completely against the grain of the man she's known, is loudly and forcefully contradicted by her sense of Baker and how he might act in a given situation.

For example: yes, Baker *might* have sold his beloved .303. But he wouldn't have done so and kept the other guns.

Yes, the hard disk of his computer might have been accidentally erased, but how? Baker surely didn't make mistakes like that.

And there's more damning evidence, like the Federal Express waybill prepaid by the same memorably named Tulsa law firm that figured in the Barnum killing.

And what about the rattlesnakes?

On her return to Maine from Utica, Lucy had found that her friend at Hearst had done just as she'd asked. An overnight envelope was waiting for her with tear sheets of the missing *Outdoor Sportsman* articles. One was meaningless, a trifle about tarpon fishing, but the other set her skin crawling: a piece about the annual rattlesnake harvest in Sweetwater, Texas.

"You'll never know what the power of life and death feels like," Baker had written, "until you hold thirty-six inches and three pounds of sinewy, writhing, hissing death in your bare hands. Not even a .44 Magnum conveys such a feeling of ultimate lethality."

The photograph illustrating the column showed Baker with another man; they were dirty and unshaven, probably half drunk, grinning lewdly under high-top Stetsons, in each hand holding up for the camera an angry, twisting, fang-baring rattlesnake. The caption identified the other man as "Sweetwater rancher and old diamondback hand Frank

Sinclair." This was the name in the caption under the empty space in Baker's photo album.

It was the clincher. After seeing this, Lucy knew she had to do something.

As she reaches the summit of Mulholland Drive, she wonders how Carlsson's going to react to Baker's caricature of him as the Pope. The incriminating sketchbook is in her shoulder bag. But where, she asks herself for the hundredth time, are the originals?

Wherever *he* is, she supposes. Tacked on the wall of a thatched shack on the Kenya coast, perhaps, or the log sides of a cabin in Finland, or the Sheetrock of a nondescript condo development somewhere in the heartland, or any place with electricity. Somewhere that Baker feels safe, where he can sit and scheme with the ingenious, focused obsessiveness of the nearly mad and then venture out, bound on deadly business. Seven faces were depicted in the scrapbook, including hers. Three down, four left: Carlsson, the Pope, Mannerman, herself. She can't make herself think the obvious next question.

How frightening anger can be, she thinks, how deadly. Baker is living proof of something Lucy's father often observed. In his experience, anger was as addictive and self-destructive as a narcotic—as heroin, or meths, or alcohol, or crack. Anger makes people crazy; crazy people do violent things. The danger in anger is that it frequently leaves the addict in full possession of his intelligence and physical capacity, allows him to be calculating where the crackhead is spontaneous, patient where the speed freak has to get off right now, in control and percipient where the boozer is weaving and delusionary.

Lucy's heard people call anger "corrosive." She thinks of Baker's anger more as on the order of flash fires: combusting in unexpected times and places, jumping from one flammable spot to the next, sweeping through his soul with a breath-draining suddenness that kills everything and leaves behind only a desolate thicket of blackened branches, a bleak and shriveled tangle of dead limbs and scorched bones. By now, she guesses, Baker's as dead to himself as he is to her.

As she turns right after passing under the Ventura Freeway, she riffles through "the Baker file" she keeps in her head, wanting to make sure she's left out nothing.

There's just one item, not as dramatic as the rest, but significant. "GK-CHUR," the mystery acronym from Baker's Quicken files. Lucy now thinks it stands for the Graubündener Kantonalbank in Chur, Switzerland. She's pretty proud of her detecting on this one. When she got home from Utica, she went to the Paster's Point library and on a hunch looked up "Chur" in a geographical dictionary. The one entry indicated a city in Switzerland, capital of the canton of Graubünden, noted as the gateway to "the beautiful Engadine Valley." She went to an atlas and located Chur; scanning the surrounding region for a clue, she saw a town whose name rang a bell. On a table at Two Moose there'd been a silver-framed photo of Baker with two members of the Belgian royal family, dressed in faintly ridiculous loden hunting outfits, posed beside a bag of three rare Alpine antelopes, the ones called chamois. It was signed by the two noblemen and dated "Pontresina, 1983."

So Baker could well know Chur. From the map, it looked to Lucy as if anyone traveling to the Engadine by car or rail would have to go through it. At home, she checked an international banking directory, and sure enough, there, in Chur, was the head office of the Graubündener Kantonalbank. Safe to assume this was the "GK" in Baker's Quicken account. But she'd hit a wall. Swiss banks, notoriously secretive, have been known to talk, but only after the right leverage is applied, leverage exertable only by a really big hitter with major connections. Someone like Carlsson.

Molly has to cut lunch short, so they barely get through the usual preliminaries—why are they working this hard, have you heard about so-and-so, where are all the men? Speaking of which, Molly wants to know, what's this about Robert Carlsson? She's seen the item in Liz Smith. What's going on? Lucy assures her nothing is, that it's strictly business.

Lucy arrives at the Aero Services terminal at Burbank forty-five minutes ahead of the rescheduled departure. The place is infernally busy. At this time of year, the lords and ladies of Hollywood are dispersing every which way, none with fewer than a dozen pieces of expensive luggage, and they and their courtiers are all shouting at the top of their voices at the two harried people behind the counter.

Lucy settles into an inconspicuous corner of the waiting room and boots up her laptop. She's quickly absorbed in what she's doing.

When she next glances at her watch, it's 1:40, five minutes before departure time. She looks around and sees no signs of Carlsson or a retinue. Well, she thinks, there's still five minutes. She packs up her laptop and walks over to the broad glass windows. Lucy knows her corporate jets; among the parked and waiting aircraft there's nothing she recognizes as a Falcon. She turns around and scans the waiting area. Still no sign of Carlsson. Ten minutes pass, then twenty.

Finally she goes to the counter.

"Excuse me," she says, "but I was scheduled to be departing at one forty-five on a General Talent flight to Aspen. With Mr. Carlsson."

The portly woman at the counter picks up her clipboard, traces down the the top page with her finger and nods to herself. She looks at Lucy with pity and asks, "Are you Ms. Preston?"

"That's right."

"Oh my goodness, hon, I sure wouldn't want to be in your shoes!"

"I beg your pardon?"

"Well, dear, I hate to tell you this, but Mr. Carlsson was wheels-up out of here at twelve-oh-five. He waited twenty minutes, which I've never seen him do, nor any such commotion either, people phonin' this way and that and Mr. Carlsson turning purpler by the minute!"

"But—" Lucy starts to explain, then stops. No point in complicating a bad situation, no point in telling this woman about the message at the Bel-Air. She looks at her watch. "Twelve-oh-five, you say?"

The woman behind the counter nods.

"About two hours ago?"

The woman turns to look at the large clock behind her.

"That'd be about right, hon."

"Which means they should have entered Aspen airspace by now?"

"I guess so, hon. Depending on traffic and the weather. It can get pretty hairy over there this time of year. You going to Mr. Carlsson's party? Let's see, hon—" She runs her finger down the clipboard again. "There's an MGM Jetstar scheduled out at four. You might be able to hitch. Just tell 'em you're Mr. Carls—"

"No, no. No, thanks." Lucy shakes her head and turns away. Her heart is beating so loud and fast she presses a fist against her bosom to stifle the uproar. Her knees feel about to buckle. Her mind is racing.

She takes a deep breath and turns back to the counter. Her throat is so tight she can hardly speak. "Is there any way to reach Mr. Carlsson's plane from here?" Her voice sounds to her like a dry squeak, but the Aero Services lady doesn't seem to notice.

"Oh, I'm afraid not through us, hon. By now, they'll be talking with the tower. But, you know what?" She brightens and points to a bank of pay telephones on a far wall. "You could always try calling Mr. Carlsson direct, dear. Here."

She lifts a telephone onto the counter, takes up the handset and looks expectantly at Lucy. "Just give me the number, dear."

"I haven't got it. I don't have it. You must have some kind of directory."

The woman shakes her head, but she dials a number, and after checking her clipboard, gives an operator what Lucy guesses must be the stabilizer number of the Falcon. There's a pause, then the woman thanks the operator and hangs up.

" 'Fraid you're out of luck, hon. The number's unlisted. Most of them out here are, what with the movie stars and everything."

At that moment the phone rings, and the woman is taken up with other business.

Lucy tries to think. Call his office! That's it! If she tells them it's an emergency, his secretaries will put her through. She walks as fast as she can to the pay phones.

No such luck. All she gets is a seductive recorded voice saying that Carlsson's agency is closed through Christmas.

Do nothing out of the ordinary, she tells herself as she hangs up. Act normal. Act disappointed. Play the good-looking girl who through sheer foolish carelessness has missed her chance at the brass ring.

She picks up her bags and makes for the exit. From behind the counter, the woman calls out cheerily, "Merry Christmas, hon! And good luck!"

That's what I'm afraid of, thinks Lucy. Right now I'm having more luck than anyone ever has had. She feels she might be sick.

It's a hazy blaze of an afternoon. She is totally out of place here. Christmas should be snowy, with a biting wind off the ocean. Not this!

Three taxis sit waiting, their drivers standing beside them, shooting the breeze about the NFL playoffs. She gets in the first one and tells the driver to take her to Los Angeles International. The faster she can get home, the safer she'll feel.

As Lucy's taxi pulls onto the Ventura Freeway, Falcon IK567J descends through 13,000 feet, banks sharply onto a southwest heading and crosses I-70 just east of Glenwood Springs, forty miles northwest of Aspen, and slows its rate of descent.

It's a brilliant, crisp afternoon. The day before, there'd been a big snow, a real "dump," and the Rockies gleam under the new powder.

Right now, Aspen's Pitkin County Airport is the busiest place for a hundred miles around, busier than Denver International. Carlsson's Falcon is fifth in a queue that comprises eighteen aircraft spaced at five-mile intervals curling west and north toward Grand Junction. One after another, shining Gulfstreams, Falcon 30s and BAEs roar in over the mountains, and now and then, like sparrows in a flight of hawks, a Lear or Westwind. The flotilla is touching down at the rate of one every three minutes. It's quite a spectacle—in the dying light, the line of incoming jets resembles a glinting necklace of silver beads, and a goodly portion of Aspen has turned out to watch.

Most of these jets are flying in for the famous Carlsson Christmas Eve party, which has literally taken over the town. The guest list reads like an all-star compendium of the richest and most famous in the worlds of entertainment and finance. The main bash will be a dinner-dance thrown by the Carlsson Talent Agency at the facility on top of "Ajax," as Aspen Mountain is known. Before that, star-studded receptions will be held at the Little Nell Hotel, the Ritz-Carlton, the Jerome and the Caribou Club, as well as numerous private functions in the great lodges in Starwood and on Red Mountain, from which an Arab billionaire has arranged for a spectacular holographic *son et lumière* executed by George Lucas to be beamed across to Ajax.

A Pan-Australian Press 727 clears the runway. Now there are only four more in front of IK567J. The pilot goes on the intercom and advises Carlsson that they should be down in seven to eight minutes.

From a window of the rear cabin, Carlsson studies the glorious mountainscape and reflects with satisfaction that he's going to get off cheap on this party. With the hologram display arranged by his grateful Brunei client, there's no need for fireworks. The Paris bank for whom he solved a *very* big problem has shipped over a hundred cases of a special bottling of Dom Pérignon, and in the Falcon's cargo hold is enough caviar—gifts from studio heads, book agents, publishing moguls, flacks and players—to supply a dozen parties: a minimum of a couple of hundred kilos of beluga, by the look of it. The stuff kept arriving at Burbank right up to the moment they closed up the cargo hold, and his executive assistant in Century City has phoned in to report that another dozen late-arriving tins will go out on an Aspen-bound Paramount Gulfstream leaving LAX in about an hour.

Carlsson's mood has improved. He had looked forward to having company on the flight and was frankly curious about what Lucy Preston wanted to talk about, but he's not one to sulk or waste time when it happens to come free. As soon as they were up, he hit the phones. As a result, tectonic plates of global commerce worth billions of dollars are starting to shiver and rumble, although it'll be a month or so by his reckoning before the tremors are felt in New York and Buenos Aires.

"Anything before I close up, Mr. Carlsson?" asks the copilot. "We're going to be pretty busy for a while now."

"You might ask the young lady to come aft, Ben. See you in Aspen."

He checks his watch. Five minutes to touchdown. Time enough. Why wait until they get to the chalet?

The copilot goes forward. A young woman is sitting in the front cabin, a decorously dressed blonde in her mid-twenties, avidly scanning *The Hollywood Reporter.*

"Mr. Carlsson would like to see you now, miss."

She puts down the paper. A minute later, she's kneeling before him, her hands busy at his fly. Carlsson relaxes, eyes closed. His last thought before he becomes captive to sensation is how important it is to organize one's life. Sex can be a terrible distraction, especially in Hollywood. Submit to sexual urges, and your eye comes off the ball. That's something he decided a long time ago, and he deals with it in logical, Carlssonian style. As a result, every Tuesday and Thursday without exception, Robert Carlsson gets a first-class, professional blowjob, just as on every other Wednesday he gets a trim from the top barber at Giorgio's.

Up front, the pilots receive clearance to land. The jet assumes its attitude for final approach and begins to lose ground speed. In the cabin, the young woman looks up and asks, "Shall I continue like this, or would you like me to finish by hand?"

By now, Carlsson's breathing hard. Still, he manages a smile.

"I think the combination plate today, sweetie. What the hell, it's Christmas."

The plane descends into a zone of deeper-colored sky as it passes a turnoff above the valley which is a preferred viewing point for Aspenites. Among the cars parked there is a mud- and salt-stained maroonish-brown late-model Cherokee. Its driver is a thickset man so bulked out by a parka and heavy wool pants stuffed into hard-used Manitou snow boots that he seems almost square. He's wearing a plain navy wool ski cap pulled low over mirrored dark glasses, which in turn top off a thick mustache. The rest of his face is concealed by a stout wool muffler. He could be anyone. Aspen is full of such types. None of the other spectators, including a Pitkin County sheriff's deputy parked four autos over, gives him as much as a glance.

He stands beside the Jeep, studying the descending Falcon through powerful binoculars, confirming the numbers on the tail. A wire runs from a tiny earpiece through the open window to a high-powered portable receiver on the driver's seat. It's tuned to the frequency of the Pitkin County control tower. Through a sputtering haze of static he listens intently to the conversation between the tower and IK567J.

Next to the receiver is a radio control device, not unlike a TV remote, connected to what looks like a cellular phone antenna on the roof of the automobile. It provides 180-degree line-of-sight signal coverage which takes in nearly all of the valley. A red light glows dully on the device, above a single orange button.

When he estimates the Falcon is down to less than a thousand feet and fully committed to land, he reaches inside the car, continuing to hold the binoculars with his left hand. The other hovers above the radio control.

When the Falcon is a mere quarter of a mile from the end of the runway, he counts to three silently and presses the button.

For an infinitesimal fraction of a beat, everything is just as it was. Then the radio pulse completes its leap from the transmitter to IK567J, where it closes a low-voltage circuit in a detonator connected to a charge of C-4 explosive concealed in a blue tin can bearing the Cyrillic markings of a leading St. Petersburg caviar exporter. The tin is wrapped in the distinctive pink-and-silver paper of Beverly Hills' fancy-goods purveyor-of-choice to the stars, and is sealed with its heavy embossed label. This package, along with others similarly wrapped but innocent, rests atop a wooden case containing six magnums of 1961 Château Pétrus.

When the detonator circuit closes, the charge—half the weight of the explosive that destroyed the Pan Am 747 over Lockerbie—explodes with a force sufficient to blow a hole in the Hoover Dam. The blast devastates the Falcon, all but severs its tail assembly, atomizes its hydraulic system. The plane yaws sharply left, poses *en point* on one wing for a hideous balletic moment and then barrels earthward and begins to cartwheel—but only for an instant, before it explodes in a thunderous fireball and the snowfields for yards around are stained and pocked with what will later be variously identified by FAA forensic teams as incinerated bits of foie gras, caviar, glass and tin, aircraft fragments, human matter and blood and a more darkly purplish liquid which the FAA investigators will subsequently identify as the finest claret produced in Bordeaux prior to 1982.

For an instant, it seems as if all life is suspended—frozen—for those aware of what has happened. At the base of Ajax, three miles to the east, the noisy après-ski festivities on the Little Nell deck babble on uninterrupted.

And then, as if a guillotine has crashed down from the sky and severed the spine of the day, there's a sudden shocking moment of tense, desperate silence, and all hell erupts.

Right behind the Falcon is a stretch Lear belonging to a Manhattan currency-trading king. It practically stands on its tail as it breaks off. The rest of the approach queue follows, making for alternative fields at Glenwood Springs and Grand Junction.

At the observation point across the valley, people get out of their cars, including the driver of the Cherokee, and stare at each other in wild confusion. In the valley below, there is an interminable empty pause before sirens break out. The deputy jumps back into his cruiser and screeches off, almost losing it on the icy, snow-rutted road.

Gradually, the watchers get into their cars and disperse, still half transfixed, barely aware of one another, galvanized by the horror of what they have just witnessed.

The driver of the Cherokee is one of the last to leave. He watches as the first figures struggle through the snow from the terminal only to halt, helpless, before the ring of flame and the great oily plume rising into the afternoon sky. Finally he climbs into his car, grunting with the effort of squeezing his bulk behind the steering wheel, and starts the engine.

For an instant longer, he sits there, engine idling roughly, and studies the pandemonium below, the antlike figures, the toylike vehicles, the column of smoke rising like a black, curling stem from a nest of flames set dead in the middle of a speckled ring of carnage and torn metal. Then he smiles and backs out. Moments later he is back on I-70, heading east, driving toward night and obscurity.

PART FOUR

PUZZLE TIME

— I —

It's while she's making dinner that Lucy has her epiphany.

She's standing at the kitchen counter chopping celery, her mind elsewhere, essentially deaf to her father's repeated exclamations of wonder and alarm.

The Chief, with Lucy's cat, Lucifer, in his lap, is glued to the kitchen TV, which is tuned to the Discovery Channel. It's *Shark Week*, twenty-eight hours of prime time devoted to the carnivorous monsters of the deep, and Lucy's dad hasn't missed a minute. Ever since his 193-pound mako won the Seniors prize at the Association of Chiefs of Police annual shark tournament off Montauk Point on Long Island, Chief Preston has considered himself a combination of Quint, the wily captain in *Jaws*, and the legendary shark killer Captain Frank Mundus. He's been especially looking forward to tonight: the entire evening will consist of great whites doing terrible things to human and animal flesh.

"My goodness' sakes, Luce, will you look at that!" He's speaking to the cat, having long since given up trying to get through to his daughter.

Lucy's been sealed up in her dilemma. It's about to be Valentine's Day, almost two months since Robert Carlsson's aircraft was blown up coming into Aspen, and she still hasn't figured out what to do. But the Chief can only see that it's as if a wall's grown up around her.

Time has got to be running out. Somewhere out there Baker's got to be setting up his next fatal scheme, settling the crosshairs on his next victim. He must be stopped. But how?

The obvious course is to go to the authorities with what she knows and suspects. And yet she can't bring herself to do it. For one thing, it might land her in prison. She's not sure that she doesn't technically qualify as an accessory before the fact of Robert Carlsson's murder.

Fortunately, no suspicion has attached to her. The LAPD, Colorado state police, Pitkin County Sheriff's Department and FBI all questioned her, and everyone accepted her story: that she simply misread the message, read "1:45" instead of "11:45," and showed up two hours late. They swallowed it whole. She could read their thinking in their faces: no woman is ever on time. It helped that she told her story well. Why shouldn't she have? For ten years or more she's been paid a lot of money to dissemble to some of the most suspicious analytical minds on Wall Street. She thanks her lucky stars that, unlike most of her countrymen when similarly flustered, she resisted the urge to tell her life story to the woman at the Aero Services desk. And on one point she was completely sincere: she had shown up in all good faith intending to get on that plane. If it had been there, she'd have boarded it.

But if she comes forward now and tells the "real" story? She can just imagine how it would go.

"You mean, Ms. Preston, you strongly suspected that Mr. Baker was alive and that Mr. Carlsson was one of his probable targets, and yet you said nothing, and now Mr. Carlsson's dead, as well as the flight crew. You as good as detonated that explosive, Ms. Preston! That's four counts of Murder Two. Read her her Miranda rights and book her!"

Of course, Lucy knows, that's not how it would go. A lawyer with half his legal wits about him would have her on the street in seconds. But that would hardly be the end of it. Next would come lawsuits from the families of the flight crew, the insurance companies and further criminal complaints. She'd impoverish herself and wear out her life in the courts, become a public spectacle. Would she end up flinging herself off Paster's Bluff into the rocky gray wash of the Atlantic?

And Baker would still be out there.

Oh, there'd be a temporary uproar, and "Have You Seen This Man?" legends and voice-overs in fifty languages would blare on television screens from Dakar to Denver. And Baker would go to ground until the commotion died away. And suppose the authorities did manage to lay their hands on him, what evidence would they be able to marshal against him? What provable connections to the killings of Betti Jo Barnum, Chadbourne Tinkry, Herbert Lamond and Robert Carlsson?

Lucy's no criminal lawyer, but like a lot of people she knows, by powers of osmosis, from *Court-TV* and the O. J. Simpson trial, from sound bites and news bits absorbed while surfing the box or skimming the papers, from the legal thrillers that have gotten her through long flights and boring rainy weekends, she considers herself to have earned something like an honorary LL.B. To try to prove the connection between Baker and each individual killing is to invite a nightmare of circumstantiality and habeas corpus problems. The connection between the four victims—all worked for Mannerman, Baker hates Mannerman, ergo Baker would have chosen them—is a syllogism laughably full of holes.

If Baker's to be stopped, it will have to be done "outside channels." But how?

To begin with, where is he? He could be lurking outside even as she stands there mincing a celery stalk. The thought makes her squeeze the knife.

It's clear he hadn't wanted her on that plane. Why?

There are many answers, some of them quite flattering, but not the one to which Lucy keeps returning. He's saving her. Reserving her just as she's reserved the water in which the dried *porcini* were soaking, to be added to the sauce for the meat loaf.

But for what? For when?

Think offensively, she tells herself for the trillionth time. Follow Mannerman's oft-expostulated dictum. She can hear him now: "A good offense is the best defense." Seize the initiative. Take control of the game. Be the one who's doing the stalking. But how?

"Darn it, Luce, you just have to see this!" The Chief's voice, loud and insistent, breaks through the shell. He's not speaking to the cat.

She looks up. On-screen, men are throwing great bloody chunks of dead horse, whole haunches and rib cages, over the side of a boat. The chum bobs in the wake, trailing ribbons of blood. Then there's a terrible thrashing of white water, and a great white boils up from below, rising a third of its length out of the water, a huge bone-strutted piece of beef vised in jaws boasting an array of cruel teeth that look to be six inches long. The giant fish shakes its "prey," terrierlike, with a force sufficient to snap a bull's spine, then crashes back to the water and disappears.

"Wow!" exclaims the Chief, "how about that!"

Lucy doesn't hear him. It's like a fissionable reaction inside her head. Through some process that will be forever mysterious to her, bits of discrete information—whisperings of intuition, remembrances of things she's read, heard, knows—that have been whirling around her mind or settling dust-covered in dark corners, all these inchoate random thoughts seem to arrange themselves kaleidoscopically and connect to one another with an explosive yet surefooted logic. Everything blows together in a great roaring coalescence. Then there's a quick, quiet interval while the smoke, debris and darkness sort themselves out, light and clarity reassert themselves, the scene clears, and there, like a splendid statue born of raw chaos, is a plan that cannot possibly fail.

The initial association was a pure and simple visual hookup. The sight of those ravenous jaws produces an instant flashback to a set of equally fearsome mandibles. At Two Moose, Baker showed her a video of a Lake Kivu crocodile bursting onshore to seize an antelope carcass carefully placed to bring the amphibian within range of a tranquilizer dart. Like the shark's attack, the croc's was explosive—a detonation of pure bestial energy imbued by its sheer violence with evil. She remembers Baker observing as they watched that with "peabrains" like crocs or sharks, whose neural machinery is pre-prehistoric, dead meat will do the trick every time; with more advanced species you had to use live bait—a tethered goat, for example. At which point he launched into a lengthy reminiscence about tiger hunting with a Bengali maharajah.

Other pieces emerge from shadowed chambers of her mind and take their places in the evolving puzzle. There's a line from the cover story of the latest *Fortune*, which anointed Mannerman its "500" CEO of the Year for the fifth time: "Fifteen years ago this coming December, in what has turned out to be about as nice a Christmas present as a board ever gave the stockholders it represents, GIA's directors brought in John P. Mannerman to turn the company around." There's a squib from *The Wall Street Journal* concerning GIA's acquisition of VIP Group, a Liechtenstein-headquartered purveyor of luxury goods and services, everything from high fashion to the interiors of private jets to five-star hotels—among which is the Regina Palace in Venice, "the pearl of the Pearl of the Adriatic," just down the Grand Canal from the Gritti, and the only challenger to the Cipriani, across the lagoon, in the ne plus ultra department. There's something Carlsson said to her on the eve of his fateful flight, about his plan for a "bash of the millennium." In the most recent bulletin of Save Venice, the conservationist charity to which

Lucy sends $500 every Christmas, there's a note that the GIA Foundation has contributed $5 million toward the restoration of the burned-out La Fenice opera house.

Just scraps, these, but like Proust's madeleine they summon other associations: everything else she knows pours in now, everything about Mannerman, GIA, Baker, the Deadly Sins, everything she's suspected, guessed at, hypothesized about, speculated on. Suddenly, Lucy's so excited she can hardly finish making dinner.

After the Chief leaves, she sits up late, working through her ideas. They're *her* ideas now, she's taken over. It's after midnight when she finishes her "script." As she slides under the sheets, she's shivering less from the frigid February air sneaking in the leaky window than from sheer anticipation.

Thanks to pure blessed blind dumb luck, she's due to be in New York this week and she has a long-standing dinner date with Spuds on Thursday. Spuds is the key, she thinks as she closes her eyes. The key—and he's someone she is absolutely certain she can count on to deliver.

On Thursday, when they touch base, Lucy vetoes both "21" and the Stirrup Cup as too noisy. Spuds has had a falling-out at Le Cirque, and he happens to know that the Mannermans, in town for the Lou Gehrig award the next evening, are dining at La Grenouille. So they decide to meet at Elio's, a favorite Italian restaurant on the Upper East Side. Lucy waits until Spuds's third martini and second trip through the bread basket before playing her opening card. It's like that shark show, she thinks. I'm chumming the waters of Spudsy's mind.

"Nice piece in *Fortune*," she says. "PL must be out to here."

"You know how the Old Man is about publicity, Luce. If you can't put it in the bank, don't call him, he'll call you." He winks at Lucy.

She plays it deadpan.

"Still, it was nice. I can't believe it'll been fifteen years, but I suppose it has." She makes a show of counting on her fingers. "Let's see. Yep, it is! Fifteen years for a CEO. My God, Spudsy, that's like fifty in a human marriage!"

By way of reply, Spuds raises his glass in a toast to the absent Mannerman.

"So," she continues with all the innocence she can muster, "I assume you've got something planned to mark the great occasion? Something like they laid on for Warner Emerson out at EmerComm?"

Emerson had finished fourth in the *Fortune* derby. Like Mannerman, he too had brought his company back from the dead. The party to celebrate *his* tenth anniversary as CEO had cost close to $25 million. As the pièce de résistance, the board had voted to change the company's name from Applied Instrumentation to EmerComm.

Spuds's eyes widen at her question. It's a look she knows well. It means he's picked up the roar of a bullet coming straight at him.

"Jesus, Luce, thanks for reminding me! The fact is, I've been so damn busy, I haven't. But I sure as hell will get on it prontissimo! Prontissississimo!"

From his coat pocket he produces a Mont Blanc ballpoint and a slim alligator case holding a thin sheaf of three-by-five note cards and looks expectantly at Lucy. "Hey, no time like the present, and this is much more your line of country than mine. How about a little brainstorming? Give me a hand just for old times' sake?"

"My pleasure."

"The first thing we have to decide is where to hold it. I'm thinking the St. Regis. The Plaza's too *déclassé*, and the party rooms at the Carlyle suck."

Time now to see if the power of suggestion is all it's cracked up to be. Lucy asks, "Didn't I see that you guys bought a bunch of fancy hotels in Europe? What's that about anyway? Hotels? You're going to put a Ritz in cyberspace? I thought PL's idea of a twenty-first-century service business is five billion electrons working their sparky little butts off, not a lot of Thais toting trays?"

"It's what we're calling the Trilateral Initiative," Spuds replies. "This is strictly off the record, *comprende*?"

Lucy nods. "*Sí, sí, señor*. The Trilateral Initiative, eh—what in God's name is that?"

"Trilateral means do a lot, do a little, do nothing. The way the Old Man sees the world working out, there's going to be just three slices of the economic pie. The rich, the poor and the in-betweens. The Initiative addresses each slice. The rich are going to end up with all the disposable money, so for them we'll do a lot—financial services, the high life, whatever! The poor have nothing to offer us except as a threat we can trade on, but as a market they're zilch, so them we ignore except for lip service."

"That's what these speeches about quote social equity unquote are about?"

"You said it, not I. And then we come to the in-betweens. That's UnivCom's power base, the market Carlsson saw. They're, well, they're just *in between,* like Spam in a sandwich. But there's a shitload of 'em, so even if you score just a little, you make out like bandit! A billion people around the world, the so-called global middle class, terrified of the homicidal underclass and barely getting by on a hundred grand a year, too scared to go out of the house and too broke to hide out in first class, stewing in resentment as they sit in front of the tube with a thumb in their mouth and the other up their behind, or jerk off—excuse my language—on the Internet. Sitting ducks for every home shopper, anger peddler or mental junk food manufacturer able to pay what we're charging for thirty-eight seconds of pitch time. You remember what the late great Carlsson said? What we used to call a captive audience is turning into a trapped audience."

Ordinarily Lucy's response to this kind of talk would be editorial, but her agenda this evening is very focused, so she merely asks, "In other words, the VIP Group deal is your way of going after the top slice, the Cipriani crowd?"

"Ooooh, language, please, young lady! The Regina Palace crowd, and don't you forget it! People who really get off by blowing ten grand a night on a hotel suite! Actually, the place is closed right now for elements of refurbishment and rehabilitation, as our greatest ambassador to Britain once remarked. Fifty mil's worth, to be exact. New suites, complete do-over by some guinea decorator, plus a roof garden that'll beat hell out of the Danieli and a kitchen that's higher-tech than NASA. I understand they copped the chef from Harry's Bar. It's due to reopen around Christmas, and believe you me, after we get done, the joint'll outspiff any place on God's green earth, including the Oriental in Bangkok! The place is going to make the Gritti and the Cip look like Days' Inns!"

"So why don't you—"

Spuds doesn't let her finish. He slaps the table and looks at her with an enormous sly smirk. "I get your drift, I get it! I dig, I dig! Why don't we combine the two, right!"

Lucy says nothing, merely beams her admiration of her friend's genius.

"A gala, the gala of galas, right!" Spuds is scribbling furiously now. "A night of nights to celebrate the Old Man's fifteenth anniversary! His glorious reign!"

"You might even call it the party of the millennium," Lucy ventures, "seeing as how next year starts with a two."

"Wow! What a grace note! Of course, that's one we'll let the columns use. It'll sound better coming from them."

The columns, thinks Lucy. Of course! And thank you now, Spudsy, she thinks, because that takes care of one of two missing pieces in her puzzle. The other she doesn't even want to think about, can't make herself face.

Spuds calls for another martini. He's flushed with excitement. Lucy's starving, but she figures she better let him run with it.

"My God, can't you just see it, Luce!" he exclaims. "Lights, camera, action! Five hundred of the best and the brightest and the greatest and the goodest. Distinction, money, celebrity and clout, we'll invite some of each! The men strictly white tie and decorations, the ladies in Van Cleef and Armani. We'll start with a champagne reception, during which the mayor of Venice or the President of Italy or . . ."

He pauses, gripped by some inner thought.

"Or who?"

Spuds's expression turns sly again. "Oh, no one in particular. Just a little thought I had."

Lucy never had any trouble finding Spuds's wavelength. She knows whom he has in mind. She thinks of mentioning GIA's big contribution to Save Venice and decides against it.

Two weeks later, Spuds tracks her down in Atlanta, so excited that he hardly needs the phone to make himself heard across sixteen hundred miles.

"The Old Man's bought the idea a hundred percent!" he shouts. "All systems are go! Christmas Eve in Venice! How about that?"

"Good on you, old boy," says Lucy as calmly as she can manage, fearful that her thumping heart will be audible. "Congratulations!" She's excited herself, exultant and—for the first time—remotely in control of events.

"Can you meet me next week in Boston? Someplace quiet? Say Wednesday at the Ritz? The show's on the road and we have a lot to talk about!"

"*We* do?"

"Yep. Come back, little Sheba, all is forgiven! Himself wants you involved. I told him it was sorta your idea. All will be made clear when I see you."

In her fondest imaginings, Lucy hasn't counted on this. To be invited to work on the inside, as it were, would be a huge advantage. Obviously Mannerman felt that this would be an offer she couldn't refuse. Mannerman and she haven't spoken in over two years. Her repeated rejections of his importunings to rejoin GIA may have been insupportable blows to his ego, especially back last summer and fall when the markets soured on GIA and he was feeling tender. That he didn't call her after Carlsson's death also spoke volumes. He would have felt entirely isolated and bereft, deprived of his right arm, and Lucy had been frankly surprised he didn't reach out. Yet in retrospect she's thankful, because she's not sure how she'd have responded, and if she'd gone back, where would she be now?

But time, as measured in the quicksilver intervals of the stock market, heals all wounds. The market was steaming ahead at a rate that would see the Dow Jones at 8,000 or better when the millennial clock struck midnight. There'd been an undercurrent of doubt surrounding Carlsson's role in the GIA scheme of things, just as Lucy had feared, a feeling that Mannerman had gone Hollywood, that he'd bet his company on the digital evanescences of UnivCom. But with the world economy firming up, UnivCom's mix of retributive and sensationalist was picking up audience share in every market worth tabulating, and GIA's preliminary year-end numbers, released in January, had been dazzling: GIA stock was up over 8 percent in just the past two weeks. Another two points, Lucy reckons, and the company will cross a near-mystical boundary and enter territory explored by only a handful of listed stocks—AT&T, GE and Coca-Cola—one of the few publicly traded enterprises ever to achieve an aggregate market value in excess of $150 *billion*! What a Valentine's Day present that would be for the stock-holders, Lucy thinks, barreling down I-95 toward her rendezvous with Spuds. Including me, she reflects: her GIA shares—she never sold a one—are now worth more than $500,000, and the main reason she can go ahead with her scheme.

Her old friend is fairly flying. To her amazement, Spuds passes on a drink and orders Virgin Marys for them both. He looks terrific: it's as if his face has been deveined. Mannerman's detached him from all other duties to work on the gala, he tells Lucy gleefully. He's having the *best* time of his life! With this kind of excitement, who needs booze!

Lucy doesn't push or pry. When the main course—sole for her, had-dock for Spuds—arrives, he picks thoughtfully at his fish and then, looking at her gravely, says in a truly serious voice, "What I'm about to tell you is subject to the Official Secrets Act."

"Understood. But first don't you want to tell me where I fit in?"

"I'll get to that. Now—you ever hear of a dude called Isaiah Berlin? Some kind of English philosopher Grover's always quoting?"

"The name rings a bell."

"OK. Well, according to Grover, this guy Berlin says people divide into two categories, foxes and hedgehogs. Foxes know lots of things. Hedgehogs know one big thing. Don't ask me why, but that's the way it is, according to Grover. So, first I want you to put on your hedgehog hat."

Lucy dons an imaginary chapeau, sets it at a smart tilt, adjusts an invisible brim. "OK?" she asks pertly.

"Hey, this is serious! Now, you remember me talking about a special guest—"

Oh please, God, please, please, please, prays Lucy silently, let it be who I think it is. "Yes, I remember." She nods.

"OK. Well, this is the one big thing from which everything else flows. This cannot get out, *comprende*?"

"You're repeating yourself, Spudsy. I'm a big girl. I dig."

"So, our special guest on Christmas Eve, who'll be cutting the ribbon on the all-new restored fifty-million-dollar Regina Palace roof garden, who'll in fact not only be cutting the ribbon but—tarantara!—*blessing* the place will be—can you guess?"

"The Cardinal-Archbishop of Venice?"

"Don't be an asshole. You think we're going to put this kind of a show together for some diddly-squat Archbishop?"

Spuds's sly look borders on the unspeakably smug.

"Not the present Archbishop," he continues, "but the last one. The world knows him best as Pope Leo XIV!"

"I don't believe it! Oh, Spudsy! The Pope! *Quel coup!*" Lucy whips off an invisible topper and tips it to him.

"Well, he is the Old Man's asshole buddy. And there were other considerations, as they say in baseball."

Lucy's so whipped up at this news she has trouble keeping in character. "La Fenice?" she asks, buying a little time to get her pulse down.

"That—and some restoration at San Marco that's turned out to cost about ninety million dollars as opposed to the sixty-odd they were budgeting, which leaves the Church about thirty million short. We'd already committed to La Fenice through Save Venice, so now we just throw in the extra."

"You're *not* going to give thirty mil? How can you do that?"

"Well, as the Old Man says, what're reserves for?"

"I'll tell you now, Spudsy, if the pro-choicers—people like me who don't have divided loyalties—get wind of this . . ."

"Don't worry, they won't. Believe me. We've learned a lot of new tricks since you jumped ship. Anyway, the symbolism here is great. We're going to play up the economic angle. Instead of Church and State, you got Church and Enterprise. Free enterprise, that is. God-fearing Judeo-Christian capitalism against godless redistributive liberalism. Dynamite, huh? Grover's working with the Vatican right now on the wording. Anyway, let's cut to the chase. With His Holiness on board, obviously the security measures are going to have to be extraordinary."

"Obviously."

"Well, you ain't just whistlin' Dixie. Hell, nowadays the Old Man spends more time thinking security than business—ever since Herby Lamond was offed and they blew away that banker in Frankfurt. We have three U.S. firms on retainer, and the Old Man's personally watched over by a team out of Tel Aviv. *Not* the guys who were supposed to be covering Rabin. Plus for this one we're bringing in another private outfit—Northern Irish, out of Belfast—that gets high marks in the bomb department. Think of them as an added extra layer of Kevlar. Then there's everyone else: the lay chief of Vatican security, the Swiss Guard, the vice-commander of the Italian carabinieri, the chief and deputy chief of the Polizia da Venezia, plus whatever the guests insist on individually."

From her bag Lucy produces a legal pad and a rollerball pen. "Mind if I take notes?"

"OK, but this is strictly for your eyes only, remember."

"Of course."

"Now, what all the security people agree on is that time is the enemy. We want to cut the lead as short as possible. The less time there is between cup and lip, the less time some lunatic out there has to pull together a gondola full of ammonium nitrate and diesel fuel. As you can see, this puts us in a bind. Our guests will not be the sort of people you call up on December 23 and ask if they're doing anything tomorrow night. We're talking *heads of state,* we're talking Bill Gates—speaking of personal security—we're talking *royals!*'

Spuds is right. The sort of people Mannerman will insist on, especially with the Pope signed up, are types whose datebooks are filled through the first decade of the coming century, and hitting them too late could cost the guest list a carat or two, which he wouldn't stand for. This occasion is to be perfect with a capital P. "So then what's the timetable?" Lucy asks. Lucy's own dead reckoning, based largely on thrillers and such research as she's been able to do on-line, is that Baker would need a minimum of six months.

"OK," Spuds continues. "We kick things off the Friday of the July Fourth weekend. Six hundred faxes will go out over the Old Man's signature asking the recipient to hold December 24, details to follow, and confirming by return fax. Subject to a twenty-four-hour grace period, if we don't hear from you, you're out. Unless, of course, we decide to make an exception—for someone like Buffett, for example. We figure on six hundred invitations netting five hundred confirmations."

"You'll do better than that. I know these people. Because it's so early, they'll figure what the hell, if something better comes along down the line, they can give you the leg. You know how they are." July 4. July, August, September, October, November, half of December at the most. Not quite enough. "What are you going to do about the logistical side?"

she adds. "What about the support troops? They have to know early."

Planning and executing a party like this is like staging D-Day, she knows from long experience. Logistics and supply are all-important: caterers, transportation facilitators, vintners, calligraphers, chefs from Paris to Hong Kong to Bombay, hairdressers, seamstresses would have to be booked, along with landing slots, Federal Express, messenger services on four continents, blocks of satellite time, quires of heavy Venice letterpress.

"We're faxing them next week on a no-names basis, using different people in New York, London, Paris, Taipei and Milan. They guarantee us the dates, we guarantee them a fat nonrefundable forty percent advance on confirmation. Plus, once the guest list, et cetera, gets out, to be chosen to work this party is going to be worth more than a royal warrant!"

"Spuds, who does know the specifics?"

"As we speak? Inside the company: the Old Man, me, Grover, TK, Marie and Bets. Outside: the Pope and—on his staff—a couple odd monsignors I liaise with, along with one very smart nun who handles internal security. The commandant of the Swiss Guard. The other security types I mentioned. You."

She does some quick addition. From what Spuds says, fifteen or so people are officially in the loop, then maybe throw in another five, make it ten, for accidentally overheards, snoops, pillow talk and so on. Say twenty-five. That's fine, that's plenty: all Lucy needs for what she's got in mind. If twenty-six people know a secret, you might as well figure fifty. Especially with a bunch of Italians in the loop. Gossip accounts for half the Italian GNP!

"Moving along," says Spuds brightly. "We hit Stage Two in early October, around Columbus Day, when we activate the support systems. These will be on a venue-to-be-designated basis with a firm delivery date."

"What about the invitations? They have to be specific. I hardly imagine you're going to run them off at the last minute on a photocopy machine. On the other hand, engravers have been known to tip the columns off."

"No flies on you, my dear Holmes! The invitations will be lettered by a team of calligraphers at a Trappist monastery in Kentucky and will not be released until the Monday before Thanksgiving, when they'll go out by FedEx Platinum Service. Only then, just three weeks and change before the actual day, will the whole world know exactly what's up!"

"You're fooling yourselves if you think there won't be leaks. You can't keep something like this secret."

"You think we don't *know* that? Hell, girl, we may be doing some selective leaking ourselves! The thing is not to put our imprimatur on the gossip."

"I dig. Now, where do I come in?"

"I thought you'd never ask. We want to engage you as our consultant responsible for the Wall Street side of the list. The Old Man wants this to be the toughest ticket short of a ringside seat at the Last Judgment, which for some people it's going to feel like! A lot of fine distinctions are gonna have to be drawn. For example, if you have Soros, do you have to have Gilbert de Botton? Or Kravis and Forstmann? If you put Buffett at such and such a table, is Sir John Templeton's nose going to be out of joint? What about the Japanese banks? How do we handle the Daiwa situation if Greenspan's going to be there? Is Jimmy Goldsmith too rad these days? You know what I'm talking about."

Lucy nods.

"So, how does a hundred K sound—plus out-of-pocket, of course?"

How about sixty thousand, she's thinking, plus four invitees to be named by her.

Spuds adds, "Plus the special bonus. Payment in kind. You attend as a guest. No different from Henry Kissinger or the King of Spain. Well, not quite. As a kind of working guest, more like it. Think of that, Lucy Preston—right up there among the world's Five Hundred!"

Oh God, she thinks, if something goes wrong, the last place on earth she—or anyone—will want to be on Christmas Eve will be the roof garden of the Regina Palace Hotel. But what can she say? Still, if there's a kind of fundamental equity to be served, it's the honorable thing to do. "Well, my goodness," she says, "how can I resist? Do you know any place that sells glass slippers?"

Because my Prince will come, she thinks. If she can buy him the time, Baker will be there, somewhere out in the dark. How could Baker resist taking a crack at Mannerman's anniversary party—and at the Pope?

And at me.

His three most hated people, all in one place at one time. At night and in Venice. He'll be there.

On the drive back to Paster's Point, she examines the problem from every angle. There are damn few loose ends. Not at this early stage. Later perhaps, but not now. She's come up with a variation on an idea taken from one of Baker's thrillers. As a scheme, it's frail and far-out, but somehow, with the right resources, with the right help, Lucy thinks she might just be able to bring it off. One thing's for certain. She's passed the point of no return. This is mortal business. It's moved from the imagined to the actual, it's no longer an artifice existing solely in her mind, confined within her contemplation.

She is no longer carrying the ball by herself. But she still needs help. With Carlsson gone, her choices are few. Two, in fact, but to walk across the bridge to the Chief, she thinks, she'll first have to crawl across a nearer one.

The next morning, she roots through her files until she finds the telephone number she needs.

"Be there!" she says out loud, as she dials.

Her prayer is answered on the third ring.

"Hello, Mr. Morland," she says, "it's Irene Martin. From Philadelphia. You remember? We spoke a few months ago about a sporting rifle?" She wishes she hadn't used an assumed name the first time she talked to Morland. Now she's going to have to go roundabout to arrive at the truth, not that it should matter.

"Oh, sure," Peter Morland replies, "how are you, Ms. Martin? The missing .303, wasn't it? Did it ever turn up?"

"As a matter of fact, it did," Lucy fibs. "It seems Mr. Baker gave it to a nephew."

"Well, good. What can I do for you today?"

"When we spoke, I recall you telling me that you are a location scout, I think you called it. You set up movie scenes, is that right?"

"Something like that. It's close enough."

"Well, Mr. Morland, I have a sister, a twin sister, actually—this is strictly personal business, by the way—who has written a screenplay in her spare time—actually I think it's what you professionals call a treatment. In any case, it involves technical details that she's worried she's not getting right. In the interests of verisimilitude, that is. Things someone like you would understand much better. We happened to be talking, and my conversation with you popped into my head, and so I said to her that maybe she would be well advised to consult you. Hire you, that is. I suppose I should ask what your fee is?"

"I don't come cheap. It's two thousand dollars a day plus expenses. I fly business class."

Lucy does some figuring. At the most she's looking at twenty thousand dollars.

"That wouldn't be a problem," she says. "My sister has a very indulgent husband. Do you have any free time just now?"

"As a matter of fact, until Easter I'm pretty much open. But UA has put a hold on April for the new James Bond picture, and after that I don't free up again until August, probably."

"This wouldn't take more than a week. Would it be all right if I have my sister call you herself?"

"Absolutely. What's her name?"

"It's, uh, Lucy. Lucy Preston. She uses her husband's name."

I should be better paid for this, Lucy thinks with a certain chagrin. Become an actress. Or an investment banker. The fibs flow out of me as easily as butter. Too easily. Untruth has become second nature. I really ought to find a new line of work.

"That'll be fine, Ms. Martin," she hears Morland say. "Just have Mrs. Preston call me."

There's a pause. Something's occurred to him. "One last thing," he adds.

"Yes?"

"This location your sister wants me to scout—do you have any idea where it is?"

"Yes," Lucy replies, "yes, I do. It's Venice."

— II —
At five thousand feet the descending airliner breaks through the crust of streaky gray overcast. In the afternoon light, the water below is the color of a dull knife. Gazing past the tip of the Air Canada 737's port wing. Lucy decides she likes the look of Halifax. Snuggled against its famous fine harbor, guarded by a hilltop fort which from the air resembles a six-pointed star curiously stretched out along one axis, the Nova Scotia capital reminds her of Portland, or a compact San Francisco. The plane sweeps across the winter landscape north of the city, passing over deep-forested country speckled with the mirror surfaces of frozen lakes, and comes around on final approach. Lucy tenses, half expecting to be blown to bits at any second—will she ever again be a relaxed flier?—but ten minutes later she's in the terminal waiting for her bag, trying to pick out Peter Morland from the crowd on the other side of customs—and wondering if this is a big fool's errand.

She's still unsure exactly what—or how much—she wants from Morland. Or to what degree she will want to confide in him. She'll have to settle for playing it by ear.

At the very least, the man's expertise should give her a sense of the target zone, in the best of all possible worlds even the bull's-eye, from which Baker would be likely to attack Mannerman's gala. Obviously this will depend on Baker's weapon; anyone involved with present-day action films, as she surmises Morland is, should know all about these —from the conventional to the exotic. Then there's the psychological aspect. Maybe Peter Morland remembers something about Baker he learned from his brother that will prove useful. Lewis Morland spent a lot of time with Baker, would have had a sense of his field habits, his tricks and turns of mind, his quirks as a hunter.

Beyond that, what can she expect? Why has she come all this way? It would have been easy to FedEx Morland the treatment reposing in its neat blue covers in her shoulder bag, a thirty-page outline laboriously confected according to the dictates of a paperback manual on screenplay writing she picked up in Boston. The treatment and a covering letter could have sent Morland off to Venice with a clear idea of the questions for the answers to which she was prepared to pay him handsomely.

Why, then, is she here?

Lucy needs someone to talk to, that's why. This Baker business has

her so penned up within herself she's about to suffocate. Just to be able
to talk with Morland will be like a valve releasing a puff of steam. She
has no intention of going into the whole business, but at least she's
doing *something*—and doing it "live." Nothing ventured, nothing
gained, and she can't stay at ground zero for much longer without losing
her mind!

"Mrs. Preston?" says a voice to her left. For a second, Lucy doesn't
respond. Then a hand touches her arm.

Peter Morland is hardly what she's expecting. Baker's photographs
showed Lewis Morland to have been a compact, swarthy, short-browed
man, muscular and unsmiling. His younger brother, by contrast, looks
like an aging graduate student, a type Lucy knew well at the Institute,
those Ancient Mariners of academe who exhaust the decades chasing
doctorates that will never be granted, whose faces reflect their awareness
that what began as a fervent, solemn quest for intellectual glory has
with each passing year become a faintly ridiculous exercise in avoiding
reality and middle age.

Peter Morland has an intelligent, long-browed, long-featured, skeptical face, with a pale, uneven complexion that suggests he takes the
sun and wind badly, surely a drawback in his line of work. He's quite
tall, and not what you'd call lean, but he doesn't come across as big,
the way some men do. Lucy guesses he's about her age: a year or so
away, in either direction, from the dreaded four-oh that she herself will
hit all too soon.

"You're a brave woman, Mrs. Preston, to venture this far north. Even
in as mild a winter as this one, Halifax is no picnic in February. And
there's a front coming through, in which case you may be here till the
thaw."

"Would that be so bad?" Lucy asks. "The city looks very agreeable
—at least from five thousand feet. And please call me Lucy."

"Delighted. And as for jolly old Halifax, it's home, it's where I grew
up, I'm used to it. But it can be cold! Now just wait inside here while
I get the car."

When she crosses the pavement, Lucy understands what he's talking
about. The wind pierces her like a sharpened icicle. She's delighted to
gain the warmth of Morland's Pathfinder.

"I've booked you into the Halliburton House," he tells her as he turns onto the southbound freeway leading into Halifax. "It's a nice enough hotel, and it has about the best restaurant around. I'd show you around the town but with this much snow and more on the way, there's not much to look at. You should come back in late June, early July; that's when this part of the world starts to show best. Especially down around Cape Margaret. Not that I ever seem to be around to see it."

"You must travel a lot for your work. Is it mostly out-of-doors?"

"It used to be. But ever since Bruce Willis took off at the box office, it's mainly big cities for me now. You know, urban, *Die Hard*–type venues. Still, I'm looking forward to Venice. I've never worked there. The rap is that it's a tough town to shoot in, and the Italian unions are the worst! I assume you're aware of that?"

"I wasn't, actually. Tell me, why didn't you follow your brother's career track?"

"I almost did. In fact, I got into my own line of work through Lewie, or rather through one of his hunting clients. That was about twenty years ago, when I was still at McGill, and apprenticing Lewie in the summers. I loved the work, the setup, the outfitting, the stalking, all that. My problem was, I hated the actual killing. I couldn't help thinking: That elk is somebody's father. And most of all I didn't like most of the people I saw. Believe me, Lewie used to say the same thing himself. When it came to big-game types, to have a client like H. A. Baker—he used to talk about Mr. Baker all the time. He must've been quite a guy."

"So they say."

"According to Lewie, he was literally one in a million. All the others were basically out there for the butchery and the bragging. Anyway, we were way up north, around Hudson's Bay, after polar bear. The client was a man who at that time was very important at MGM. We got to talking one night around the campfire, and after a few hits at the whisky what I would later understand to be his native Hollywood idealism came out—I'm being sarcastic—and he got going on how the trouble with life is the people, that ninety-nine point nine percent of the people you end up dealing with in any line of work are total scum. So the thing to do is to figure out one's particular aptitudes and abilities and then look for wherever it was that you can get the best money for using them, because if it isn't for the money, what's the point of living?"

"I take it you agreed?"

Morland looks at Lucy sharply. "I did not!" he says, but with more good humor than offense. "But I did take him up on a job offer to scout locations for him. I liked the work, still do. Shooting a movie's a lot like organizing a hunt. It takes planning. If you want a rhino, you don't just grab your trusty Weatherby and head for Nairobi, any more than if you want an Oscar or three hundred million dollars at the box office, you tell Jack Nicholson to say cheese and jump off a ten-story building. Say the script calls for Chechnya: that's out because there's a war going on, so the location scout has to find a place that can be put across visually as Chechnya, which these days, given the IQ of the audiences, is not very hard. Or maybe they have to shoot in New York, say, so I explore Manhattan from top to bottom to match place to script, an adaptable piece of ground or water where the action the screenplay calls for can be filmed several different ways. If you shoot the scene on 147th Street from this angle, you get this, and from another, you get that, so you can shoot it either way—what we call twinning."

He looks over at Lucy with a knowing little smile that makes her squirm inside. "Now and then," he continues, steering smartly off onto an exit ramp, "I end up virtually rewriting or restaging a scene or a sequence. Over the years, I've picked up a lot of technical and special-effects stuff, so sometimes we'll end up with a scene that's basically my invention as far as the action's concerned. The big change is how important the computer's become. As in practically everything else in life."

"How so?"

"It's easier to demonstrate than explain. I'll show you later. Basically, let's call it a function of costs. These days, shooting on location is killingly expensive. To redolly an exterior take probably runs thirty thousand dollars. Insurance alone costs what used to be the entire budget of a decent feature. People like George Lucas and this Pixar outfit can materialize whole continents on their computers. Still, audiences want the real thing, so to compete with that, I have to find ways to come up with location specs so precise that the suits in the studios can send a crew to Transylvania knowing to the inch and to the penny how it's going to be shot and what it's going to cost—assuming the talent stays in line, which is practically never the case. If we could computer-control Hollywood's proneness to intragalactic lust, keep the stars' hands off each other, most of the industry's location-cost problems would be solved!'"

Lucy's not really listening. The talent? she wonders. Is that how I should think of Baker? In the next flash, she wonders if she should let on that she knows all about Hollywood's studio suits? She has an uneasy feeling that Morland has more of the measure of her than he's letting on.

It's getting on for four o'clock when they reach Lucy's hotel. She'd like to freshen up, she tells Morland, and make a few calls. He suggests that he return at six-thirty.

That's fine with Lucy. What she really wants is time alone to regroup. It's nothing Morland's said—it's more a matter of barely noticeable inflections of voice and glance—but she's getting a sense that she's not in control here. The feeling's not quite so pronounced as on that fatal —there's no other word for it, not after all that's happened—night at Morton's with Robert Carlsson almost five years ago, nor is it so shot through with apprehension, but it's there.

Well, she tells herself, so what? If she keeps her lips zipped, what can go astray?

Over an excellent dinner she succeeds in doing most of the talking while he sips, eats and thumbs through her treatment. The scene she wants him to lay out for her in Venice, she tells him, is to be the climax of a story of a serial killer whose victims in his mind personify the Seven Deadly Sins.

"They made that picture a few years back," he comments with a smile. "It was called *Seven.* Morgan Freeman and Brad Pitt. A stinker, if you ask me, but really grisly and it did some business, as they say."

"I know it," Lucy answers quickly. "That is, I rented it. My picture's different. My killer's not a sicko, not at first, at least. Actually, he's kind of an idealist." Trying to keep any warmth out of her voice, she describes her central character as the viewer will first see him. It's the Baker she fell for, the Baker of the BEECO closing and "21," of certain unforgettable Italian hours, the Baker who turned out to be a fiction cooked up by her romantic imagination.

"Not to be a wet blanket, Lucy, but they made that one too. *Lonely*

Are the Brave, with Kirk Douglas. A lone cowboy takes on the twentieth century. Nice little picture—basically *Don Quixote* with cars instead of windmills."

"I suppose if you look closely everything's already been done at least once."

"Not everything," Morland replies, "but most things, I suspect. I beg your forgiveness. This business of seeing everything in terms of this or that picture—I'm afraid it's an occupational hazard for me, a kind of tic, like that wrist thing people get when they type too much. The fact that I teach a course in film here at the university doesn't help. I'll try to be careful. And I look forward to reading this."

It's still early when they finish dinner, and Morland suggests they go back to his place so he can show Lucy his setup.

Is he coming on to me? she asks herself as he goes for the car. It's been months since she had a beau: her Bowdoin professor didn't survive the close quarters of the barge trip, and as for the one after him—

She has trouble recalling him at all—beyond the catastrophic weekend on St. Bart's. The name, yes, but little about the face or the rest of him. The fact is, since Carlsson's death this Baker business—who's got time? Or energy, or passion, or creativity? Under normal conditions someone like Peter Morland would be immediately "possible." He's obviously intelligent, at first blush reasonably pleasant, physically acceptable. He chews with his mouth closed, drinks and eats neither too much nor too little, neither too quickly nor too slowly. He listens. Definitely under normal conditions a man worth a preliminary Lipscomb. But these are hardly normal conditions! She's in a box, she's in a trap, she's in a prison—and until she somehow fights free, she must keep all her wits and energy for herself.

Morland lives in a pleasant old stone house in the lee of "the Citadel," as the fort on the heights is called. His studio boasts as elaborate a computer and video setup as Lucy can recall seeing outside a studio. He pours them each a brandy and puts his array through its paces.

"What we're really looking for is to narrow down our choices for camera setup," he tells her. "For instance, this"—a rocky outcrop seen from the middle distance appears on the 32-inch Sony monitor—"is a key exterior for the new Stallone picture. We're looking for a sense of depth, of absolute breath-clutching fall-away, we want the audience to experience virtual vertigo, let's call it, so what I've done is photograph it every which way, both still and video, from above and below, from a helicopter, from a Skywing—"

"What's a Skywing?"

"One of those oversized kites powered with a two-horsepower engine that can carry a man. Anyway, then I scan the images into the computer, and let some proprietary software I've developed digitalize and massage them, and finally what gets spit out are optimum camera angles and placements for certain effects and contexts. At which point the bean counters take over with their sharp pencils and cost each alternative out, and the producer and director huddle with the camera operator, and they decide which setups to shoot, and these go in the budget, and that's that. Until Sly decides he prefers another setup which emphasizes a little more jaw or a little less shortness, at which point everything goes out the window, starting with the budget and up to and frequently including the producer, but by the time that happens I'm on to the next project."

"Very impressive," says Lucy, sipping her brandy. It's good stuff: smooth and full. "And that's what you'll do for me in Venice?"

Morland, sitting across from her on a sofa, settles back against its old, stained leather and looks at Lucy. Looks at her so hard and so dubiously that it's difficult for her not to wince.

"That's what I *could* do in Venice," he says. "My problem, *Mrs.* Preston, is that I don't think I'm going to take on this assignment."

"You're *what*!" Reflexively Lucy drains her snifter and without thinking holds it out for a refill. When she realizes what she's doing, she starts to pull it back, but Morland, with a smile whose warmth belies what he's just said, is already pouring. She sets the snifter on the table beside her. "Come again?" She doesn't feel the least bit high.

"Something here is bothering me. A number of things, actually. To begin with, it bothers me that you're not wearing a wedding ring."

"My God!" Lucy exclaims, and makes an appropriate production of examining her left hand, naked except for a silver-and-gold Tiffany twist on the little finger. "I must have forgotten to put it back on when I washed my hands at the hotel."

"Please. That's the least of it," Morland says nonchalantly. "The resemblance between your voice and your so-called twin Irene's is uncanny. I'd lay a lot of money that the voiceprints are identical. In fact, *Mrs.* Preston, I'll bet you ten thousand U.S. as I'm sitting here. Meet me tomorrow morning at the RCMP station, where they have a voice-printer."

"RCMP?" Lucy bobbing and weaving.

"The Mounties. It's a short walk from your hotel. The desk clerk can tell you."

Lucy glares at him.

"But those are just symptoms," Morland goes on. "My intuition—yes, men have intuition too—is that something's going on here. I don't want to wake up and find myself named an accessory to a contract killing. As a co-conspirator in the extermination of a ballroom full of people with someone who's represented herself as a housewife with a hot movie idea but is actually an agent for Red October or whatever they call themselves. I heard about a fellow to whom something like that happened. Not that the idea isn't chockablock with interesting technical possibilities, depending on how close in you want your villain to work."

He lets it all sink in, then adds, "You know, Lucy, I spend my life around movie stars, most of whom are vocationally required to be two people: whoever they happen to be and then the persona they are on-screen. After a while you develop a sixth sense about when someone's doubling you. You're doubling me. That bothers me, although as long as I don't go for whatever it is you're *really* pushing, my guess is that I'm out of harm's way. So thanks but no thanks."

Lucy's thinking feverishly. She sees that she's been careless, so focused on Christmas Eve, Baker and Venice that she's overshot the fact that, come July, indeed come May—according to her own plan—the world will become aware that the world's great names will be congregating in Venice, and unless Morland removes himself to another planet, he won't fail to be aware of this himself, especially since he's going to be working for Disney, and Eisner will surely be on Mannerman's guest list. What will his response be?

Suppose she opens up to Morland, how is that likely to work out? What does she know about the man sitting across from her, brandy cupped gracefully in the palm of his right hand, observing with evident relish as she stews in the juices of indecision? She *knows* practically nothing, but her sense of him is that he's smart, he has the knowledge and resources she needs, and he's discreet: he hasn't dropped a name all evening, a restraint which in Lucy's experience is practically unthinkable for someone with his connections and résumé. He's a bit arrogant, she judges, and that's a quality worth probing to see if she can turn it to her advantage.

"You're right," she says with a shrug. "There's more to this—to everything—than I've told you."

"Feel free," he replies, reaching for the brandy bottle. *Tinker, Tailor*—

"Pardon?"

"The TV adaptation of the le Carré novel."

"I never saw it."

"One of the best things the BBC ever did." He slips off into recollection for a few seconds before speaking again. "You never saw Hywel Bennett as Ricky? Pity. None better." He continues, in a thick, fairly convincing Cockney accent: "I'm going to tell you a story, Mr. Smiley. It's all about spies. And when I'm through—"

"Please," says Lucy. Does this man see everything as a movie?

It's two in the morning when he returns her to the hotel. She's told Morland everything: all she knows, suspects, theorizes, connects. She's gone from the very beginning, with the sale of Baker's company to Mannerman, and she's left out nothing. She's taken him through her deductions and speculations, led him through her behavioral arithmetic, laid out the mental sums she's arrived at. He listened quietly and intently, now and then asked a question that was more of a prompt. At times, Lucy felt that he was shaping her recitation.

"In other words," he said when she finished, "you think Baker's still alive, and out there killing people."

"I think right now he's deciding who's next. I want to make up his mind for him."

"And you won't go to the police or the FBI?"

"Would you? I've told you. It isn't just that they both leak like sieves. Look at the record! Not to mention my own position. If I'd spoken up earlier, Carlsson would probably still be alive. So what does that make me now?"

And then, of course, he asked the sixty-four-jillion-dollar question, the one Lucy herself can barely make herself murmur to her mirror.

"And what do you plan to do when you do get him?"

"I don't know."

"It usually comes down to dead or alive."

Lucy said nothing. Morland studied her watchfully, then changed course. "And you're guessing he's watching the Internet?"

"How else would he have known I was supposed to fly to Aspen with Carlsson? Liz Smith has her own Web page now. All the celebrity services do too."

"In other words, you're all well-known targets of opportunity on whom he can maintain continuous on-line surveillance."

"Not me."

"You too, if the company you keep is fancy enough."

"I'll make a note of that."

Now, outside Lucy's hotel, with the engine running for warmth, he says, "You know, Lucy, this really would make a hell of a movie. The suits love serial killers. Audiences love the killer sneaking up on someone while the good guy sneaks up on the killer. How old did you say Baker was—is?"

"Almost sixty, I think. Why do you ask? I wish you wouldn't call him a serial killer!" Her vehemence surprises her, but Morland doesn't appear to notice.

"Sixty! Perfect for Clint Eastwood. I know his people at Malpaso Productions; would you like me to give them a call? Just joking. Anyway, according to your hypothesis, Baker's responsible for nine deaths over the last two years and some. Eight by his own hand so far—seven adults, including Carlsson's flight crew, plus Lamond's little grandson. The part I can't understand is, how'd he sucker you in?"

She shakes her head helplessly. "He was different. He wasn't about money. Also, there were—well—resonances from the way I grew up. Town-gown stuff. You know how it is."

"Mercifully, I don't. That is, I haven't—not for a dog's age." He gives her a rueful little smile. "I think you're right about the publicity angle. If word got out, all hell could break loose. The gun nuts would call it the Second Coming of John Wayne, and so would the bleeding hearts: the lone rider coming down from the hills and cleaning up Sodom. As long as he doesn't blow off Mother Teresa, he's a hero. He's the logical extension of Peter Finch in *Network*—'I'm fed up and I'm not going to take it anymore'—or Michael Douglas in *Falling Down*, except that he's not a boozed-out suicidal wacko like the former or a Mr. Nobody with a plastic pocket protector like Douglas's character."

"And he's real—not a character in a movie you can make go away by changing channels."

"Exactly. No, this is the legend made flesh, the dream of vengeance come true. One man against his crummy time. The Wrath of Achilles, the Anger of Baker. It plays. He could become, overnight, the patron saint of every person with a gun and a grudge, the inspiration by example for a multitude of individual bloodbaths that, taken together, might add up to an ocean. Hey, if he can blow away a Tinkry, why can't I! Lord knows, the anger's out there, and the firepower to match. That's one reason I live in Nova Scotia. Once every century or so a ship blows up and levels the town, but those odds are OK with me. The only trouble with Halifax is that the world has shrunk. I can get from here to Los Angeles in less than ten hours. In a justly ordered world, it would take ten days."

At the thought of Hollywood's proximity, he falls silent. Lucy wants to ask the obvious question—Will you help?—but holds back. Time is her ally. Give him long enough, she thinks, and he'll turn this into a movie in his own mind, and then he'll be hers.

She stirs as if to go. Morland jumps out of the car, rounds it and sweeps her door open with a flourish.

"You know," he says, with exaggerated nonchalance, "this plan of yours might just work. Perhaps I was hasty. Let me sleep on it." He breaks out a big smile. "You can't possibly know this, but you've ferreted out my secret ambition. I've always fancied myself in the role of Sanger Rainsford."

"Sanger Rainsford?"

"The hero, I suppose you'd say, of a real chestnut of a story called *The Most Dangerous Game*. I read it as a boy and never got over it. They made about three lousy movies from it. In the story an experienced sportsman named Sanger Rainsford, kind of a Baker type in fact, falls overboard from a yacht and is washed up on a remote island owned by a crazy Russian general or baron or something, one of those types with a monocle and a cigarette holder and a brace of wolfhounds at his heels.

And before Rainsford knows what's hit him, he's out there on this weird island being stalked like an animal. So he stalks back. You can guess the ending."

He walks her to the hotel door. "One other thing you ought to think about," he says. "Whether I'm involved or not, you're going to have to have someone along for the ride who can pull a trigger if he has to. A pro."

"I've thought about that. The question is, where do I find one?"

"Beats me," Morland says. "Ask your dad. He was a cop, wasn't he? As for me, well, frankly, m'dear, I don't give a damn—just as long as the son of a bitch can shoot straight."

— III — "I figure it's better to see where he actually *did* do someone in before I try to figure out how he *might* do in someone else."

The frozen fairway squeaks underfoot as Morland and Lucy push against a spray-wettened northeast wind whipping off the dunes, churning the surface of Hook Pond into a racing froth. It makes an eerie counterpoint to Morland's half-shouted words, and so do the creaking limbs of the tall maples guarding the third green two hundred yards away.

Under her down vest and polyfleece pullover, Lucy shivers. This is a terrible idea. East Hampton on the first day of March is colder than Halifax in February ever was.

Morland has declared himself "in." When Lucy picked up the phone a week ago, his first words were "Quick, Watson, the game's afoot!" He's flying to Venice tonight. But he's "in" conditionally. He'll scope out Venice, make a report—but any further involvement is subject to Lucy finding "a shootist," as he irritatingly puts it. He definitely wants to be in on the Baker plot, but if anyone's killed, he wants it odds-on that it won't be him.

His choice of words—this talk of "kill"—irritates Lucy, but she knows he's right. She and Morland aren't killers, and Baker is.

To whom can she turn? Spuds gave her the names of outfits in the

United States and Italy that supply armed bodyguards, and she's faxed for rate sheets, but she can't bring herself to pop the real question. Her behavior reminds her of a teenager buying his first rubber: she put one of her early beaux through that agony once, and watched through the drugstore window as he edged up to the counter, shifted from one foot to the other, unable to get the words out, until finally he turned diphtheric scarlet and fled, while Lucy collapsed in giggles on the pavement.

There's always time, she tells herself—until, one day, there isn't.

Morland has agreed that Baker will need six months. "It's his outside time frame," he told Lucy on the way from LaGuardia, where they rendezvoused, to East Hampton. "That's assuming he's hiding out in the Antarctic and has to make his way to Venice by dog sled."

This afternoon, Lucy will drive Morland to JFK, where he'll catch the overnight Alitalia to Milan. She'll drop off the rented car and return to Maine, and they'll meet again on March 15 in Halifax.

Lucy counts backward, six months from Christmas, to mid-June. Say Memorial Day, to be on the safe side. That's still three months away. As preparations for Mannerman's gala get up to speed, the likelihood of a leak increases with every conversation, every purchase order.

"Of course, a lot will depend on his ordnance requirements," Morland had said. "There's a logic in these things he can't get around. He'll work backward from his target location. He has to figure out first where he wants to hit it from. Up close and personal is one thing, but if the security perimeter extends out four or five hundred yards, he would have to use different weaponry. From everything we know, Baker's no suicide bomber. He who kills and runs away, lives to kill another day. His choice of weapon will be a function of range and accuracy, as well as portability and availability—something Baker can get hold of discreetly and handle himself, but with a lot of power. Then he's got to have documentation, disguise—"

"I think we can assume he has those already," Lucy had interrupted. He could have grown a beard, dyed his hair, had his eyes "done" or changed their color with contact lenses, taught himself to walk funny.

"You're probably right. I may be overgenerous about the time frame, but all I'm doing now is trying to figure out what kind of needle he'll choose and which haystack it's likely to be in, come the day. Things tend to take longer than we think. Those guys in Oklahoma City used a year to go after a facility with zero security with a bomb made from stuff you can pick up at your local Agway. Baker's going after the richest and most powerful people on earth with probably ten in security for every guest, and that's not counting high-tech."

Now they are walking out to the narrow plank bridge connecting the fourth tee to the fourth green. Lucy looks around, for it's a long while since she's been out this way. It's strange to see the place so deserted. She gave up the Hamptons years ago, but she hasn't forgotten that without the people the dunescape is really very beautiful: the high, deep-arched sky makes her feel as if she's in a Dutch old master painting, a Koninck or Van de Velde.

She and Morland stand silently on the bridge, gazing across the pond's wind-whipped water at the green.

"Lamond and the boy would have come from there," Morland says, pointing at a massive shuttered shingled house in the middle distance. He takes a few steps farther along the bridge, kneels down and peers under it. Lucy follows suit.

"Here's where I'd have him shooting from if I were directing this picture." He points to the fretwork of struts and pilings through which courses a pair of medium-diameter white polyethylene pipes. "Hard to pick out, especially in the early glare off the water, and a can't-miss angle. Now—"

He stands and surveys the pond again, beginning with a stone bridge well off to the left and finishing at the rush-fringed southwestern bank, where subterranean tides seeped beneath high dunes mantled in sea grass.

"Where he would go after that is the kicker," Morland says. "In a movie, it'd be there." He points to the seaward edge. "Dramatic, but too far and too shallow in real life. He'd have figured he'd have maybe fifteen minutes tops. My bet is he went either there"—Morland gestures to his right, to a great stand of rushes dividing the pond from the perfect lawn of a subtreasury-size white "cottage"—"or there"—he points diagonally across the water to a bulging, bush-covered spit perhaps a hundred yards away. "Not far, good cover, and shielded from the road. In August, he'd have figured there'd be people about very early. Onward!"

He strides off. They traverse other greens and fairways, pausing briefly to study the Lamond house, boarded up for winter. Eventually they reach the top of the dunes running parallel to Maidstone's ninth fairway. The sea, a dreary grayish dun, is running rough. The winter beach seems brown and uninviting.

"C'mon," Lucy says, and they scramble down. She crosses to the water and sticks a hand in the foaming outrace. It's paralyzingly cold; unimaginable that it can ever be swum in. With a little cry, she backs off, and she and Morland stroll eastward, close to the water, where the sand is firm. On the unprotected beach, the wind feels twice as savage. Lucy zips her pullover to her chin.

Lucy's happy to be here. I like you, Morland, she thinks, behind the screen of gentle, random chatter. You're smart, you're young in spirit, you haven't thrown away your enthusiasm. You may be boring to look at, but you're articulate, you're inventive, you're good company. *Simpático*, Baker would have said. Morland stops, gazes out to sea, picks up a stone and skims it ineffectually at the incoming waves, grimaces at his ineptness like a little boy. Lucy likes her men boyish. She senses the familiar stirrings of that urge to Lipscomb. No time for that now, Lucy, she tells herself sternly. Perhaps later.

If there is a later.

They reach the eastern end of the Maidstone golf course, where the unbroken stretch of dune ends and large houses emerge from a background of pine scrub.

"This way," says Morland. "I want to see something."

A narrow path through the dunes takes them to a small parking lot and a paved road that runs along Hook Pond toward Dunemere Lane, where their rented car is parked. The gates along the deserted road are chained and padlocked. No car passes. In the summer it would be different, even at six in the morning. This would be a popular walkers' route to the beach and back. The vans and trucks of those who service the wealthy would be up and about.

"Here," Morland says. He stops and points.

They're looking back across at the narrow bridge. From this angle, the fourth green can't be seen; it's hidden away behind the curving pond bank and obscuring tangles of marsh vegetation. He leaves the road and prowls briefly in the rushes and thornbushes.

"He could have stashed his getaway rig here," Morland says. "Walking shorts, Nikes, a T-shirt, a couple of towels. He could have swum underwater from the bridge, surfaced amid these rushes, crawled into those bushes and changed."

"What about the rifle?"

"Sank it. No one would think he'd jettison it, a thirty-thousand-dollar rifle! Anyway, where would *you* start looking? A lot of the stories surmised that the shots came from over there." Morland points northwest, to the far bank of Hook Pond, nearest the town. "But personally, I think they settled on the wrong point of the compass. Baker once swam with the SEALs. I think he came back this way, wrapped the rifle in his wet suit, assuming he was wearing one, tied 'em up together with some weights and sank them or buried them under the bank. It's been what? Almost two years? By now the stuff's probably a foot under silt. Anyway, then he changed, emerged from the bushes, and to anyone who happens along he's just another fiftyish WASP, another Bank of New York VP enjoying his month in the sun, creeping out of the tules after having a pee."

On the way to JFK, Morland seems reflective.

"This is a man who knows his own strengths and skills and works with them. What he doesn't know about, he doesn't try. No on-the-job training for Mr. Baker. He likes to work on territory he knows well before he gets there, so he can concentrate on the niceties, not have to hunt around. Did you know he'd been a member of the Maidstone Club?"

"No." Lucy wishes she'd taken a closer look at the golfing photos in Baker's albums, tries to recall whether any of the backgrounds resemble this place.

"Well, he was, for about ten years. He rented—I guess—a house down here back in the late sixties."

"How do you know that?"

"Played a hunch. Dialed up *The Social Register*—the Forbeses, the magazine people, own it and they took it on-line a couple of years ago —and ran a search on H. A. Baker. He was there, all right—from the time he got out of college until he quote died unquote. I ran the entries for every year, and what do you know: for four years he listed his summer residence as 'The Gatehouse, Middle Lane, East Hampton,' and Maidstone as one of his clubs. He knows the lay of the land here. So, assuming he had a bee in his bonnet about Lamond, and if he saw the piece you told me about where Lamond talked about putting over there by dawn's early light, his mental lightbulb probably clicked right on."

Baker had never mentioned his East Hampton life to Lucy, but she can understand that. Like some other declared "ex-Hamptons" people she knows, he probably hated what had happened to the place in the 1980s and had mentally disavowed any youthful connection as out of keeping with the serious image he wanted the world to see. Most men she knew reinvented themselves three or four times; they were revisionists who edited their own histories, who searched in themselves for the one with the ball with the same determination that she searched in them for the one with the ball. It strikes her that only when the two searches end with the same man will hers be over.

Morland pulls over to the curb outside the Alitalia lobby and gets out.

"Well," says Lucy, "happy hunting." She doesn't mean to sound flip.

"Not to worry. And to you too. Any progress on our shootist?"

She considers fibbing, but what's the point? "Not really. I've got some names. Security firms, Kroll, people like that. The whole thing scares me."

"I can see why. Use a big licensed firm and we're back in Leaksville, no matter what they say."

"That's my feeling. Peter, you must know someone." It's the first time she's called him by name. She never called Baker anything but "Baker."

"In Halifax? In *Canada*? Hardly!"

"No, no, no! On the Coast? One of those tough studio security people? Or a private investigator?"

"You mean like Fred Ward in *The Player*? Or Sam Spade or Philip Marlowe? Hey, give me a break! If such exist, I've never seen one."

"Damn!" Lucy can't hide her chagrin. This wouldn't have been a problem for Carlsson!

For a moment, both are silent. She feels her spirits plummeting.

"Say, what about your father?" asks Morland. "You told me he was a crack shot who had done what he had to do in the line of duty. Back in his FBI days. And he hates extremists and vigilantes."

This is what she's tried to stay away from, and now here it is, right in her face.

If the Chief were anyone else, the suggestion would make sense. He *was* a crack shot who in his day could fill up the bull's-eye at thirty yards. For a while, in the early years at Paster's Point, he practiced diligently, kept his hand and eye in, but that was when Lucy was a little girl. Paster's wasn't the sort of beat that required quick-draw, Deadeye Dick policing. The only shots her father had fired in recent memory were at his monthly forays after duck and Canada goose. Still, how many times had he told Lucy that shooting was like riding a bicycle: once you got it, you never lost it.

Moreover, her father and Baker never met. So there would be no danger of the quarry recognizing his pursuer.

And then there's this: it's one thing for Lucy to confess to her father and ask his advice, but it's totally different if she gets him actively involved, if she—there's no other word for it—entangles him in her own dilemma. Still, the Chief's feelings about people who take the law into their own hands give Lucy a certain leverage.

"You might be right," she tells Morland.

"Or maybe he'll know someone. These ex-FBI people run a pretty good old-boy network."

"I'll try the idea out on him." And for the first time, she means it.

Suddenly Lucy realizes that she'd fallen into a familiar trap in thinking about the Chief, a tendency toward tunnel vision that she'd always had to work consciously to avoid. Mentally she'd consigned her father to the role of advisor, counselor; she'd thought of him as wise parent and extrapolated from there. But Morland is raising the possibility of bringing the Chief in as co-adventurer. And now, suddenly, speaking frankly—confessing all—to him seems entirely possible. The Chief walks the bluffs in every kind of weather, hoists a sail in white water, waits through freezing nights in duck blinds, smokes cigars, drinks bourbon, keeps his venerable sidearm oiled and polished even if he seldom fires it. He's a tough old coot who led an active front-line life in which he wasn't treated fairly. Lucy knows the seam of vindictiveness there that can be bored into and mined.

I've been too busy being busy, Lucy thinks, to recognize how bored and useless he must feel, trying to build a life from television and recollection. This is a man who in his time tracked down and faced down killers and lunatics, including one who dismembered children across six states. If she holds out the golden apple of one last big adventure, it's her guess that the Chief'll probably snatch at it.

"Good enough," says Morland. "As long as there's a real shooter on this trip, I'll keep up my end." He checks his watch. "Anything else?"

"Just this. When you get back, I may want you to find me an island."

"An island? What kind of island?"

"We'll get to that later."

Morland smiles, shakes his head. Women! And he disappears into the terminal. As Lucy pulls away, she thinks: Say what you like, it's not an entirely crazy idea. Baker still has some kind of hook on her, some hold that makes it repellent to think of dealing with him as cold-bloodedly—in his high-handed way, he would probably say "objectively"—as he's dealt with others.

I'm damned if I do, she thinks, as the airliner descends toward Portland, damned if I don't—and she decides, like Scarlett O'Hara, to think about it tomorrow.

The next evening, as she climbs out of the car and walks quickly up the path toward her father's front door, Lucy's feet turn to ice. Am I nuts, she thinks, or am I nuts? Her father is—has been—an officer of the law to whom the law is sacred. All Lucy's life he's told her: America is a nation of laws, not men. In the last year, she's heard the Chief explode time and again with rage at the notion of Americans—anyone —trying to impose a private vision of the way things ought to be with guns and bombs, and he's always finished up with the same old declaration: America is a nation of laws, not men. She's heard it from his lips perhaps a thousand times, yet Lucy's never really grasped the concept of "law" as a sacred ideal. To her, "law" means lawyers, means Mannerman's sharp and oily attorneys drilling loopholes like pipelines through the very ventricles of equity. Never having had to test the proposition, she's simply assumed that at the sticking point, as Morland would say, her father would rate family ahead of law. Now—can she be sure? She wishes Morland were here to help out.

She finds the Chief in the kitchen, boiling water for coffee.

"Daddy," she says, taking a deep breath, "I've got something to tell you."

He looks at her sharply. "Don't tell me you're pregnant!"

The question draws a smile from Lucy. Where would I find the time? she thinks. "Nothing as simple as that." In as commanding a voice as she can muster—a good offense is the best defense—she tells her father to sit down.

What ensues comes as a terrible anticlimax, what Lucy will regard as a waste of many a sleepless hour, many an edgy self-questioning minute. After an initial outburst, basically about how stupid she's been, how she's put herself in a box, the Chief behaves neither as a paragon of law enforcement nor as an outraged parent. His reaction is emotional and personal, and Lucy realizes she's guessed right. She's understood her father better than at first she let herself think. Under that terse New England personality there's a powder keg of old resentments, and she touches them off.

The Chief practically licks his chops at the prospect of showing up his old service, of making scapegoats and fools of the Bureau that years ago scapegoated him and exiled him from the center of the action to this rockbound outpost on the near shore of nowhere. Her legal exposure he dismisses virtually out of hand. Beside the larger issue, it's irrelevant. It's her plan for bringing Baker to book that he cares about, and he probes, critiques, questions, challenges: asking but not waiting for answers.

"Count me in," he says finally, and starts to rise from the kitchen table, as if to go upstairs to start packing.

"Sit down," she says quietly. I can count you in, she thinks. What I have to know is, how am I going to count on you? "Daddy, I have to ask you this. If you had to, could you shoot a man? Could you shoot Baker?" She hates the question so much, it's an effort get the words out.

"Honey bear, the way I feel, if I had to shoot *you* to pull this off, I'd do it!" the Chief answers vigorously. His face flashes thoughtful. "Shoot *at* him I could, but hit him—ah, that's something else. It's been a long time."

For a moment he falls silent. Then he brightens. "I'm being silly! Shooting's sixty percent instinct, forty percent practice. You either have it or you don't—you and I have it, honey bear—and once you've done it, you don't forget, like riding a bicycle. You may be a bit wobbly off the mark, but after a hundred yards, you're as good as ever. How much time did you say we have?"

"Till Christmas."

"Not to worry, then. As long as these don't betray me—and why should they—when the time comes I'll be as sharp as ever." He holds out his hands, palms down. Not a tremor, not a tremble. He looks at his daughter with an enormous, confident smile. "By Thanksgiving, honey bear, you can expect to see a lot of one-eyed gulls around these parts."

Later that week, when Lucy drops by to leave off some groceries, the moment she's inside the Chief's front door her nose picks up the almost-forgotten scent of Hoppe's #9 gun-cleaning solvent. From the workroom comes a contented humming. She peeks in and sees her father vigorously polishing his old Smith & Wesson .38 Police Special. He's intent on his task, his bluff, hard-worn face child-serious, dead earnest, but lit with a freshness Lucy hasn't seen since her mother died. He's humming the "Maine Fight Song" as he squints down the barrel. He looks twenty years younger.

— IV — In the wake of a big nor'easter, the crossing from Portland is a rough one. Lucy, who's never seasick, is up three times in the night, cursing her father between retches. To come to Halifax by ferry was his idea. He argued that he'd never have another chance, and Lucy'd given in to his plaintive reminiscences of romantic holidays in Nova Scotia with her mother. When she staggers topside at seven for coffee, with the ferry making calmer way in the lee of Digby Neck, with the southern coast of Nova Scotia looming darkly against a darkening sky, she's pleased to see that her father and his friend Ormerud look as gray-gilled as she feels.

Raymond Ormerud is the Chief's choice to fill out the team. He's a cool customer, a spare, unsmiling Southerner a half dozen years younger than Lucy's father, an old colleague from the FBI (who'd also put in time at Alcohol, Tobacco and Firearms and the Secret Service), who presently works as chief of security for a gated community just north of Palm Beach. According to the Chief, Ormerud, a three-time FBI pistol champion, knows all that needs to be known about surveillance and shooting, but he doesn't suffer fools, period, an attitude that's caused trouble at every agency he's served in. In the mid-1980s he was driven from government service when an FBI special investigations team he headed up tracked down and killed a team of kidnappers, one of whom unfortunately died on the wrong side of the U.S.–Mexico border. Ormerud became the focus of a diplomatic incident, was publicly pilloried at televised hearings conducted by an ambitious junior senator and forced into early retirement. Like the Chief, he believes that the greatest threat to the rule of law is the people who put themselves above it, and that the once-sacred calling of law enforcement has been so weakened by corruption, politics, special interests and general moral spinelessness that it has become all but powerless to prevent the nation from toppling into anarchy.

On the basis of the few hours she's spent in his company, Lucy reads Ormerud's condition as like her father's: a combination of boredom and brooding resentment. That's why Ormerud signed on so willingly, she guesses, for what Morland's taken to calling "Lucy's Excellent Adventure." She'll be interested to see how Morland reacts to the new recruit.

The ferry docks in Yarmouth shortly after ten, about an hour behind schedule. Not long after they roll off, a front sweeps in, accompanied by high winds and snow, and it takes them six hours instead of the usual four to reach Halifax by the coastal highway. It turns out not to matter, however. When they check into the Sheraton at the waterfront, Lucy finds a message that the weather has stranded Morland in Montreal and he probably won't make it to Halifax until much later.

Still, at eight the next morning the phone rings in Lucy's room and Morland says, "I'll be downstairs in forty-five minutes. Time to get cracking."

When they get to the nice old stone house—this is the first time Lucy's seen it in daylight—his studio is set up for a presentation. Three chairs have been placed in front of his 32-inch Sony monitor, connected, Lucy supposes, to the computer on a table off to one side at which Morland seats himself. He fiddles with his computer mouse as he studies the standard monitor in front of him, and the big Sony displays, in vividly colored split-screen mode, two bird's-eye views of Venice, one cartographic, the other photographic, with the main geographic features labeled in large red letters, with compass points and distance scales also clearly readable.

The map is similar to one that Lucy's been studying back home in Maine, a standard tourist map that takes in most of the city—with separate inserts for the more prominent islands of the lagoon: the Lido, Murano, Burano and Torcello. The same field of view as the aerial photograph. Morland clicks his mouse and the photograph is replaced by another, shot from a much higher altitude, that covers nearly the entire Venetian lagoon.

From the air, Venice resembles the heads of two reptiles devouring each other. The jawline of the topmost, lunging from the right, follows the east—San Marco—bank of the Grand Canal from its beginnings by the railroad station, hinging at the Rialto Bridge, then curving back, and then back again to form a lower jaw which includes the city's most famous sights, the Piazza San Marco, the Campanile, the Basilica of San Marco. The upper beast's gaping jaws are set to clamp down on the other reptile's snout, a protuberance coming in from the left and shaped by the western bank of the Grand Canal. The lower reptile's ferocious mouth, which seems about to swallow the San Marco quarter whole, hinges where the Foscari canal runs into the Grand Canal, near the three great palaces of Rezzonico, Foscari and Balbi. The jaw—the so-called Dorsoduro—runs out into the lagoon and finishes in a savage hook set off by the noble sixteenth-century church of Santa Maria della Salute.

Below and roughly parallel to the Dorsoduro is a fierce inverted talon of an island: this is the Giudecca, where Lucy and Baker stayed at the Cipriani and lunched with Baker's friends the Volsis in the garden of their villa. Below lies the populous eastern portion of the Lido, with its grand resort hotels and casinos and, at the very tip, in the place called Alberoni, the golf course where Baker played nine holes with Count Volsi.

"This is just to give you a sense of the whole," Morland says. He clicks again, and a concentric set of bright yellow circles appears, centered on a point on the upper bank of the Grand Canal roughly, as Lucy eyeballs it, a quarter mile up from San Marco.

"Range diameters," Morland says, "calibrated in hundred-fifty-meter intervals. For our purposes"—he clicks again and all but three circles vanish, and the second panoramic aerial view is replaced by its predecessor—"we need concern ourselves only with a target radius of between four hundred and eight hundred yards from Ground Zero, here." A fat black arrow materializes out in the lagoon off the Piazza San Marco, and moves erratically left, in time with Morland's manipulation of the mouse, into the mouth of the Grand Canal and a few inches along the upper bank until it settles on the point where the circles meet. Another click and the arrow vanishes, replaced by the legend "Grand Hotel Regina e Imperatrice."

"Queen and Empress?" Lucy exclaims. "What happened to just plain old Regina Palace?"

"I'm more interested in your assumptions about range," says Ormerud impatiently. "What's your thinking?"

"Good question. We're trying to predict someone else's behavior, and we have to make certain assumptions based—well, in this case based on what Lucy knows. One of my principal givens is that Baker obviously knows that the closer in he works, the better will be his chances of success, but that he won't venture past the point where he'd have to give himself up. He's not a suicide type—we're not looking at Beirut-by-the-lagoon here, and he won't want to be caught. I'm guessing his no-go point to be roughly four hundred yards out from Ground Zero. For instance, right here . . ."

Another staccato series of clicks. The concentric yellow circles disappear. On the waters of the lagoon, a shallow, thick orange arc, chopped into six unequal trapezoidal segments, materializes on the blue ground that indicates the lagoon. It extends in an oblate sweep from the tip of the lower left-hand jaw, a point Lucy remembers as being dominated by the Salute, across the opening of the Grand Canal to a point on the lower right-hand jaw which she identifies as right under the Doge's Palace.

"Right here is where any spectator fleet would assemble," Morland continues, "no closer. Of course, a lot depends on how they choose to move the party from the hotel to the church. I'm guessing by barge, behind a screen of police boats. The spectator fleet, out here, would be fenced off by a second screen of picket boats between it and the police boats. They'll probably split it into segments: media here in the middle, say, then VIP sectors for big shots and the uninvited rich and famous here, and the hoi polloi in rowboats here, here and here. The segments'll be separated by water alleys—let's call them—for emergency or official water traffic to move in and out. They'd patrol these alleys electronically with very sophisticated recognition sensors, just in case any unauthorized soul should get the idea of trying to sneak through disguised as a water ambulance. There's no way anyone could attack from within this nautical crowd scene without being spotted."

"Do you mind if I ask how you know all this?" Ormerud seems both impressed and skeptical.

"I don't *know* anything. I'm just trying to think through how I'd set up security if it was up to me. If you have anything to add, Ray, for God's sake speak up! You're the security expert!"

"Just curious. Looks to me like you're on the right track."

Morland clicks again. Two yellow circles reappear. The diameter of the smallest circle encompasses only a portion of the tourist's Venice: the Piazza San Marco but not the Basilica or the Doge's Palace; the Grand Canal up to the Accademia Bridge but not the Rialto; only the Salute end of the Dorsoduro. The next largest takes in most of the central city on the right bank of the Grand Canal, looking north; it includes the "mouth" of the Dorsoduro and reaches inland just short of San Rocco, Tintoretto's masterpiece. Its bottom arc runs along the edge of the Giudecca, incorporating most of the up-angled claw of that island—although not the Cipriani—and crosses the little Canale della Grazia to gather in the portion of the neighboring island of San Giorgio Maggiore nearest the city, including the great church and its lofty campanile.

Looking on, Lucy can't help feeling a twinge, as she remembers going to those places with Baker. It's odd, sitting here, studying this great city not as a monument to civilization but as a venue for savagery, as a killing ground. Remembering lunch with the Volsis at their *palazzino*, she studies the screen carefully, trying to locate it exactly.

"OK," Morland says, "here's the bottom line. These two circles represent firing radii of four hundred and eight hundred meters. Realistically, I think we should only concern ourselves with the latter." A click: the smaller circle disappears.

"Why?" asks Lucy's father.

"Choice of weapon, mainly. And—as I said—the prospective perp's MO."

"What about a hit-and-run from a boat?" asks the Chief in a doubtful voice. "You sure you can rule that out? It'll be nighttime, people will be excited. If he positions himself in the right place and unloads a couple of bazooka rounds . . ."

"I'll give you partial credit, Chief." Morland smiles. "But think about it. With a bazooka, he has to have line of sight, he's on the water, he's got to shoot between two picket lines of security craft and God knows what else."

The Chief looks at Ormerud. The latter shrugs.

"Just for argument's sake," Morland says, "let's say he gets himself a high-speed motorboat, something like a Donzi, capable of fifty knots, and he tries a running shot, with his bazooka in one hand while steering with the other—"

"He could have an accomplice," Ormerud observes.

Morland looks at Lucy. She shakes her head. "I don't think so," she says.

"Even if he does, he'd have to shoot from within a very short stretch beginning roughly here, just past the Dorsoduro, before he'd have to break off for open water. Fact is, Chief, an attack over water blows all his percentages. He'd hit them when they're packed together in the roof garden." Morland glances at Lucy again. "Didn't your spy say there would be fireworks at midnight?"

"Before midnight," she replies. "So you have to give the Pope time to get from the hotel to San Marco. The fireworks—personally supervised by George Plimpton, I hear—will begin around eleven and go for half an hour."

"That's what I was guessing," says Morland. Now it's his turn to look at Ormerud for endorsement. Ormerud nods.

"What about from the opposite bank?" Lucy asks. "Why wouldn't he try a *Day of the Jackal*? He loved that movie."

"Let's assume the carabinieri have seen the same movies he has. They'll have sharpshooters on every roof within probable firing range of the hotel."

"How about from the air? Like that nut who crashed into the White House?" asks Lucy's father.

"Ah, here's a man who's read his Tom Clancy. Actually, Chief, I tried that on for size. I've worked on a couple of pictures where we used drones, model planes, but the problem is, it's hard to come up with one that has enough wingspan and horses to lift and then deliver the explosive power he'd want. Plus, in a film, you shoot the drone in one take and then the explosion in a second, and then you splice 'em. In the real world it has to be continuous. Besides, this is Venice. I'm damned if I can see where he'd find enough room to assemble a good-size drone and get it airborne. And then you've got weather to worry about, and finally if the Polizia decide to jam frequencies as an extra precaution, your radio control is shot—and all this assumes no air cover, but I'll lay you ten to one that we're going to see air cover starting with choppers at sea level and going up to around ten thousand feet."

"What about something larger, fired from farther out? A handheld ground-to-ground rocket launcher, an antitank missile, something like that?"

Morland grins. "Chief, I've always said great minds work alike! Basically, I see only two types of weapon filling Baker's bill: either mortars or some kind of shoulder-held, hand-fired launcher with a smart rocket. My guess is, Baker's familiar with both—from his time in Vietnam and that stint in Afghanistan when the Russians were there. But that doesn't solve our problems. With a line-of-sight weapon, anything from a pistol to a bazooka, your accuracy tends to be a function of range and elevation. But you're going to have all sorts of trajectory problems—this is a hint, students—shooting at a roof garden nine stories up."

"Unless you're at that elevation yourself!" Lucy practically shrieks. She feels like a kid in school, waving her hand frantically for the teacher's attention. "What about from up on the portico of the Salute?" she asks, looks at Morland and subsides. "No, that'll be patrolled, won't it?"

"What about one of these towers here?" asks Ormerud, rising and tapping the screen. "Wouldn't they give you a straight-in shot?"

Morland grins at him with a thumbs-up. "Exactly my thought, Ray. Let's come back to that. Now: choice of weapon. Baker would want something with a high degree of accuracy, portability and killing power.

With handheld rocket launchers, you're looking at line-of-sight, infrared tracking. The military record isn't all that good where accuracy's concerned, but then again, that's largely because the gunner has to expose himself to a target that either is shooting back, which doesn't exactly encourage ready-steady aiming, or is moving. Neither would be the case in Venice."

"So what are you thinking about specifically?" Ormerud asks.

"Specifically, the latest Swiss refit of the old Army Dragon II. It's what they call an MAW, a medium assault weapon. Basically an all-in-one, one-off gizmo."

"One-off?"

"Like a disposable razor, Chief. It's just a fiberglass tube that comes complete with missile inside and a tracking assembly you screw on. You fire the missile and throw the tube and tracker away. It weighs fifty pounds and measures less than four feet, and its effective range is a thousand meters, which is comfortable for our boy."

"Fifty pounds is not exactly feathers."

"No, Ray, but it's manageable. As I say, it'll fit in a golf bag, a big duffel, an oversize rod case, anything you could push along on wheels. Or something like this."

Moving like a showman, Morland goes across to a closet and brings out a fat graphite tube almost five feet long.

"I picked this up in Milan. It's a carrying case for the new Nikon 3800-millimeter video lens that recently performed so well in combat conditions in the Caribbean."

"What combat conditions?"

Morland smirks at Lucy. "Just kidding. This is the lens the *National Enquirer* guy used to grab those shots of Princess Di topless. If you take out the lining, it'll hold a Dragon very nicely. But my main point is: who'll notice? Can you imagine how many paparazzi are going to be in Venice? Except for whatever pool your friends allow in the actual gala, the photographers are going to have to work at long range. This is a really fast, digitalized piece of optical machinery. Come Christmas week, they'll be as common in Venice as those masks!"

"But surely Baker will want more than one shot?" asks the Chief.

"Probably, depending on the warhead. My guess is, he'll figure on no more than three."

"That's a hundred fifty pounds."

"Why not take it as a given," says Lucy, "that he'll find a way. He always has."

Her father nods doubtfully.

"The question I have," Lucy asks, "is where is he going to buy these things?"

"Only from one of about five hundred discreet sources. Nowadays, with national defenses winding down and guerrillas and private armies stocking up, the arms trade has gotten to be like Home Depot. Let's be more exact: he buys from a dealer he locates on the Internet. From wherever there's a war going on or there's been one. About the only place you can't buy weapons is . . . well, you can't walk into Fort Devens, say, waving your Visa card, and ask to have one gift-wrapped. My sources tell me the Iraqis bought a ton of these off the Swiss via Algeria and have been selling their overstock to Serbia, which means you can probably lay your hands on them anywhere from Trieste to Ankara."

"Can I ask something?" says Ormerud.

"Sure."

"Well, you're pretty committed to line of sight—"

"Baker's a crack rifle shot, don't forget. Firing from the shoulder with a rest is his style."

"I'll buy that, Peter. But what about an alternative? Wouldn't a mortar make sense?"

"Definitely a wavelength I looked into, Ray. Portable, available, accurate. We'd be talking theme and variations on the M224 60-millimeter, with a sideways glance at the M252 81-millimeter. The 81-millimeter gives you all the bells and whistles and five thousand meters of range, which means Baker could cut loose from the Lido, but it's a big sucker: ninety pounds. Throw in the ammunition at ten pounds or so per round—though two rounds of high-explosive with a fifty-yard lethal radius would more than do the trick—and you're looking at a commuter situation to get it set up, and that might draw attention."

"If it's a mortar, I'd take the 224," says Ormerud. "That's what they should've gone with at Waco."

"I agree. Eighteen pounds plus the ammunition for the handheld version, forty-five plus ammo for the model with the bigger baseplate.

One man can fire five or ten rounds per minute from as far out as nine hundred yards. That would give Baker all of Circle Two to work with. If he gets himself one of those global-positioning devices you can order out of a catalogue for around eight hundred bucks, he could drop a round on a gnat's eye. The problem is, mortars are lob-type weapons. You're usually firing at an enemy you don't see, and so you're deprived of the relish of watching what happens when the round strikes."

"You really think that makes a difference?"

"What do *you* think, Ray? You know how people like this think, what they get off on."

Ormerud considers his answer. Morland looks at Lucy; his expression asks the same question. She nods.

"I come back to the fact that a shoulder-mounted rocket launcher's the closest you'll get to a rifle, physically and operationally. If he can find the right spot to shoot from, he would take the Dragon. I'd bet on it!" It's hard to resist Morland's infectious excitement. He's a man in the grip of certitude.

"And you think you know what the spot might be?"

"I do, Ray. So do you. Right here!"

The fat black arrow reappears, crosses the narrow neck of the lagoon, settles on the tip of the island of San Giorgio Maggiore and begins to blink furiously.

"For this particular caper," Morland declares, "there's no better firing platform in all of Venice. I went up to the observation deck, about a hundred feet above sea level and practically eye-to-eye with the Regina roof garden, which is roughly six hundred meters away. I had a pair of twelve-power glasses with me, and I could just pick out the roof columns. Beyond the range of the longest photographic lens in commercial use today, including the Nikon 3800. I checked this out with George Lucas's people at Industrial Light and Magic; outside of the stuff NASA uses, there's nothing more powerful around, and please make a note of this point, because I'll come back to it. From a shooter's point of view, look at it! A straight shot of less than half a mile, an optimum range for a Dragon II, and nothing in the way! You'd be shooting right over the spectator fleet. There's even a parapet you could rest the launcher on. Nobody's likely to see you at night, especially after the fireworks show begins and everybody's going 'Ooh' and 'Ah' at the night sky."

"If we can see this, won't the security people?" Lucy observes. "It'll be under lock and key, or there'll be guards posted on top."

Ormerud shakes his head. "I doubt it. It's a half mile away, well off the processional route."

Lucy studies the screen. She wishes she could be as certain as the men. "I don't know," she says. "You seem so adamant about San Giorgio Maggiore, but look at all these other places."

"Strictly nonstarters," responds Morland in an irritatingly confident tone. "Once he's decided on the Dragon, his options are set."

"How do you get into the place?" asks Ormerud.

Well, thinks Lucy, *his* mind's made up.

"Through the church." Morland's mouse clicks. On the screen appears a floor plan and elevation of San Giorgio Maggiore and its campanile. "From right here, tucked away in the left-hand corner as you face the altar and not generally visible from elsewhere in the church. The entrance is manned by an old geezer who sells votive candles and postcards. According to the signs, the tower's open only four or five hours a day, including holy days, but I ran a little field test of Venetian venality and knocked on the old boy's cubicle and asked him for a special trip to the top, making sure he saw the five-thousand-lire note I was palming."

"How much is that?" asks the Chief.

"About three bucks. Peanuts, but real money if you're living off the generosity of Rome, which these days probably means half a crust, a piece of yesterday's fish and a spoonful of olive oil. Plus whatever you can get from the postcards and candles, and hundred-lire tips from tourists. Anyway, away we went! Nobody saw, nobody cared.

"Now try this on for size. Mannerman's invitations go out around Thanksgiving and then the world knows all the details: the venue, the guest list and the Pope! The press descends on Venice to set up. You can't turn around without tripping over a paparazzo. Just imagine that someone claiming to be a photographer from one of the scandal sheets, or maybe just an amateur with a video hard-on, shows up at the campanile. He comes around a few times, checks out the custodian, softens him up with a glass of wine, a coffee, a grappa, a sandwich, slips him a five-thousand-lire note for a private view, then another and another. He learns about schedules, if there's going to be any security. The custodian takes him at face value. You think he knows from telescopic lenses, reads *Popular Photography*? Finally, after some days of this, by now the old man's feeling like a trust-fund kid, the fellow gets to the point. He wants to rent the campanile Christmas Eve. Take some pictures from it. All the custodian has to do is leave the gate and the elevator unlocked. The sum of, say, fifty thousand lire is mentioned. Plenty, but not too much. There's a haggle. They settle on a sly hundred *mille*. You get my drift?"

"Yes," says the Chief enthusiastically, "like bribing the custodian for an hour alone on a certain floor in the Texas School Book Depository."

"What if there's competition?" Lucy asks. "What if a real paparazzo hits on the same idea?"

"That's the point about the lenses! A real photographer's limited by his equipment. As I told you, even a Nikon 3800 won't make the carry! For him, the campanile's out of bounds. But *our* quote photographer unquote isn't using a camera."

"This is too easy," remarks Ormerud. Lucy agrees. Peter's fallen in love with his theory, she thinks.

"OK, Ray, let's go worst case," says Morland with a patience born of certainty. "The old guy demurs. *'Non è possibile,'* he says. The Pope is going to be here. The Polizia have been here. A guard will be posted. 'Fine,' says our so-called paparazzo. 'The more the merrier. You can watch too, both of you. I'll make it worth the cop's while, and I'll bring a bottle or two and some Christmas *dolci*. Make a real party of it.'

"Can't you just see it? An old man and a cop whose mind is elsewhere up there alone with Baker! They'd be better off with Jack the Ripper. Or if the cops are there to start with, he will deal with them somehow —maybe with his unaccounted-for .44 Magnum. As Lucy says, he'll find a way."

"What about the rocket launchers?"

"He brings them over the morning of the party as part of a pile of stuff he says is camera and video equipment. Boxes and cases and tubes, all sizes. You know how photographers are these days. Whatever happened to Cartier-Bresson with his one lousy Leica? Anyway, he asks Signor Custodian to store them in the grimy hole he probably lives in behind the elevator shaft. Another twenty-five thousand lire change hands. By now it's a game."

Lucy looks at her father and Ormerud. She's damned if she can see holes in Morland's logic.

"Let's assume for now you're right," says Ormerud. "What's our strategy?"

"Start with our biggest advantage: total surprise. Baker doesn't know we're on to him. He's never laid eyes on us, apart from Lucy, at least not in person. If he's disguised in the Piazza San Marco and sees you strolling by, Lucy, that's no problem: you have to be in Venice, you're on the list, which you can be sure will be published in the *Cronaca Venezia* and every other rag or gossip glossy. But you have to stay away from the battlefield. Leave that to us."

"Aren't you going to need some kind of credentials?"

"Leave those to me. I don't want our names appearing on any lists. Ray and the Chief can surely use their FBI connections for cop-to-cop courtesies."

"Meaning what?" Suddenly the Chief is all protocol, very correct.

"Meaning, Chief, that you two can bring your personal sidearms into Italy without a flap."

"And what exactly do you consider personal sidearms?" Ormerud, too, is being tough.

"Whatever you like to pack, Ray. The Chief's S and W. And something for me, *s'il vous plaît*, something that shoots fast. An Uzi, something like that."

Ormerud purses his lips, shakes his head doubtfully. He'll see what he can do, he says.

"Look, Chief," Morland continues, "here's how I think it could go. We three fly in separately on December 15—me via Alitalia to Milan and then by fast train to Venice, you from Boston to Paris and Venice direct by air—I don't want you to get lost in Milan looking for the train station—and Ray from Miami; BA has a good connection. Once news of the party is out and the media are scrambling, there won't be a hotel room in Venice, so I've already booked two rooms under your names in the Elisabetta, which is a nice comfortable hotel across the Grand Canal and up a bit from the Regina."

"And what about you? Where are you going to stay?" asks Lucy.

"I'll use my Mr. Hollywood persona, a Wyatt Earp quick-draw artist with the Platinum Card. I made a reservation at the Gritti."

"The *Gritti!*"

"Not to worry, my dear. From here on out, I'll be using my dime. This is going to be a riot! Provided I get first dibs on the screen rights, that is. Anyway, we three will stake out the San Giorgio campanile the day after we arrive. My idea is that we can rotate in three-hour shifts. One inside the church, two outside. Does that make sense? Ray, you look dubious."

"Aren't they likely to notice three Americans hanging around day after day?"

"I really doubt it. There're always tourists in Venice, and everyone dresses alike these days, especially if it's cold, which it probably will be, so everyone'll be bundled up. We'll position ourselves strategically and we'll be able to pick up Baker and follow him back to where he's holed up. There are only two jumping-off points for San Giorgio from central Venice—the No. 5 and the No. 8 water buses, which connect from the Riva degli Schiavoni"—click, and the arrow moves to a point down the waterline from San Marco—"and here"—the arrow zips across to a sharp tip of land separated by a narrow stretch of blue from San Giorgio—"on this quay that they call the Zitelle, on the Giudecca. Setting up shop on the Schiavoni is a cinch, and on the Giudecca, there's a little park here right at the tip that will do nicely. Once we make him, see which way he goes, we can alert whoever's on that picket duty at the time and follow him to his lair."

"Communicating how?" Ormerud wants to know.

"Cell phone." Morland's tone is that of a man with all the answers. "I called in a due bill I had on a guy at RAI in Milan. I got him onto the set of the last Stallone, the one we shot up in the Dolomites. So he's lending me three cellular phones plus noiseless pagers, the kind that vibrate instead of beeping. We'll be in constant communication. Yours'll be waiting for you at the Elisabetta. Now, Lucy, the only no-no is you. No matter how curious you become, do not wander around either San Giorgio Maggiore or the Giudecca."

"That won't be easy. My friend tells me I'll be holding hands at the

Cipriani, where the big finance hitters are billeted. That's right around the corner."

"Then stick with your glitterati. Confine your roamings to the hotel grounds or the central city. Use the hotel launch. None of those people will want to see San Giorgio anyway."

There's something flip about Morland's tone that irritates Lucy, something condescending. He doesn't think this is real, she reflects. It's a video game to him, all clicks and arrows and shifting screens. It's a movie. "Hold the pig talk, please," she says sharply. "OK, suppose you—as you say—'make' him and find out where he's hiding. Then what?"

"Then we take him. Probably not in his hotel. Depends on a lot of things. Maybe on the way from his bolt-hole, but more likely in the actual act, up in the campanile. It'll be dark, he'll be concentrating on his work, he won't hear us coming."

"Coming from where?" Ormerud again.

"Through the unlocked wicket and up the bell-tower stairs with cat-like tread."

"And if there's a guard?"

"Chances are he'll be in on the candy. Either the custodian will take him and Baker to the top in the elevator, and come back down, at which point I think you can color the cop dead, or they'll both stay up, in which case Baker will need two crayons."

"What if the tower's locked?"

"I'm counting on you and the Chief to handle that, Ray. Somehow, between the two of you, I doubt that there's a padlock in Venice that can resist your charms. Anyway, five minutes after Baker goes up, and the situation looks set—whatever it is—our little SWAT team materializes. Up we go and that's that."

"That's *what*?" Ormerud again.

"That's the end. We get the drop on him, bind him hand and foot and steal away. And when we've safely melted into the teeming throngs, one of us notifies the police."

Morland looks at Lucy before continuing. "That's Plan A. Then there's Plan B. We bind him hand and foot, somehow manhandle him down the stairs and through the crowd gathered on the quay to watch the fireworks and to some kind of high-speed boat. And from there we make our way somehow to a private airfield—I'm not even going to go into how we'll get from boat to airfield—where a chartered jet will be waiting with engines running. With the help of a flight crew, who will ignore the fact that our papers are not in order, we'll fly our prisoner to a secluded retreat where he will spend his remaining years in shackled but well-cared-for contemplation of the error of his ways."

There is a long, disbelieving silence. "I'm sorry, Lucy, it just won't wash," Morland says gently. "I've heard stories about private sanitariums in the Guatemala mountains, but getting there's the trick. You need to be in touch with people I just don't know. Perhaps Carlsson could have swung it. Perhaps Ray knows someone—"

Ormerud shakes his head.

"It's a nice fantasy," Morland concludes, "but it's a fantasy."

"What about Plan C?" asks Ormerud.

"Plan C?"

"We have to shoot the son of a bitch."

The three men look at each other. Ormerud has spoken what's been at the back of their minds.

"I mean it," he continues quietly. "If he resists, and he's got a gun, we're going to have to shoot back. Or—preferably—shoot first!"

Lucy is still scratching a mental itch. "What about another worst case, as you call it, Peter? What if your compelling logic is all the way off? What if he doesn't show up?"

"Then we sound General Quarters, Dive, Air Raid—the works! If Baker doesn't turn up at the bell tower by ten, we hit the cell phones!"

Suddenly, that seems to be that. All threads accounted for, all i's dotted, t's crossed. It's as if, in Morland's cinematic terms, the "second act" of the screenplay has ended: everything from now on is climax and resolution.

For a moment, all four of them look at each other, Morland triumphant, the Chief sanguine, Ormerud and Lucy pensive.

It's too perfect, she thinks. It's like a kit. Too much Tab A into Slot B. Too pat, too equational. "It's too much like a movie," she blurts out.

"Of course it is," says Morland. "Movies are life. That's why we go to them."

That night, Lucy and the Chief return to Maine. Morland leaves the

following week for Hollywood, then Central America, and won't be heard
from until early May. There is nothing to do now but wait.

Spring comes and goes, the eastern seaboard from Norfolk to Halifax
suffers from a sweltering unseasonable heat wave that lasts from late
April to late May. As Memorial Day approaches, the heat abates. The
frenetic pace of the Northern Hemisphere's great cities slackens as people ripple outward to open their summer palaces; in the Southern, autumn rigidifies as winter comes on. By the end of the month, the great
eastern resorts are poised and quivering in the blocks, ready to explode
into hyperactive high season at the first sound of the traditional starter's
gun, the Memorial Day weekend.

Lucy is thankful that her own business provides a rich measure of
distraction. Apart from the meetings she attends with Spuds and his
team to finalize the invitation list—triaging, compromising, often going
to Mannerman himself for ultimate Solomonic judgment—she keeps in
daily touch by phone and E-mail. Nothing changes, however. The party
has taken on an inexorable logistical momentum. The schedule is set.

On Friday, July 2, at precisely 11 a.m. Eastern Daylight Time, fax
machines around the world will warble and trill with the arrivals of
requests to hold the week before Christmas free and to confirm by return
of fax. Administrative assistants, social secretaries, keepers of the gate
and in a very few cases the addressees themselves will examine the
newly arrived messages with routine curiosity until they come to Mannerman's signature and his personal postscript. This latter ingredient
requires high-level, immediate consideration. In all but a very few cases,
notably where Death beckons from the sickroom door, and even in a
couple of these, the answer will be an instant yes. Six hundred faxed
invitations will go out; five hundred sixty-nine will respond in the affir-
mative.

But in May, Lucy knows none of this as yet. What she does know is
that a July 2 kickoff doesn't give Baker enough time. She has set the
Memorial Day weekend as the point at which she herself intends to shift
the course of events.

She takes extreme precautions. Spuds has reported that PL has gone
ballistic about the possibility of leaks. It wouldn't surprise her if all her
lines—phone, fax and computer modem—are under surveillance. Lucy

is due to spend the holiday weekend with friends on Martha's Vineyard, which she knows to be the summer retreat of at least eleven recipients of Mannerman's fax. On her way to Hyannis to catch the ferry, she pulls into a rest stop off I-95 and locates a pay phone. I suppose this is paranoid, she thinks as she dials a New York number from memory. But Liz Smith's line will be clean, she knows; ever since that business with Disney, the gossip columnist has her phone checked every morning. She told Lucy the last time they lunched, "These days, dear heart, you just can't trust anyone, not even your worst enemies!"

"Hi, Dennis," Lucy says, when the other end picks up. "Oh, sorry— hi, St. Clair. Is herself there? Sure, I'll hold."

Two quarters later, a familiar drawl comes on.

"Listen," Lucy says, after a brief exchange of pleasantries, "I've got something really good for you, but if this little bird gets found out, it'll be shot and mounted." She speaks quickly and intently for about a minute. "Remember now," she finishes, "this just dropped from the sky."

"Doesn't everything? Bye, dear heart, and thanks."

And now, Lucy thinks as she rings off, there is nothing to do but wait.

Four days later, on the Tuesday following the holiday weekend, when Liz Smith's loyal readers have returned safely within her circulation radius—one hundred fifty papers nationwide, scores of English-language journals widely dispersed over four continents, "pages" scattered across the Internet—they learn that, come Independence Day weekend, six hundred of the luckiest people in the world will receive a mystery invitation. The column goes on to disclose the nature of the special occasion, the date and setting, the planned entertainment, the names of the three big stars who will sing to the fireworks, as well as a mouthwatering sampling of the guest list—although the Pope's attendance is merely hinted at.

True to her mentor's philosophy that a good offense is the best defense, Lucy, who is by then in California, is on to Spuds at 7 a.m. Pacific time.

"Hey, I just read the *L.A. Times*! What the hell is this in Liz Smith?" she demands to know. "PL must be gnawing the carpet."

"He is shitting bricks!" There's a slur in Spuds's voice. Lucy guesses he's been at his file cabinet. "Indeed, even as you and I speak, he is considering calling the whole thing off!"

No, he won't, Lucy thinks. He'll bluster and he'll roar, but Jack Mannerman's ego bows to no man, not even himself.

"The fortunate part is, my dear, that we here who are privileged to kiss the very hem of greatness, including your own wee self, have been exonerated, thanks to the miracle of modern communications, if you get my meaning."

"Phone tapping is against the law."

"Not if you consider yourself above the law. In the event, what does it matter? We think the leak came from the Vatican, from God's lips to the lady's own ear, you might say."

"Did anyone try to find out from Liz?"

"Aye, that we did, indeed the Old Man personally himself offered to trade an invitation to the grand affair for just the initials of the malcontent who's done this awful thing, but alas, the lady's not for talking."

Another pause, another swig. He's going Celtic on me, Lucy thinks; he always does when he drinks that Irish gin neat. Another couple of pops, and he'll be incomprehensible—provided he stays conscious.

"You know," she says, "I can think of a dozen people on that list who'd trade their mothers for a promise of a mention in Liz Smith."

"As can I, m'dear, as can I. Ah, but it'll make no matter. We'll just tighten up all around lest anyone in a Newark mosque get any ideas. Grover's onto the Secretary of Defense t' see if the Sixth Fleet can leave the Gulf long enough to give us a hand, and the Speaker's goin' to have a word with the FBI and . . . I don't know. It'll be jus' fine, jus', jus' fine. . . ."

His voice trails off. Lucy tells the void at the other end to call if there's anything she can do.

Within thirty-six hours, the Liz Smith column is picked up and recirculated to subscribers of a multilingual variety of on-line services providing celebrity and socialite news, and has been posted on *their* Internet bulletin boards and Web pages.

One of these has been automatically downloaded to a SuperMac that sits on a table in the study of a well-kept apartment in one of the more stylish quarters of a large city far to the southwest of Martha's Vineyard and Manhattan. When the apartment's occupant returns in the evening, he goes, as he always does, to his computer, which is programmed to cycle through various on-line sites in search of certain names. He pulls up a chair, flicks on the monitor and, with a few keystrokes, scrolls through the information collected during his absence.

As he reads, he betrays no emotion, but when he is finished, he starts in again from the top. When he has read it through a third time, he gets up, hangs up the outer coat he has been obliged to wear, the weather outside still being blustery, and goes into his well-appointed kitchen to prepare his evening meal. As he works, slicing and sifting and simmering, he considers this new development. When his meal is ready, he uncorks two bottles of a nice Chilean sauvignon and makes his way laboriously through a meal which has by now become so boring he could barely get it down, were it not essential to his special diet. At length, finished at last, he pours the dregs of the second bottle into the sink, loads the dishwasher and returns to the computer. On his way, he pauses to examine a set of seven neatly framed old drawings hanging above a bureau.

A few keystrokes, and he is back on-line. He is soon lost in concentration, his mind hard, clear and close-focused in spite of the wine he has drunk, as he studies alternative ways of traveling to various European cities that have one thing in common: reasonable and discreet overland access to Venice.

PART FIVE

AFTER THE
FIRST DEATH . . .

— I —

"And so, Signor Bonte, which will it be today, Tofana or Cristallo?"

"Tofana, I think," says the man at the table to the hovering waiter. "I prefer the afternoon light over there. Better for the coloration, you understand."

His Italian is correct, but pronounced with a heavy guttural accent. Like most of his countrymen, the waiter is no snob when it comes to the sound of the mother tongue in the mouths of foreigners, but he cannot entirely suppress a twinge of pity that so accomplished and civilized a man as Signor Bonte should have the bad luck to have uttered his first words in Portuguese. Such a harsh language, he thinks.

"Signor has an excellent eye for nature."

Bonte looks around and takes a deep, appreciative sniff of the morning. He likes it here. The inn is comfortable, the food more than tolerable, the staff on the whole unobtrusive and the setting incomparable. Even though it's the first day of the last month of the year, the mountain air retains traces—like the delicious perfumed trail a beautiful woman leaves behind—of the leafy pungency of autumn. Altogether quite bearable, as his Italian friends would say.

Nestled in a deeply wooded fold of the Dolomites a few kilometers northwest of the grand ski resort of Cortina d'Ampezzo, the Albergo Re dalle Nevi—the King of the Snows Inn—overlooks a wide sweep of peaks and valleys, from the rugged, almost overdramatic cluster of Tofana eastward to the undeveloped, granite-toothed crags of Pomagagnon, a primeval area open only to hikers and ski trekkers. At its rear is the relatively busy Highway 51, the main road to Venice, which lies a mere two hundred kilometers to the southeast.

What wonderful mountains these are, the man thinks, ladling a generous dollop of frothing milk into his already cream-lashed cappuccino. It's not on his diet—he's trying to watch his weight—but how harmful can one more cup be?

The Dolomites have a striking ancientness, a ruddy, vivid quality that reminds him of the red-rocked Sonora, scene of his vain stalkings of the desert ram. He expects to have better luck in this part of the world.

The season is still in its infancy; indeed the inn only reopened the previous week, and there are but a handful of other guests. The mountains are barely dusted with snow, and hikers and rock climbers remain the principal traffic carried by the two funiculars to the station at Tofana di Mezzo. Down in the town, shopkeepers and restaurant owners are already complaining. If this keeps up, the season will be a disaster— *disastro*! Behind the wailing, however, if you know the Italian spirit and listen carefully, the man thinks, you can pick up a faint antiphon of confidence that the gods will make it all come right by December 15, when, as if on autopilot, the Venetian and Milanese upper crust abruptly put aside the finery of autumn and head for the mountains and the luxury resorts of Sestriere, Bormio and Cortina d'Ampezzo.

"Ancora un' caffè, signore?"

"Sì, grazie."

The waiter buzzes off. This early in the season, his is an undemanding job; moreover, Signor Bonte has shown himself to live up to his name. A generous tipper and easy to deal with, a man who knows how to treat the people who make his life agreeable, a man obviously at ease—as these days so few seem to be, when money can be acquired at several times the speed of manners—with servants and working people. A Brazilian he may be by passport, but there's Italian in the man's soul, thinks the waiter. Perhaps he's Argentine—that must be it, since half the Argentines are of Italian descent.

The guest savors the landscape. His sojourn here has been most pleasant, but next week he must be going. The end of the mission is in sight. More urgently, people he knows will be arriving in Cortina for the season; he doesn't dare risk a chance encounter, even as he looks now, the supposed victim of a chronic and debilitating glandular disorder that had the customs official at Istanbul nodding in profound sympathy and touching the brim of his cap as he absorbed the profound difference in appearance between the man standing before him and the picture in the passport.

The passport he presented at Turkish Immigration was the only one of the three he's carrying that he's entitled to on the basis of birth and citizenship, although the name, photo and other information are skillful recent alterations. It still has six years to run. Thank God, he often thinks, for whoever it was in the Passport Bureau who decided to go to a ten-year expiry.

This passport, along with the two acquired later, in a place where such things are more easily done, is a key element in his arsenal of disguise. He can still hardly believe how smoothly it went once he decided to test the waters. The process was all laid out for him in a collection of newspaper stories and books he assembled. He could even have obtained a mail-order text on how to disappear, but this he had passed up, not wanting to appear, under any name, on a computerized mailing list. Tempting as it was, he also shunned several specialized sites on the Web/Internet from which he could have downloaded all sorts of helpful hints. It never occurred to him to seek out one of the "consultants in disappearance" he's read about. On this kind of mission, a man must go it alone.

He started by scanning his own original birth certificate into his computer, then altering certain of its particulars, using an old corporate stamp he found in a drawer to give it an embossed authenticity that he was certain no one would examine too closely, and finally soaking it in tea briefly. In a sequence that in retrospect seems almost organic, the birth certificate midwifed a new Social Security card and driver's license, eventually a passport. Under the new identity, he opened accounts in various out-of-state brokerages, using bearer securities, which he margined, and used *those* proceeds to open accounts in various out-of-state banks. In short order, those institutions put him in possession of a useful array of credit and debit cards. The statements were mailed to various addresses of convenience he opened at commercial mailing and package forwarding outlets in three cities within a day's drive of his home base. It all went so easily that over the ninety days following receipt of his new passport, he replicated the documentation. "Franklin Smithers" was joined by "Arthur Travers."

All the while, during the eight months it took him to do this, he continued to live the life he was born to. A solitary life, a reclusive life, mountain-bound and forest-girt, with Nature his only companion. No one to look over his shoulder, ask questions, worry at his silences, ponder the intense nights he spent at his computer. No involvements of any meaningful kind, nothing beyond driving to town for mail and groceries. He'd taken care of that the moment the inspiration hit him, the conception which he's since recognized had been building in him for months—sometimes revealing itself like lightning flashes, more often as a continuous, distant, barely audible rumble of thunder. The moment of truth, of decision, had arrived not all that far from where he now sat. An odd coincidence, now that he thought about it. Small world.

Everything he needed could be obtained on his computer screen. He devoted every waking hour—and a good many dreaming—to putting it all in place, to giving his inspiration the bone and heartbeat of actuality. After that, he took a broom to his past, as it were, effacing every track and trace, the tiniest displacement of dust or irregularity in the surface which might arouse the curiosity of anyone—a lawyer, investment manager, testamentary—who might chance on the path he was about to take. When he was certain that all had been taken care of, that the roadway behind him was swept absolutely clear, he went to Africa and died.

Speaking metaphorically, that is. The only real, physical deaths were those of the boatmen. He was regretful about that, but there was no other way, really. Besides, if one objectively considered living conditions in present-day Rwanda, the qualitative difference between life and death was hardly worth discussing. He had assured the two Tutsi fishermen who agreed to take him out that this was merely a nest-spotting mission preparatory to evacuating hatchlings to a preserve farther up the lake where they would be safe from the war moving closer each day. When they were well out on the water, he killed them.

He had only once before cut a man's throat, but once turned out to be practice enough. The first time had been in Vietnam, the night the company he was following went into a village and a VC came running at him from between two huts. The gook's weapon had misfired as his momentum brought him within orbit; by then Bonte—not his name then—had his knife out, it was the first thing he could lay his hand on, and with a mighty swipe he damn near took the fellow's head off. Out on the water, it proved easier; the first boy was no problem, and the second preferred to take his chances with nature: he jumped overboard and managed to splash twenty yards or so before the first croc hit him. A foul crash breaking the surface, a scream that died in the darkness after no more than a double dotted half note, and then nothing.

He'd lowered the sail and rowed the boat into shallows he'd mapped out earlier, about ten miles north of Kolohe, the town from which they'd put out into Lake Kivu two nights earlier, and twenty miles from Bukavu, where there was an airport from which he could connect to Nairobi and the rest of the world. The locals gave these croc-filled lake waters a wide berth. The night was moonless; it was a simple matter to prize out a fat, stick seam of caulking from between the bow staves, so that the craft with its grisly crew would gradually fill with water and eventually swamp head-down. When the night wind off the savanna came up, he rigged sail and rudder to direct the skiff back out onto the lake among the heron-dotted sand spits which lay a few hundred northerly yards away. The agile fifteen-foot-long crocs whose domain this was were known man-killers, known to have swamped more than one boat with a lash of their heavy, armored tails. They would make short work of the boat and its occupant. His own corpse would be assumed to have been dragged off and consumed by a croc with a taste for pale flesh.

This was country he knew, so the overland trip down to Bukavu, roughly fifty kilometers, was no problem. He had his backpack and—in addition to the .44 Magnum he'd brought in case a croc got any ideas about him—a sporting rifle he'd bought during a layover in Frankfurt with one of his new Visa cards. He kept off the truck route, was careful not to stray over the Rwandan border and made haste slowly. Outside Bukavu, he donned the red wig he'd bought in São Paulo, which matched the photo in his new passport, flourished an armband and stethoscope, along with hard-worn documents identifying him as a representative of Doctors Without Frontiers, and let himself be carried along in the wailing stream heading for the refugee camps on the city's southeastern border.

The next day, still disguised, he flew to Nairobi, thence to London and Toronto. He entered the United States two days later—the day before news of his disappearance reached CNN—near Sault Ste. Marie, using his second U.S. passport. Two days after that, he purchased—for $137,500 drawn on a Merrill Lynch cash-management account—an isolated lakeside cabin on Michigan's Upper Peninsula, and for roughly $26,000 from the same CMA a new gray Jeep Cherokee: the funds had been remitted to Merrill Lynch's Geneva office two months earlier via a bank in Chur, Switzerland. The cabin was equipped to his specifications by his credit cards—now billing to a Mailbox Inc. in the nearby city of Ishpeming—in the course of a three-day excursion to the Mall of America near Minneapolis.

For the next two years, he lived in Michigan, a watchful hermit. Not that neighborliness was ever an issue: the nearest cabin was four miles away, and occupied only in summer.

His comings and goings were limited. Except for excursions to Texas, Arizona, the eastern tip of Long Island in New York, he stayed close to home. Twice a year, he traveled to Detroit for no good reason other than that he wished to reexperience, briefly, the fevers of a big and troubled city.

By now he was fully immersed in a long-term scheme whose objective was to achieve a level of concealment and flexibility that would allow him to respond quickly and effectively should an attractive opportunity present itself. He was certain there would be such an opportunity. Unlike his skittish mountain sheep, the game he was now stalking tended frequently to come together like a glittering school of brilliant brainless reef fish. Such a gathering might represent a unique opportunity to kill an entire herd, as it were, with a single shot. To do that, he needed to be able to get close to them, if not actually in among them, without arousing suspicion. He needed an impenetrable disguise. Here fate took a hand. A film accidentally seen on pay cable suddenly gave him the inspiration for a strategy of personal concealment that he regarded as breathtaking in its simplicity, and therefore likely to succeed.

The problem was one of implementation. The normal means available to him were either too risky or too slow. Then, one day, he happened to pick up a well-thumbed wrestling magazine in one of the randomly selected barbershops he patronized in towns well outside his normal radius; the barbers who cut his hair would have been surprised by the same orangey-red thatch by now familiar to the people who worked in Bud's Mobil, the Lakeside Deli Market and the local 7-Eleven, the only businesses near his home that saw him regularly. An illustration to an article on expatriate colonies around the world caught his eye. He studied the photo and its caption, read the article top to bottom, stared thoughtfully at the flyspecked ceiling and then read it over again.

Here was what he was looking for! In addition, he could see important collateral benefits.

He acted with a decisiveness that most people might consider downright impetuous. The local representative of a firm of nationwide freight forwarders arranged for most of his effects to be packed up and shipped south to the movers' central Florida storage facility, to be held there while—as he told them—he found a suitable house in the Orlando area. He prepaid three years' storage; he was persnickety, he explained to the movers' rep; it could very well take him that long, especially in Florida (this with a wink!), to find exactly the right place to live. He closed up his lakeside cabin and headed for Chicago, making an easy two days' drive of it. He placed the Jeep in a long-term storage garage, and prepaid for a program that combined a year's parking with regular engine and maintenance checks. A year seemed a long time, and the fee large, considering he never expected to return, but one never knew, did one?

Two weeks later, six months to the day before Robert Carlsson's jet exploded in midair, he stepped off a Varig Airlines flight at Guarulhos, the international airport serving São Paulo, Brazil.

The teeming city suited his purposes to perfection. It was huge—15 million inhabitants!—cosmopolitan, accessible, fecund, diverse, industrious, civilized, modern. A hive in whose busyness a man could easily lose himself, a great city where he was likely to find anything he might need. After two weeks in an apartment-hotel, he located an apartment on the Avenida 23 de Maio, on the edge of the Liberdade district, which housed the largest Japanese population outside the home islands. This was the consideration that had directed him south.

It was easy to replicate his Michigan setup in São Paulo. Within days of Senhor Bonte's signing the lease, technicians from a local computer store had a system up and running. He programmed it himself, and established the on-line links that allowed him to sweep the vast landscape of America's publicity culture like a radar beam. This done, he set about making a life for himself in Brazil's second city. There was method in the apparent randomness with which he explored São Paulo's districts, but over a few months he drew his focus closer, habituating himself to certain quarters, then neighborhoods within quarters, then certain streets within neighborhoods, displaying an enthusiastic desire to become knowledgeable, but never overstepping the subtle boundaries of form and deportment that rule Japanese life and culture. By the end of November, by Thanksgiving—no, by the feast of St. Clement (he must stop thinking in terms of the American calendar!)—in his first year in São Paulo, Senhor Bonte had efficiently insinuated himself into the community he had targeted; he had, in effect, become a "regular," so much so that he was scarcely noticed anymore, a feature of the daily landscape as taken for granted as the fish market at the end of the block.

Just at that point, when he was scarcely a month into his new dietary regimen, his computer sweep fastened on an item from an American gossip column that made him sit up and take notice, an innocuous item that to him spelled M-I-S-S-I-O-N. His grasp of the broad possibilities was instinctive and immediate. To refine his thinking, he investigated certain recondite sites on the Internet/Web. From these, he learned all he needed to know in terms of sourcing. Within a day, he had a plan.

He flew from São Paulo to Rio and from there to Oaxaca, Mexico. In Oaxaca, he rented a Hertz car and drove south into the state of Chiapas, flourishing press and related credentials which his now-impressive computer graphics expertise had found a cinch to create. The Chiapas revolution was at that time both floundering and simmering. People were desperate for money; it was a simple matter to obtain what he needed in San Cristóbal.

He then drove steadily north, and four days later crossed into the United States at the Juárez–El Paso junction. He was running some risk, he knew; if for some reason the customs people decided to search his vehicle, they would surely find the six brick-shaped one-pound blocks of C-4 plastic explosive he had concealed in the well holding the spare tire. He considered the likelihood of this so remote as to make his apprehensions groundless, but as an added precaution against the sharp noses of the DNA dogs sniffing incoming traffic for drugs on the other side of the bridge spanning the Rio Grande, he bought a large bottle of Joy perfume at a Juárez duty-free and then spilled its contents in the trunk.

As he expected, he reentered his native land without incident. At El Paso, he returned the car, paying an exorbitant drop-off fee, and flew via Dallas–Fort Worth to Chicago, where he reclaimed his Jeep. Two days after that, he reached Denver, where he left the Jeep in a lot at the new airport, and flew on to Los Angeles.

At LAX he rented another car and checked into a motel. Over the next day and a half, using various credit-card identities, he acquired what he needed—the "mechanicals" at a Radio Shack on Sepulveda, the packaging at Milton's House of Caviar on Rodeo Drive in Beverly Hills. In his motel room, the afternoon of his planned departure, he assembled his "tribute": a five-pound cooler in which a round two-pound tin of the finest beluga available west of St. Moritz was packed with coolants guaranteed for forty-eight hours, the whole done up in Milton's House of Caviar's famous pink-and-silver gift wrap and placed in a Giorgio shopping bag. He then telephoned a Santa Monica messenger service which he knew had the Hollywood warrant, and arranged for the package to be picked up the following morning and delivered by no later than 10 a.m. to the Aero Services terminal at the Burbank airport.

He checked out of the motel late that afternoon, arranging for the package to be stored overnight in the small refrigerator in the office behind the desk. He recognized that there was a risk here too. Americans are notoriously inefficient in such matters, but he covered as many bases as he could, including advising the messenger service of the package's location.

His flight to Denver left on schedule and arrived a few minutes early, thanks to strong tailwinds over the Rockies. He reclaimed the Jeep and drove hard for three hours on I-70 to Glenwood Springs, some forty miles northwest of Aspen.

It was just after midnight on the morning of Christmas Eve when he arrived. He immediately patched through from his laptop to São Paulo and, via a LapLink remote, collected whatever information had been gathered there.

One item—from Liz Smith's column—made him sit up.

He thought through the implications. Let it stand, and that would be one less to deal with. But he didn't feel ready. Not yet. For her, nothing less than special treatment was called for.

The next morning, bright and early, he called the Aero Services operator at the Burbank airport, where he had ascertained the CTA jets to be based, and represented himself as one of Mr. Carlsson's assistants, calling merely to verify the flight plan and make absolutely sure there would be no trouble about the reserved takeoff slot. Yes, they were still due to be rolling at 11:45 a.m. sharp, and three minutes had been cleared on either side of the prereserved slot just to make sure.

"OK. Good. Mr. Carlsson'll be pleased. Now—can we check the manifest?"

"Certainly."

"Fine. Crew—I don't know who'll be flying this trip—"

"We're showing Captain Harmer, Captain Lancy and a Miss O'Leary."

"OK. Passengers: Mr. Carlsson and a Ms. Preston, L.?"

"That's correct."

Hanging up, he looked at his watch. Seven a.m. Los Angeles time. Too early. Give it another hour. Knowing the way Lucy uses up the clock, it's a sure thing she'll have scheduled a breakfast.

At 9 a.m. his time, he reached for the phone again, thought better of it and went outside. Give her another quarter hour, just to be safe. It had snowed during the early hours, he saw, not much more than a cosmetic dusting whitening the crusted drifts left over from a big snowfall three days earlier. The road was clear. So was the sky. There'd be no problem for anyone to get to Aspen today.

He got in his Jeep and drove a half mile down the road to a seedy strip mall, where he located a pair of pay phones outside a doughnut shop. Using one of his phone cards, he called the Bel-Air and asked for Lucy Preston.

"Miss Preston is breakfasting outside the hotel," said a crisp voice. "She expects to return by nine o'clock."

"This is Robert Carlsson's administrative assistant, Tom. Would you please give Miss Preston the message that there's been a change in plans, Mr. Carlsson's been delayed at Universal, and the plane won't be departing Burbank until 1:45 p.m. Unfortunately, it won't be possible to reach Mr. Carlsson before then."

He hung up, went into the doughnut shop and downed three cream-filled crullers and two cups of despicable coffee. By eleven, he was back on the road. He stopped for a quick hamburger at a country-and-western theme bar in Snowmass, then regained Route 82, continued

toward Aspen, then took the Woody Creek turnoff up into the hills. By
one o'clock, he was parked at the overview site he remembered from
the last time he'd skied in Aspen, as the guest of a Saudi construction
mogul who had a 15,000-square-foot house in the gated colony of Starwood. When he arrived, two cars were already there, their occupants,
like himself, bundled up against the sharp afternoon chill, watching and
videotaping the skyborne parade at the airport below. In the next hour,
other cars pulled in, including a sheriff's deputy in a mud-flecked
cruiser. By two the site was full.

Part of the time, waiting, he read fitfully. He'd brought along an old
book of essays on upland shotgunning by his late friend Jack O'Connor.
O'Connor had the right stuff; reading his easy sportsman's prose was
more calming than Prozac. Now and then he checked his watch, got out
of the Jeep, peered at the airport through the new Zeiss 8 × 40 sporting
glasses he'd bought in São Paulo, put a finger to the wind, checked his
watch again, calculated the CTA Falcon's probable EDT, recalculated.
Wheels up at, say, 11:50 Pacific time, give or take ten minutes; two
hours' flight time; one hour time-zone differential; 11:50 plus 3 equaled
14:50, or 2:50 p.m. Mountain time. Say quarter of. In any case, pretty
soon now.

Inside the sporting essays was tucked a page torn from an *Aviation
Technology* spotter's guide; it showed the silhouette, from several angles,
of the Falcon 30E turbojet his quarry would be flying in on. He had it
memorized, but it never hurt to keep the memory refreshed. When
it comes to preparation and outfitting, he told himself, you're a real
belt-and-suspenders type, a real old—what did she call you?—
"fussbudget."

He thought now and then of Lucy. Not with much emotion. In the
great scheme of retribution that now ruled his life, she occupied a higher
order of damnation in his mind. Right up until Como he'd been honorably interested in her, had even wondered once or twice whether she
might be the one. Harming Carlsson would maim Mannerman, but it
would not be the final, ultimate stroke: when that came, Lucy's head
would be next to Mannerman's on the block. She was his whore. She
belonged with Mannerman, with Lamond; she was a card-carrying member of the group that had raped his honor and then left it for dead in

the gutter. It did not occur to him, as it might have occurred to a shrewder, more worldly soul, that he had come into the world honor-blinded.

Lucy would surely marvel at her wild good fortune. She might even wonder at the message that had spared her. Would she put two and two together? How could she? Carlsson was a man with a million enemies. How could she home in on that one or this one? Any of Liz Smith's readers could have known she was scheduled to be on that plane.

At 2:30 p.m. Mountain time, he got out of the Jeep. At 2:36 p.m., through his binoculars, he picked up the unmistakable Falcon silhouette swinging out over Woody Creek to vector onto its final approach. At 2:37:32 p.m., he confirmed the stabilizer number: IK567J.

At 2:41:19 p.m., he actuated an intermediate-distance electrical circuit, and at 2:41:21 p.m. had completely satisfied himself that nothing had gone wrong, that there had been no slip 'twixt cup and lip. He hung about for a while, seeming to participate in the general shock and horror. To leave a choice seat at a catastrophe too early would be unnatural, might draw attention. Finally, as the thrill of the first adrenal shock wore off and as stunned, disbelieving silence fell over the viewing site, he judged it would be OK to leave, and he climbed into the Jeep and drove off.

Two days later, the day after Christmas, eleven months before the morning on which Senhor Bonte contemplates the sun on the Dolomites from the terrace of his hotel, the 10:30 a.m. shuttle from Rio deposited him at Congonhas Airport, São Paulo's domestic terminus. Back at base, to wait for whatever destiny will next deliver.

At the end of May, he learns.

The early details are sparse but sufficient. It would appear that if he is successful, he may confer on mankind the single greatest blessing since God touched Adam's fingertip. Remove at a single stroke the sources of its worst afflictions.

As he studies the information on the Web page, a map of Venice forms in his mind. He fastens immediately on the Giudecca and the adjoining island of San Giorgio Maggiore. He will need to know more, much more, but he knows enough to make a start.

At a bookstore at the Iguatemi shopping mall, he buys the one map of Venice they have in stock, a good, large Hallweg with enough detail for his present needs, along with a simple student's compass. At home, he searches the Internet/Web for bulletin boards and sites dealing with arms, armament and ordnance. A *Soldier of Fortune* forum suggests half of what he needs, which he confirms quickly with his map and compass; with this particular weapon, the target is well within range of the spot he wants to fire from. Another, more esoteric Internet forum, originating, it would appear, in Peshawar, Pakistan, suggests three arms bazaars where he is likely to be able to acquire, with a maximum of discretion, the weapon he has selected: in Peshawar itself, still active, although with increasingly limited stocks as its glory period of supplying the Afghan mujahideen against Soviet occupiers winds down; Trieste, Italy, which appears to be the clearing point for off-the-books weaponry destined for the Bosnian conflict; and Khartoum, in the Sudan, the funnel for armaments being fed into the raging tribal bloodfests of equatorial Africa.

Commercial and sourcing considerations being equal, Trieste seems a clear winner. By late October he has arrived in the capital of Friuli–Venezia Giulia via a leisurely route that takes in Caracas, Dakar, Lisbon and Vienna, with overnight layoffs at each junction. He has purchased, using different passports, three complete sets of tickets for the journey, the airline computers showing three different names traveling in four different classes of service on various legs of the trip; he switches between these as he goes, pulling and discarding unused flight coupons along the way. Clearing customs is no problem. What he requires for his specific mission he intends to buy in Italy; so, apart from the usual personal items, his luggage contains only the tools of his avocation. Indeed, he shows samples of his work to the customs officer, who expresses grave and gratifying admiration. This has been true at each stage of the journey. The nearer he draws to Europe, the greater the respect for high culture and the more perfunctory the inspection he's given, especially since it is clear from his appearance that he's not a well man.

Ending his air journey in Vienna, "Ilario Doucão" stays overnight in a modest hotel on the fringes of the Schwabing district, and the next morning travels by train to Innsbruck, where "Franklin Smithers" rents a nondescript Fiat van, which he states he will return on December 27. He intends to spend the next sixty days working among the splendid prospects of the Dolomites, in the cheery all-confiding manner that Europeans have to come to expect from Americans. Crossing into Italy by the Brenner Pass, he stops overnight in Bolzano and Pordenone before arriving in Trieste on October 29.

Trieste is a bustling industrial and trading center, with no time for the past, no time to waste, as a place like Florence off-season might, on the quirks of a stranger in its drowsy midst. He remains there for more than a month, establishing himself at a modest, comfortable hotel on the Via della Geppa. Here again he displays his work to the concierge, whom he tells he is putting together a book of key places in the life of D'Annunzio, the celebrity-poet who briefly reigned as dictator of Fiume, as the city of Rijeka, in neighboring Croatia, was known. He establishes himself as a regular at a caffè on the Piazza dell'Unità d'Italia, the crossroads of Triestino life, and in certain trattorias around the city. He makes himself accessible, buys drinks, leaves no quarter of the city unvisited by day or darkness. He's trolling, with himself as bait, hoping to be defined as a man with an agenda by those with a talent for sniffing out such intentions. He's banking on the assumption that large cities on the edge of, but not principal to, a war breed profiteers and traffickers, and that sooner or later the connections he needs will emerge.

In the sixth week of his sojourn, when he is beginning to wonder if he should shift to Plan B, he becomes involved in a series of circuitous conversations, at first political and theoretical, with a middle-aged man whose light-haired, square-featured appearance is completely at odds with the ratlike characteristics one associates with sub rosa types "who can get you anything for a price." The conversation evolves; the two men are like two praying mantises circling each other; finally, confidence is established. This kind of arrangement involves much trust. While the bona fides of "Senhor Doucão" cannot be established with absolute certainty, it is well known that parts of Brazil are in ferment, are indeed combustible, and the genuineness of the senhor's cash is beyond dispute. A deal is finally struck.

Four days later, then, in the late afternoon, almost exactly one hundred hours prior to this very glorious morning in Cortina d'Ampezzo, Senhor Bonte parks his nondescript Fiat van in a back street of Gorizia, a city of 44,000 of mixed Slav and Italian descent set squarely on the Slovenia border. He clambers down, gets out his kit, and makes his way to the cathedral square, where he sets to work. At the end of the day, around four o'clock, with twilight settling fast, he packs up, takes a coffee and aperitif at a nearby caffè and returns to his van.

In the failing light, he can make out the shape of two large black duffels. Taking out his key, he opens the rear doors of the van, feels quickly through the thick canvas of the duffels and satisfies himself that the hard tubes are there as expected. He stows his other gear and heaves himself into the driver's seat, pausing to lift the floor mat and recover the keys, duplicates to his own, that had been made a few days earlier in Trieste. He unlocks the glove compartment. The envelope containing $10,000 split equally into dollars, Swiss francs and lire is gone. For the first time since regaining the car, he smiles to himself. He had budgeted $15,000—based on the quotes on the Web—so he's $5,000 to the good.

He spends that night in Udine and the next day drives straight through to Cortina d'Ampezzo. It is November 28 when he arrives. He is exactly on schedule.

Over on the Tofana massif, the brilliant early-winter sunlight glints off the polished roofs of the funicular cabins moving up the mountain with the obstinate smooth pace of shooting-gallery decoys.

Yes, he thinks, I'll work there today. It helps make up his mind that the restaurant at the lift station serves an excellent pasta with squirrel sausage.

Everything seems in order. Better than in order, in fact.

The week before, something he had anxiously been anticipating happened: the magazine *Oggi* somehow secured and printed a complete guest list of the gala planned for Christmas Eve in Venice to celebrate the leadership of the American industrialist John P. Mannerman. It will be the most splendid social occasion to take place in the city since the Bestegui and López-Willshaw balls nearly forty years ago.

He studied that list carefully, each time with mounting joy and anticipation. The greater names he's known about for some time, since the first leaks back at the beginning of summer. These names are his reasons for being here.

What gives him added joy now are certain omissions. Names he hoped not to find on the list. Names whose absence gives him the last key piece of his elaborate plan. He'd been almost certain from the beginning that his friends wouldn't make the cut. Americans are deeply provincial, he thinks. He could reasonably expect that Mannerman's list, being a peasant's projection of who and what counted, would pass over the first names of Venice. But until the complete list appeared, he couldn't be certain. Now he is.

The day after *Oggi* published the list, he telephoned a Milanese banker whom he had met some years earlier through Italian friends, representing himself as an American lawyer on vacation in the Dolomites, acting urgently on behalf of important New York clients who had tracked him down. "You know how it is, signore, when the very wealthy want something, they must have it!"

The banker sympathized. He quickly confirmed that what was wanted could be done. As it happened, his bank had a branch in Cortina; if it suited the American signore's clients, a local transfer of funds could be readily arranged. As for access when the time came, provision was made for keys to be picked up in Venice, at a lawyer's office on the Riva del Carbon not far from the municipal offices in the Palazzo Loredan. That afternoon, "Arthur Travers" presented himself to the manager of the Banco Centrale e Mercato on the Largo delle Poste, handed over a check drawn on a CMA in Merrill Lynch's Geneva office, in the sum of $8,000 plus a $2,000 security deposit, and executed the necessary papers "as agent."

All that is left now is to wait. To fill the time. Yes, he thinks, with this light, Tofana will definitely be better.

Bonte slides a five-thousand-lire banknote under the saucer and pushes himself from his chair. The waiter beams effusive thanks.

Back in his room, Bonte examines himself in the mirror as he takes his blood pressure with a small portable device. One-ninety over eighty: not bad, considering the medication he's taking, considering everything. His pulse is seventy-eight—also not bad. He stills his breath, tries to get a sense of the general condition of his cardiac estate; it seems OK.

He gathers up what he needs and grabs his vest off the back of the chair; it could be cold up on the Tofana, the bright day notwithstanding. His eye falls on yesterday's *Gazzettino di Venezia*; the lead story is about the massive security precautions planned for the Pope's visit and Mannerman's party. He runs through it quickly; it's more or less as he anticipated.

He goes downstairs. Acknowledging the greetings of the day manager and the concierge, he goes out and walks around to the hotel parking lot. As he gathers additional kit from his van, he reflexively touches the topmost duffel. To the casual hand, the hard, round shapes within might be fishing-rod cases, or draftsman's tubes designed to protect rolled-up blueprints.

He doesn't feel like hassling with the van this morning. Parking at the Tofana station is likely to be difficult. Even though there's virtually no snow yet, the regular winter parade is already forming: last night, the Corso Italia was crowded with flamboyant women—the ones the locals call "*cafone* girls," no more than peasants strutting huge hair, huge furs and tiny dogs. From streetside caffè tables, men in carefully creased velour hats and faultless loden coats draped over their shoulders talk gravely and keep watch on the *passeggiata*. Bonte considers taking a table himself, but he doesn't. He's not yet entirely secure about his new appearance.

He loads his gear into his oversize backpack, straps on the folding work stand and slips into the shoulder harness. Locking the car, he ambles down the driveway toward the main road. There's a stop less than a half kilometer away for the bus that will let him off at the funicular station.

From the terrace, the waiter watches Senhor Bonte pass from sight around a fir-shadowed bend in the driveway. An amazing man, he thinks: in such an unhealthy condition to have such energy.

— II — Just after noon, the sun finally slices away the crown of the eggshell-colored cloud cover that's lain over Venice for the best part of a week; blue sky appears, at first pale, no more than a hint, but then coming into its own, expanding in space and deepening in hue until finally the city glories under a dome of perfect, purest winter brilliance.

On the point of the Giudecca, near the landing of the Guardia Finanza, Morland keeps watch on the portico of the great church across the way. He's seated on a bench with a stack of magazines and newspapers, which he pretends to read. Now and then he lifts his field glasses and peers across the neck of the lagoon called the Bacino and tries to make out Ormerud on patrol over on the Riva degli Schiavoni. Morland's satisfied they have the exits covered.

There are few people about—a couple mooning on another bench, a uniformed knot of men staring down at an official launch bobbing at the dock, men and women in raincoats with briefcases on official business.

Morland unbuttons his oiled-cotton jacket. Earlier, when the mist still lay on the water, you could see your breath; now it's perfectly agreeable out. As the day improves, people emerge. A few yards down the Fondamenta San Giovanni, toward the Zitelle to the west, a waiter sets up tables outside a caffè; an enormously fat man waddles out onto the quay from a narrow side street, sets up an easel, and begins to paint; a fashion team—photographers, assistants, models, makeup people—clambers out of a snazzy launch and goes to work, using San Giorgio Maggiore as the backdrop for summer ready-to-wear.

Loitering nearby, Morland cocks an ear: the crew's German, the model English, he guesses. He returns to his paper and wonders if anything's happened inside.

Just now, Chief Preston's on station in the church. He's sitting hunched up in a dark blue parka, head bowed, watch cap on his lap, halfway along a pew all the way back on the right-hand side, the best place to monitor the church's main entrance and the traffic to and from the campanile elevator tucked way over in the far northwest corner, on the left facing the altar. Mustering as much simulated Catholic devotion as his rock-simple Down East Presbyterianism is capable of, he pretends to mutter, in the fashion of other worshippers he's observed, and now and then looks disapprovingly at the altar, whose busy splendor he finds obnoxious.

The Chief, Ormerud and Morland have been rotating at one-hour intervals, changing hats, outer jackets and other props, pretending to be tourists or worshippers while keeping watch on the entrance to the campanile elevator. The bell tower keeps short public hours in winter: from ten to noon and two to four.

He looks at his watch. Another fifteen minutes until Ormerud will cross over on the *vaporetto* and spell him.

On this Christmas week morning, San Giorgio Maggiore is doing precious little business. Worshippers are few: the rows and rows of pews in front of the Chief hold no more than a scattering of worshippers, women mainly, in black dresses and shawls, murmurously praying. A handful of tourists prowl the chapels lining the side aisles, looking faintly embarrassed as their twenty-lire pieces rattle noisily into coin boxes to buy a scant minute's automated illumination of a darkened something that the guidebooks say mustn't be missed; here and there, stretched out or slumped in a rear pew, an obvious derelict or crazy winds down his muttering days in the comparative warmth of what, if you ask the Chief, is a drafty, chilly stone icebox. Still, it's better than being outside, where a sneaky breeze off the water cuts right through L. L. Bean's best-quality goosedown, and the whole city is as damp and smelly as a bilge.

A noise off to the left prompts him to sneak a peek while he fakes a prayer and tries not to cross himself the wrong way.

It's a pair of Japanese tourists talking to each other.

The Chief's beginning to feel this whole thing's a wild-goose chase. They began the stakeout four days ago. It's Morland's theory that Baker will cut it close, delay his arrival in Venice to the last, and the Chief agrees—but so far no one who's passed under their scrutiny has exuded a whiff of suspiciousness.

Morland's theories! he sniffs. Morland this and Morland that! He's getting fed up with Morland and his theories. He thinks Ormerud is too. Morland's a nice young man, but it's obvious he's seen too many movies. Just the other night he and Ormerud got into a terrific argument about *JFK*. The Chief kept his thoughts to himself, but he's seen the picture too, and he agrees with Ormerud that it's hogwash.

The Chief's not much of one for theories. In his day, theories didn't put criminals behind bars, shoe leather did. What does Morland know about the criminal mind, or deviancy, or how real sociopaths behave? During his days at the Bureau, the Chief saw any number of cases that got screwed up because the agent in charge tried to reason like the criminal. Now everyone thinks that way, he hears; everybody walks around acting like a character in *The Silence of the Lambs*, as if the Bureau's successes were attributable to mind reading and not to dogged hard work and long hours of sifting, sifting, sifting! In the Chief's view, this business of trying to catch a serial killer by thinking like him is stuff and molasses. No normal man can think like a psychopath, not even like a calculating thief planning a burglary. The criminal mind is as distinct from a normal man's as a woman's is: anyone who bets on the superficial similarities is asking to be sheared.

He's not about to stir things up, however, not this late in the day, with only two days to go. He might have earlier, but Lucy seemed to hang on Morland's every word, and . . . well, the young fellow may not be a criminologist, but he's presentable, intelligent, attentive, obviously makes a good living, and Lucy's closing fast on forty and not yet married.

Morland's setup is excellent, that the Chief has to admit. One to watch the way in, the church itself, and two to watch the ways out, the *vaporetto* stops on the Zitelle—just across the narrow channel of the Canale della Grazia—and at the Pontile San Zaccaria a quarter mile away on the far side of the Bacino. To keep in touch each has the noiseless beeper and preprogrammed cell phone—as well as a sidearm.

All the planning and preparation in creation doesn't cover the one big gap: they don't know what Baker looks like. It's safe to assume he's changed his appearance, but what was the appearance he's changed *from*? All they have to go on are some old photographs. A formal full-face taken twenty years earlier for the NRA annual report, the same camera portrait that most of the newspapers that reported his disappearance in Lake Kivu had used. A picture taken in front of a huge grader from a sales brochure issued by BEECO in 1985. A photo Lucy scrounged from somewhere: a safari shot, with Baker's face half hidden in the shadow of a wide-brimmed hat, although it gave a useful feeling of his lanky body type. A self-portrait Baker drew of himself on his trip to Italy with Lucy: naturalistic but sketchy, more useful for divining how Baker saw himself than how he might look to someone else. Finally, there was Baker's caricature of his features on the face of Anger—their latest evidence, close to five years old.

Not much to build up a mug shot or composite. Not enough for a police artist to go on.

None of this bothers Morland. If you see X doing Y, he believes, then X by simple power of deduction will be Baker. The Chief doubts it's that simple.

He shuffles his feet back and forth on the stone floor, creating friction for warmth. Absently, he studies the main altar, trying to puzzle out from this great distance who the different saints in the niches are.

He feels a quick draft on the back of his neck, hears a racking cough. Someone's come in the side door. He pretends to stretch as the new-comer crosses behind him. Then he crosses himself, turtles his neck down into the heavy, high collar of his parka, slowly revolves his head, muttering a pidgin Rosary for all he's worth.

A tall, thin man is standing at the back of the church, framed by the great entrance portal. He studies the interior, never looking in the Chief's direction, and then makes for the far left-hand side aisle. He walks with a distinct limp, dragging his right foot theatrically. Too the-atrically, the Chief thinks. As the man passes down the aisle, he begins to cough again, deep, sobbing, smoker's coughs that shake his entire frame.

As he proceeds toward the choir, the newcomer pauses now and then like any tourist to study the individual chapels set into the church's north wall. Whenever he stops, the Chief notes, he takes audibly deep, asthmatic gulps of the damp interior air. The flip side of the coughing, the Chief thinks disapprovingly: a smoker in terrible physical shape, lungs shot to hell. A smoker—or someone who wishes to be taken for one.

He's so stooped it's hard to say exactly how tall he is. Over six feet, the Chief guesses, and then some. Thin to the point of emaciation, but all he's wearing on this chilly day are a denim shirt and jeans and a too large, multipocketed, putty-colored vest that makes him seem even skinnier. The upper part of his face is concealed by aviator-style dark glasses, an odd choice given the gloom of the church's interior, the lower by a flowing pepper-and-salt mustache that would have done credit to a Civil War general. His thick, rough hair, almost entirely gray, so un-evenly tended and dressed that it seems like an ill-fitted wig, is pulled back in a fat pigtail that descends below his bony shoulders. One shoul-der dips low with the weight of a bulging, professional-looking camera bag. Around his neck hangs one of those viewfinder gadgets the Chief recognizes from pictures he's seen of movie directors, along with a 35-millimeter Leica.

When the new arrival passes the transept, he moves beyond the

Chief's field of vision. The Chief doesn't move. He sits there mumbling, pretending to tell a cheap set of rosary beads Morland bought for him in a tourist trap over by the Rialto. A few minutes later, the coughing grows louder and the fellow reappears, coming back up the aisle, again pausing to study each chapel, very much the photographer carefully casing a setting for a setup. And yet there's something in the way he looks around whenever he halts that bothers the Chief. The man pretends to study what's in front of him but keeps flicking quick little glances right and left, seeming to sniff the air with the furtive wariness of a rabbit on a lawn. This fellow's on full alert, the Chief decides. Too typecast, too perfect.

Might he be Baker?

The Chief reviews what he knows. According to Lucy, Baker's six foot two, and weighs 170, 180. This man, standing straight up, could be the right height, but there's no way he weighs more than 140 to 150 pounds dripping wet. From 175, say, to 145 is a big drop. Can you do that? Of course you can, the Chief thinks. Look at what concentration-camp survivors went through! So just suppose Baker managed to take off thirty pounds on, say, a killer diet helped along by pills. And then enhanced the newfound skinniness with clothes a size too large. Got a wig and false whiskers, or maybe just grew the darn things, dyeing them to suit. Now he's changed his basic type, the overall physical understanding registered at a first glance by eye and brain—from stylish, fit Ivy Leaguer to aging, infirm hippie. Every other impression would be altered by this change.

Damnation, the Chief realizes, this could be Baker!

He wishes he could have a better look at the man's face, the eyes in particular. Even in this dim interior light, they're screened by those tinted wire-rimmed aviator glasses. Wouldn't this thorough a makeover surely incorporate tinted contact lenses? Are these the hawk eyes Lucy kept swooning about?

As the Chief watches from behind a hand cupped to his brow, the newcomer concludes his study of the final chapel, with its huge painting of a female saint being done to death. He looks around him again; this time the Chief feels the eyes settle on his own neck for an instant, so he mumbles and fingers his beads with renewed fury, keeping his face averted. Then the man turns away, facing the entry doors, hesitates and then limps off in the direction of the entrance to the campanile.

The Chief counts to ten—the way he was taught at the FBI Academy—and gets up and moves quickly on the balls of his feet to the side aisle. He saunters halfway down, then reverses direction and comes back up, walking with the purposefulness of someone who's just remembered an appointment, and leaves the church by the northernmost of the three entry doors. As he goes by, he shoots a quick glance in the direction of the campanile and sees the suspect in murmured conversation with the old fellow who runs the elevator.

Outside, the Chief quickly takes stock. Just across the way, on the little plaza at the tip of the Giudecca, he can make out Morland on a bench. Ormerud will be over near San Marco, at the first eastbound water-bus station. A westbound No. 5 *vaporetto* is rapidly approaching the San Giorgio stop. The suspect has not yet emerged from the church.

The Chief crosses rapidly to the *vaporetto* station, pulling out his seven-day tourist pass with one hand. He boards the water bus and moves to the rear open deck. The wind and motion kick up a fine spray. It feels good on his face, it feels like Maine. He takes out a small cellular phone and punches out a preprogrammed auto-dial number. He shifts his gaze back and forth between the facade of San Giorgio Maggiore, growing smaller with each throb of the water bus's engine, and Morland, reading on the bench. He sees, with some amusement, Morland jerk involuntarily as the phone in his pocket goes off, set to vibrate furiously instead of ringing audibly.

No one takes notice of the Chief. If there's one thing Italians love as much as their spaghetti, the Chief's concluded, it's the cellular phone. At least two other passengers are chatting away busily.

"I think we've got him," he murmurs when Morland comes on.

He quickly describes the suspect and hangs up. As the *vaporetto* passes the tip of the Giudecca, he sees Morland get up from the bench and saunter to the edge of the quay, where a fat man is painting at an easel, as he has for the last few days whenever there's been a break in the winter damp. He and the Chief have developed a nodding, silent acquaintanceship. The Chief knows nothing about art, he's not like his daughter, but he knows what he likes and the fat boy's brightly colored landscapes have lent a pleasant summery note to those hours spent waiting in the cold.

Watching Morland study the panorama, moving his small but powerful spotting binoculars along a wide arc that takes in the Dorsoduro and the far tip of the San Marco quarter, each time resting for an imperceptible instant on San Giorgio Maggiore, the Chief has to admire the younger man's excellent surveillance technique. It's really pretty good for a nonprofessional. You take advantage of what the terrain offers, whether artificial or natural, and take on its coloration and rhythm, and Morland's doing just that. Of course, if you've worked on perhaps dozens of cop movies, as Morland has, you can't help picking up a few tricks of the trade.

The water bus slows as it approaches the Zitelle landing, where the Chief disembarks. He pauses briefly, as if undecided which way to go, makes a bit of a production about consulting a green Michelin guide, then heads back up the Fondamenta San Giovanni. He has to admit it: he likes the role playing, the stagecraft. It's like being in an old Orson Welles spy movie.

Morland's still standing there by the painter, studying the view over the lagoon. Nodding to the painter, ignoring Morland completely, Chief Preston makes for the bench Morland had occupied and sits down. From the small stack of papers and magazines Morland's left behind—a nice touch, that!—he picks up a copy of *Allo!* and idly thumbs through it.

After another minute or so, Morland turns away and comes back to the bench. Obviously their man has left the church. The Chief feigns small embarrassment and replaces the magazine. Morland shrugs in a gesture that says: It's nothing. He sits down, takes out his cellular phone, and punches out what must be Ormerud's number. Speaking just loudly enough for the Chief to overhear, he gives Ormerud a description of the suspect, who's just boarded an eastbound No. 8. Ormerud will pick him up at the San Zaccaria stop and stay with him to wherever he's hiding out.

"It's him all right," Morland mutters when he hangs up. He doesn't look at the Chief. "You stay here. I'm going across the way to have a word with our trust-fund baby. Great job, Chief!"

He gets up and leaves. The Chief remains, until his curiosity gets the best of him and he crosses over to the fat painter at his easel.

The painting today, a full-frontal study of San Giorgio and its bell tower, is a lot better than yesterday's, in the Chief's opinion. It's very blocky and indelicate, the colors lashed on as much as stroked, and not always faithful to reality, so that San Giorgio's facade appears more pink than its actual orange. This guy really goes for the wild colors, the Chief thinks. Look at the way he's dressed: under a much-spotted down vest of an improbable bright green all he's wearing is a scruffy white velour warm-up suit with the zips at the ankles wide open. Not much for a nippy day, the Chief thinks, but if you're that fat, you bring your own insulation with you, and besides, at his size, these're probably the only kinds of clothes he can fit into. His feet are shod in leather sandals, wide straps buckled over heavy black wool socks. Definitely not a fashion plate, and his painting style shows it. Still, the picture's got a feel to it, something that grabs the Chief.

Across the way, he sees Morland cross the piazza and enter the church. He returns his attention to the picture.

"*Bello*," he says, jabbing an enthusiastic finger at the canvas. Like all Americans, he thinks he has a God-given right to interrupt anyone at any time. "*Bellissimo!* I—me—like, uh, lika thisa pict'!"

The painter looks up and smiles. He nods his appreciation.

"For sale?" asks the Chief. "You sell it?"

The painter shrugs. He doesn't understand.

"Sell. Sell. You sell"—the Chief mimes peeling bills off a bankroll —"it"—the Chief points at the painting—"to me"—he points at his own chest.

"*Ah, sì, comprendo,*" the painter says. His ruddy, rotund face, heavily bearded, with frank dark brown eyes sparkling behind lightly tinted, heavy-framed glasses, breaks into a large, jolly grin. "*Lei vuol' comprarlo.*" He pauses, obviously working hard to get the translation right, then asks, "You wish to—buy?"

"*Sì, sì, comprado,*" the Chief replies, then carefully pronounces the only Italian phrase with which he's thoroughly comfortable. "*Quanto costo?*"

The artist pauses, obviously has to think about this new development. The Chief looks down on him expectantly.

"*Non è finita, la tavola,*" he says. "Is no finish."

"When you maka da finish, I—me—buy," the Chief replies, nervously adding a bit of pidgin to the extra vowels that Americans think will make them understood in Latin languages. He nods vigorously and repeats the bill-peeling sequence.

The painter smiles and nods back. "OK, OK," he says.

"OK, OK, too." The Chief sticks out a large rough hand. As they shake, a thought jabs at him. "But, uh, but . . . *quanta costa?*" he asks. "How much is?"

The artist purses his lips, strokes his beard, studies the Chief staring at him anxiously. Finally he says, more as a question than a demand, "*Settemille lire.*"

The Chief reacts with an expression of utter bafflement. The painter holds up seven fingers, then bends over with a grunt, picks up a small sketch pad and a bit of drawing charcoal, flips over a leaf filled with rather crude renderings of the facade of the great church across the way and on a blank page carefully writes "L700,000" with the tip of a brush. He rips out the page and hands it to the Chief.

The Chief indicates with a series of shrugs, grimaces and eyebrow lifts that he wants to think it over. In the same lingua franca, the artist responds that that's no problem.

"Tomorrow, then, or the next day?" the Chief says. From his wallet he extracts a small calendar and points to the next day's date.

"*Non. Sta migliore il dopo domani. La Vigilia di Natale. La tavola serà finita, sicuro.*" Seeing that the Chief has no idea what he's talking about, he points to the canvas and says, "Fin-ish, for sure, eh?" then takes the pocket calendar and pokes a vermilion-stained finger at December 24. "Is good?"

"*Buono, buono,*" replies the Chief, and they shake hands.

Back at his hotel, the Chief finds a message to call "Giacomo," Morland's "work name." He punches up Morland's beeper number on his cellular phone and waits for the callback.

"It's him, all right," Morland tells the Chief. "Ormerud's run him to ground. I'll fill you in tomorrow." He then gives a detailed set of instructions.

The next morning, following orders, the Chief catches an early train for Padua. Morland travels by the same train in second class; Ormerud goes by bus.

In Padua, they arrive at the cathedral square within minutes of one

another and rendezvous at a rear table in a caffè crowded with tourists
and shoppers. Lucy is there already. She has been in Padua for two
hours, detailed by Mannerman to act as one of several shepherds to a
VIP tour of Padua and the Palladian villas along the Brenta Canal. She
has detached herself from the group, which is now off inspecting Giotto's
frescoes in the Arena Chapel under the guidance of a Princeton art
historian, and will rejoin it at lunch.

As she sits waiting for the others to arrive, toying with a cappuccino,
thinking what she's going to do about the latest jerk on her case, a
major hedge-fund manager who's complaining about being billeted in
the little Hotel Bucintoro, in the very room Byron slept in, who's threatening to dump seven million shares of GIA unless they find him something at the Gritti or Cipriani.

Some people shouldn't be allowed to travel, she thinks vexedly, but
she also doesn't want three-quarters of a billion dollars of GIA coming
on the market. The stock closed yesterday at $99 and change, and there
are buyers out there still, so there's at least a shot it might get to or go
through $100 by the time of Mannerman's party. If that happens, GIA
will be worth more than Coca-Cola! Wouldn't that be something! Lucy
may no longer work for the company, but there's no doubt that GIA still
has a piece of her heart.

Padua brings back memories of Baker. Despite herself, Lucy can't
help thinking back to when they looked together at the Donatello reliefs
in the Santo, the cathedral, and the great bronze candlestick, high as a
man, by the sixteenth-century sculptor Riccio. "You come to Padua for
sculpture," she remembers him saying, licking his lips around the words
the way a Frenchman might when speaking of truffles. She remembers
him as he was then, full of enthusiasm, green eyes so alight with enthusiasm they seemed almost turquoise, talking a mile a minute, no
longer sulky as he had been in filthy, despoiled Venice.

Now she tries to imagine him as Morland says he has remade himself:
a scrawny overage dead-eyed hippie, with a lank gray pigtail and aviator
glasses and a patently phony limp, dressed top to toe in denim and
coughing like a tubercular patient. It doesn't seem possible that he
could lose so much weight. She remembers him naked, remembers how
startling it was to see a man his age with barely an ounce of extra fat.
How could he be thinner? When they'd been together, when she'd lain

beneath him as he slumped after coming, he was easy to support. She thinks she recalls him saying that at 170 pounds he was down to 10 percent body fat—and he never did more than pick at his food . . . but what does she know? Pills, probably, that had to be it. By now, he was probably so wired up on whatever he was using that he could barely keep his feet on the ground. And Baker had never smoked.

One by one, the others show up, more coffee is ordered, and they get down to business.

This is to be the final run-through, Morland says, speaking in a rapid, low voice. There's no doubt they have their man. He's registered as "Arthur Sachem" of Coral Gables, Florida, at a small hotel near the Accademia Bridge, much favored by fashion people and the like. "Sachem" claims to be a photographer working the Mannerman gala on assignment from an American newspaper.

"Which newspaper?" asks Lucy.

"Don't know."

Dollars to doughnuts it'll be one of the scandal sheets, Lucy thinks. Mannerman's excluded them all from the press pool, which is strictly glossy paper and uppest-market.

Morland continues with the information—acquired by Ormerud from a bellboy in exchange for five thousand lire—that "Sachem's" luggage includes at least three extralarge lens cases, each more than a meter long, and each weighing perhaps twenty-five kilos, according to the informant.

"I did a little Internet lens shopping via laptop this morning," Morland says, "just to see if anything's come on the market we ought to know about. The Nikon 3800 still rules the roost. Unless, of course, you can get NASA to lend you a Fiberoptex 603."

"What's that?" asks Ormerud.

"One of Uncle Sam's newest toys. It'll give you virtual see-in-the-dark capability with electronic-exchange imaging that'll pick out the warts on the Pope's nose at six hundred meters."

"So this guy might be the real thing. Assuming he's got one of these?"

"Forget it, Ray. NASA doesn't rent."

It's a perfect cover, Lucy thinks. All year round, paparazzi bribe custodians, hotel staff, guards to look the other way. Right through the year, Venice swarms with photographers working with big, complicated equipment on fashion and architectural shoots.

"OK," says Morland, "let's go over the setup."

He unfolds a section cut from a larger map of Venice covering the tip of the Giudecca, the island of San Giorgio Maggiore and some of the surrounding lagoon. On top of it he places a photocopied guidebook plan of the interior of the church of San Giorgio.

"Because the equipment's heavy, he'll need help—a porter with a hand truck is my guess—to get the stuff over to San Giorgio. He'll most likely bring it across earlier in the day and stow it: either in the church, probably somewhere back in here, where the elevator machinery is, or maybe in the Cini gardens, which are closed to the public, but the custodian probably has a key, and there's probably a shed he can use. He'll want to keep an eye on his stuff, so he'll sort of fold into the hustle and bustle and wait. Christmas Eve, you can figure the church'll be doing a lot of business. The campanile shuts down to the public at four, but the church stays open around the clock and a lot of people'll want to watch the show from the steps and the piazza, so you can figure between the mamma-mias setting up the folding chairs right after supper and popping in and out of San Giorgio to say a prayer for the Holy Father, no one'll notice him.

"We'll rotate our surveillance. The Chief made him in the church and Ray here's done the tailing, so I'm the only one we can be certain he hasn't had a chance to notice. I'll keep an eye out for him when he comes over; after that, once we've established he's on the island, it's just a matter of keeping an eye on the campanile."

"Why not follow him to see where he stores the rockets?"

The Chief jumps in and answers. "Why take the chance, honey bear? We want to blend with the crowd ourselves. Morland's right. Be too curious too early and Baker might spook."

"I see."

"This way," says Morland, picking up the thread, "we have him where we want him. I figure that at four, or just after, when the elevator is supposed to shut down, he'll ride it to the top and stash his gear. Then he'll descend and the old boy'll lock up. That way, any carabinieri happening to stroll by can see that the elevator cab's where it's supposed

to be. I expect he'll go out and have a nice dinner, maybe a shave and
a shower, come back around ten, let himself into the campanile and
climb up to the observation deck."

"Climb?"

"Elementary, my dear Lucy. The elevator cab standing empty and
locked at the bottom is his best cover. The climb takes ten minutes
tops, allowing for a nice pause at each landing, assuming there's no
need to limp. So he's where he wants to be by around ten-ten or quarter
past. He's not going to fire until eleven at the earliest, and probably not
until some time after, when the rockets are at their reddest glare and
the entire city's oohing and aahing. He'll use this half hour or so to
relish the event before it actually happens—he's sure as hell not going
to have the time to do so afterward. Anyway, the more noise and commotion the better, so he waits. The fireworks start, and he sights in, and
then—at eleven-twenty, say—he lets off two rounds into the Regina
roof garden, and maybe a third into the spectator fleet or the Piazza San
Marco for diversion. The chances of anyone tracking the exhaust flares
are virtually nil, not with the sky spilling fireworks. So while roughly a
million people are running around in circles, he strolls down the stairs,
probably donning a new wig and whiskers as he goes, and maybe he
has a change of clothes in his kit, and he's outta here! Well, probably
not until morning, because my guess is he's leading a double Venice
life, registered at another hotel with a second passport. Don't forget, we
know him by only one identity, but he's probably got two or three. These
days, that's a cinch!"

"Not if we nail him first."

It's the first time Ormerud has spoken. The finality in his tone chills
Lucy. She looks at him. "*Nail* him, Ray?"

Ormerud doesn't answer. He lets his expression do the talking. For
the first time, something about him scares Lucy. Up to now, she's been
very glad to have him along; he's competent, collected, fit and tough.
Now she senses he's something more. She supposes the right word is
"deadly."

You don't mean "capture," do you? Lucy thinks with a shiver. You
mean "kill." But for her own certitude, she repeats the question. "You're
going to come in shooting?"

"If he throws down on me, I'll have to," Ormerud answers calmly.

Even as late as today, Lucy's managed to suppress the likelihood—
the virtual certainty—that this must all end with Baker dead. She's
been in what Spuds would call "major denial," suppressing the reality
that, all things considered, Baker cannot be allowed to go on living.
Everyone's best interests, hers, her "co-conspirators'," the world's, demand it. The complications implicit in any alternative are beyond her
resources, unaffordable in terms of time and money—too late now for
that.

Baker alive and brought to book seems no better. She can imagine
the media circus—she's in the business of orchestrating such things
herself. It would make O. J. Simpson look like traffic court. And the
ripple effect, with Baker as a Promethean model for every crazy out
there with a gun and grudge, spawning schools of would-be Bakers,
could be truly terrifying.

There's only one answer. The only good Baker now is a dead Baker.
What she sees in Ray Ormerud's face tells her she had better get used
to the idea.

Morland seems eerily to sense Lucy's mood, and he tries to take the
edge off the moment. "Look," he says sharply to Ormerud, "it all depends. When Baker shows up at the church and makes for the bell
tower, whichever one of us is on station will beep the others and then
begin a measured count to a hundred, to let Baker get well up the stairs.
At 'ninety-nine Mississippi,' we'll have joined forces and we start up—
don't forget to wear your best Nikes, fellows—keeping a landing apart
until we reach the floor below the top. Then we go up that last flight
hell for leather—or should I say hell for Air Jordan?—with Ray first,
the Chief second and yours truly bringing up the rear. The firepower,
in other words, first."

"I'd better have the Uzi," says Ormerud in the voice of a man vol
unteering to carry the picnic wine.

"You'll go in shooting?" Lucy asks. She still can't believe it.

"Depends," says Ormerud. "We'll be locked and loaded and scream-
ing like banshees. The surprise should give us a few seconds' advantage,
maybe more. If he drops the launcher, OK. If he doesn't, I'll have no
choice."

"And if he surrenders?"

"That's your call, Lucy," says Ormerud with a thin smile. "Then it's your show again. Personally, I kind of think it'll be better if he doesn't."

There, Lucy thinks, someone's finally said it.

"Chances are, he won't," the Chief adds, piling on another brick of reassurance. "Not this man. Not after what he's done."

"Don't be so sure," she rebuts, the words out before she realizes what she's saying, what she's doing. "Baker can figure where his best interests lie. The interests of his crusade, that is. If he lives to talk . . ."

She doesn't need to finish the thought. Although not in so many words, she's pronounced Baker's death sentence. The table falls silent. "And then?" She feels remarkably at peace.

"Then we clean up," Ormerud answers. "We take documents, clothes, anything identifiable. Maybe we strip the . . . strip Baker down. Then we get out."

"You just leave him there?"

"Why not? The Chief and I will deal with his hotel room—he'll be carrying the keys, most likely—and be on our way."

"Having saved capitalism and mankind," Morland continues, jocular, "we go back to where we came from. We say nothing. I turn what's more or less happened into a screenplay, which I sell to Spielberg for six million—which we split four ways. Then it's sayonara."

"Suppose something goes wrong?"

"What can?"

"Well, just suppose."

"Then it's your call. You are playing center field, as they say, circulating with the great and glittering, but with beeper tucked in your garter and cellular phone in your bejeweled evening purse—you can get it through security as a professional necessity—and we can keep you abreast of our progress. If you don't hear from us by ten forty-five—"

"Ten-thirty," interrupts Ormerud quietly.

"Ten-thirty," Morland repeats obediently. "If you don't hear from us by ten-thirty, you go to Security Control Central and yank the emergency cord, and then you get the hell out of there!"

"If something goes wrong, why wouldn't he just open up right away?" Lucy asks.

"He might—but also might not. Say he blows us away. The smoke clears. But there's no sound of backup. He's going to wonder about that, put himself in our shoes, ask who we are . . . were! Either way, you'll have a few minutes' leeway. This is a methodical, fearless man who swims with crocodiles. Men like that don't panic; they rationalize. He'll want to know who we are. He's never seen any of us, don't forget. He'll search us but we won't be carrying identification, not so much as a hotel matchbook, although we'll be wearing those blue windbreakers the Italian plainclothes guys fancy. Since he won't have a clue who we are, Baker will do exactly what we've been doing: apply behavioral logic. He has to conclude that we have someone on the outside primed to hear from us by such and such a time. That's when he'll open up. You can figure you have until ten forty-five, no later, to clear the roof garden."

Ormerud nods confirmation.

"I hope I can," says Lucy quietly.

The others look at her.

"There's Mannerman, don't forget. When I tell him his great party of the millennium must close down because over in the campanile of San Giorgio Maggiore is a man about to blast him to kingdom come with ground-to-ground missiles, a man supposedly eaten by crocodiles four years ago in Africa, the man who made him wet his pants in public— it is not going to be easy. This is Mannerman's shining hour, his parade, and he won't want anyone or anything to rain on it! Especially me. Because I'm someone who deserted him for"—Lucy hesitates—"for love of the man who's about to blow him and the Pope to kingdom come."

"Look," Ormerud says impatiently, "you can argue this way or that. But if we don't get Baker, then the decision is his. The fact is, he has an alternative and that leaves us one. Suppose he deals with us—and then, to his surprise, sees or hears no sign of backup, no suspicious activity on air, land or water. He checks the roof garden—he'll probably have a twenty-power spotter scope; Baker is not someone who under-equips himself—and sees no change in the pitch or rhythm. So he waits. The fireworks start at eleven sharp. Still nothing. Now he knows that if he leaves quickly, while things are still in flux, he may live to destroy another day."

"But I thought by ten-thirty I've already sounded battle stations?"

"I'm thinking out loud. Suppose you don't? Lucy, you're the one who knows Baker best—hold that, you're the *only* one of us who knows Baker *at all*—so only you can judge the man. If you do nothing when you don't hear from us, he may not. I have a sense of a man who likes living. Living, as Pete said, in order to be able to kill again."

"Don't bet on it," says Lucy. "This would complete his Grand Slam, don't you see? The single, unrepeatable shot he's pointed his entire hunting life toward. At one blow, he'll finish off Baker's Dozen. He must be getting tired, living on his nerve ends, feeding his obsession. It must be like keeping a piranha. You say he's terribly gaunt? I can believe that. He may have the psyche of a terrorist but I don't think he's got the metabolism, not at his age. This is it for H. A. Baker. His final bow."

Ormerud purses his lips, looks at the others. "That being the case," he says slowly, "he gets a count of one."

Morland checks his watch. "Time to be going." Standing behind Lucy, he places his hands on her shoulders and presses gently. It's the first time he's touched her. "Considering whose bacon we're saving, it seems only fair that your client pick up the check."

"No argument here," says Lucy, signaling to the waiter.

"There is one thing," her father says.

"Yes?"

"Pete, OK if I take the noon shift on the Giudecca tomorrow?" The others look at the Chief. He doesn't wait for the question, but plunges right in with his answer, looking more than faintly embarrassed. "The reason is, I got to see a man about a painting."

"A painting?" Lucy looks at her father with pleased disbelief. "What kind of a painting?"

"I guess you'd call it a Venicescape," the Chief answers. "You remember, Peter, the fat guy with the easel?"

"Sure. How could you miss him? Must go close to three hundred pounds."

"Well, he's doing this picture sort of across the lagoon, with a little bit of San Giorgio. It's weird, but I kind of like it, so I'm going to buy it."

"And . . . ?" Lucy can't believe this. *Her* father, her *father*, buying a painting! "For how much, may I ask?"

The Chief digs in his jacket pocket and pulls out a folded sheet of drawing paper.

"How much is this in dollars?" he asks, displaying it to the others.

"A hundred thousand lire?" says Lucy. "About sixty bucks."

"No," says the Chief, "this is supposed to be seven hundred thousand."

"Wrong," Lucy replies. "If it was a seven, it would have a crossstroke through the stem. That's how they write it here—to keep it from being confused with a one. That's not a seven, not an Italian seven, that's a one."

"Honey bear," her father says plaintively, "it's gotta be a seven. I asked how much—*quanta costa*—after he wrote it, and he held up seven fingers. And he said 'setty.' "

Lucy shrugs. What does she know? "OK," she says, "it's a seven. Seven hundred thousand lire's about four hundred and fifty dollars. That's not peanuts, Dad. Are you sure? You want me to have a look?"

The Chief shakes his head vigorously. "Listen, I like it. What else'm I going to with four hundred and fifty dollars? See Paris and die?"

"It's Naples," says Ormerud quietly.

"Naples?"

"The saying is: See Naples and die. *Vede Napoli e poi mori.*"

"I didn't know you spoke Italian," says Morland.

"I don't," Ormerud replies, smiling. "You just heard all of it. Somebody said it at my old man's funeral. He was killed there in '43."

What did he think he was fighting for? Lucy wonders. Probably the same things Baker'd tell you he's fighting for.

The waiter arrives with the bill. As Lucy pays, the others leave and are soon lost in the hubbub of the piazza. Outside, she pauses in the lee of Donatello's great equestrian statue of the fifteenth-century soldier Gattamelata. Another hired gun, she thinks, an Ormerud of his time. Men and their weapons, she sniffs, and hurries off toward the cathedral to rejoin her group. But sometimes, it occurs to her, there is no answer but the gun.

— III — From one end of Venice to the other, right through the fine December day, sweeping like an aberrant hot wind through the narrow alleys and across the lagoon, the excitement mounts. The day begins calmly enough: at chilly first light, it's quiet, the streets and canals deserted but for shopkeepers and workers beginning another day's routine, here and there revelers returning to their lodgings from parties before *the* party by gondola or water taxi—even some on foot. But by high noon the agitation's grown palpable, shivery and intense: a reedy tenor fizz of near-hysteria audible above the city's normal clamor. The combination of Christmas Eve, a papal visit, the world's great and glamorous schooling at the hotels like bejeweled minnows; it's all too much, even for jaded, cynical Venice with all its centuries of weary experience.

To the oldest-timers, the day brings back odd, displacing memories of wartime. The city is once again full of uniforms. With several heads of state in attendance and the Pope in the wings, a security setup unmatched in memory is in place; police and military officials of twenty nations, along with some eight thousand representatives of various branches of the Italian security forces, have turned out in full fig. The effect is both gala and ominous: the marvelous dress uniforms add to the festive mood; the grim faces of their wearers bring a dark note. The security forces are operating under great pressure: the previous week, a high Egyptian dignitary was car-bombed while on an official visit to Naples; people are jumpy, the politicians are under pressure, the media are furious about the tight restrictions.

From A (Addington, Lord—chairman of British Aeromotive) to Z (Zaragoza, El Duque de), Mannerman's guest list seems to feel the tension most. The general unease coalesces with social anxiety to yield a general neurasthenia. In Harry's Bar, the possessors of $9 billion of aggregate global net worth trade punches over first call on a pitcher of Bellinis. The police are summoned to a smart hairdressing parlor off the Campo San Moisè to separate a kicking, scratching English countess from the clawing, spitting wife of a Central European prime minister. A top seamstress at a major couture house, who has made the journey from Milan on speculation, smiles to herself as she leaves the Gritti Hotel to catch the *vaporetto* for the railway station. Her hunch has paid off: in her purse rests $50,000 in crisp new 1,000 DM notes, the fruit of a silent auction for exclusive use of her services in setting to exact rights the drape of one of three identical couture ball gowns purchased, for $15,000 each, from her employer's salon on the Via Montenapoleone, Milan's premier shopping street, by the wife of Liechtenstein's most prominent tax lawyer, a Bogotá investment advisor's Dutch mistress and a German grocer's widow whom *Forbes* rates as being worth $6 billion.

Tension of a different sort—a more focused anxiety based on speculative expectation—grips Morland, the Chief and Ormerud. By nine, they have taken up position: Ormerud outside San Giorgio, Morland opposite on the tip of the Giudecca, the Chief near the San Zaccaria water-bus station.

At eleven they rotate. The Chief comes across to the Giudecca on the No. 5, Morland having just left the Zitelle minutes earlier on a No. 8 for San Giorgio; disembarking, Morland notices Ormerud waiting to embark for the Riva degli Schiavoni, a short walk east of San Zaccaria. As the *vaporetto* chugs off, Ormerud goes forward, and sees the Hotel Cipriani launch vectoring toward the shops and salons of the *sestiere* San Marco; it's filled to the brim with fancy folk, men and women clad alike in fur, and packed together they resemble a single animal. A single torpedo right now would probably take out $10 billion. The sight of those satisfied, insulated faces prompts the reflection, not for the first time, that it may truly be God's work that Baker's about, but then he spots Lucy's blond head, scarfless and windblown on this fair winter day, and returns to his senses.

At 11:20, just as Morland has forecast, a water taxi, strakes polished, brass glistening, all done up in bunting for the occasion, arrives at the San Giorgio landing and Baker disembarks. Accompanying him is a hotel porter, the name picked out in gold serifed capitals on his cap. As the speedboat bobs unsteadily, a hand truck is manhandled out of the boat, followed by a collection of duffels, hard camera boxes and three extraordinarily long tubular lens cases. The luggage is stacked, and the hotel porter trundles off toward the church, followed by Baker, looking more wraithlike and scruffy than ever. The water taxi remains moored, presumably waiting to take Baker back across the lagoon.

No one pays any attention as these two men lever the hand truck up the steps of the church. Morland watches them enter by the left-hand door, then follows at a cautious distance. Inside, the two head for the left-hand aisle and make their way toward the front of the church. A few praying heads look up incuriously at the sound of wheels on stone, then resume their devotions. Morland halts before the Chapel of St. Lucy, puts a thousand lire in the box, takes a votive candle and lights it, breathing an unheard prayer for them all. A covert sideways glance down the aisle yields nothing, but he knows what he needs to know: so far, Baker is following Morland's script to the letter. He completes his false devotions and takes an outside pew halfway down the aisle, waiting.

A few minutes later, he hears the sound of wheels and Baker and the porter reappear, the latter pushing the empty hand truck. Morland watches them leave the church, cross the piazza and reboard the water taxi. This surprises him. He'd expected Baker to stick around. He must be very confident, Morland thinks—a good omen. As the launch accelerates off in the direction of San Marco, he beeps Ormerud to let him know Baker has gone back to his hotel to wait out the day. Ormerud will keep an eye on him until relieved.

The Chief, stationed across the narrow ribbon of water, checks his watch. Promptly at noon, he sees his new friend the painter emerge from a side street in the direction of the Zitelle and waddle up the quay to his favored spot. The Chief gives a merry wave. The painter nods. He can't wave back because his hands are full. Under one arm is a rectangular brown-paper parcel tied with fat twine, presumably the Chief's picture. Under the other is a blank canvas. His paint box and easel are carried in an ingeniously rigged backpack arrangement slung across his shoulders.

The two men converge at the painter's usual spot. He sets down his parcel and canvas and shakes hands with the Chief. The parcel is opened, the Chief inspects his new acquisition, pronounces it entirely satisfactory by vigorously nodding his head and digs out an envelope stuffed with currency. The painter thumbs it quickly, nods, and the deal is done. The Chief heads back to his hotel. He is due to spell Ormerud outside Baker's hotel at six. The artist sets up his easel, attaches his paint box, places a new canvas on the easel and begans to lay on a new painting with thick, abrupt scrapes of charcoal. Life and art go on.

By four the bright day is fading fast. At 4:19 on the western horizon, down past the Malamocco channel and the southern shore of the Lido, the sun delivers a fantastic curtain line: a blazing winter sunset, vivid orange and vermilion streaked with earthwide lashings of violet—hard to imagine that any fireworks fabricated by man will come near that! Across Venice, lights twinkle on in rooms and lobbies, in multicolored chains strung across narrow *calles* and framing the rotted elegance of sixteenth-century lintels, here and there, in no pattern, as if a spirit with a taper is dancing through the streets. The excitement in the city, already feverish, builds toward bursting. By 6:30, with an hour and a half still to go before the first guest will arrive, the electricity in the city is ungovernable: everyone seems to be speaking in tones pitched an octave higher, to cover a meter of space in fewer seconds and more paces, to blink faster, to gesticulate more extravagantly.

At 7:10 a silver-and-gold World Express II, Mannerman's brand-new personal jet, its stabilizer emblazoned for the occasion with the papal seal, touches down at Marco Polo Airport and the Holy Father deplanes. Mannerman is waiting on the runway to greet the pontiff, along with the Cardinal-Patriarch of Venice. The three men and their retinues, attended by a contingent of Swiss Guards, half in traditional dress bearing halberds, the remainder in bulletproof vests and armed with semi-automatics, are borne by a small convoy of motor yachts through a seven-mile-long corridor of closely spaced picket boats while Agusta helicopter gunships of the Italian Air Force and the state police weave a protective thatch overhead. At a landing on the Riva degli Schiavoni, with *Alpini* sharpshooters lining the quay and stationed along the roof-line of the Doge's Palace and buildings opposite, the Pope bids Mannerman, with whom he has been in nonstop deep conversation about the situation in Mexico, a temporary adieu and transfers to a transit barge that takes him up a narrow canal to the Patriarchal Palace. As the transparent bulletproof canopy glides under the Bridge of Sighs, the Pope gives his blessing to the sharpshooters ranged along the palace battlements; in the distance, out of sight, can be heard the uproar of the crowd pressed in upon the very edges of St. Mark's Square, where it's held back in by a human wall of police.

At seven sharp, a splendidly bedecked armored gondola propelled by a gondolier dressed in eighteenth-century festive livery embroidered with a coat of arms devised for the occasion by Versace leaves the Gritti

Palace Hotel. It has been searched bow to stern before leaving and will be so searched again upon arriving at the Regina's landing. It presents its credentials at the floating security checkpoint off the Calle Traghetto, is waved through and makes its smooth way the eighth of a mile down-canal to the Regina, where it discharges its passengers, the first to arrive at the gala, a Taiwanese mogul said to control the world market for virtual memory chips and his wife. After clearing voice- and palmprint checks, the couple pass through the metal detector described by its designer, a New York florist, as a "Guardi-esque mini-triumphal arch," submit to a discreet but thorough body search and exchange their passports for color- and magnetic-coded place cards. When the chip king checks these against a gold-framed table plan, his eyes crinkle at the corners in a pleased expression which would bring forth massive sighs of relief in certain Taipei sweatshops, and he seems to swell with satisfaction. A steward appears with two escutcheoned champagne flutes —specially blown at Murano for the occasion—filled with a special cuvée of Veuve Clicquot, and the new arrivals are taken in hand by an elegant young Englishwoman who curtsies deeply before leading them to the elevator that ascends to the roof garden, where Mannerman and his wife are stationed to receive their guests.

The troubleshooting team, including Lucy, is strategically positioned around the room. She's been on hand since 6:30, checking place cards, touching up flowers, lining up knives and forks. When the Taiwanese mogul makes his appearance, she's standing at the southeast end of the roof garden, where she can keep an eye on Tables 19 through 27, where most of the financial strength present tonight will be seated. She's persuaded Mannerman that at this kind of function it doesn't do to mix people too much. You have to recognize and accept a certain amount of intragroup homogenization. The very, very, very rich, for example, with a cutoff of roughly $8 billion in Forbes wealth, will only be really comfortable with each other. They have the same toys, look for the same things, know to the penny how much their brethren in wealth are worth. Outside their homes and the lackeys who make up their immediate business circles, they're at ease only in the company of others equally rich. It's the same way with corporate chiefs, who are Studs's responsibility, with the great speculators and moneymen she's tending, with TK's pride of peers of the UnivCom realm and other media potentates and with the Washington eminences and dignitaries of state who are being watched over by Grover and by a former UN Secretary-General hired for the occasion. The only group to be widely dispersed—one or two to each table—is a double diadem's worth of celebrity and stardom: Hollywood names, golf champions, luminaries of the opera and concert stage, Nobel medalists, artists boasting Metropolitan Museum retrospectives. These are scattered throughout the room so as to sparkle individually, like diamonds in the splendid coiffure of a diva. As well they should, since all but one or two are being paid six-figure sums of "appearance money."

Lucy looks pretty splendid tonight herself. In the past, she's done a couple of useful favors for Oscar de la Renta—who'll be on hand tonight—and he's come through for her with a lovely, wide-sashed gown of soft deep taupe chiffon that sets off her supple pale looks to perfection. She can hold her own against most of the women in the room, thanks to the final ministrations of the woman whom Oscar had Balmain send down from Paris to do her final party fitting. The dress isn't merely beautiful; it's practical. The full, gathered skirt is easy to move around in and the sash hides her beeper without a discernible bulge.

As the early trickle of arriving guests becomes a steady stream, the temperature in the enclosed roof garden rises. The garden's outer walls are made of vertically louvered glass panels that are supposed to work in electronic harness with the hotel's internal climate control system to balance the comfort level, but the technology has been defeated by the heavy velvet hangings—all the Fortuny fabric between Venice and Genoa has been commandeered for the gala—chosen by Milan's decorator of the moment to set off the splendid company. Lucy, feeling hot, seizes an unoccupied moment and goes to a window. Pushing aside a drape, she looks out over the Bacino. The basin is a madhouse of marine traffic. Boats of every size have gathered in rows that stretch back across half the lagoon. In front are a dozen sleek launches bristling like frigates with the cannonlike long lenses of the paparazzi who have chartered them. These edge up as close as possible to the cable barricade which the Marine Police have strung between the Dorsoduro and the *sestiere* San Marco. This is backed up by a chain of boats moored in a line running from the Customs Dock in the lee of Santa Maria della Salute to the Riva Ca' di Dio a half mile away. Inside the rope lie the half dozen squat barges from which Long Island's famed Grucci family, along with a team of pyrotechnical specialists dispatched by the Governor-General of Hong Kong, will work their spectacular artistry after dinner while George Plimpton narrates.

Beyond the spectator flotilla, on San Giorgio, she can make out a crowd forming in the piazza. Towering in the background, the church and its campanile are brilliantly illuminated. The tall black slits of the campanile's belfry, carved like the teeth of a jack-o'-lantern into the weathered orange stonework, look like gunports. Below them lies the pale girdle of observation-deck windows from which Baker will have planned to fire. Lucy wonders if he's there yet.

By eight, three-quarters of the guests have arrived. The atmosphere is merry, the service fleet and efficient. Mannerman, handsome—almost distinguished—in a croupier-slick tuxedo, moves easily among his guests, dispensing his presence in precisely calculated dollops of familiarity and bonhomie. Never in her life has Lucy seen grander jewelry or more elegantly turned-out women, never again will she. By rough-and-ready reckoning, she figures there's a half billion dollars' worth of apparel and gems under the pale gentian tent.

At 8:15 the Princess Royal of Belgium arrives, handed gracefully onto the Regina's landing by the Mayor of Venice and Cardinal Huenens of Antwerp. She's followed ten minutes later by a Royal Prince of England. Lucy crosses the roof garden and checks the roster. All the dinner company present save one. Time to be seated.

At that moment, Spuds sidles up. He's resplendent in a new double-breasted dinner jacket with lapels the width of a promenade deck, and he's sporting the ribboned boutonniere of what Lucy knows is a minor Costa Rican order of merit.

"Change of plans," he mutters. "His Holiness can't stand missing the fun. He's coming over for dessert. We're giving him a nine-thirty ETA. Gotta tell the Old Man." He wheels and plunges into the chattering throng in search of Mannerman.

Damn, Lucy thinks! In the original plan, the Holy Father wasn't scheduled to appear until 10:45, just in time for coffee and the fireworks. That gave her some extra room—to save the Pope at least. She checks her watch. It's 8:37.

Ten minutes later, roughly a half mile away, Ormerud tenses and his eyes narrow as Baker appears in the doorway of the small hotel across the narrow piazza.

Baker's appearance is startling. He's all duded up. Literally dressed to kill. He's head to toe in black, stovepipe jeans studded with big silver stars and belted with a silver-gilt buckle the size of a postcard, a full-sleeved shirt with brilliant buttons, a black brocade vest. His lank hair, washed and brilliantined, is pulled back tight. The effect is striking, ascetic—like a long-faced satanic matador in a raven *traje de luces*.

No one who sees this man tonight will forget him—which doesn't make sense, Ormerud thinks, as he rises to follow. Moreover, this style isn't in keeping with Baker as Ormerud has come to think of him. Baker is an old-school type: if he were going to dress for the occasion true to type, chinos and Top-Siders would be more like it, and this getup is hardly what you'd choose for an inconspicuous getaway. Yet what's really strange is how natural he looks in it. It's possible to change and imitate, and Ormerud's seen some first-rate switches and transformations, but this is as good as, if not better than, any of them: he walks the walk and looks the look, as if he's had it his entire adult life.

Ormerud's still wondering at the incongruity when he hands Baker off to Chief Preston at the No. 5 *vaporetto* station at the Ca' de Oro. He continues to ponder the matter through the arrival and departure of two more San Giorgio–bound water buses before he boards the third at 9:32. As the boat sputters free of the landing and eases into the channel behind the spectator flotilla, he mentally checks his arsenal. In his Adidas sports bag are three blue nylon windbreakers, a silenced Glock 9-millimeter automatic with a firing rate of a round a second for Ormerud, as well as Ormerud's personal .32 Beretta, which Morland will carry. The Chief already has his Police Special tucked in his waistband.

Morland is waiting at the foot of the campanile. He looks nervous. When the Chief comes out of the church, it's clear that he too is having trouble putting on his game face. Ormerud's not surprised. It's been a long time for the Chief, and for Morland it's been never. He's glad he's going in first.

"God almighty," the Chief exclaims, looking toward San Marco, "how about those small craft! Must be a thousand out there! Like seabirds when the baitfish are running."

At that moment, a roar goes up from the eastern fringe of the flotilla and ripples smoothly westward, beating time to the progress of the richly bedecked barge that has emerged from the canal running behind the Doge's Palace and now moves into the mouth of the Grand Canal, swept along by sixteen oars manned by the crews of the Italian Navy's number one and number two eight-oared shells. At each oarsman's feet lies a .305 Beretta semiautomatic.

"E-viva il Papa! E-viva! E-viva!" The cheer is like a coxswain's rhythmic call to his oarsmen. The effect is hypnotic: the great blades dip and pull, dip and pull, the throng out on the water responds in cadence. It's hard not to be swept into the mood.

Ormerud, Morland and the Chief have mounted to the top step of the church porch to get a better view, and are transfixed by the spectacle. The papal barge is too distant to permit a clear sighting of the Holy Father himself—the Chief curses himself for not having brought his field glasses—before it vanishes behind the twinkling hulks of the Customs House and Santa Maria della Salute. The cheers from the barrier cable subside as the barge slides into the Grand Canal.

Mannerman, alerted by Spuds, is waiting on the Regina landing when the papal barge draws up. He kneels and kisses the pontiff's ring. Upstairs, the glittering company has risen from its seats and studies its protocol cards, while ten million dollars of entertainment value cools its heels in separate air-conditioned suites on the floor below. With crisp little gestures of blessing, the Holy Father makes his way through the press of security, hotel factotums and local VIPs, and leads the Cardinal-Patriarch and Mannerman into the elevator. It's 9:53.

Morland and his colleagues are inside the church now. They enter one by one, spaced by about a minute's interval, and by different paths make their way toward the northwest corner. The place is virtually deserted, empty save for a handful of people, worshippers so blinded by the habit of faith that there might as well not be a world outside.

When Ormerud arrives, Morland is gently rattling the iron-cage door. A shiny padlock secures the edge of the door to the iron-barred frame.

"The goddamn lock's been changed!" he mutters. Ormerud moves in, examines the new lock and scowls at Morland as he produces a ring of skeleton picks. "No problem," he says quietly. The lock is a Saturday-night special: cheap and easy. Hardly what you'd expect a pro to use.

It's a matter of minutes for Ormerud to pick the lock. The Chief and Morland keep watch. The church is dead still and deserted, although outside they can hear the uproar swelling as the crowd increases and its excitement intensifies. It's 9:54.

Across the way, to enthusiastic applause, Barbra Streisand, clad in the same Oscar model as Lucy's but in gunmetal blue, makes her way among the tables haloed in a single spotlight. Before the throne on which the Pope sits, flanked by Mannerman and the Patriarch, she executes a deep, graceful curtsy, then moves off to the side where a single stool and microphone stand are set up.

Lucy's standing in the shadowy back of the tent with her colleagues. The evening so far has been a total success: there have been no catastrophes and everyone seems to be having as good a time as people seriously constrained by their sense of their wealth and importance are capable of. As the band launches into "People," and applause blots out a few early measures of Streisand's rendition, Lucy steals a glance out the window. Above its bustling quay, San Giorgio's campanile thrusts nightward like a magnificent orange spike.

Her watch reads 10:07. They must be in, she thinks, and murmurs a quick, silent prayer of Godspeed before her pounding heart seems to drown out every other noise.

Across the lagoon, on the second-floor landing, Morland and the others don the blue nylon windbreakers, along with Navy baseball caps marked with an X that Morland's brought along as an afterthought. There's a series of clicks as Ormerud checks the Glock and releases the safety on Morland's pistol, while the Chief thumbs the cylinder on his Smith & Wesson. Then, guns in hand, they begin the seven-landing climb to the observation deck, moving slowly, practically on tiptoe. On each landing, they check their watches, there's plenty of time.

Two floors below the observation deck, they pause to get their breath. Only the Chief is showing the slightest signs of exertion. They can hear the sound of someone moving about upstairs. It's 10:19.

Across the lagoon, Streisand concludes "Ave Maria" by sinking low in a ballerina's deep bow, arms open as if to embrace the applause. The Pope beams his approval, and claps stiffly, palms upright. The singer rises, curtsies, kisses his ring and exits to a standing ovation. The lights come up briefly, no more than a minute's pause to let people reorient: to clear their minds of the entertainment just past and ready their sensibilities for Julio Iglesias, who will follow.

Lucy's heart is beating faster. She fingers the beeper in her sash as Iglesias appears at the back of the room and begins to sing "La Vie en Rose" as he moves toward the front of the roof garden. In the dim light, Lucy's fancy Cartier party watch is difficult to read. She wishes she'd been more practical. Finally, by holding it just so, to catch a wink of illumination from one of the crystal-faceted globes revolving slowly at the corners of the tent, she can make out that it's 10:21. Pretty soon now.

In the campanile, the three men take the last two flights slowly. Their rubber-soled jogging shoes make no noise, but the mounting crowd noise rising from the piazza is now so loud that the tramp of jackboots would go unheard.

The door opening from the stairwell onto the observation deck is ajar. There's no interior light anywhere. Across from the doorway, they sense rather than see their quarry. He's hunched and still, intent on whatever he's doing.

Morland checks his watch: 10:23. He looks at Ormerud, who gestures them into their order of battle. Ormerud first, then the Chief, then Morland. He gestures with his pistol. Locked and loaded! Geronimo!

Ormerud looks at his mates one last time, edges closer to the door. He crouches, seems to count silently to himself, then with a mighty cry of *"Polizia"* hurls himself onto the deck, followed by the Chief and Morland.

Baker's back is to them when they crash in, and that gives them the seconds they need. He's standing on the far side of the deck, aiming something at the brilliantly lit roof garden; a pair of lethal-looking tubular devices, hard to make out exactly in the dim light, lean against the wall next to him, muzzles up. At the disturbance behind him, he begins to turn, but by then he's dead meat. Ormerud crosses the intervening space in a single bound, launches himself across the deck and hurtles into the man. His shoulder takes the quarry in the breastbone with enough force to make him cry out, as if a rib or two might be cracked, and sends him reeling along the wall. He brings his pistol up and presses the muzzle against Baker's jugular.

"Don't even think about it," he says quietly.

With his free hand he takes the device Baker's holding by its barrel and, without looking, hands it behind him to Morland. Baker stops wheezing, catches his breath, makes what sounds like a sob and then starts to say something in an angry voice, but a touch of added pressure from Ormerud's gun stops the words in his throat.

"Cameras," says Morland, from somewhere behind Ormerud. "These are fucking goddamn cameras!"

Instinctively, Ormerud eases the pressure against Baker's neck and looks at him carefully. He sees the fright in his captive's eyes replaced by indignation. A terrible worry courses through him.

"What the goddamn hell is this about! Who the fuck are you people!" Baker's excited voice, almost an angry shout, is coarse, is redolent of "Noo Yawk," the streets.

Morland nudges Ormerud. In his left hand, muzzle down, he holds his useless semiautomatic. In his right, gripped halfway up the lens barrel, is a Nikon Model 5EXEP single-lens reflex to which is affixed an extremely long, thick lens, almost three feet from focal plane to sunshade.

"Who the hell are *you*?" he asks. "What the hell is this?"

"That, asshole," says "Baker," "is a Fiberoptex 603. So are those! Hey, asshole! Be careful, huh! You drop those fuckers, someone owes NASA a hundred fifty G's plus three people are gonna get canned because these lenses are AWOL, not to mention that my ass is gonna be grass!"

This tirade is directed at the Chief, standing behind Morland, revolver jauntily jammed back into his belt. In each hand, he's brandishing similarly equipped Nikons. "Lenses," he says forlornly. "Damn lenses!"

"May we see your ID?" says Morland, trying to sound officious, trying to save the situation, trying to buy time.

"You bet your ass, asshole!"

From the bosom pocket of his vest, "Baker" produces a plastic sheet about the size of a file card and hands it to Ormerud. The clear laminate encloses a press card in the name of Arthur Sachem, a staff photographer for the *National Enquirer*, Coral Gables, Florida.

Morland studies the card, then shows it to the others.

"You assholes want more?" asks "Baker."

Ormerud shakes his head. What does it matter at this point who this guy is? All that matters is that he's up here with three cameras— cameras!—not rocket launchers, and somehow they've got to deal with it. He's thinking so hard it doesn't occur to him to blow off at Morland—and Lucy—for drawing him into this damn fun-house movie script!

"Tie him up," he says finally.

"You outta your fucking mind!" screams Sachem. "This is a one- twenty-five-K gig, you sons of bitches! This isn't just the *Enquirer*, you assholes, I got *Match* in on this, and *Hola!* I'm on fuckin' deadline! Not only that, these fuckin' lenses gotta be back at Cape Canaveral tomorrow night!"

"Tie him up, Chief."

Sachem moves angrily at Ormerud, but a brief flicker of the Glock's muzzle stops him as effectively as if Ormerud had pressed the trigger.

"Get on to . . . you know who," Ormerud mutters to Morland and jerks his head in the direction of the hotel across the lagoon. Morland backs across the deck, turns away from the others and dials Lucy's beeper. The Chief moves toward Sachem.

When her beeper starts to vibrate, Lucy comes to with a start. The close atmosphere and Iglesias's dreamy rendition of "All the Things You Are" had briefly lulled her. She slips out of the main room into a waiters' foyer and fumbles in her purse for her cell phone. A moment later, Morland's on the other end.

"We've got the wrong guy!" he tells her. "It's not him."

"What!"

"This isn't Baker. It's a damn *National Enquirer* paparazzo!"

"What!"

"That's it! What do we do now? We'll truss this guy up like a turkey. Someone'll find him tomorrow, no harm done except to his dignity and a big fee. Can't be helped, though: go around looking like someone else is supposed to look, you pay the price. Anyway, what do you want us to do?"

Lucy is stunned. It had all seemed so certain, so logical, so pat, so in keeping with every hunch, clue, connection, suspicion, intuition!

"If you still think Baker is out there," she hears Morland say, "you'd better get your ass to Security!"

Lucy is rushing toward the elevator, hardly hears him. Her feet have sent her on her way before her mind has processed its instincts. How could she have been such a fool?

As the elevator doors close, a quick glance at her watch tells her it's 10:33.

There's time. Just. Thinking more clearly now, she mutters a series of terse instructions into the cell phone. "Got that?"

There's no answer.

Across the lagoon, in an instinctive act of frustrated, fuck-you rage, Sachem has broken loose from the Chief, who was trying to secure his hands with an electrical cord, seized Morland's cell phone and dashed it against the stone floor.

Lucy hasn't time to figure out the reason for the new silence. She reckons she has fifteen minutes. Her special bar-coded, voiceprinted five-star VIP pass gets her through the security gates and out the back entrance of the Regina Palace Hotel. A half block away, at a special landing, Mannerman's personal speedboat is parked and waiting to water-lift the Pope, when the time comes, to the Piazza San Marco.

The driver recognizes Lucy, knows she has 100 percent clearance. It's not his job to ask questions. Five minutes later, they race up the security alley carved through the spectator fleet by the police. Two minutes after that, Lucy's bounding up the steps of the Cipriani landing on the back side of the Giudecca.

It's 10:42. Back on the Regina roof garden, there's a tremendous outpouring of affectionate applause as Iglesias steps aside and Ol' Blue Eyes, firm of step but in his eighties a little confused, makes his uncertain way, his son Frank Jr. at his elbow, to center stage.

Lucy flies through the hotel lobby to her room, changes her evening slippers for running shoes and grabs her shoulder bag and pistol. She'd like to change everything but hasn't time. She slips down the back stairs, lets herself out through the rear gate by the lavish pool and cabanas and minutes later is running along the back streets of the Giudecca. A few blocks in front, the noise of the crowd lining the entire north bank, facing San Marco, swells all the way from the Guardia Finanza dock at the tip to Santa Eufemia at the western extremity. It seems to ratchet up by the second in anticipation of the fireworks show. That's in a quarter of an hour.

It's 10:46. Lucy pauses in the street, looking this way and that, trying to match reality to a picture in her mind. A picture dating back four years. There's no helping it: it's all she's got. She's past the point of no return. She knows Baker's out there, and she knows where he is. *Knows!*

If she can only find the place.

Now let's see. She tries to make herself remember in an organized, methodical fashion. On their way to lunch, she and Baker came through the back gate of the Cipriani and turned left. She's sure of that. Then, here, just past this doorway with the fancy ironwork, now bare in winter but then refulgent with early autumn flowers, they'd gone right, up a block to within a few feet of the Fondamenta San Giovanni, then . . .

Then right again here. Her feet, propelled by powers of memory now so forcefully concentrated that Lucy's scarcely aware she's actually thinking, take her into another narrow street. 10:49. Across the lagoon, Sinatra has forgotten the lyrics of the second stanza of "My Way" and is mouthing along with the band. The Pope doesn't seem to notice; he's as transfixed by his proximity to this star of stars as everyone else.

It's here, Lucy is certain. At the end of this little cul-de-sac off the Calle Carolina. She's sure of it. She turns the corner and there it is, the Villa Volsi, where she and Baker lunched a million autumns ago.

A mortar or a rocket launcher: according to Morland, those would be Baker's alternatives. To fire a mortar, Morland had said, Baker would want an open space secluded from view. A place where he could set up, get his coordinates with his global-something gizmo and fire in an unhurried fashion. A place that he knew. A place that would be available and empty, deserted by its owners—she recalls Countess Volsi pridefully recounting their inflexible seasonal schedule—unless, of course, they had been bidden to Mannerman's gala—which Count and Countess Volsi were not.

Lucy stares at the villa's prim facade, feeling full of memory. So full that it takes a second or two for her to register that every window is alight.

Why? The Volsis would be away, skiing.

And then it hits her. Of course! Of course, of course, of course! There had been a voracious demand for rented accommodation from guests too grand to accept the lodgings the better hotels were left with after the early rush for reservations. Yesterday's *Gazzettino* reported that a small canal-front palazzo on the Dorsoduro had been rented to a Mexican biscuit queen for five days for the lire equivalent of $50,000. The Volsis would have seized the opportunity.

She fumbles in her shoulder bag for her cell phone and tries Morland again. No answer.

She checks her watch: 10:54. There's still just enough time to clear the roof! Time at least to get the Pope out—and possibly everyone else. Morland said he thought Baker would wait until the fireworks were peaking before firing. Mortars drop their deadly fire straight down, she knows. She mounts the low stoop and yanks hard at the bellpull. Fireworks are a better cover for a mortar attack, she thinks, hearing a bell sound in the recesses of the villa, than for the fiery exhaust of rockets streaking across the lagoon. Baker can afford to take his time. And if he's firing a mortar, it's unlikely he'll be in a place where he can see the Regina's roof garden being evacuated.

She pulls on the bell, hears it ring again and again. Finally, she hears heavy footsteps, and—a few seconds later—the door is opened by an enormously fat, bearded man dressed in a butler's off-white jacket and dark trousers.

"*Sì, signorina?*" he asks, smiling at her with the inborn courtesy of good servants. "*Cosa vuol' la signorina?*"

"*C'è il Conte Volsi?*" Lucy hears herself asking. "*Il conte?* The Count Volsi?"

"*Ah, non c'è, non è qui.*" The gracious smile remains fixed, attentive, solicitous. Isolated by the thick, surrounding beard, it seems to have a life of its own, as detached as the grin of the Cheshire cat.

"No here, *il conte*," the butler says. His English is uncertain, almost comically accented. "*La villa è affittata.* Ees ren-ted." He gestures helpfully at the night sky behind Lucy. "*Per la festa.* For ze par-ty. *Nel' albergo Regina, quartiere San Marco.*"

She glances at her watch. Eleven sharp. Please run late, she prays.

Across the way, her prayers are answered. Sinatra has launched into a rambling recollection of Las Vegas after the war that will last ten minutes. The Holy Father seems entranced. Mannerman looks significantly at Spuds, who fades behind a curtain and gets on the intercom to the Grucci command barge. If necessary, the fireworks display can be shortened by a couple of segments in order to get the Pope to San Marco on schedule.

At that moment, on the Giudecca, Lucy makes her mind up. Wherever Baker may be, it's not here, and time is running out. On a Renaissance cassone that serves as a hall table, she spots a telephone. Instinctively, without thinking, she heads for it, shouting over her shoulder at the butler, *"Emergenza!* Emergency!"

He shrugs, smiles and gestures open-palmed at the phone. *"Prego, Signorina."*

She snatches up the handset and starts to dial Spuds's beeper number. Then she stops.

The line is dead.

Slowly she replaces the phone. With an awful clarity, she grasps that something is wrong here. There's no clutter about the place, no coats on the hooks in the vestibule, no signs of life or occupancy. Renting or owning, people make their presence felt. Not here. The furniture may not be sheeted, but it might as well be. The place has an unaired, unoccupied feeling.

A terrible certainty thrills up her backbone. Bits of information present themselves, whirl about, then organize into a pattern that makes sense. A pattern that includes a fat man painting day after day on the Giudecca, watching for strangers; a fat man who writes "7" not in the Italian fashion but the way an American would. Which makes him an American lapsing for just a single moment in all this time in one unconscious, careless slip. An American who needs the use of a nearby garden.

Baker.

"Il telefono sembra . . ." She fumbles for the words, trying to seem cool. She can't make herself turn around to face the man behind her. If she could only make a break for it . . . but not the way she's dressed, and besides, the most cumbersome beasts in nature are lightning-quick for five yards. She remembers Baker saying that. "Crocodiles, sumo wrestlers, defensive linemen: for the first five yards, they're as quick as cheetahs." She can hear those words, his voice.

"Sembra spezzato . . . is broken," she says, edging back down the hall, nervously touching the front of her gown. "Kaput! Telephone ka-

put!" Tough it out, honey, she tells herself. Make him think nothing's amiss.

She turns firmly toward the front door. "*Ebbene,*" she starts to say— "Oh, well"—when a mighty blow to the side of her head propels her out of this night, this world and—as she thinks, drowning in blackness—this life.

— IV —
At first, there's a whistle, a sharp report, then another, followed by the sound of thousands sighing and exclaiming in awe and delight. Lucy claws her way through a thick veil of pain and confusion and looks up blearily. The sky above is a magical, multicolored garden of phosphorescence: green and gold, scarlet and vermilion, violet, ivory and silver.

She fights for her bearings. She's lying on her side, she realizes, her torso on a pebbled walk, her legs on dirt worn thin and hard by winter. Her arms are tied behind her at the wrists, but her legs are free. She rolls onto her back, still struggling to come to, and prizes herself into a sitting position. Swiveling on her behind, a movement made difficult by the full skirt crumpled under her thighs, she sees the fat man emerge from a low garden shed with a square piece of metal. She guesses it's a mortar baseplate. He places the plate carefully on a raked and leveled patch of ground, comes across and stands over Lucy. The dark glasses are gone. His eyes are hazel and languid. The eyes of a thin man.

"It *is* you, isn't it?" she asks. She can't make herself call him by name.

He doesn't answer.

"How?" she asks, trying to keep her voice firm, a screen behind which she can think her way out of this.

"That's *my* first question," he says. "We'll come to that. First, let me get set up."

He makes four more trips to the shed and back. Another baseplate, then the mortar tubes, which he affixes to the baseplates, finally a heavy duffel which he half carries, half drags across the bare garden floor.

The ammunition, she guesses. How many? Six rounds? Eight? Does it matter?

He seems to guess at her thoughts. "Four rounds each of standard and fléchette, my little love. Do you know what a fléchette is? It's sort of a little dart. Traveling end over end at Mach Three it does the most extraordinary things to flesh and bone. There won't be a piece of Mannerman and his fancy friends larger than a half-dollar when these get through. The straight explosives are more for effect, you might say."

"You're mad! You know that!"

"Am I? There're millions out there who would call me the sane one. Who would say that it's you and your lot who are crazy, to think you can go on behaving as you have while all the rest of the world sinks further into the muck, without ever being called to account. Rubbing our noses in it ad infinitum, ad nauseam. Anyway, that's no longer here or there, is it? Now, Luce, give it to me straight. How'd you tumble?"

"You left a trail a mile wide. You're an amateur."

"Really? Well then, why aren't more people thundering down my mile-wide spoor?" He pauses. "It was warning you off Carlsson's plane, wasn't it? That must have been it. An uncharacteristic act of mercy on my part. Of course, I had larger plans for you. I had to wait to find out what they were."

Overhead, the sky is lighted up by a brilliant blossom of yellow and pink sparkles.

"Considering you're someone who kills small children, I suppose I should be grateful for small blessings," Lucy says, and throws him a contemptuous smile. Keep on the offensive, she tells herself. Stay brave, stay feisty. "You're right, though," she adds, fibbing. "After Carlsson, a lot of things started to fall into place."

He doesn't answer. The sky is aflower again, this time with a bed of flaming scarlet peonies. Baker looks at his watch.

"Nine after eleven exactly," he remarks. "I think zero plus thirty-five or so will be about right to start the big show. How about a drink? No? Well, suit yourself." He disappears into the house and reappears with a bottle of champagne and two glasses.

"The tincture of choice for grand occasions. You're sure you won't? I must say, I find that surprising. You used to fancy the bubbly, as I recall."

He pours himself a glass and sets the bottle and the other glass on the ground. "Just the one, I think," he says with a grin. "A clear head and a steady hand, that's the stuff!" He sips his drink, then spreads his arms and makes a little bow in Lucy's direction, as if encouraging applause.

"Quite something, the new Baker, wouldn't you say?"

Lucy nods.

"Amazing what you can do when you put your mind to it, isn't it?" he remarks in a pleasant conversational tone. "I got the idea from Brando. Have you seen him recently? The man's the size of a hippo! It made me think that fat was the way to go. So I asked myself: How does one get deliberately fat? Tie a pillow to one's gut like a schoolboy Falstaff? Live at McDonald's? It would take me fifteen Big Macs a day three hundred sixty days a year for five years to do it—maybe. Anyway, I didn't have five years. Then I had a bright idea."

"Really?" Lucy wants to sound offhandedly curious. Not overwrought, not anxious. She needs to keep him talking. Every second is an ally— well, no worse than a standoff. She prays that Morland, unable to get through, will have had the sense to go to Mannerman's security, and yet somehow she doubts it, she doubts he could penetrate even the outermost barriers of the fortress of checks and credentials that encases the Regina.

Overhead, a series of rockets burst without warning into bloom. Their sharp reports startle Lucy and she has to clench her bladder.

"Sumo," she hears Baker saying. "Sumo wrestlers need to keep their fat up. I decided to find out how. So I went to São Paulo."

"São Paulo? Sumo wrestlers in Brazil?"

"São Paulo has everything, my dear, including the largest Japanese population outside the home islands. Where there are lots of Japs, I figured, there has to be sumo. I was right. The wrestlers have a special diet, a kind of thick gruel, more like a stew, called *chanko nabe*, which is made from rice and beef and vegetables. I lived on it, along with a few steroids and veterinary supplements to speed the process. I wanted to be ready when the call came."

Lucy's having trouble thinking. She's cold, damp, her head aches, her dress is heavy. Keep him talking, she tells herself. Let him gloat.

He's flying right now. Keep him up there while you figure how to make him crash.

"I'm surprised you didn't kill yourself."

"I was careful. I stayed aerobic, I watched my blood pressure. Funny, isn't it? A hundred pounds of bloat, a bad wig, a music-hall accent and a bit of optical glass, and I'm as safe as if I was riding in a tank. I might as well be invisible!" He looks at his watch. "My goodness," he exclaims, "how time flies when you're having fun!"

He lowers himself to a kneeling position and sets to work. From the duffel he takes eight lethal-looking shells and places them next to the mortars in two rows of four, fussily making sure the snub-pointed tips align precisely.

"You said something about a call," Lucy asks. "What do you mean?"

"The usual. The call to judgment, call to action, call to righteousness. The divine signal. You know, when God tells Gabriel to sound the last trumpet, chances are it'll go out on the Internet. A wonderful thing, that. You meet so many interesting people and learn so many interesting things."

"You are absolutely fucking nuts!" Lucy spits the words at him.

"Oh, I disagree. Actually I'm testing a theory. You remember that old game, rock, scissors and paper? That's all that you people are playing, except that your so-called grown-up version might be called pen, sword and dollar. Which is mightier, the pen or the sword? Or take it to the next level: the pen, the sword or the dollar? I tried the pen, as you know. While I was, so to speak, alive. Nothing came of it. I considered trying one of those complicated computer scams you read about in thrillers. Too complex for this old head, too tech, as they say. In the end it came down to the dollar or the sword, and the choice was obvious. For me, that is. Someone like your Mr. Buffett over there across the way, or that Soros fellow, might see it differently. Anyway, as for dollars, I simply didn't have enough."

"Nothing much has happened as the result of the sword either," Lucy interrupts rudely. "Net net net, that is. You blew away Carlsson, but UnivCom rules cyberspace and GIA isn't exactly falling apart. Mannerman still walks on water! Only BEECO's dead. Shit in, shit out!"

Baker's smile doesn't waver.

"You may see it any way you choose, my dear. Still, all things considered, when it comes to getting things accomplished in a way people can relate to, I'll stick with the sword. What it comes down to is a matter of scale. Of sheer numbers. Of body count, as we used to say. You have to get people's attention. Tonight will do that."

The evening sky continues to erupt. Baker looks at his watch again.

"Oh my goodness," he says mockingly, "I'm running late, as the White Rabbit might say, I'm running late!"

"Spoken like a true child killer, you miserable son of a bitch!" Lucy shouts at him. "There are innocent people over there!" She clenches her jaw in anger.

"In today's world, at that level, there are no innocent people," Baker says calmly. He starts to say something else and then stares hard at Lucy.

"Well, I'll be damned," he says. "I should have seen it before. It's the jaw. The chap that bought my painting, a picture as bad as I could make it and you might have thought we were talking about Titian! That would be Daddy, wouldn't it?"

Lucy doesn't answer.

"Of course it is! That square-featured Down East face peering over my shoulder. There's a lot of your daddy in you, my dear, at least by the light of the rockets' red glare. How could I have missed it!"

Lucy remains silent. The sky continues to shower sparks.

"Does Daddy know where his little girl is tonight? What's he doing here anyway?"

She tries to sound coolly confident. "He's my bodyguard. We have them, you know. He's never been here. I got a freebie for him out of Alitalia."

Baker seems hardly to listen. Now that he's made one connection, he's making others. When he wasn't looking over Baker's shoulder, Lucy's father was either standing over by the Guardia Finanza dock, studying San Giorgio, frequently through binoculars, or talking to another man, a younger fellow whose face Baker now knows he's also seen before—and where.

"What is Lewie Morland's kid brother doing here?" he asks abruptly.

"I don't know who Lewie Morland is. Am I supposed to?"

"Of course you do. You've heard me mention him time and again. He was my guide. We were going to do the Grand Slam together. He was in my will, for Christ's sake! You must have gotten a copy. Knowing how your sort is about money, especially someone else's, you sure as hell would've read every line!"

"Oh yes, I remember the name now. Morland's dead, you know. Died not too long after you did. Cancer."

"Is that true? Poor Lewie!"

"God's truth. The difference is, he really is dead." Lucy pauses, does some quick figuring, decides to play the hand differently. "That's how I met Peter."

"Peter?"

"Peter Morland. You got it right. The brother. The one you probably saw talking to Daddy. The one who helped me track you."

Now it's Baker's turn to remain silent.

"As I said, you're an amateur." Lucy slams her facts down like a kid playing slapjack. "A .303 killed Lamond and his grandson. I knew you had one, it was your favorite, God knows you talked more about guns than about people. That was your game from the beginning, wasn't it? Revenge—with me as the pipeline serving up whos, whys, wherefores and whens? Anyway, that .303 wasn't among the guns you left Lewis Morland, wasn't in the inventory, wasn't anywhere. Where is it? At the bottom of Hook Pond in East Hampton?"

"My lips are sealed."

"After that, it was easy," she goes on, "provided you knew where to look. I did. Considering the quality of the opposition, it wasn't hard."

Baker says nothing. A flaming tracery in the shape of the San Giorgio bell tower lights up the sky. The first of a series of pyrotechnic "monuments of Venice," Lucy knows. Roughly ten minutes to go, tops. She's running out of time.

"You're working together, aren't you?" he asks while she considers her next lead. "Just you, your father and this Morland kid?"

Lucy nods.

"Just the three of you? Against *me*? And you're calling *me* crazy? Why wouldn't you go to the police?"

"We figured they'd scare you off, send you back down your hole. And then—well, there was Carlsson. By then I knew you were out there. I knew for sure."

A brilliant purple rendition of the Salute facade twinkles overhead, dissolves into a drizzle of sparks. It's followed by a golden phoenix: La Fenice risen from the ashes. The city roars its approval.

"Is anyone else with you?" Baker recaptures Lucy's attention.

"No."

"Where are they? You're not wearing a homing device, are you?"

Lucy shakes her head. She doesn't want him to search her.

"They're wondering where I am. We made a mistake. We thought you'd come at them from San Giorgio. It's the first time you've fooled me."

"San Giorgio? Really? Hmmm." He ponders that.

"With rockets."

"Rockets?" The thick lips purse in thought. "Ah, sure: ground-to-ground. It's an idea. Too complicated, though. For these old bones."

"You seem to get around. We figured San Giorgio'd give you a better view of your handiwork. Madmen like that, they say. It's why arsonists hang around to watch the fires they set."

Baker smiles. When he speaks, his voice is calm and easy. "Oh, I think we'll have a perfectly satisfactory sense of the occasion from right here. Are you happy with your seat, or would you like a closer view? As the man says, it is now showtime. And, believe me, Lucy dear, I'm not mad. Not angry-mad, not any longer, and not crazy-mad. I'm just getting even." He returns to the mortars. From a leather case lying on the ground, he takes a device that looks something like a television remote with dials and a map and makes a series of computations. Azimuths, Lucy guesses. The gadget must be the global-positioning device which Morland had mentioned. The GPD will give Baker an exact reading—to the second—of his longitude and latitude. Lucy guesses he's already done the same for the Regina.

On a pocket calculator, he makes some computations. Correlating, Lucy reckons. Then he goes to the mortars and fiddles with their aiming scales, double-checking against the readouts on his calculator and GPD. Above the garden, the night sky blossoms with great scintillant peony-shaped starbursts that hold together for an instant before breaking up and drifting back to earth amid a great gasping roar of admiration that seems to fill the bowl of heaven. He kneels by the mortars and picks up a round. With both hands, he holds it aloft, a bit above eye level, like a priest elevating the host.

"Any last words?" he asks, looking at Lucy with a huge, mad smile. He doesn't wait for an answer, but turns back to his work.

Lucy reckons she's got five minutes. Now or never. She plays her hole card.

"Baker," she says in a strained voice, using his name for the first time, "I have to pee. Badly."

"So do it."

"Oh, for God's sake, Baker! Not in my dress! Untie my hands, damn it! Be a gentleman!"

He considers her situation, then sighs, sets down the shell and with a grunt gets up and comes over to her. He jerks her to her feet. Standing behind her, he unties her right hand and grips her wrist. His fingers are like cables. She remembers shaking hands with him the first time, an eternity ago, in Pennsylvania. He brings her left arm in front, controlling it with the cord, then moves quickly around her and renooses her hands. In a few seconds, Lucy's hogtied once more, except that now her arms and hands are in front.

"There," he says. "Now be quick. Stay in the light where I can see you." To emphasize his point, he picks up something she hasn't noticed until now, a pistol of some sort, its stubby barrel unnaturally elongated by a silencer.

She moves to the edge of the garden, just outside the deeper shadows in which the thin night light loses itself, turns her back to Baker and squats. She goes through all the motions, rucking up her skirt, which is difficult because of the length and the heavy, bunched fabric. This is a man she's peed in front of many times, so she tries to seem matter-of-fact. It's hard to maintain her balance, and she has to shift forward on the balls of her feet and use her fists as a tripod, then rock back to a position where she feels steady. She doesn't dare try to look back over her shoulder. She senses he's busy fine-tuning his ordnance. He'll wait until she's ready before firing.

"Get a move on," he calls over in a low voice.

"I'm trying, it's not easy."

The way he's retied her wrists makes it awkward to get her hands under her panty hose, but finally she manages, pushing the tights down to where her fingers can close on the checkered handgrip of the Colt Woodsman .22 she stuffed in her underwear back at the Cipriani. She had brought it from Maine, just in case: broken down—with its disassembled parts scattered in with her makeup and computer impedimenta.

Now, thanks either to sheer nerves or to sheer willpower, she manages to unleash a thin but adequately noisy stream while, beneath her skirt, she works the gunsight free of the waistband of her tights. With her right thumb, she edges the safety off. The pistol feels comfortable, familiar—but she hasn't fired it since leaving Maine.

It's one thing to plink a plastic Clorox bottle on a fence post, another to shoot something that's alive and menacing, something that's human. The chamber holds the bullet that came with the pistol from Baker's attorney's, the bullet meant for her, a bullet she likes to think will be lucky. Backing it up in the magazine are six others, but she doubts she'll have a chance for more than one shot.

The fireworks seem to be reaching an interim crescendo. The patterns are more complex now, the colors richer and more varied. She can see her watch in their light: 11:32.

"Come on, damn it!" Baker has to make himself heard over the crackle from the sky and the great collective murmurs the Grucci display is drawing from earth and sea.

"I'm done," she says over her shoulder. She feigns wiping herself, counts slowly to six to get her pulse steady, then pushes herself erect with her leg muscles. Her back is still to Baker. Her arms point straight down in front of her, a single continuous vector running to the muzzle of the Colt between her legs, concealed by her long skirt. Now she turns, bringing her arms up as she moves, slightly relaxing the tension at her elbows, letting them flex, keeping her wrists firm, raising the pistol to a point where she can sight easily along the barrel. When she has fully turned around, she calls out, "Baker!"

Her voice sounds to her like a pistol report.

At first, he doesn't notice. He's fiddling with his artillery. Now he picks up a shell, and she calls out a second time.

"Baker!"

Her sharp tone swings him around. When he sees the pistol aimed unwavering at his face, Lucy thinks she sees his eyes widen in shock, but for no more than an instant. He grins at her, his eyes take on an untroubled cast, his body seems to relax. He carefully sets the mortar round down beside him. It's a bland facade, too easy, too cool. Lucy's not fooled. Behind it the wheels are turning at full throttle; his hunter's instincts are in command: calculating angles, distances, ground to cover. He's kneeling, but even on all fours Lucy reckons he can be across the small space of dead ground that separates them so fast she may blow it, so she takes a half step back, adjusting her aim as she does.

"You haven't got the guts," he says.

"Try me."

He doesn't move, simply smiles.

"At your leisure, then," he says, and rocks back to rest his weight on his upturned heels. But his right hand, a half yard—no more—from his pistol on the ground, stays put. When he seems settled, he looks at her expectantly, and says, in a voice as casual as if he were discussing the weather, "No blindfold, please."

The Woodsman is starting to feel heavy. Lucy loosens her elbows a little, imperceptibly flexes her wrists. She thinks the sight is beginning to waver.

A .22 isn't much of a weapon against someone the size Baker is now, she thinks. His bloat will neutralize its stopping power. The bullet will have to be placed just so.

She wants to fire, but she can't. She needs him to give her cause, to try something. She can't simply blow him away as he kneels there. She senses he knows this about her. In the small of her back, she feels a dappling of perspiration. Behind Baker, a splendid rosette is etched on the night in silver and pink.

He sits there dead still, waiting, letting her disable herself. The muzzle of the Woodsman is wavering faster now, it's a strain to keep it steady. She's breathing hard now, working hard now, sweat beads her forehead, a drop courses down and gets in her eye and she tries to blink the salt sting away.

At that moment, the beeper still hidden in her sash begins to vibrate furiously. Morland is back in the loop, but a lot of good it does Lucy. It's late, she thinks, time's a-wasting, Baker has to move now or it'll be too late. The thought scares her. She shifts her weight and flexes her arms; once again the sight wavers. In the sky, a long staccato series of reports takes golden form in a rough approximation of the papal arms. She shakes her head as if to free her eyes of further perspiration; as she does, she lets the Woodsman's muzzle drift leftward and down, and her shoulders seem to sag.

Baker buys the fake. With a great yell intended to discombobulate, he snatches up his pistol and hurls his bulk to the right, trying to bring his weapon to bear. Halfway up, however, his gun arm loses motion and stops in mid-swing as if spiked: it's like a freeze-frame. Baker, his gun arm frozen, staring up at the single black unflinching eye of Lucy's Colt.

"You're too right-handed, Baker. You need to learn new tricks."

The sight at the end of the barrel is centered on the space between his eyes. She shifts her aim a micromillimeter left and one bright hazel orb settles atop the black metal bead. A tiny fraction upward, just as he taught her, so that the gunsight blots out the pupil, and now squeeze.

She senses Baker's gun hand start to move again. But not to shoot, she senses. Bringing his gun up is just Baker's way of dropping the handkerchief. She sights along the barrel; the hazel circle at the end of her pistol, so steady a target that it might as well be attached to the muzzle by a skewer, seems to change in a nanosecond from an eye into the *O* of the floridly lettered label of a plastic detergent bottle. His gun hand is still moving. Goodbye, Baker, whoever you were, you murdering bastard, she sighs somewhere deep in her being, and squeezes the trigger.

Lucy will never be sure she heard the report or felt the pistol kick. All she knows is that Baker taught her well. The sight stays steady on the target. The circle around the bead turns in an instant from light to dark, from hazel to near-black, then blossoms in dull, dark petals the color of brain blood. A single thick tendril, scarlet-edged, deep, dark crimson in the middle, breaks loose and starts its twisting journey down a corpulent cheek, and Lucy lowers the pistol.

Baker lies collapsed on his right side, head up, his one good eye lightless, his right arm outstretched, his left loose along his side. He looks, Lucy thinks, like an antique marble Roman on a temple relief. Some force beyond nature holds the lifeless body in that pose for one beat, for two, then the head slumps sideways and the torso rolls slowly over on its back and lies still.

"Jesus God," Lucy murmurs. Her pistol is still trained on Baker's corpse as if her arms have turned to stone. Finally, she makes herself lower them, sinks down herself and places her pistol on the ground.

Her beeper goes off again. The insistent vibration at her waist snaps her back to reality. Her shoulder bag is over by Baker's body. She crawls across the short space, keeping her eyes averted, and digs with bound wrists inside her shoulder bag until she finds her Swiss Army knife. She cuts herself free, locates her cell phone and dials Morland as she goes inside the Volsis' brilliantly lit and empty house. She can't bear another second alone with Baker.

"Where the hell have you been?" he asks angrily. He doesn't allow her to answer. "That goddamn idiot paparazzo broke my goddamn phone, the Chief forgot his and Ormerud's died—just bad luck. We had to go back and get the Chief's. By the time we did, you'd gone off the screen. We're in a caffè on the Zitelle trying not to look like complete assholes. Anyway, it looks like we're home free. The show's almost over and no Baker. Maybe the guy was a figment of your—of *our*—imagination. Where the hell are you? You must be about winding it up over there."

"I'm not there," she says quickly. "I'm here. Not more than five minutes away. Get your butts over here pronto!" Lucy gives him the address, hangs up and throws herself on a sofa. Now it all lets go in her, and she gives way to great racking, wheezing sobs somewhere between grief, relief and hyperventilation.

The spell lasts no more than a couple of minutes. Then she's all right, looking like hell, she judges from a mirror, but back in control. Minutes later, she admits her three colleagues.

She quickly recounts what's taken place as she leads them into the garden.

"Jesus holy Christ!" cries Morland. The Chief is struck dumb. Thank God for Ormerud, she tells herself. It takes him only about ten seconds to get the picture. He issues a series of crisp orders, and tells Lucy to wait inside.

In fifteen minutes, the body's been stripped bare, the ordnance packed away in the duffels, the bare ground swept. The villa is gone over for Baker's effects: one florid nylon warm-up suit, size XXXL, and a stained leather backpack which appears to contain the sum of his several existences: four passports and a range of birth certificates and other supporting documents, various credit cards and licenses, $15,000 in various currencies, principally Brazilian and Italian, a small notebook with what look like computer keyings.

"The rest of his stuff must be in a hotel or *pensione* somewhere," Ormerud observes, "but who cares? If and when they find it, if and when they find *him*, so what? Anyway, you're some piece of work, Lucy. You can fly on my wing anytime. Of course, I hate to think what would've happened if he'd just let you pee in your tights."

"He never would have. I knew that. He was a gentleman. I think that may have been all he cared about."

"And it got him killed," says Ormerud thoughtfully. "Anyway, you can figure he's on his way to Potter's Field. We have this stuff—so what'll anyone have to go on? Two days outdoors in this weather and no one'll know what this thing was. Now we need to get the hell out of here."

"You go," says Lucy. She goes back into the garden and looks down at Baker. The naked corpse is gross and pasty, bloated and mottled, a disgusting, suety, shit-stinking pile of nothing she remembers. Whatever man it was she knew is lost forever in this heap of flab. That's fine with her and she hopes it suits him, wherever he is. He wanted to be invisible—so now he is. Forever.

She feels suddenly sick—sick at heart, sick at stomach. All this anger, all this waste. She takes deep gulps of the night air. The sky is still alive. She needs to be alone.

A door in the garden wall leads to the street. She eases the bolt and slips out. Skirting the Cipriani park, she walks swiftly toward the south bank of the Giudecca. It's deserted. The entire population of the island has turned out on the opposite shore to watch Jack Mannerman's great show.

Bread and circuses, she thinks. They never fail.

Outside the bright orbit of the fireworks the night is moonless, gauzed with a high haze that masks the stars, except for an unnaturally bright one high in the east burning with a strangely constant light. The sky is deep black, purpling in its depths, bordered at its base by the pale-edged golden aurora upcast by the lights of Venice. Out on the water, looking toward the Lido, the darkness is punctuated by the bobbing lights of moored yachts and, now and then, the sweeping searchlights of police launches. In the farther distance, Lucy can make out the brilliant strings of lights decorating a large cruise liner, some multicolored, most pale gold at this distance, and farther still, the red, white and blue neon filigree spread across the "island" of the enormous USS *Forrestal*.

She breathes deeply—sucking in the night. The weather seems to be changing, the air feels thick and wet. The moisture strikes her skin like microscopic hail; her breath forms wispy cones of condensation.

Someone comes up behind her. She turns warily and sees it's Morland.

"Ormerud got hold of a boat. He'll bring it over once the Pope's in San Marco and the rubberneckers disperse and we'll dump the ironware and the other stuff in the lagoon, probably down by the Malamocco where it's deep and the seaward tides are strong."

She nods. "What about the guy in the campanile?"

"He'll be all right. They'll find him tomorrow. I doubt much will be said, especially if it's that old custodian who stumbles on him. Someone at NASA's going to have to do some fancy explaining how a tabloid photographer came to be using lenses that are classified for the space shuttle."

"And—"

"We have to leave him where he is."

Lucy can't help thinking back to the orderly family plot high on a hill above Bakerton. Baker had called it "the family's little private Arlington." A long way from a corpse rotting in the garden of a shuttered villa in Venice.

Morland stares out at the spectacle on the water. "You know *Amarcord*," he says, "that picture of Fellini's? There's something about this that reminds me of that scene when the liner *Rex*—"

Lucy puts her forefinger to his lips.

"No more movies, please," she says. "Not for a while."

Just life for now, she thinks, just life.

She turns away and starts toward her hotel. Her watch says it's 11:49: time for the next act of Jack Mannerman's gala, for another small chapter in that saga of ambition and hype.

The sky to the north, off to her left, is rent with a dozen sharp, simultaneous reports. A huge UnivCom logo stitched from a thousand flaming sparks materializes a thousand feet up, drawing a sound from the watching multitude that's almost a shriek.

"Wow!" Morland exclaims. They watch in silence as it wavers on

high, then collapses in a drizzle of tiny lights. Then it's dark except for
the stars, silent except for the lapping of the water. Morland walks
beside her, but there seems to be nothing to say. For a few seconds,
everything seems to stop. Even the crowds spread across the city and
the lagoon have fallen quiet. The only noise that carries over the water
is the busy crystalline clamor of Mannerman's revelers awaiting the next
display.

"Well," Morland says, "that's the end of it."

"Do you really think so? I have a feeling Baker may just have been
the beginning, especially if the world keeps going the way it has. Just
think: what we've done here tonight seems to ensure that the world *will*
keep going the way it has. Bummer, eh?"

"I meant the fireworks, stupid!"

Without thinking, Lucy reaches out and takes his hand, and they
walk in silence beside the water. The entire world seems mute. Even
the sounds of the party have faded away.

Then, suddenly, there's a final upreaching rush of spark and flame
above the domes and towers of San Marco as a last rocket chugs into
the sky. It climbs in a stately manner for a few seconds before its tail
of fire vanishes. There's an instant's silence, an instant's darkness, and
then—all at once—a huge, glorious, sparking blossom appears in the
sky. It's GIA's new corporate symbol: an incandescent, scintillant chry-
santhemum of flame and color that seems to fill the entire dome of night
with countless petals of white and scarlet, gold and violet and green.

The crowds start to cheer, but the sheer beauty of the moment cuts
them short. The great flaming flower hangs in the sky for perhaps five
seconds, held together as if by prayer and magic, by the will and hope
of the people below, before it breaks up into brilliant points of light
floating earthward, going out one by one as the festive noise and radi-
ance of the city fade away, until all at once there is nothing left but
night, silence and, above the far horizon, the Christmas star.